THE PASSIONATE GAMBLE

When Cara yielded to the Shawnee warrior chief, Ousa, she knew full well what she was doing. She would be going to live with him in a strange tribe, surrounded by the hostility of those who would never accept her as one of their own.

Ousa, too, knew what he was risking—his position as leader and the respect of the tribe that only he could save, and that now would despise him for yielding to so unmanly an emotion as love.

But as they held each other in the wilderness night, nothing else existed but the perfect mating of their flesh, the perfect joining of their spirits. No matter what they might lose, they would not lose this. . . .

SHAWNEE DAWN

BOOK 2

SHAWNEE DAWN

THE INDIAN HERITAGE SERIES

by

Paul Joseph Lederer

A SIGNET BOOK
NEW AMERICAN LIBRARY
TIMES MIRROR

NAL BOOKS ARE AVAILABLE AT QUANTITY DISCOUNTS WHEN USED TO PROMOTE PRODUCTS OR SERVICES. FOR INFORMATION PLEASE WRITE TO PREMIUM MARKETING DIVISION, THE NEW AMERICAN LIBRARY, INC., 1633 BROADWAY, NEW YORK, NEW YORK 10019.

SIGNET TRADEMARK REG. U.S. PAT. OFF. AND FOREIGN COUNTRIES
REGISTERED TRADEMARK—MARCA REGISTRADA
HECHO EN CHICAGO, U.S.A.

SIGNET, SIGNET CLASSICS, MENTOR, PLUME, MERIDIAN AND NAL BOOKS are published by The New American Library, Inc., 1633 Broadway, New York, New York 10019

First Printing, January, 1983

1 2 3 4 5 6 7 8 9

PRINTED IN THE UNITED STATES OF AMERICA

Prologue

In the days before the great canoes sailed up the Hudson River, the Iroquois nations dominated the continent. There were only the Algonquins to oppose, and against these barbarians the Iroquois had the succor of the Great Manitou. But then the canoes came and the men from the far side of the moon stepped onto the shores of the Hudson. The white men came, and the end of the world began.

In that time Crenna was the headwoman of the great Oneida people, a tribe of the Iroquois nation. She was honored, composed, competent, skilled in war and in negotiations. But the curse that the moon men brought came upon her, and she fell in love with the Dutchman, Van der Veghe.

They went away together to try to live in peace along the great river, but the moon men continued to come. The French, as they called themselves, and the English, and they made their war.

They made their war and the Indian fought with them, died with them, and there was nothing Crenna could do to stop it. She had shamed herself by marrying the white Dutchman.

She waited and watched and saw her people die. And when the land belonged to the men from the far side of the moon, when the old way was gone forever, she moved on to a distant land with her husband, the Dutchman, her sister, the ethereal Sachim, and her children. The land was free and wild and none lived there but the Shawnee.

1

They saw the first runner as they paused at the river crossing. He was only a shadow, a blur, a specter beyond the screen of willow brush, but Crenna's sharp eyes saw the man. Within hours their arrival would be known to every member of his tribe.

"Mother." Cara, who had clambered down from the cart while they searched for a ford, lifted a stubby finger and pointed across the silver breadth of the river. "I saw a man running away."

It was an incident to be remarked. They had seen no other human being for two weeks. Crenna picked her daughter up, noting the gangling length of her legs. Her beautiful chubby daughter was no longer a baby. Each day the sunshine, the fresh air, contributed to her healthy growth. Soon she would be long, sleek, and beautiful. Crenna kissed her daughter and set her back on her feet.

"Who was it? What did he want?"

"He wanted nothing," Crenna said. "He was sent to see who is passing through the land of the Susquehanna."

"I think there's a ford a little north, around the bend!" Peter Van der Veghe was walking toward the horse-drawn cart, the breeze shifting his long, thinning blond hair. At his

…ked William, flailing out at the wildflowers with a …d stick.

Crenna waited for her husband to arrive. "I walked out a hundred feet. There's a gravel bar which should be wide enough for the cart."

Peter Van der Veghe wiped his forehead with the back of his hand. The autumn morning was warm. Frogs grumped in the brush along the broad Allegheny. The sun glittered off the shifting mirror of the river. Mottled shadows fell across the bright new grass beneath the oaks.

"What happened?" Peter asked his wife. He nodded at the little girl, who still stood staring across the river.

"Nothing. A Susquehanna runner, that is all."

"Will that mean trouble, Crenna?" Van der Veghe asked with concern. He had brought his family into this wide Ohio Valley to escape from the bloodshed, the horrors of the war which was building between the French and the English in the East. They had seen enough of trouble, this Dutchman and his beautiful Oneida wife. Van der Veghe had only to look at the empty left sleeve of his shirt to be reminded how close disaster had come.

He had lost that arm fighting a frenzied Iroquois warrior, Crenna's brother. The Europeans had brought a plague of warfare with them, and it had infected the eastern tribes. The Iroquois and the Algonquin were spilling their blood for the ambitions of the French and English.

When there had no longer been any hope of avoiding the war, Van der Veghe had packed his goods into the wobbly two-wheeled cart and brought his family west into the broad valley.

"Where is Sachim?" he asked.

He had no sooner asked than the fifth member of their small party emerged from the woods, her hands behind her back, her dark, wide eyes flickering to them. This was Crenna's sister, the quiet one, the one who walked with spirits.

"Am I making you wait?" Sachim asked breathlessly, hurrying up to them.

"No. We've only now found a ford," Van der Veghe replied, wondering if the word he had chosen for "ford" was the correct one. His knowledge of the Oneida tongue was still imperfect, probably always would be. It was Crenna who had the gift for languages, among so many other gifts. She spoke her own tongue, that of the Algonquin, her people's blood enemies; she was excellent with Dutch, and her English was as good as Van der Veghe's.

But then, she was good at so many things. He looked fondly at his wife, this beautiful Oneida woman with the dark, sleek hair, proud, bright eyes, full mouth, long legs which could carry her effortlessly over distances. She had been born to rule, and in her own time, her own country, she had done so magnificently. Until she had given it up for him. That perhaps was her greatest strength—her ability to give.

"Are we ready?" Crenna asked.

Van der Veghe looked up, his eyes distant, and he nodded, kissing her lightly on the cheek. "Yes."

The children were placed on the seat of the cart, and Peter Van der Veghe turned the horses northward. Crenna handled the reins while Sachim walked behind, a deep distant smile playing on her lips.

The river was broad, its surface glittering, bright so that they could not look at it for more than a moment at a time. Van der Veghe moved ahead of the cart, knee-deep in the water. He looked across his shoulder and smiled at Crenna. He nodded; the ford would do.

Fans of silver rose from the horses' hooves. A long V of southward-winging ducks cut dark silhouettes against the white skies. William, his yellow hair flying in the wind, his eyes eager and bright, stood in the wagon box as the horses achieved the far side of the river.

Home. Home, they had told him, was on the far side of this great rambling river, and now he stood surveying this land which was not much different from that they had been passing through for weeks—except that this was home, and with that title it took on special, immediate significance.

"Not yet, William," Crenna said, reading her son's thoughts. "This is still the land of the Susquehanna. We must travel a little farther to where no one lives, no Susquehanna, no Iroquois, no English or French."

"But then we shall be all alone, Mother," William said.

"Yes, I know it, William."

Deflated, he sat down. There would be no one, no friends, no craftsmen to observe, no hunters to follow. But then, there had been few enough people back home on the Hudson. Those who had come had not always been friends. The boy sat down, watching as his father, long-striding and confident, led the horses through the deep oak grove. His mother walked beside Van der Veghe now, and it struck him, not for the first time, how unlike they were.

He was tall and fair, blue-eyed like William himself. His mother's eyes were black, her face oval with arched brows, her mouth wide and determined, but likely to break into smiles which brought rainbows to William's world.

"May I get down, Sachim?" he asked his aunt.

"Yes, William," she said. He paused to make a face at his older sister and then slipped from the cart as it rolled on through the oaks. He hit the ground, slipped, braced himself with his palms, and hurried on, walking three paces behind his mother and father, near enough to hear their intermittent conversation, although he paid little attention to it. There were more important things to occupy his mind. There were red squirrels in the oaks, and a saucy blue jay which followed them, fluttering from bough to bough, squawking loudly.

"There will be no trouble?" Peter asked.

"I don't think so," Crenna answered. "We're nearly out of their lands now."

"And the other land? This broad valley you've spoken of?"

"It belongs to no one. It is a common hunting ground used by the Miami, the Susquehanna, and the Shawnee."

"But will they want us settling there?"

"We will not bother them," Crenna said, knowing it was no answer. The truth was, she did not know. Their only aim had been to find a broad land where no one dwelt, where the children would be free to roam the forests and to grow without danger. Behind them was a war, ahead wilderness.

"Other Iroquois have come west," Crenna told her husband. "Even some western Oneida. Come west, as we have, to avoid the conflict. They are calling themselves Mingoes, which means travelers. It would be possible to find one of these tribes and live with them." She looked expectantly at Peter Van der Veghe.

He shook his head. "We are better off to ally ourselves with no one, to depend on no one."

Crenna agreed. "The next river," she told him, "is that called the Monongahela. When we have reached it, we will know we are in the hunting ground. There we shall build our house. There we shall plant our corn."

Van der Veghe frowned slightly. "I'm not sure how much

good I will be with an ax now." He glanced at the empty sleeve.

"We will all help, Peter. It has always been that way with us, hasn't it?"

"It has." Van der Veghe slipped his arm around his wife's shoulder and kissed her forehead. She smiled in return and patted his waist. "There is a place out here, Crenna, I know it. A place where we can be happy. I have you. I have the children. I want no more out of life but enough time to enjoy you."

"Until you are a hundred summers old!" She laughed. "William! You're straying too far."

They watched the boy scamper back, turned to look toward the cart to see a solemn Cara sitting beside her aunt, Sachim. Crenna smiled and waved, and Cara flashed her own smile.

Sunlight streamed through the oaks, spattering the dark earth underfoot with gold. Mockingbirds sang in the high branches. The day was good, the land was fair.

That evening they camped within sight of the Monongahela. The late sun gilded the river, lighting it like a promising beacon. A wind came up with the dusk and it carried a low, twisting fog off of the river. It crept through the pine and oak forest like a curious gray beast.

But their fire was warm, a haunch of venison roasting over it. It was more meat than they had cooked for a single meal in weeks, but it seemed a time to celebrate.

Crenna stood beside her husband at sunset, watching as the sun lit the tips of the dark ranks of pines with golden stars in the last moment of its life. Her man was silent and stood erect, his blue eyes sparkling with light reflected from the quiet river.

"It is a fair land, Peter, Manitou's land. We shall have a home here."

He turned and held her close for a long minute. She could feel his breath against her cheek, and she smiled up at him. Together then they walked back through the forest toward the camp. The fog was thickening now and the red cone of the fire seemed unnaturally bright. Sachim sat on a fallen log with the children, telling them a tale of Raven and the Bear.

Crenna and Peter sat side by side, cross-legged on the earth, eating their meal of venison and parched corn. Van der Veghe became more animated after eating, and he sketched out in the dirt several plans for a new house. The firelight glowed on his cheeks, and Crenna, watching him, listening without hearing his words, thought again how much she loved this tall yellow-haired man who had come from across the seas, been tortured by her own people, fought and become strong, proven his devotion to her and to the children. She had never regretted marrying him, not for a moment, although she had given up her position as headwoman of the Oneida people to marry Peter, although she had left home under a cloud, shaming herself in her father's eyes. At the end, even the old man, Yushta, had admitted that she had done what was right, that which made her life a joy and not a burden.

"We will need a smokehouse, I think, although temporarily we will just use racks as your people do," Van der Veghe said, looking up. His eyebrows drew together as he caught the speculative light in Crenna's eyes. Then he smiled and drew her to him. Sachim's voice droned on.

"The Bear told Raven, show me where the silver fish swims and I will catch him. He will make a good meal for both of us."

"Is this the end of the journey or the beginning, Crenna?"

"A beginning I hope. Always a beginning with you, Peter."

"Never an end?" he asked, tilting her chin up.

"In a hundred summers, perhaps, as I have told you."

"That will not end it," Van der Veghe said, his voice oddly husky. He still held her, watching the fire.

It was growing damp, and so they moved closer yet to the fire ring, listening to Sachim as she told her tales to the children. Crenna watched their young faces, fire-bright, fascinated, content. Peter Van der Veghe too was happy. They had found their place. They were healthy, and the land was rich. With their own hands they would build a home.

Crenna leaned nearer to Peter, resting her head on his shoulder. He was content; she could not bring herself to shadow his contentment by telling him about the watchers in the forest.

There were at least three of them. Crenna had seen them moving, shadowy, wraithlike as the fog itself. What they wanted, she did not know. For the time being, they meant her family no harm. If they wanted to, they could easily overpower them. No, they were only watching, waiting. Who could say what they waited for?

* * *

They came upon it in late afternoon. The timber crowned the low knoll overlooking the small sunlit valley. Van der Veghe, walking before the cart, exchanged one quick glance with Crenna. No word passed between them or was needed. This would be their home.

They had crossed the Monongahela a day earlier. They walked now across a wide virgin valley. A silver rill ran down from the timbered uplands and wound its way across the meadow, which was flushed with the pink of wildflowers. A doe, drinking at the rill, lifted its muzzle, and sunlight caught the water on its muzzle, silvering it. The doe bounded away through the tall grass.

Crenna had seen signs of beaver and of otter along the river; the tracks of a bear had crossed their trail. The deep forests were alive with deer and squirrels. The small river they had forded this side of the Monongahela was rich with fish.

Van der Veghe had halted now, and he turned to look back down the valley. The timbered slopes behind him cast a long shadow down onto the meadow.

"I think the source of the stream is up there," he said. "A spring, perhaps."

"Where will the house be, Peter?" Crenna asked.

"Why, I think . . ." He stopped and smiled. "How did you know what I had in mind?"

"It's a fair land, Peter Van der Veghe," Crenna answered.

"Will it do for a one-armed Dutchman and his Oneida bride?" he asked her, resting his hand on her shoulder.

"Ask them," Crenna responded. Van der Veghe looked to where the children romped across the meadow, vaulting into the air, the long grass bending to mark their passage. A cry of laughter escaped William's lips. Peter Van der Veghe grinned. Crenna looked to the cart, where Sachim sat in silence.

She did not have to ask a question. Sachim nodded her head and then clambered down from the cart, unhitching the two horses. The children played themselves into exhaustion while the three adults unloaded the cart, finding a hollow carved by nature up along the knoll to use for temporary storage.

They built a fire and ate, the children falling asleep almost immediately after eating. Then Crenna and Peter made their bed, and they lay together watching the stars wheel past overhead.

"Do you never wish for your home, Peter?" Crenna asked unexpectedly, her voice soft and musical in the night.

He lifted himself to look down at her. "Home?"

"Holland, Peter. Your home across the sea."

"This is home, Crenna," he told her with all sincerity. "Here with you. What causes you to ask such a question?"

"Perhaps the night," she said after a moment's pause, "perhaps wishing for my own home." Her fingers ran up along his strong arm, and she gripped it tightly. "I only want you to be happy. That is all I have ever wanted."

"And you have given me happiness. Ask me no more foolish questions." He smiled, bent down and kissed her eyes, her lips, and lay back beside her.

Crenna lay awake for a long while listening to the deep breathing of Peter Van der Veghe. Smoky clouds trailed across the pale, pocked face of the rising moon like banners of starfire. She recalled being very young and speaking to the stars, asking them questions they never answered. They did not mock you, those distant, winking eyes, but hung cold and aloof, seeming to promise something—what, she never knew, when she, as a young girl, had attempted to learn from the stars as the shaman Yo claimed to do. Now she did know. They promised a moment of life. Pain and often joy; travail and moments of ecstasy. It was a part of Manitou's wise plan. Without pain, the pleasures of the world mean nothing; without work, play is essentially meaningless. And so it was her lot to endure the terrible moments they had had so that the moments of peace would be that much sweeter.

"Still a foolish girl," Crenna told herself angrily. There were tears standing in her eyes, and she wiped them away with irritation. She rolled to Peter and clung to him in the night, feeling his warmth and strength.

She walked a star-shadowed world. She wandered the long, crooked corridors among the pines, their scent alive and palpable in the brittle cold. The dry brown pine needles underfoot were glazed with a thin frost which crackled as she placed her moccasined feet.

Still she was as silent as a velvet-footed cougar, more quiet perhaps, because Sachim moved with the slight weight of one who has no real substance. It had always been so with her. She dragged her slender body around with her, bumping it across the face of the earth, a terrible burden. Wretched thing.

Sachim was a soul bound to the flesh. A moonbeam captured and swallowed by this world. It had molded a clay woman around her soul, and it was an awful weight to carry.

Now she stopped in the clearing. Tilting her head back, she looked up through the gap between the ranks of towering black pines. Starlight funneled down through the distances. The treetops swayed in the cold wind. Manitou breathed, and the small ones dwelling in the hearts of the pines whispered to her.

There were other voices as well—the murmuring of souls. Real men, with their hot blood and hard muscles, with their unseeing eyes, lurked in the forest, and Sachim felt their presence like a prickling weight on her eyes and heart.

They were only human; she did not fear them.

She knelt, hands outstretched, and looked into the heart of Manitou. It was a time before it began. There was a humming deep inside her ears, which gradually became louder, more insistent. The stars became silver pinwheels against the black night. Behind her eyes the tumbling fountain of flames began. Crimson waterfalls. Golden sparks gouting up, forming mysterious figures. Great fiery-winged eagles which lurched upward, winging across the purple skies. Beyond the tumult was the peaceful glade, ancient, silent, and cool. There sat the man in white robes, his eyes glittering, his voice soft, and he stretched out a hand to Sachim, drawing her through the flames.

It was silent. He spoke in whispers. The trees were thick with downy bluebirds with amber eyes. He took her body from her and cast it aside, and Sachim too became a bird, blue, soft, eyes bright and curious.

His hand touched her head and she tried to fly away. Failing, she tumbled to the earth, but he scooped her up and held her in his cupped palm, whispering to her until dawning brought the harsh light which faded his features and caused his body to change to mist and drift upward and away as Sachim lay trembling against the earth.

Then for a time she slept. Awakening, Sachim blinked. The sunlight through the pines was harsh and yellow. It formed long straight-edged bands of brilliance. She rolled to a sitting position, yawned, and dusted away the pine needles from her buckskin dress.

The girl stood silently watching.

"Cara!" Sachim stood, smiling gently.

"What are you doing here, Aunt Sachim? I heard you singing, saw you clap your hands together, and then you were still. I called to you, but you did not move. I thought you were sleeping, but you were not."

The child's eyes were puzzled. Her forehead was furrowed with worry. Sachim put her hand on the girl's brow and smoothed the wrinkles away.

"I was dreaming, child. Only sleeping and dreaming."

"No!" Cara was emphatic. "I know you were not sleeping. You spoke to someone and listened for an answer. You listened and heard something. Something, but what?"

"I was only sleeping," Sachim repeated. Then she put a gentle hand around Cara's shoulder and walked with her back through the dewy morning freshness of the forest. *She knew.* Already the girl knew that Sachim had the gift. Did that mean that Cara too would one day walk with the spirits? Better not to place too strong an interpretation on the girl's comments, Sachim thought. It could encourage her. Some became eager to learn. In their rush toward holiness, they starved themselves, mortified the flesh, injured their bodies and souls. Sachim had seen it many times.

She kissed Cara's dark, glossy hair, and as the soulful eyes turned up to her, she managed a smile. "How do you like your new home?" Sachim asked with enthusiasm.

"Why are they watching us?" the girl asked instead of answering.

"Who, Cara? Who is watching?"

"I don't know. But they are out here in the forest. I know it."

"You saw them?" Sachim asked.

"I know they are out here," Cara said again, and then she would say no more.

Below, the ax rang against the trees. Crenna, who had begun marking out the house, which would stand against the bluff on the southern edge of the meadow, stopped to watch her husband.

He had one arm, but—she thought—two hearts. There would never be another man like Van der Veghe. He worked slowly but with great precision. The ax, biting deep into the reddish-white wood of the pines, sent small showers of chips frothing from the trees. The strokes of the ax, metallic and solid, were like the beating of Crenna's heart.

Van der Veghe was shirtless, and perspiration glossed his pale back. His hair was damp and dark with sweat. He had tied a cloth around his head.

"You must watch him, Crenna. He was ill for a long time."

Crenna turned to find Sachim standing with Cara. "I will," Crenna promised.

"Now, what is it you would have us do?" Crenna's sister asked.

"Fish traps? Snares? It is already time to start thinking about food for the winter, Sachim."

"I think fish, then. Come, Cara, I will show you how to make a fish trap."

"Oh, I already know how," Cara said with childish arrogance. "But I will help you."

"Good!" Sachim laughed. "Then the work will go twice as fast. William!" She called the boy to them. "We are going to fish. Would you like to come along?"

"No." He turned blue eyes to his mother. "Must I?"

"I suppose not, but you must do something to help, William," Crenna told him.

"I intend to." He drew himself up to his full height of nearly four feet. "I am going to kill a bear."

"You haven't seen a bear?" Crenna asked with some trepidation.

"I will find one," he said, his words quite sober.

"If you do, he'll eat you," Cara said.

William turned disdainful eyes upon his sister. "I am a warrior; I'll do a warrior's work."

"A warrior! You are a white man! Look at you," Cara said. Almost instantly she was ashamed of herself. William turned his pale eyes on her. From across the meadow she could see her father looking their way. She turned and walked away, muttering an apology. Sachim shrugged at Crenna. William's face was crimson.

"William?" his mother said. But the boy had already turned to stalk away. In his hand was a small bow he had made, and three arrows. His narrow shoulders were rigid.

"She has crushed his game, his image of himself," Sachim said. "But in a moment the strength of his dreams will return. Then he will laugh again, and become bold and brave."

"Yes," Crenna said absently. It was the first time either of the children had commented on the difference in their coloration, and it worried her.

William was fair, with Dutch blue eyes like his father. Cara could have been nothing but one of the People. She was dark, her skin like mahogany, her eyes black as coal. Would they always live in a world where such things mattered?

Where could Cara have found the impulse to make such a remark? She and Peter had always been careful to make no comment. Perhaps it was deep in the blood, this mistrust of those who were different, this need to point out the differences. It reminded Crenna all too sharply of the fear and prejudice her own people had held against Peter in those early days.

"Down!" Peter called, cupping his hand to his mouth, and Crenna's head swiveled that way as the great pine swayed and then toppled to the earth, lifting a fine cloud of dust.

She walked toward him, her thoughts still distracted. Peter was glistening with sweat. His long recuperation had not left him fully fit. She glanced involuntarily at the stub of his left arm, recalling the pain and anxiety of the night when she had been forced to amputate it as he lay feverish and pale.

"The first tree," he said happily, and she walked to him, holding him tightly. "That," he said, nodding toward the great fallen pine, "is the beginning of our new world."

While Van der Veghe chose a second tree and began to cut it, Crenna, using the old methods of her people, began trimming the fallen pine into lengths. The bark she scraped away at measured intervals. That bark was then used to start a fire in a hollow beneath the tree at the spot where the log was to be sectioned.

Van der Veghe's ax rang in the clear cold air; the small fires burned brightly. Crenna continued to level the ground near the bluffs where their house, half-dugout, half-log, would abut the bluff.

William, tired of being given a child's jobs again, went wandering, searching with a sharp stick for the elusive bear of his imagination. The woods were deep and cool. Twice he saw deer; once a waddling, outrageously fat porcupine.

He climbed a rocky prominence and looked down upon the meadow. The creek which wound across the valley jogged at this point, tumbled over a bared outcropping, swirled around a deep stony pool, and then continued toward the Monongahela. William sat watching the frothing of the white water, tapping his stick against the stone on which he sat.

He would have his father help him make a larger bow, he decided. Then he would be able to go hunting properly. What was there to do around home? That was going to be slow work, building the house. He wasn't strong enough yet to lift the logs. Even Sachim was stronger than he was. A man had to stand around and listen to women's silly talk. Cara, who thought she was a woman fully grown already, was a torment.

But one day—he lifted his eyes to the broad blue-green land—he would walk the woods and hunt, living alone. Well, maybe his father would travel with him. They would have great times. When winter came he supposed he would have to come home, but he would come with an armful of warm furs and be welcomed as an honored guest.

William sighed, and leaning forward, picked up a handful of small stones, which he flung at the pond below him. Something had happened. The moment of his triumphal return from the wilderness, which had seemed around the corner moments ago, in imagination, now seemed years away, impossibly distant. He was trapped in his boy's body, and it momentarily angered him. But that too soon passed, and he worked his way down the hillside, coming suddenly upon a thicket of wild raspberries. With childish greed he decided to eat all he could hold and to return home empty-handed. Let Cara find her own berries.

He prowled the berry vines, stuffing plump red berries into his mouth, staining his face, catching more than a few thorns. When he could eat no more, he found a large flat rock which overhung the pool where the water from the narrow, silvery falls plummeted from the heights to swirl around in constant, peaceful motion. He lay and watched it, his stomach full of tart-sweet berries, the sun warm on his back, the stone warm beneath him.

"What was that?" Cara held a fish trap in her hands. She looked toward the bluffs, frowning.

"What?" Crenna asked. She stopped her work, which was moving stones of useful size to where Van der Veghe's chimney would be. She straightened, wiping her brow.

"I heard something, Mother."

Crenna shielded her eyes with her hand and looked toward the bluffs. She saw nothing, heard nothing.

"Aunt Sachim?"

"I heard nothing, Cara."

"But I do. . . ." Cara took three steps forward, dropping the fish trap. She lifted her head and looked southward toward the pine-covered bluffs. "I do!" she said with an intensity which startled Crenna.

"What, Cara?" she asked. "What do you hear?"

"I can't . . . Oh, no! It's William, Mother. It's William. Hurry, please!"

Cara started off at a dead run across the meadow. Reaching the bluffs, she clambered up, spilling stone and earth behind her as she clawed her way upward, her face a tight mask, her eyes wide.

"Mother!" she shouted, and Crenna, lifting her skirt, followed.

Sachim wasn't far behind. She stopped long enough to shout at Peter. "Van der Veghe!"

Van der Veghe's head came around, his ax poised overhead for a downstroke. He looked at the women running for the bluff, and his first thought was of a hostile attack. He threw the ax aside and started downslope toward the homesite, cursing himself for having discarded the ax, which might have made a useful weapon.

Yet he saw no warriors, no wild animals, only Sachim waving furiously, Crenna cresting the bluff and disappearing into the tall pines.

"What is it?" he asked breathlessly. He had forgotten himself and spoken in Dutch. Now he asked Sachim again. "What?"

"William!" She pointed up the bluffs.

"What's happened?" he demanded, but Sachim was already off and running, and Van der Veghe loped after her, his head throbbing with alarm. "What is it? What?" he shouted.

"I don't know," Sachim panted. She kept climbing, and Van der Veghe did the same, not feeling the rocks which tore the flesh from his callused palm.

He passed Sachim and ran on ahead through the pines, dodging blindly as he called to his wife. "Crenna!"

He saw her dip down into a fern-clotted ravine and emerge on the far side. "Crenna! What is it? What's happened?"

She paused, shook her head, and rushed on. Van der

Veghe, smothering an oath, ran on even faster. A pine bough whipped across his face, and he was momentarily stunned. He shook it off. Plunging into the ravine, he came down hard, jamming a heel against an unseen stone.

He paid no attention to it. Why was he running? What had happened? Had his entire family gone mad? He clawed his way up the bank through the underbrush and ran on.

Cara, far in advance, rushed onward, still hearing the voice, the fear and anxiety in it. She glanced once across her shoulder and saw her mother, her face drawn, skirt lifted, running after her, and beyond her mother, Van der Veghe, rapidly closing ground, his face pallid.

She knew. *She knew.* She knew. Cara's heart was hammering against her rib cage. Still she heard the sounds, the cries for help, and she ran on without hesitation. She leaped a rocky ravine, landing hard, briefly sprawling against the earth. Lifting herself to her feet, she stumbled on, her breathing ragged, labored.

She knew.

She reached the prominence and without hesitation turned to her left, half-skidding down the winding game trail toward the pool below.

He was there. She saw his hair, damp gold against the blue of the pond. Her heart leaped. She noticed with clarity the red-and-white-beaded belt he wore around his buckskin trousers, remembered vividly the nights Crenna had sat making the surprise gift while William slept.

Cara was off the trail, onto the rocky outcrop, and before she knew what she had done, she was hurtling through the air feetfirst. Then she hit the icy blue water and went down. Not far. Her feet hit the stony bottom of the pool and she came up beside her brother's still form.

She turned him and yanked his head from the water. There was a splash and a shout behind her, and she saw her father fighting his way toward her, his face a gray-white, dismal mask. Crenna stood above them, hands to her mouth. Sachim was rushing down the hillslope.

"Lift him up. That's it!" Van der Veghe was shouting madly. His mouth was drawn down with intense anxiety. His blue eyes were wild with fear. "Is he all right! Can you feel him moving?"

He was beside Cara then, and he pushed her aside with unthinking roughness. Then he was walking toward the shore, carrying his unmoving son. Crenna was rushing around the pool toward the far shore. Cara stood rigidly in the cold water, breast-deep, her eyes blurred, her ears ringing.

She waded toward the shore, the weight of the water against her body cold and swift.

Cara climbed from the stone pool, her buckskin dress heavy with water. She scraped a knee on the rocks and struggled to her feet.

Van der Veghe, still ashen, was working over William. He had placed the boy facedown, head turned, against the earth, and now he lifted him by the abdomen, his motions rhythmic, cautious. Crenna stood biting her lip, staring with disbelief at the scene. She did not seem to notice when her daughter stepped up beside her, wet and cold, but her arm went around Cara's shoulder.

"Do you know how to do this?" Van der Veghe asked loudly, with the irritation anxiety produces. "I only saw it tried once years ago. A boy fell into the Zuider Zee . . . we were fishing for haddock . . ." Van der Veghe's words were rambling; his face, formerly ashen, was now flushed crimson. "Breathe," they saw him say. "Breathe!"

But the thing on the ground, the thing which should have been Cara's brother, William, did not move. A pool of water and slime lay near his slack mouth. His hair, like spikes of cornsilk, looked lifeless; his fingers were blue. Cara wanted to turn her face, to look away, but was unable to. Some dark fascination riveted her vision to the motionless sheath of flesh which was not her brother. Not just now.

She saw the body convulse suddenly. One eye opened, looking yellow and glassy. It flickered open, looked at nothing, and closed again. The convulsion was repeated, and Cara felt her mother's hand tense on her shoulder. The hand gripped her tightly, the fingers digging in roughly. It should have hurt, but Cara didn't feel pain. All of her attention was on the small boy before them, on the tall blond, one-armed man who worked frantically over the still, cold figure.

When he coughed, it was a strangled, gouting sound accompanied by an expulsion of liquid. William took in a deep, high breath and then paused as if his lungs could not expel the breath. He coughed again, a choking, wrenching cough which lifted more fluid from his lungs, and then he lay still, shivering, breathing in shallowly.

His fingers, which had been blue and lifeless, pinkened as

blood and oxygen rushed to the extremities. Cara felt her mother sag against her, felt the warm brush of her kiss, and she realized that her own heart was raging still, thudding against her ribs.

She turned, buried her face against her mother's breast, and cried.

Sachim, who had been standing by silently, helped Van der Veghe to lift his son. Then the tall man turned, and with William's arms locked around his neck, he began walking back toward the homesite.

"Cara . . . ?" Crenna looked at her daughter. She was dark, cold, and damp. Her long hair was plastered to her skull. Her eyes were nearly anxious, nearly troubled. Crenna simply held her, letting her question fade away.

It was not until that evening when they sat near the fire, William's damp clothing and that of Cara steaming next to the flames, that Crenna finished her thought.

"She has the gift," Crenna said.

Van der Veghe held his son, who was wrapped in a red-and-blue blanket. He had been sitting motionlessly by the fire for many hours. He looked at Crenna, but she was not sure if he had heard her or not.

"Yes." It was Sachim who answered. Her voice was soft, and it came as if from a great distance. She looked at Cara, who slept now, bundled in blankets and furs near the fire.

"Is it so, sister?" Crenna wanted to know.

"What are you talking about?" Peter Van der Veghe asked, looking from one sister to the other.

"She heard William when none of us did," Crenna told her husband. "When it was not possible for anyone to hear him. He was too far away. Yet she heard him, and she knew. She has the gift."

"The gift . . ." Van der Veghe frowned and shook his head, not understanding.

"She knew, you see? She knew that there was danger. She heard his cries. She can see across the distances, Peter. She can hear what we cannot hear. She *knows,* Peter."

"I'm sorry. I don't understand what you're telling me."

"It is this, Peter," Sachim said. "The girl has special powers. I've thought before that it might be so. Now and then she will hand you what you wish before you have asked. Now and then she will do what you will before you have put it into words; now and then she knows what is on your mind."

Van der Veghe looked at Sachim's thin, dark face, watched the fire redden her cheekbones and deepen the hollows around her eyes. He was ready to laugh, but he did not. He knew something about these people. He knew that they did not take cynicism lightly; he also knew that more often that not their seemingly preposterous explanations had proved sound. At least he had not been able to disprove them.

"Crenna?" He looked at his wife, that elegant, fine woman whose hair, he noticed for the first time, now showed a touch of wintry gray.

"Sachim is right. I have known it for some time, but I did not mention it. Not to you, not to Cara. It is a gift, Peter, but it is also a burden. To know the future, to foresee tragedy . . ." She shook her head. "That sounds like a wonderful, golden gift, but it can bring sorrow. To see all that is to come, to feel pain twice—to suffer through foreknowledge and then to accept it when it does come—it is a mixed blessing, Peter."

Peter Van der Veghe's eyes lifted toward his daughter, who slept on, heaped over with blankets and furs. "It must have frightened her," he said reflectively. "To have these ideas . . . What should I call them, premonitions? To have them burst upon her. She is so young, Crenna. How can she understand?"

"She understands, my husband, because to her it is natural. It doesn't frighten her." Crenna smiled, her eyes lighted with dancing fire. "But I think it does frighten you just a little."

"Yes," he answered after a pause. "It does frighten me, Crenna, it does. Yet, without that gift . . ." He looked down at his son, still pale and still, sleeping on his lap. She had saved her brother's life; there were no two ways about it. He accepted his wife's contention that Cara would not be frightened by her gift of prescience, but he wondered how it would not be disturbing to anyone, adult or child. Vague knowledge beyond the senses, sudden bursts of insight. It was a frightening gift, and one to be handled carefully. Most carefully.

The house went up slowly. The first snow had come before the roof, of bark and thatch, was in place. Finally the door made of the planks of the horse cart, was hung on leather hinges, and together the family went in. Before, it had been a work project; now, when it was completed, it was suddenly transformed. It was hearth and home. They stood loosely together, watching the fire burn. It was a silent ceremonial moment. Crenna, looking at the stone fireplace, could recall each stone as it was put in place, the concentration on her husband's face, the pleasure when the job was done.

On the wall hung a braided rug which Sachim had made. It was dull red and orange, the only decoration or touch of brightness in the room which did not come from the fire itself.

The floor was of packed earth. There were no windows, but only two narrow slits high on the walls, where the winds of winter, blowing through into the house, would not hit them full force.

"It's done." Van der Veghe turned toward Crenna. His expression was half-satisfied, half-questioning. Was the small lodge enough of a home for a headwoman of the Oneida?

"It's done, and done well," she said, putting an arm around his waist. "And we have enough food to last this winter."

There were a hundred dried fish in the larder, two fine deer. The root cellar was filled with chestnuts and acorns as well as what parched corn they had left from their journey. If the winter were long, it would be difficult, but they would survive, and in the spring they would plant the seed corn and squash they had brought with them.

Warmth. Food. Love. Crenna hugged her husband more tightly. "We have all we need, all we can use," she whispered.

It snowed lightly for two days, long gray clouds sweeping down the Ohio Valley, hiding the sky. On the third morning the snow was already melting as Crenna went out of the house into the golden light of dawn. This was a brief respite before hard winter, and it was time for all of them to gather stores.

William and Cara had built a sled of wood left over from the cart, and they used it to go into the hills to collect firewood. The hunting was left to Crenna. It was impossible for Van der Veghe to use a bow. He was realist enough to know that she was a better hunter anyway.

She had spent a lifetime in the woods, playing, observing, learning. When she moved, her feet were silent against the earth. She knew the game trails, the animal signs. She knew whether a deer was a buck or doe by its hoofprints, by the way it braced itself. She knew how long ago and how frequently the animal had visited the water's edge. And there were skills beyond understanding. The jays which fluttered away screeching when Van der Veghe came near, sat their perches as Crenna, silent and swift, moved through the tall pines.

The sun glittered intermittently through the blue-black boughs overhead. The snow lay in patches in the clearings. The air was crisp; a deep breath was a menace to the lungs. Crenna moved lightly, taking small, shallow breaths.

It had been there each morning for a month. A great buck with much antler for tools, with a fine hide for moccasins and shirts, everything they needed to survive.

There he was, his muzzle lifted attentively, his eyes wary. An old grandfather who had fought many a rutting battle, mounted his harem, sired spotted fawns. He who had walked the long forests, fled from fires and prowling panthers. He who was wise in the ways of his world. He whom Manitou had put on this earth to die so that Crenna's people might live.

She notched an arrow, slowly drawing the sinew-wrapped hickory bow. She spoke wordlessly to the deer: Forgive me for taking your life, Grandfather, but my children will be cold in the winter and their bellies will be empty. You have lived long; let us live a little longer.

The arrow was beside her ear, and then it was gone, a whizzing great insect, its barbed stone head seeking the heart of the stag. The bowstring twanged; she saw the deer go down, flopping on its side, and she rushed toward it, heeding the antlers, remembering Ta-Ka-Linte, a hunter from her own village who had been killed by a frantic buck.

But this deer was not to rise again. The arrow had been true. It lay steaming against the earth, its black nose leaking fluid, its scarred, fawn-colored coat being slowly stained crimson.

And then it was still and Crenna apologized again to the spirit of the deer. Then, ceremony observed, she knelt and began skinning the great buck.

She did not see him at first. She sensed him. The back of her neck prickled and an uneasy current crawled up her spine. She glanced first at her bow, which lay ten feet away leaning against a fallen tree, and then up into the hungry yellow eyes of a prowling gray wolf.

He stood there massive and shaggy, his eyes unblinking. Crenna saw immediately that he had a forepaw missing, that his huge head was scarred, an ear torn.

"Go back, Wolf," she said quietly. She did not move. She sat hunched over the deer, its blood scent rising into the air. She looked beyond the great wolf, wondering if there were more of his kind, but he seemed to be alone. A massive, terrible hunter with fangs which seemed as long as Crenna's fingers.

"Go back, Wolf, find your own kill," she said. She could see the demons lurking in his amber eyes, however, see the gauntness of his belly, his concave flanks.

It was well over a hundred pounds of killing beast. A savage, fearless instrument of an angry nature. Designed to kill, ridden by the dark demons. His eyes never wavered. His jaw drooped open, revealing a purplish tongue. He slavered, took a step forward, and halted again . . . challenging?

Crenna quickly cut out the liver of the deer and threw it to the wolf, which gobbled it up, swallowing it nearly whole in two gagging efforts.

"I will leave you half," she said, and the wolf cocked his head. Far from being appeased by Crenna's gift, he seemed inflamed by it. He had tasted meat, but that was not enough to assuage his savage hunger.

Crenna again looked at her bow, knowing that it was impossible. She would have to reach her bow, notch an arrow—and a killing arrow—before the ravaged wolf could reach her.

She wrenched the entrails of the deer free, feeling their warmth against her hands. She tossed them toward the wolf, which snapped them up voraciously, his great body quivering as he forced the food down.

Even that was not enough. He came forward another step, his amputated foot forcing him to hobble. Crenna stood cautiously; through her mind flitted images of her son and daughter, of Peter Van der Veghe. There were other deer; she would not contend with this dark beast over it.

But would he let her go! She rose cautiously, knowing that her body smelled of deer blood, that she could as easily be a victim.

"Take it and go, Dark One. Eat. Eat and then leave. Do not trouble me."

She was erect now, slowly backing toward her bow and arrows. The skinning knife was in her hand. The wind was chilling; it drifted her dark hair across her face. The wolf came forward, eyes yellow, feral, body quivering, his gait ungainly, his sides heaving. Then he lunged.

Crenna nearly fell, backing away. The wolf lurched forward, and reaching the deer, he halted. He looked up with glaring, mocking eyes at this weak human. Then, his eyes still on Crenna, he lowered his muzzle and tore at the heart of the deer, swallowing it whole. His bloody, shaggy face lifted toward Crenna, and seeing that she still backed away, more rapidly now, he crouched and began methodically to rip the meat from the bones of the great buck.

Crenna was a hundred feet away, still backing slowly. Now she had the bow in her hands, an arrow notched. Her heart palpitated rapidly; her blood was hot in her arteries. Her mouth was dry, cottony.

She did not run; she didn't dare. He watched her still, slavering jaws working as he gorged himself on the raw meat.

Finally, when Crenna could no longer see the wolf and his dinner, she turned her back and walked homeward through the pines, her legs shaky, her heart still racing.

She could not keep herself from turning her head at frequent intervals, watching for a loping, sharp-toothed attack, although her logic told her that it was foolish. The wolf had what he wanted. He would not be hungry for a long while.

She told Peter about it when she got back to the house.

"Lord, Crenna! Are you all right now?"

"Quite all right now." She managed a smile. "He is an evil one, Peter."

Van der Veghe did not laugh. He had lived with the woman too long. To Crenna and all of her people, spirits lived in the bodies of animals, in the trees and rivers. Most were friendly spirits, easily appeased. A deer, for example, was fair game. You had only to apologize to the spirit, and seeing your need for the hide and horns, for the liver and meat, the spirit would depart to find a new home. But there were evil ones in the forest. Rogue bears, killer wolves.

If Van der Veghe would have explained it all by understanding that the wolf had been injured—mark his lost forefoot—still he could not deny that an evil spirit of sorts now resided in the animal. He had come to grips with Crenna's beliefs long ago. They were, he decided, only a matter of terminology. Yet . . . at times he too had seen things which bordered on the supernatural, things which would have made his fellows at the university split their sides laughing.

But then, they had never lived here. To exist beside nature day by day was entirely different from studying it in the halls of a university. Van der Veghe, who had been a naturalist by training, had learned more from Crenna than from all the otiose texts in the great musty library in that university at Delft.

He wiped his hand on the plank which he had propped up on the backs of the two chairs brought from Albany. There he had his yellow clay brought up from the riverbank. The clay was used to chink the gaps between the logs of the cabin walls.

"What should we do?" he asked.

"Do?" Crenna shook her head. "There is nothing to do."

"The children, Crenna. We can't have them wandering the forest while the wolf is out there."

"They seldom attack a human being," she said.

"Not even this one?" he asked, and he saw the sympathetic response in her eyes. Yes, she knew. This one might do anything. He was an evil one.

"That," Van der Veghe said, "is what I thought." He turned half away and said as he dabbed at the clay, "I'm going to go after him."

"You can't!" she said, coming to him, turning him around. Her eyes were dark and fiery.

"How can I not? We are speaking of the safety of our children, Crenna."

"But you . . ."

"I have one arm. I am not an Oneida warrior. I have never stalked a killing wolf."

"Yes," she answered slowly. "All of that. I won't have you killed, either, Peter Van der Veghe. Don't you know—haven't you learned by now—that I have no life without you, my husband?" Her eyes searched his. Her hands were on his capable shoulders. She felt him shrug slightly.

"I am talking about my children's safety, and yours, Crenna. Nothing can mean more."

"But you are not equipped—"

"Will he go away?" he demanded in a tone sharper than she expected. The sharpness was brought on by anger, by concern, yes, and by fear. Fear for family and loved ones. That was something Crenna understood, for it was uppermost in her mind at this moment. She feared for Van der Veghe, her beautiful tall Dutchman. This kind man who had come across the sea and suffered for her, who had given her only love and happiness and was now ready to sacrifice his life if need be.

"He will go away." Crenna moved closer, lifted her arms, and intertwined her fingers behind his neck. Her breasts pressed against his chest. "We will keep the children close to the house for a time. There is no need to take foolish chances, my husband. If you . . ."

She did not finish her sentence. Instead she lifted her face to his and kissed him, smiling as she did so, although tears stood in her eyes. One broke free and streaked hotly across her cheek.

"I won't take an unnecessary chance," Peter told her, stroking her hair. "Do you think I am ready to leave you?" He smiled then, deeply, and kissed her forehead, his arm tightening around her. "But," he asked, "what if the wolf does not go?"

"He will go." Crenna turned her eyes down. Her fingers continued to toy with the fringes on Van der Veghe's buckskin shirt. "Why would he stay?" she asked with a light shrug.

"And if he does not go?" Van der Veghe repeated, lifting her chin.

"*Then* we shall discuss it. Give it time, Peter. So many problems resolve themselves. This is nothing. I met an Evil One. He grinned at me and I ran away, a foolish woman."

"Yes," Van der Veghe said, pressing her to him. *A foolish woman?* Not this one. He had never known her to do something utterly foolish, never known her to panic or to feel unwarranted fear. But she had seen enough of that wolf to fear him. Now she was trying to protect her husband, and he could only love her the more for it. He held her close, touching her ear with his lips, until he laughed and stepped back, saying, "I've gotten clay on you. Look at you!"

Crenna too laughed, and she turned away, brushing the yellow mud from her dress. But she had turned only so that he would not see the lingering apprehension in her eyes. *He was an Evil One,* and he had come hunting.

Cara knelt by the river's edge. Reaching below the surface of the icy water, she found the tether and began pulling the fish trap in, already knowing by its weight that she had caught something.

Soon there would be no more fishing. Soon the river would be sheeted with ice, the great oaks along the river standing gray and leafless.

She drew the trap from the water. It was simply a conical contraption of rush reeds. The fish swimming downstream went into the big end of the trap, and kept there by the current, were unable to escape. A small happy exclamation escaped her lips as she saw the great silver fish, one with much meat, wriggling in the trap.

She pulled the trap onto the bank and set it aside, still listening to the flapping sounds the fish made. Finally it was still, its pink gill slits showing as it tried to find oxygen in this foreign environment.

Cara felt dizzy, and she sat down, back against the elm which shaded this small covelike bend in the wandering river. Her legs trembled as she eased back, and she felt a warmth creeping down her abdomen. She closed her eyes and leaned her head back, the rough bark of the elm against her scalp.

The river whispered past; the clouds fashioned sky cities overhead. Somewhere a lark called to another of its kind.

The warmth between her legs increased, and Cara simply sat there, eyes shut, feeling her body transform itself. She was not frightened, for Crenna had told her that this would happen. That her body would ripen and alter. But she had not expected it to feel quite like this; she had not expected it to come quite so soon.

There had been a little stiffness in her spine, a slight bloated feeling for nearly a week. Cara opened her eyes, watching the clouds transform themselves into hatchet heads, hulking towers, running silver horses. She smiled and closed her eyes again. The river ran past. She was a woman!

"What is the matter with them?" William asked. He sat near the fire, watching his father, who held a clay pipe between his knees and was now filling it with the last of their tobacco.

Peter Van der Veghe's eyes lifted to the far corner of the house. Sachim, his wife, and his daughter were huddled together, speaking quietly. Cara was beaming with physical pride.

"It is woman's business, William," Peter said. He tossed the tobacco sack to the mantel, poked the long-stemmed clay pipe in his mouth, and lit it with a brand from the fire.

"Secrets now," William grumbled.

"And don't you have your own, boy?" Van der Veghe asked.

"Sometimes." William looked at the writhing golden flames in the massive stone fireplace. A stew pot hung there from a hook Van der Veghe had fashioned from iron stripped from the old cart.

"Then leave them to their secrets, William."

"I am always treated like a child."

"Because you are!" Van der Veghe laughed. The laughter didn't transmit itself to William. He stared broodingly at the fire. The smoke from Van der Veghe's pipe lay heavy in the room, forming itself into silver-blue spirals which hovered overhead.

"I'd really like to know," William said finally, and Van der Veghe nodded.

"Very well. Cara has become a woman today."

"Is that all?" William said with disgust. He shook his head and slapped his knee. "Women—and those are their secrets."

Van der Veghe smiled softly. "They will have a small ceremony. We are not invited. It is the old way."

"What old way?" William asked with surprising virulence.

"The Oneida way, the way of your mother's people."

"Why is it always *their* way? Why?" The boy's eyes were earnest. "Tales of Ravens and Bears, of Great Heads and Stone Giants! Why don't you speak to me of Europe, of the English and French. *Of our home*."

Peter Van der Veghe looked into the boy's pale blue eyes, surprised not at the request but at the almost desperate force of his words. *Our home*.

"It is all so far away, William," Van der Veghe said gently.

"And so are my mother's people," he pointed out. A bit of pine pitch caught fire and flared up hotly, sending off a small shower of tiny golden sparks.

"Yes." Van der Veghe looked down at his pipe and frowned. "But Europe is much farther. Across the sea."

"I know that. But a man could travel there, couldn't he?"

"Why would he want to?" Van der Veghe asked with irony. "I came a long way to be rid of Europe and its ways."

"Perhaps all men aren't the same," William said. "Perhaps some men would want to travel to Europe and . . . know. Just know what is there. Castles, canals, highways of stone."

"And corruption and plague."

"Still . . ." William's voice was faraway. "A man might like to know."

It was then that the distant howl sounded. Atavistic, mournful, chilling. Van der Veghe was to his feet in an instant. Crenna had already gone to the door.

Outside, a pale half-moon floated behind a screen of dark clouds. The wind shook the pines on the high bluffs. To the east the moon-silvered river ran slowly southward. The howl came again.

"What is that?" William asked.

Crenna glanced at Van der Veghe. "Only a wolf, William. Only a wolf baying at the moon."

"I've heard a wolf before," he said, and she felt him shudder. "But this—it's different."

The mournful sound drifted again across the meadow. A tragic, lost, and bloody sound which seemed to echo off the moon, to summon dark spirits from it. Evil calling to its brothers. A lost mourner on the dark earth, a clan chieftain. Which? All of these, Crenna thought. He stood alone somewhere, the dark one, calling to his tribe, complaining bitterly to the moon spirits that his people no longer obeyed, that they shunned him now that he was crippled and scarred. Angrily he proclaimed his defiance.

"Crenna?" Peter was beside her, his hand on her neck. "Are you all right?"

"I don't like this one, Peter. I do not like him at all."

"No," he agreed. "I don't like him either." He had his coat on now, the one Crenna had made of buckskin stuffed with the down of ducks.

"Where are you going?" she asked, her voice catching.

"Not to fight our Evil One," he replied with a comforting smile. "I thought I should bring the horses in closer. If the wolf is as much the renegade as he seems, he may try for them."

"He cannot run swiftly with his bad foot," Crenna said. "That is why he stays here, around us."

"I think you're right," Van der Veghe said. "You killed the buck for him, and he hopes to have such luck again." A lone wolf who could not run well was a desperate creature. The deer, the rabbits, eluded him easily. He had no pack to circle behind the prey, to distract them while he pounced. The horses, penned up as they were now, were a tempting meal for the Evil One. Once the horses were dead, there would be no others. Although they had heard of wild horses farther south, horses escaped a century ago from the Spanish paddocks—or liberated by the Indians—they flourished now on the plains.

But here, in Ohio, horses were few. True, the Shawnee had some, traded for from the allied western tribes, the Sioux and the Omaha, but they were unlikely to let Van der Veghe have any—they were still too dear in this part of the country.

He walked out, watching the glitter of the stars, the moonshine on the frosted earth. The horses, their whiskers frozen into icy spikes, watched his approach warily.

"So you heard him, and you know what he wants," Van der Veghe said softly. He stepped into the rough corral and stroked the horses' necks. Looping a rope around the bay's neck, he led it back toward the house, tethering it to a picket pin driven into the ground.

Returning with the roan, he tethered it similarly. Then for a minute Van der Veghe stood looking toward the piny bluffs; but he saw nothing. Only the cold dark skies, the moon falling behind the towering black pines, the formless black mass of the high ridge.

"But you're out there, aren't you, you bastard wolf," Van der Veghe said in a whisper. "You're out there lurking, and you're growing hungrier with each day."

It began to snow again overnight. Heavy, dry flakes which settled softly on the roof and smothered the earth's green. The fire blazed away day and night as the long storm hovered overhead, the temperature dropping overnight to freezing and below, rising no higher for days on end.

The eaves were hung with icicles. Water had to be boiled and carried to the horses. Van der Veghe and Crenna decided that because of the wolf the children would no longer go out, at least for the time being, and they grew restless and irritable.

Van der Veghe and the women took turns going into the hills to hunt for firewood, which had to be dug up from beneath the snow. Still it snowed. Day was not much different from night, except at night the wolf howled and the wind carried his cry to them.

Sachim told tales. "The little people, the pukwudjinnies, conquered a very wicked giant. The giant, Kwasind, was an evil weedigo, a bad giant, and very strong. But he was not smart. Once he told the little water spirits, the nibanabas, that he could be killed in only one way. At the back of his head was a hollow where no skull bone had grown. If he were hit there, then Kwasind would die. But it was of no use to the little spirits to know this. Kwasind was as tall as a pine tree, and they could not strike him, and so he trampled through the woods, killing everything that grew.

"But the pukwudjinnies tricked him. Their singing was very beautiful and had the power to lull you to sleep. One day while Kwasind was in his great canoe, the water spirits began to sing, and soon the terrible giant was sound asleep. The water spirits then gathered up pine cones, and swimming to his canoe, they climbed aboard, and while he slept facedown, they struck him in the back of the head with the pine cones, killing Kwasind."

"That's a child's story," William said irritably.

"You used to like it, William," Sachim said in soft reproach.

"So . . . I used to be a child; I'm not now."

"No." Sachim shook her head. "One forgets."

Crenna looked at Van der Veghe, who said nothing. They realized that Sachim told the children tales not only to divert them but also to instruct them. William, too old for this amusement, was too young to learn from the stories.

"I think, then, bed," Crenna said, her voice a little stiff.

William started to plead, saw the set expression on his mother's face, and thought better of it. He turned toward his bed of furs in the corner, yawning.

They heard the terrified whinny of the horse above the shriek of the wind, and Van der Veghe, grabbing his ax, was out the door and into the teeth of the storm before anyone else could move.

Crenna was at his heels. She didn't bother to close the door either as the horse's shrill whinny sounded again. The terrible force of the wind drove the snow into the cabin as Sachim tried to shut it, keeping the children behind her.

Crenna emerged into the whirlwind of snow, her eyes searching desperately for Van der Veghe. It was impossible to see a thing; even his tracks were already filled by the wind-whipped snow.

She started toward the sheltered side of the house where the horses had been kept close in against the hollow in the bluffs. Before she could reach the corner of the house, she saw the gray phantom.

He loomed up out of the snowstorm, yellow eyes bright, crazed. Crenna pulled back so quickly that she tripped and slammed into the cabin wall, her head jolting off the logs.

She saw him crouch, saw him leap, and she threw a hand up defensively. But it was too late. The weight of the wolf slammed her back again. She felt his hoary coat against her flesh, saw those malevolent greedy eyes, the slavering jaws. She could smell the stench of dead meat about the animal.

She thought she screamed, but she wasn't sure of that. She only knew that the wolf had hit her, that he lay upon her, that the snow was falling in heavy swirls, that the wind was bitterly cold.

It was a long minute as she sat there, hand over her face, hip deep in snow, before she realized that the wolf was not moving. He glared up at her with sightless eyes, his tongue lolling from his mouth.

"Crenna! Crenna!"

She saw Peter rushing toward her from out of the snowstorm, saw the anguish on his face, the ax in his hand. And it was then, only then, that she realized that the gray wolf was dead and that it had been killed by the arrow which protruded from its heart.

"Are you all right! My God!" Peter pushed the wolf aside; the animal was already stiffening in this cold. Then he pulled her to him and held her, his frosted mustache against her face, a hot tear from his eye freezing against her cheek.

"I'm fine, fine," she kept repeating. Finally, laughing now with relief, they stood, staring down at the wolf, at the arrow which jutted from his rib cage just behind the right shoulder.

"Who in God's name . . . ?" Peter peered into the swirling storm, seeing nothing, no one. He reached out and yanked the arrow from the wolf's body.

"And so," Crenna said, "that is done with. The Evil One is no more."

The Evil One was gone. But there was another presence out there now, hidden by the dark and the storm. Crenna was worried. They knew what the wolf wanted. Blood and meat. But this other one. The one who walked on two legs, who moved like the wind, who struck surely, with deadly accuracy—what was it *he* wanted?

2

The winter passed slowly. The storm was a never-ending sweep of clouds, gray days, and dark, dark nights. Cara had nearly forgotten that the sky could be blue, that there were such things as green grass, flocking birds, and butterflies.

The snow on the windward side of the tiny house drifted to the eaves. The fire, always blazing, seemed never to warm the house completely, and they wore as many blankets and furs as they could carry.

Meals took on an insipid sameness. Jerked venison, dried fish, and corn soup, with sometimes a pudding made of chestnuts and a bit of their precious maple sugar.

There were the tales of Sachim to occupy them, always Sachim and her tales; and the lessons of Crenna. She taught them the language of the English and the Dutch, although Cara could not see what good it did to learn English when England was across the sea, the nearest Englishman hundreds of miles from Ohio.

William took to conversing with his father in Dutch, and he prodded him constantly to tell him about Europe.

And so the days passed, tolerable but with creaking sameness. It was the nights which Cara found nearly intolerable.

She slept but did not sleep. She took mind voyages to distant places, to the star towers which Manitou's hand had built beyond the storm clouds. She rode a fiery comet and laughed with the Weenks—those tiny dragonfly-riding warriors who brought sleep and dreams and lightness to the world.

And then, at times, with her new womanhood upon her, she would lie awake when the cabin was still, with only the low grumbling and hissing of the fire, the wailing of the wind. Her body would stir, warm, and even ache as she wondered when he would come. Who? A tall young brave, very strong and daring. He would come with horses or with furs, and he would purchase Cara from her father. Then he would set her on a spotted pony and take her into the wilderness to be his bride.

The idea was frightening, but deliciously exciting. She could see the strong young warrior, but his face was not clear. She could feel the weight of his body against hers. And again she shivered with fear and girlish anticipation.

All dreams—all foolish dreams to pass a winter's night. Yet at times it was real, all too real, and Cara's heart would drum in her breast and she would *know*. She whispered to the night: "I know he is coming."

Then, satisfied with the end of her twilight dream, she could roll over, bundled in her furs, and as the cold winds blew, she could sleep.

Then it happened that Hinu, the Thunder God and the West Wind, took pity on the people and together they chased Ka-tash-huaht from the land, sent him skulking and snarling back to his frozen north, and the West Wind breathed gently on the earth, warming it with his touch.

When Van der Veghe opened the door on this morning, there was a burst of nearly white light which flooded the cabin, blinding them momentarily. Still they could see muddy gray clouds pasted against the skies—Ka-tash-huaht's footprints. But between these clouds lay patches of brilliant blue. The icicles which hung like translucent fangs along the eaves were slowly melting.

Cara went out to see to the horses. The snow still lay deep and virginal across the land. The glare off the snow was blinding.

She walked slowly through the knee-deep snow to the hollow in the bluffs, finding the horses shaggy, suffering with the ice which still clung to their coats, but healthy.

With a piece of rough sacking Cara rubbed the ice from

their coats, talking to them gently as she worked. They had little enough hay left, and what there was was mildewed and black, but there would be green grass soon enough. Fields of it, an entire valley ripe with lush new grass.

She finished her work and started back toward the house. Cara halted, surprised. There were footprints in the snow. She looked around, expecting to see her father or mother. There was no one.

Perplexed, she walked back to the cabin. She glanced at the floor, seeing no damp patches, looked at their feet and then at their faces. No one had been out that morning but her.

"I saw footprints in the snow," she said simply, and no one answered her. They all knew by now that there was a man in the hills—they assumed it was a man—a man who killed wolves, who watched them silently, a man who was capable of living a winter alone out there. His arrow still rested on the rough-hewn mantelpiece.

"The horses?" her father asked obliquely.

"They are gaunt and long-haired, but healthy," Cara answered.

Crenna looked up from the corner where she was making her preparations. "Winter is over," she announced in a way which admitted no contradiction. Van der Veghe knew she was right; she had always been right. It would snow no more. "We must burn tobacco to Hinu for delivering us from Ka-tash-huaht."

William made a small disparaging noise and Van der Veghe shot his son a rebuking glance. The boy shrugged.

"It must be done," Crenna said quietly. "It is only proper."

She rose now with a bit of tobacco, her flint and steel, and a small clay bowl. She went out into the blinding white of morning, and they followed, watching as Crenna struck fire to the tobacco and then stood, chanting: "Our thanks to Hinu, who has driven away the North Wind. Our thanks to the West Wind, who has brought his warm breath to the land. Summon the Sisters from their deep sleep, for soon we will be planting our crops. Let them sleep in our corn seeds and, stretching from their winter's nap, let them make our corn grow tall and straight."

William watched sullenly, Cara noticed. He was determined, this one, to be a European, and Cara wondered with a pang of guilt if she hadn't helped to do this to her brother.

She recalled the times she had told him he was no warrior, that he was a white man.

Crenna rose, hands over her head. She sang a brief, joyous song like that of a lark, and then she turned, touching her forehead. With a start Cara realized suddenly that her mother was not young any longer. This hard past winter had run frosty fingers through her hair and touched it with winter white. Not so much white, only a strand here and there, but it was noticeable. Cara, whose own youthful belief in physical immortality was shaken by this realization, shuddered a little. Her eyes shifted to her father. He was drawn and pale from the winter. His hair was thinning. She remembered a bald Dutchman she had seen as a child, remembered the shocked amusement. She had asked her mother why the man had plucked his head, and Crenna had explained promptly and with conviction that the white men had once offended a mighty spirit and the spirit had decreed that they should lose their hair, a fate spared the Indians, who respected all of the spirits and honored them.

. . . As her mother did now, burning tobacco to the Thunder God, Hinu.

The ceremony completed, Peter Van der Veghe stood in the yard looking about him at the snow-smothered valley. "There is so much to do," he said. "It's time to begin."

The first order of business was to restock the depleted larder. They must have meat. The deer would be out of their thickets now, searching for fodder. Crenna herself would hunt, and she agreed to take William, who was desperate to learn how to use a bow properly.

Van der Veghe went out in search of firewood—the nights would still be cold for a long while.

Cara went off by herself to the river, fringed with ice, with only here and there a gap where the gray water was visible through the frozen surface.

She had taken a length of iron—once a cart strut—with her, and she chipped away at the ice until she had a hole large enough for fishing. Then she lowered her antler-bone hook baited with a cornball and stood back, arms crossed beneath her breasts, breath frosting from flared nostrils, to wait.

It was a long, cold morning, but when she returned she had three red carp and one fine silvery trout. Van der Veghe took an uncommon interest in the fish, cleaning them happily. Cara remembered her mother telling them that Van der Veghe had been a naturalist, and recalled the tale of the Oneida camp. There the Indians had assumed that Van der Veghe was a sorcerer, divining the future from an animal's entrails as other shamans did. It had nearly gotten Van der Veghe murdered.

When Crenna returned, a beaming William beside her, she brought a young deer, thin from the hard winter, but carrying enough meat to last them a good long time. Proudly Crenna revealed that it had been William's arrow which killed the spikehorn, although Cara doubted it.

Van der Veghe and Sachim were careful to heap praise upon this young blue-eyed youth who would be a warrior. Cara managed to mutter some compliment and was rewarded with a scornful glance from her brother.

The following day was warmer yet, and by the end of the week the snow had nearly melted. The earth was muddy and dark; the ice in the river had broken up, and milk-white floes drifted downstream on slate-gray water.

In another week it was possible to work the earth, and the entire family was out planting their precious corn, Crenna singing to the Sisters, the spirits of the crops, as they went with their dibble sticks, tucking each seed carefully away in the dark, loamy earth.

The grass was already springing from the earth, metallic green, bright, fresh. In another month it would be tall, a rare treat for the long-suffering horses.

Van der Veghe had begun a smokehouse and a shed for the horses. He had plans to add another room to the cabin. Cara helped him more often than not. William spent long hours in the forest with his bow, bringing back more stories than game.

One afternoon, late, when the dying sun bled crimson and deep orange onto the sheer fragments of clouds above the pine-clad bluffs, William came home, struggling beneath a weight.

"He's got one!" Van der Veghe shouted happily, and Crenna came around the corner of the house and stood, hands on hips, watching William walking down the long grassy slope. On his back was a whitetail buck. He lifted a hand, and Van der Veghe smiled at the assumed casualness.

The boy was flushed with excitement, his eyes bright. "Not a bad one," he said, dropping the deer from his back to stand panting before his parents.

"It is a magnificent animal," Crenna said.

"I saw better." William shrugged.

"There is plenty of meat for the family."

"One shot," William blurted out, able to hold back no longer. "One arrow as he paused before leaping the brook. At first I thought I had missed." His words tumbled after each other. The sundown flushed his cheeks still more. "I saw him go across the brook and into the brush. He didn't get far."

"And now you must come and eat," Crenna said, hugging her son. "You must be hungry."

"I must skin the animal."

"I will do that, or Cara, William. You eat. Wash first."

Crenna, her arm around William, escorted him into the house. He had begun to tell his story over again, embellishing it, each detail important.

Van der Veghe hefted the deer and walked it to the hook which hung under the eaves of the house for that purpose. He lifted the buck high, and it settled on the hook.

"So I must skin it."

Van der Veghe turned to find his daughter. Lovely she looked in the dull glow of dusk. He hadn't really noticed before how mature she looked. Her breasts, which had been buds before winter, were now full, proclaiming her womanhood.

"You will eat it," he teased her.

Cara had to laugh. "I suppose so. I heard the mighty hunter." She nodded her head toward the house.

"It's important to him. He doesn't feel that he has been contributing. Now he has."

"He could have been working in the garden—that would have been a contribution." Cara held her skinning knife and a stone. Expertly she sharpened the knife with long, half-circular strokes. The small rasping sound of steel against stone was clearly audible in the twilight silence.

"I worry about him sometimes," Van der Veghe said unexpectedly. He looked toward the house, mingled fondness and concern in his eyes. The expression held for only a moment.

"And sometimes, Father," Cara said to him, coming to stretch out on tiptoes and kiss his ruddy cheek, "we worry about you."

"Me?" Van der Veghe, genuinely surprised, laughed. "I

want nothing else for myself. But I want you two to be whole, to be happy.'' He gave her a playful push. ''To your skinning now, woman.''

Cara smiled and with a sigh knotted back her long dark hair. The hour was late, but she needed little time for this task now. Her hands were swift, the knife sharp, and she set to work.

She found it beneath the ribs, and when she was through, she walked into the house with it in her pocket. ''Father?''

Peter Van der Veghe was sketching an oriole with charcoal. The fire backlighted him. He glanced up, and then, placing his paper aside, he walked to where Cara waited. ''What is it?''

''May I speak to you outside?''

''Of course.'' He set his pipe on the puncheon table and followed her out into the starlit night, noticing the sliver of moon behind the oaks across the river. ''What is it?''

''I found this.'' She slipped it into his hand, and Van der Veghe, turning it over in his fingers, frowned. It was an arrowhead, but not one of William's. Its style was unique. Of glassy white stone, heavily barbed, finely chipped.

''Someone else killed the deer.''

Cara nodded. ''He said he thought he missed his shot. He did miss it, apparently.''

Van der Veghe's eyes lifted to the dark hills. The arrowhead was unique, but he had seen one like it before. There was a duplicate of this one on the arrow inside the house, the arrow which had killed the wolf that winter night. So he was still out there. Wanting . . . ?

''Say nothing to William, Cara,'' he cautioned her.

''Of course not. But does it mean what I think it does? That he's still there, still prowling around at night? Perhaps—?''

''We don't know what he wants,'' Van der Veghe said quickly. ''It may not even be the same man. Perhaps this is the style of arrowhead which is used here. Perhaps the deer carried that arrowhead for a long while.''

''Perhaps.'' Cara kissed her father and went into the house. She was not convinced; neither was Van der Veghe. Someone lived in those hills, one as sly as a fox, as silent as a shadow. Perhaps it would be a good idea to seek him out and make friends. But then, if that was what he wanted, he would have come down already, long ago.

Whoever he was, he had a reason for hiding. He had

helped them twice—Crenna owed this stranger her life. Van der Veghe made a sudden decision. Going back into the house, he crossed to his tobacco pouch. While his family watched curiously, he placed it into an earthen pot. To that he added a small sack of salt and, on an impulse, the sketch of the oriole he had been working on.

"What is it, Peter?" Crenna asked.

"I am going to propitiate a spirit," he replied laconically.

Only Cara understood what he meant, and she looked up anxiously from her chair at the table.

"But that is all of the tobacco you have left," Crenna said.

"More is growing." He looked at it wistfully for a moment, then smiled, kissed his wife on the forehead, and said, "I shall be back soon."

They watched him walk out of the house, closing the door behind him. The night was cool; the sliver of a moon was peering over the dark blisters the oaks made against the night horizon. The river muddled past. Van der Veghe walked the long meadow, went into the pines, where there was little moonlight to guide his steps, and, walking on swiftly, went to the brook which burbled out of the stony ravine among the trees.

There was a small clearing with a single bedraggled cedar tree growing in its center, and it was there that Van der Veghe hung the clay basket.

He stood looking around for a moment, seeing nothing but the dark pines like ten thousand cowled monks, the thin star shadows, the faint silver of the creek.

"Thank you," he said aloud, and then he turned and walked back downslope, hearing nothing, seeing nothing in the silent night, although once—for reasons he could not explain—he was certain, somehow certain, that his path was being paralleled by another presence.

The warm winds ruffled the leaves of the river oaks; the sun glittered on the face of the fast-running river. Gentle rains nourished the crops the Van der Veghes had planted, and soon green corn stood waist-high in the meadow. The squash, all vine and no fruit as yet, crawled across the earth, taking nourishment from it. Crenna watched the borer-plagued beans anxiously; Van der Veghe observed the tobacco crop, stunted and pale, morosely.

William wandered the hills, and now he brought meat

home twice a week. The house grew. Van der Veghe had added another room, completed his smokehouse and the corrals, and reset the chimney which a high winter wind had toppled.

Day after day passed in gentle warmth, in rich sameness. They saw no one but themselves. The only smoke which rose into the pale summer skies lifted from their own new chimney. There might have been no one else in all of the world.

If William was restless with his new approaching manhood, Cara with her ripening womanhood, Crenna and Van der Veghe were only content. The days were hard, the sun warm. The evenings were a time for a simple meal, for conversation—frequently out-of-doors, where they moved the chairs on hot summer evenings, and later, after bathing, a restful, deserved sleep in the arms of their loved one.

Van der Veghe lay awake at times, contemplating his Indian wife, this beautiful, devoted, clever, resourceful woman, and he wondered how such fortune had ever come his way. Silently he would kiss her and then lie against her in the warm night. He did not know how many nights Crenna, awakening, looked at her man and had many of the same thoughts.

Cara felt alone. It was her age, they had told her, and she was wise enough to believe that it was so. But she—neither child nor woman—felt restless awakenings, vague yearnings, and she lay awake long after the others were asleep, watching the starlight glimmer through the high windows, thinking about . . . him.

That warrior on his spotted pony; he who would be too rough, yet gentle underneath it all. A man used to man's ways, to the warfare and the hunting. A man with bark on his soul, but with gentle dreams in his eyes.

She saw him often in her hours of darkness, in her half-sleep.

To see him in broad daylight, of the flesh, and to see him return her astonished gaze with a haughty, utterly composed glance was enough to weaken her knees, to cause her head to spin, to intimidate her soul.

It happened in midsummer. Cara, looking up from her hoeing, saw the long line of Indians moving northward along the river, and she dropped her tool, rushing toward the house, long braids flying.

She slammed open the door. "Strangers!" she said breathlessly. Van der Veghe and Crenna had been at their noontime meal; now they leaped up and rushed to the door in time to see the Indians, all but their four leaders traveling on foot, ford the river and come toward their land.

"Who are they?" Peter asked.

"Shawnee, I think," Crenna told him. "We should go down to meet them, Peter. Let them see who we are, that we have no weapons in hand."

"Yes, you're right." It would be a mistake to try to hole up in the house.

Van der Veghe let Crenna lead the way. He walked behind with Cara. Sachim, standing farther up the meadow, an armload of hay before her, stared after them.

The strangers were moving with deliberate insouciance. As they came nearer, Cara could see that of the four mounted men, two were her father's age or older. The two others were no more than boys. One of these had a crooked mouth and a nose which had obviously been broken. The other! Cara nearly stumbled. Her breath caught. It was the man from out of her dreams.

Young, haughty, sun-bronzed, wilderness-tempered, he wore only a loincloth and moccasins. He sat his spotted pony like the prideful god Menabozho. His black, black eyes met Cara's and they smiled, although his mouth remained firm, set in a hard line.

She could only stand and gawk. The wind drifted a loose strand of hair across her eyes, but she made no move to brush it away. She felt incapable of movement.

Crenna had gone forward to talk to the Shawnee men; Van der Veghe hung back. They would speak to Crenna sooner than to him. He, as spokesman, was a white invader with an Indian wife. Crenna, on the other hand, might be regarded well as a headwoman who had through some quirk obtained and now kept a white dog.

Yet the Shawnee had no headwomen, Crenna knew. Their women did not enjoy the status the Iroquois women did. Theirs was a man's society.

"Welcome to our poor land," Crenna said.

"It is not your land," the young man with the crooked face shot back.

Crenna studied his face. There was a bitterness lurking in his eyes. He was a boy who rushed to become a man, and so would never be one at all.

"It is Manitou's land," Crenna responded. "And so we must use a portion of it to live, as the Shawnee do."

"The Shawnee do not cut at their mother's breast," the young one said, nodding at the neat rows of corn.

"It is the way of my people," Crenna answered. She spoke to the older of the two men now, ignoring the young warrior.

"Iroquois?" the old one asked in a gravelly voice.

"Yes. Oneida," Crenna said.

"*Mingoes*," the crooked young man said disparagingly. It was a term of contempt on his lips. "We have seen others. None with a white dog." He looked at Van der Veghe and shook his head.

"Once I was with the Iroquois in a winter camp," the second older warrior said. "The Seneca, your brothers. They treated me well."

"They are in the hunting grounds!" the young man objected again. This time the older of the mature warriors cast a withering glance his way.

"And so are we. This is no one's land." The old man shrugged. "They come to live upon the land. We come to live from it. We are making our summer hunt," he explained, his manner friendlier now. "Our home is to the south and west, across the second river. You will not go so far?"

It was a subtle warning to do no such thing, and Crenna answered quickly, "We are here and will go no farther. I am called Crenna," she said.

"Turtle Back," the elder man replied with a faint smile. "This is my brother, Stone Wolf. These are my sons." He nodded toward the crooked young man and the other warrior, he who had said nothing, he whom the gods had formed perfectly. He would be a leader, this one; it was written in his eyes. Perhaps that was what caused the bitterness in the other young man's expression.

"We have but a little, but we would be happy to make tea for you. We have berry juice for thirsty warriors."

"No." Turtle Back smiled. "We are too many. But I thank the Oneida woman."

"I wish you good fortune on your hunt," she said.

"I thank you for your wish." He had started to turn his horse when he asked across his shoulder, "There are no more white men here?"

"No."

"No strangers?"

"No," she lied. Well, it was half a lie. They did not know if the Secretive One was still in the hills. A look passed between Turtle Back and his brother, but Crenna could not interpret it.

"Good-bye, Oneida woman," Turtle Back said. Then he led his party out, the wind twisting the feathers which were knotted into his hair.

The young warrior who had not spoken sat his pony a minute longer. Crenna could not decide immediately what it was that held his interest. Then, with a mother's sudden insight, she turned to see Cara, her face immobile, her eyes bright, looking back at the man.

He lifted a hand carelessly then and rode after his father. The crooked young man waited still another moment. Then, with a faint, malignant smile, he rode his horse through their corn, trampling down the green stalks, before he raced to join his father and uncle, a wild whoop escaping his throat.

"Dirty boy!" It was Sachim who said it. She stooped over now, futilely straightening a crushed cornstalk. "I do not know what his name is, but it should be Thunder Face."

"What was he asking about?" Van der Veghe, who had not caught it all, wanted to know. "More white men?"

"Yes, that is what he asked. Then he asked about 'strangers.' "

"I wonder why," Van der Veghe said.

Sachim stood up now, hissing between her lips. "Dirty boy," she repeated. "Did you not think so, Cara?"

"What? Yes," she replied, but Cara was not thinking about the youth with the crooked face. She was still in a distant land where fantasy and reality merged, where dream men took on substance and walked out of the clouds, their eyes bold and challenging.

It was silly. *Silly*. He probably had not noticed her. Likely they would never see this man again. He would return to the mists, return to the dreams, and in time she would not even be sure that he had come to her in the flesh.

"Cara?"

Her mother was studying her closely, and Cara could detect probing humor in her eyes. "Yes, Mother," she said quickly.

"I asked if you would help your aunt with the hay."

"Of course," Cara said, carefully keeping her eyes turned down. She walked away, arms folded, head still down, and Crenna, standing beside Van der Veghe, watched her cross the meadow.

"I know," Van der Veghe said when she was out of earshot. "Well, what harm is there? A young woman needs dreams."

"We all do, Peter Van der Veghe," Crenna said. "We all do."

Summer passed quickly. Twice more, hunting parties crossed their land. Once it was a small group of Miami Indians, cousins to the Shawnee, and another time the Shawnee themselves, but Turtle Back was not with them, nor his sons. Cara stood in the tall, summer-scented grass and watched them walk away, following the course of the long river northward.

With the coming of autumn, they saw no more of the Shawnee hunting parties. The maple trees, the oak, and the Buckeye transformed into waves of crimson and gold spread across the wide valley, with the blue-green spruce, standing aloof and untouched by winter's threats, among them.

It was a time of harvest, and the harvest was good. The corn crib was full, there was much sweet hay for the horses. The smokehouse was hung with venison and fish. Van der Veghe's small crop of tobacco had cured.

When the rains came, it was too late for them to damage the crops. The house itself, in the manner of Crenna's people, was hung with strips of pumpkin and whole squash. It would be an altogether easier winter than the last.

Still William, growing tall and capable, stalked the muddy uplands, taking deer and porcupines, rabbit, and once a small bear for their winter stores.

Crenna and Van der Veghe were warm and content in their small house; it was the young ones who were restless. William hunted in all sorts of weather, only to be out of the house, it seemed. He knew that when winter came there would be no more walking the long valley, no careful stalking among the pines and deeply scented cedar, no refreshing bath in the icy river.

Cara was no less alone, no less restless. She walked the valley, losing herself in the pine forest, watching the wind sway the dark trees, the rain slant down from out of silver-gray, rolling heavens.

She went to the bluffs above the valley, and from there she

looked down upon the river, the wide virgin forest, the grasslands, straining her eyes to see how far she could penetrate the distances with her vision. As often as not, she looked to the south and west. Toward the land of the Shawnee.

Once she thought she saw a distant figure on horseback, a lone rider, moving toward her, and her heart leaped. But in another moment the figure was gone and she knew that her mind had projected her wish out onto the valley floor.

He would not come. Why would he?

The wind was cold from out of the north. Cara stood on the rocky outcropping, watching a distant pinkish flash of lightning, listening to the hollow, faint muttering of Hinu, the Thunder God.

It was all imagination, like the rider in the valley. All imagination, like the voices from the night stars, like the soft whisperings of the spirits in the forest. All of it!

He was a man of another nation; a man traveling through their valley, surveying all with his masterly eyes, studying all with faint mockery.

Probably he was dirty, savage, brutal, stupid! But she knew he was none of these.

This she *knew*. And it was no quirk of the mind, no subtle prescience which told her that. It had been spelled out in his eyes, all of his character. Those black, black eyes.

It had begun to rain steadily now. Low clouds crawled across the valley toward her, and lightning raked the skies. She watched the storm slowly advance, watched a solid, darker wall of clouds succeed those which already roofed over the sky. Soon it would freeze, soon it would snow. And still he did not come.

She started back toward the house, her head bowed, arms crossed beneath her shawl. She didn't see him until she rounded the tight bend in the trail, until she stood precariously balanced on the gray, rain-slick stone underfoot.

He was there suddenly. A wolf on hind legs. A gaunt, bearded man in buckskins. A terrible jagged scar crossed one blind eye.

He was as surprised as Cara. He had been squatting against the earth. Now he stood, a hare in his hand. He held a bow in his free hand. A filthy buckskin quiver hung down his back. Rain washed over his face. Gray hair hung in his eyes. She noticed his hand, saw that there were three fingers missing. And then she screamed.

It was the first time in her life Cara had screamed. It rose of its own volition to her lips, and hung in the air, dueling with the racketing of the thunder overhead.

He lunged toward her, his clawlike hand stretching out to grasp her, and Cara sidestepped, nearly plunged over the edge of the bluffs, and regained her footing. She ducked under his arm and ran on blindly down the slippery path.

She looked over her shoulder once, but he was not there. She slowed. *Maybe he had not been there at all.* Perhaps she was going mad. These visions! These fantasies. But she shook that notion aside.

He was real, and he had tried to grab her. She could recall every detail of his scarred face, the pleading look in his good eye, the mangled fingers. He was real, but who was he; what did he want?

She ran on down the trail, dipping through a ravine where water already ran, then up the far side and into the close ranks of the towering pines, where it was dark as night.

Now she was safe, surely safe, but she did not slow her pace. She rushed on, tripping once, falling roughly on an elbow, not slowing until she saw the smoke rising from the gray stone cabin in the meadow, until she could see the safety of home.

She entered the cabin soaked to the bone, her hair plastered to her skull, her buckskin dress heavy with water. But she said nothing. Not then.

She dried off and changed her dress; then silently she sat to the table to eat. Her conversation was terse.

Later she slept, awaiting dreams of contentment, awaiting the coming of the warrior on the spotted horse. He did come, riding from off the plains which were made of soft clouds. His head was thrown back with joyous laughter, his arms strong and bare. His eyes were entrancing; yet when he reached out for Cara, his eyes went blank and cold. His hands, Cara saw, had turned to claws, and he pawed at her, tearing at her dress while his throat emitted groaning, subhuman sounds.

She awoke with a start and stared at the cold ceiling. Now she did not even have her dreams. Cursing the man on the hill, she rolled over angrily and beat her fist against her blankets before, settling with a sigh, she fell off to a restless sleep.

It was snowing. Cara walked to the door and looked out at

the gentle drifting flakes, watching the world go white and cold. "Summer—it passed too quickly."

"They all do," Crenna said. She stood at her daughter's shoulder, a faint smile on her lips. She stretched out a hand and stroked Cara's hair lightly.

Crenna recognized and understood the girl's longings. They were identical to Crenna's own at that age. The girl wanted to be a woman of independence, to spread her wings and fly, to frame her own way of life, to escape from what suddenly seemed the intolerable sameness of her parents' chosen way. She wanted to find a man, to find her purpose, to be the first—the very first—to defeat the subtle agonies of life, the long procession of tedium and frustration, to stride among these grasping adversaries with confident strength, shrugging them off. To be the first—that was what they did not, mercifully could not, know at Cara's age; they were only the last, the last of long lines of men and women who finally had to take life on its own terms or be torn apart.

That did not make the dream less magnificent; it only meant that it could belong only to the very young or the very foolish. To them it was a great treasure, this wispy dream of freedom. It should be respected; it is the best part of mankind.

"Come, let me show you the beadwork I'm doing," Crenna said. Her daughter sighed with reluctance. Her mouth set with youthful petulance. Cara nodded. And so they would sit in the cabin as it snowed, as the long winter passed, doing beadwork, retelling the old tales—family history, which now seemed dry and, in its familiarity, tedious.

Yet outside the wild winds blew and the unseen distances beckoned.

William grew astonishingly over the winter. He was as tall as Crenna now, and there was a lean sureness about him. Since coming to Ohio, he had lost all of his softness. The pink skin had tautened over his cheekbones and been stretched by new muscle on his arms and chest.

He hunted even in the worst weather, coming home only to warm up, to eat, to sleep. "We're losing both of them, Peter," Crenna whispered to her husband as they lay in bed one long winter night.

"Losing them?" he asked with a soft, inquiring laugh.

"I mean they are outgrowing the nest."

"And is that something new, woman?" he asked, kissing

her bare shoulder. "Or is a mother's sorrow at such moments something unexpected?"

"It has never happened to me before. I see them grow, change. I hardly know their minds."

"It is the way things are, the way they are meant to be."

"But it makes it no easier."

"No." He held her head against his chest, stroking her hair. Crenna listened to his heartbeat, slightly accelerated it seemed. "It makes it no easier."

They passed the winter in comfort, the older people content with the warmth of the house, the food which was there to be placed on the table. The younger ones passed it impatiently, watching eagerly for spring, hoping that it might bring changes in their lives. They wished for adventure, romantic, challenging, fulfilling.

When spring did come, it brought change with it. But it was upheaval, fiery cataclysm, despair, and bloodshed. If Cara and William could have known then what they would know later when they looked back with warm reverie at that last winter, they would have prayed to North Wind never to let winter end, but to smother the earth eternally with snow, to let the wild winds howl endlessly. For their lives were never again to be so secure, so warm, so filled with peace.

William strode the long spring-bright valley, pausing in the shade of the giant oaks to watch the river run. He sat and ate from his war sack, where he carried jerky, arrowheads, rawhide thongs, and bannock cakes.

He wore buckskin shirt and pants, soft deerskin moccasins. His long yellow hair was tied back with a rawhide string. He sat cross-legged against the earth as he ate his dry, salty meal, chewing slowly as he studied the wild land, the empty day.

He was alone upon the earth. Three days earlier he had passed a hunting party of Susquehanna Indians, but they had paid him no mind. His yellow hair had once been astonishing to them, but now they knew the young man who moved and hunted, who thought like an Indian, and he was a familiar sight.

Since that day he had seen no one. Once the tracks of a lone traveler—a Shawnee, by his moccasin prints, by his direction of travel. Not a hunter, but a runner. He carried no extra weight, his strides were long.

William had seen many fine bucks, one fat, heavily larded black bear, a ranging panther, but he had chosen to take none of them. If he killed, he would have to return home with the meat, and he was not ready to return home. The spring mornings were warm, inviting him to stretch his legs, to see what lay beyond the next hill rise or forest, and so he followed his instincts, which were those of a wanderer.

He was alone. The day was good. The river slithered by, dappled by the shade of the oaks. A red ant crawled across the back of his freckled hand, and he watched it wind its random way. He leaned back against the rough bark of the oak and stretched his legs.

He halted abruptly, his muscles frozen.

He was not alone. He narrowed his eyes and got to his knees. Smoke rose into the crystal skies in a long, thin curlicue. Twisting into the blue vastness until the sky swallowed it.

There were no Shawnee in the area. Their large hunting party, broken into small groups now, had swept westward days earlier. Miami Indians? Very far south for them, and the fire seemed large. It was early still; there was no need for a fire. Not for warmth. William Van der Veghe got to his feet, dusting the ant from his hand.

He stood for a minute peering into the brilliant sunlight, and then he snatched up his sackful of provisions, picked up his bow, and slung his quiver over his shoulder.

He forded the creek and walked northward, his eyes alert, his senses registering all that belonged there—red-winged blackbirds, a scurrying otter making for the creek, the rustle of a snake in the dry leaves beneath the oaks—alert for a single thing which did not belong.

He walked two miles through the scattered oaks, the wind fresh in his face, the sun warm on his shoulders. Then, emerging from the trees, he halted, crouching immediately, with a hunter's instinct.

There it sat. A small log cabin, smoke rising not from its chimney but from a tiny outdoor forge. He saw no one, heard nothing, and he frowned. Moving cautiously, he slipped nearer. Now there was a sound, metal ringing against metal, and lifting his head, William saw a burly man hammering on an indistinct metallic object.

His movements were rhythmic, easy. He obviously possessed great strength. He wore a leather apron, a gray flop hat tilted back on a round, broad skull. His shoulders were hunched, rounded with muscle. And he was as white as new snow.

William went to his belly, just watching. A white man, here! This was the second white man he could remember seeing in his life, although they told him that there had been many Dutch at their old home along the Hudson. Those men were just vague, shadowy memories.

This one was real enough. Didn't he know where he was, know that the Shawnee would never tolerate this? Perhaps not. He was, perhaps, a fool. Perhaps a man of great courage. Then, almost immediately, William decided it was the former. He was a fool.

He had a son. William saw the boy moving up toward the house, carrying a sack in his hands. He was white, had dark hair and a lithe body. He was nearly as tall as William himself, and near the same age, perhaps seventeen.

Yet he moved like a child, his feet crushing twigs; his approach would have chased away any game nearby. He paused as William studied him through the screen of grass and blackthorn brush. His eyes lifted to where William lay, passed by, and then returned.

Yet he did not see him; William was sure of that.

Fools, he thought. "You will not last long."

He felt a sudden contempt rise up, but accompanying it was curiosity, strong and impelling. These were white men. Europeans. With blood like that of his father, like his own blood.

He had never seen a youth of his own age in this valley, never a white man. He decided to have a closer look, and so he slipped back into the ravine at his back, followed it for a quarter of a mile, and then reentered the oaks, moving like the silent wind toward the other boy's position.

He came upon him suddenly, and he stood unseen in the shadows of the tree, watching the boy gather acorns and pine cones from the ground. He wasn't selective, picking up this year's drop as well as last year's, destroyed by borers. He would find only hollow husks in those seeds.

He walked past a huge, layered growth of fungus clinging to the side of an old white oak, giving it a single discrediting glance.

"It is very good to eat," William said, stepping from behind a tree. His choice of language had been English, and he was correct. The young man turned his head, his eyes showing much white before they settled into calm appraisal. William was surprised to see that he already wore a mustache. Thin, perhaps, but dark and flourishing.

"This?" he said, touching the fungus. William had to admire the youth's composure. He had been ready to flee, to fight, and abruptly he had gained control of himself, pretending that there was nothing unusual at all about blond Indians stepping from the forest tangle to advise him on foraging.

"It is excellent. Even raw. But I prefer it baked. Is my accent terrible?" William asked.

"No, not so bad," the boy answered. "But are you . . . who are you?"

"William Van der Veghe."

"Dutch?"

"Yes," William answered after a brief hesitation. It seemed the proper answer. *I am Dutch,* he told himself.

"Where are your people? Oh, I'm sorry . . ." He stuck out a hand, white and soft. "I'm Richard Dawes. My father has a farm over there."

William shook his hand, finding it agreeably dry, friendly.

"Where have you come from?" Richard Dawes asked with a smile. He looked across William's shoulder as if there were an answer to be found there. "We've heard of no settlements out here. Certainly no Dutch settlements."

"We have been here for quite a few years," William said. He nodded at the tree mushroom. "This really is quite good, but some are deadly. I'll have to show you how to tell the difference."

"Yes. Thank you. That's quite good of you." Dawes ran a hand over his long dark hair. "But where in heaven's name did you come from? You say you've been out here for quite some time? My father believes he is the first man into this valley, makes quite a thing of it, he does. But then, we're Cornishmen on Grandfather Lewis' side, and a prideful lot . . . I'm rambling on, aren't I?" Richard asked.

"Just a little too quickly for me. My English is poor."

"It seems quite good to me," Richard said insistently. He broke off a bit of the tree fungus and lifted it to his lips. "Raw, you say, is all right?" He took a bite. "Not much flavor. But with a bit of butter—if one had butter—it would be superb. I don't suppose you people have a milk cow?"

"No," William answered. He understood the gist of Richard's jabber, but the words, one treading on the heels of the next, came much too quickly from the Englishman's lips.

"Well, Father will be pleased to find I've learned something about wilderness living. I think he despairs of my becoming anything. The Cornish blood didn't seem to transmit this urgency—intensity, if you will—to me."

"Uh . . . no," William replied.

Richard Dawes laughed, and it was an appealing laugh. This young dark-haired, dark-eyed Englishman had a sense of humor, a sense of self-appraisal. Humor lurked in his eyes at all times. "I am sorry, William. I speak too quickly and too obscurely, I suppose. But, dammit, man, you can't know how long it's been since I've had the chance to speak to anyone my own age. Father was a seafarer, but once here, he decided to stay. He fought briefly with Hobbs against the French in the northeast. Then, deciding that a Cornishman is a freedom-loving man—and despite the fact he's only half Cornish—he sent for us, determined to take land for himself in a country where it was still possible. *Im*possible at home, you know. All owned by the landlord . . . well, I do ramble on! Finally the governor-general received word that the Ohio Valley was opening to settlers. To keep the French out, you understand. Well, we've jumped the gun, I'm afraid. Started early, that is. Not supposed to be here, but here we are."

"More will come?" William asked.

"Many more, I expect. But I am jabbering. Come down to the house, please. Let's have some tea. Meet my father—you'll like him, rough old man he is."

John Dawes was indeed a "rough old man." Forty years of age, with hands twice the size of William's, with the calluses of a lifetime's manual labor on them. His eye was hard, appraising, his shoulders were heavy with muscles, and William knew immediately that this man had never known fear.

"Come into the house, boy, it's time for my noon meal," he invited in a tone which could have been as easily the voice of command.

Inside, a small, graying woman in a gray wool dress bustled about, lifting the heavy pots from the fireplace, lugging a huge teakettle to the table, where John Dawes settled himself for his meal.

She said not a word until Dawes announced in his rumbling voice, "Here's a boy named William Van der Veghe come to sup with us, Martha."

She murmured something which sounded like "Pleased" and got back to her work, her head shaking nervously. Dawes got to his meal, which he went at with conviction. Ham, sweet potatoes, greens of some sort. William declined all offers, but accepted tea.

"So your people are farming here already," Dawes said around a mouthful of food.

"Yes," William answered, somewhat intimidated by this bull of a man.

"I thought I was the first," he said with a chuckle. "I didn't wait for the government to make up its mind." He jabbed at William with his fork for emphasis. "Can't wait for 'em. I know they'll open the Ohio to settlers, they know it, but waitin' gets the tail end of the dog. Did you know that Duquesne is building a fort upriver not fifty miles?"

"Duquesne?"

"The Frenchy, son. Don't you people keep track of what's going on?"

"We haven't seen any white man in a long while," William said, feeling a slight flush crawl into his cheeks.

"No, I suppose that's so," Dawes said with a mildly apologetic, slightly softened tone. He lifted his fork, and Martha Dawes rushed to refill his plate.

"The French," Dawes went on, "know now they've lost the seaboard. They're going to put all they've got into salvaging something out of their American expedition. They want the interior, boy, all of it."

Richard Dawes nodded, but said nothing. William had the feeling that in this family one didn't interrupt the master when he was holding forth.

"So they'll be encouraging the English people to come in here soon enough, you can mark that. They're batting it around in Parliament. Where the colonial boundary is, all of that. But in the end, a nation's boundary is drawn at the point where it can be stretched no farther. Martha, tea! You mark it." Again he pointed with his fork. "This will be English soil."

"What about the Indians?" William dared.

"They'll have to move back. Lord, boy, they've got the rest of the continent, don't they?"

"Yes," William said. He was deciding whether or not he should add more to that, to equivocate his agreement, when the door opened.

She stood there for a moment, holding a basket full of blackberries. A girl of fifteen with long reddish hair worn loosely across her shoulders, with green, sparking eyes, and a turned-up nose. She looked only once at William, then crossed the room, William thought swaying her hips a little more than was normal.

"Louise," her father barked. "We have a guest."

"Oh?" She turned as if it were a great surprise, as if she hadn't seen the tall blond youth in buckskins at all. "Hello," she said, blinking her eyes to great effect.

William took a moment before realizing he should stand. By the time he had decided to come to his feet, the girl had turned away. She walked to the kitchen, beyond the main room, but not before she had turned and given him a coy glance across her shoulder, one her father could not have seen from his seat.

"She's a sly one," Richard murmured. William flushed, the vision of the red-haired girl, green eyes inviting, imprinted strongly on his memory.

He realized that father and son were both staring at him. He must have been blushing, because John Dawes broke into a loud, crude guffaw.

"William knows the Indian ways," Richard said, rescuing his friend from the embarrassing situation. John Dawes, pushing his plate away, looked at his son.

"Does he, now?" He appraised William again. "Yes, I suppose a man living out here would learn their ways."

William started to mention that his mother was an Indian, but something held him back. In the end he just nodded silent agreement with Dawes's remark.

Later, as Richard and William stood alone in the shadows of the pine forest, the English boy said, "I hope you'll come back again, William. I'd like to hunt with you, to learn about this land. My father likes you," he added, as if reading the hesitation in William's mind. "It's just his way. I told you he was rough. He growls, he's opinionated. But that's his way. A man has to have a little of that to survive out here, don't you think?" He looked to the broad forest. "A timid man wouldn't last long here, I don't believe."

"I'll try to come back."

"Do," Richard said eagerly.

Looking beyond Richard, he could see the red-haired girl come out of the house, toss a basin of water out, and stand negligently patting her hair, looking far beyond the forest, as if aware of nothing, of no one. But there was one last careless glance before she entered the house, one which sought and found William Van der Veghe.

Then she was gone, the heavy door closing behind her. "I'll be back again," William said. He shook hands with Richard and then was on his way, moving lightly through the deep woods.

He forded a small creek and walked up into a low wooded glen. The air was rich with the scent of cedar and pine resin. Her hair wasn't actually red, he decided. It was deep brown with highlights of red. And there were strands of gold in it when the light caught it properly. No, it wasn't red. But there was a life to it, a richness. It had a life of its own. But the eyes—they were a true green. Green as new spring grass, with a subtle mockery in them, a glint of invitation.

He lay down on the wooded hillslope and looked upward through the pines toward the deep blue sky beyond. Then suddenly he laughed out loud, pounding his fists into the loamy soil beside him.

"Yes!" he shouted to the empty forest. "I shall be back." His voice quieted. "I will be back again, and soon."

Then he closed his eyes, and chewing on a blade of grass, he pictured it all, recalling her hair, the sparkle of green eyes, the coy glance, the gentle swaying of her fluid hips as she moved. And the rest of the world simply drifted away.

It was two days before William returned home, packing the meat of a young buck. Cara noticed he was oddly distracted. He smiled at odd moments, and seemed in unusually high spirits. "Why, he even offered to help me clean the house," she told her mother. "There's something going on."

"He's growing up, Cara, as you are," Crenna said. "He's abandoned his childish ways."

There's more to it than that, Cara thought, but she said nothing. Pondering it, she could find no possible reason for the change in her brother, who, normally sullen, silent, now laughed and chatted about nothing at all.

It was Crenna who discovered the source of William's new personality, although at the time she did not place that significance on it. She stood on the high bluffs at sundown, gazing northward, and she saw the smoke.

It rose like a challenge into the coloring skies, and it lifted her pulse rate, narrowed her eyes, and tightened her fine mouth.

"Crenna?" Peter walked to where his wife, arms folded, stood motionlessly. He frowned and came to her. Then he too saw it, and he said, "My God."

"They can't be five miles away," Crenna said without turning her head.

"Shawnee?" he asked hopefully.

"No, Peter. They are white men."

He nodded. "I'll have to pay them a visit."

"No." Crenna turned to him, her eyes pleading. She placed her hands on his shoulders and squeezed. "Do not go there; we must have no contact with them."

"What can it hurt?" he asked, surprised at his wife's vehemence.

"Do you not see?" Her dark eyes searched his. He was aware of the red-streaked sky beyond and behind her, of the chill which came with approaching night. "One white man there. One here. One beyond the river. Soon the Shawnee will come and say, 'No more. This is enough.' "

Peter laughed, unsuccessfully. "Surely you are making too much of this, Crenna. One white family. Two. What does it matter? The land is wide. They have left us alone, after all."

"One family they will leave alone. Perhaps two. But when two come and are unmolested, others will follow. I see blood and thunder, my husband. I see war and tragedy, and I see it now. Rising like the smoke from that distant fire before my eyes. There is warning written on the smoke, war sign sketched across this flaming sky. We must go; it is coming again—war. And this time we will not be able to flee from it. This time, my husband, it shall be a rapidly moving fire, a wind-fanned flame, a roaring great destruction which will sweep us away, leaving only ashes in its wake."

❁ 3 ❁

In the daylight the menace seemed less palpable, less immediate. Peter and Crenna spoke quietly of it over the breakfast table. They spoke to each other alone, but the ears of Cara, of Sachim, of William, were attuned to the conversation.

"We have neighbors, that is all," Peter said, trying to place it in the best light. "We can hardly move each time we have a new neighbor, Crenna. We have put our blood, our perspiration, into this home. We have come to this land, harmed no one. How can we run away? Where would we go? We cannot return to the east, to the land of the Iroquois. There all has been destroyed. The world you knew is gone. We cannot travel to the west or south, across the second river, the Kanawha, as they call it. Turtle Back forbade that. Where, then, Crenna, if not here?"

There was no answer to that. Where, indeed?

"They are good people, Mother," William put in unexpectedly. "I mean . . ." he stammered, "they are certain to be only simple farmers, not soldiers looking for battle."

Crenna wasn't to be put off so easily. "What do you know of them, William?"

"How could he know anything?" Van der Veghe asked.

"What, William? You wander far. *Have* you met these people, these simple farmers?"

"Yes!" he said with some passion. "I've met them. They're good, solid people who only want to farm the land." He touched his chest with the tips of his fingers. "Like us; they are only like us."

"There will be many hundreds," Sachim said, but no one seemed to hear her.

"How can we abandon our farm?" Van der Veghe repeated. "Where would we go? The Shawnee may not be our friends, but they have given us tacit approval to live upon the hunting grounds."

"I will not leave!" William said hotly.

"There must be a daughter," Cara said lightly, and William turned on her, eyes flashing. "And if there is? Yes . . . all right, it's so. A woman. A young woman. She's beautiful. The family is a good one. They are my friends. What right have the Shawnee to bother them? They were here first perhaps, but what does that matter! They have wandered the earth. So have these people. So have we! Looking for a home, for peace. If there is a Great Manitou, then he has given us all this earth to live upon, to share. They have the same right as the Shawnee, as we do."

He turned then, and snatching up his bow and arrows, he stalked from the cabin, slamming the door behind him.

Van der Veghe said, "The boy may be right. What do you think, Crenna? Can we move because of this? Can we abandon what we have worked for?"

"I don't know. I honestly do not know. Let us see what happens, my husband. The boy, as you say, may be right. Perhaps I am growing old, anxious to avoid any hostility. The young live for change, for adventure; perhaps I have reached an age when I find my only solace in habit—and so I do not want to leave, no. But I fear for them, Peter. We have seen war."

"Yes," Van der Veghe agreed thoughtfully. "That war is behind us, however. It was a war between whites, one into which the Indian was dragged by trickery and his own greed in some cases. This situation—surely it is different. One family. Ten families. Can that mean war?"

"If I knew that, my husband," she answered, lifting her eyes, "then I would know what answer to give to you."

But she did not know. She only knew that the subtler

senses of her body had been alerted, that something distinctly dangerous was in the air. But as Van der Veghe said, they need not expect trouble. They would stay away from these new settlers. They would hope that Turtle Back, who seemed a reasonable man, would read no danger in their presence. That was all they could do.

She stood on the high ridge, and the wind swept coldly past. Sachim saw the long gray-green valley, the darker river, the single patch of tilled earth, the distant smoke. That was what she saw with her eyes, but her mind recorded other scenarios. Flickering behind her eyes like ghostly images, like distant thoughts of long-ago times now barely remembered, but these were not events which had happened once, which she had heard around the smoky fire inside an Iroquois longhouse. They were events which would come to pass. She knew this as she knew the wind off the north would bring rain, as she knew the forests, the dark eyes of a startled doe, as she knew the beating of her own heart.

She knew. There was a distant rumbling in her ears as the sounds of Hinu's thunder, as the beating of distant war drums. And accompanying them were the wails of mourning women, the shrieks of the injured and frightened, the heated war cries of the young warriors.

Her eyes saw the long sheets of war flame, saw the red of blood staining the green grass, saw the armies in blue-and-white uniforms marching forward. She saw the forests fall and the grass burn, the smoke rising to the heavens like a filthy blot, a symbol of man's blasphemy, a dark, wretched, whimsical monument to his own impotence.

They came, and they would kill because they had no other way to prove they were alive. They came, and they would kill because it was a game. They came for a hundred reasons, for the sake of pretenses which hid the last, final reason—he was a savage thing, this Man, steeped in bloodlust. He loved his warsport as long as he believed he would win, as long as he believed the other would die.

His face was red or white, a hundred colors, he wore uniforms or breechclouts, and in his heart the bloodlust lifted its misshapen head and clawed at the heart with eager, crooked paws. It whispered one message, and was always obeyed. It always would be.

If man had built the heavens, the stars would be blood-red.

The moon a rising crimson eye, the seas tumultuous vermilion waves, each child born with war ax in hand.

It was never-ending. "Peace" was a word used by those who saw nothing to gain by war; it was only a momentary aspiration.

That was what Sachim saw. She saw it all in the thin bluish tendril of smoke rising from the distant house. She closed her eyes and shook her head. The wind had increased, and it ranted against her, tearing at her clothing, her skirt and buckskin jacket.

Run away, then. Go to Crenna and tell her they must run.

But you cannot run away from it—that is the truth of it. It came stealthily, but in the end it touched every corner of Manitou's world. It is the great pursuer. It can only be accepted.

Sachim knew she would stay. She would always remain with Crenna and with Van der Veghe, the two people who gave her life meaning, who gave her love. Their courtship had been Sachim's, in a way. The birth of their children the same as Sachim herself giving birth. And when they died, she knew it would be exactly as if she had died herself.

Was that a sign of uselessness—to have no real life of her own? Or simply an indicator of her own tenuous grip on the corporeal? For Sachim did not belong on this earth; she received little pleasure in being here. She should not have been born—some mistake had been made, and she lived on, the eternal outsider, only to await the moment when she could return to the stars and leave this clumsy, useless body behind.

"Good morning."

He had come out of the thicket of blackthorn and scrub oak so softly that she hadn't even heard him. Now, with a start, she leaped back, her fingers going to her breast. William laughed at the expression on her face, and at his laugh Louise's eyes suddenly hardened.

"Anyone would be frightened," she said defensively.

"Perhaps." He perched on a rock, one long leg dangling, watching the girl gather the chestnuts she had spilled. She was irritated still. Her face reddened as she picked up the spilled nuts.

"What are you doing here?" she snapped.

"I am your neighbor!" William laughed. "I came to see

you. I went to the house, but your father and Richard are gone."

"They're out hunting. You shouldn't be here."

"Why?" He stretched his arms overhead in a lazy, feline gesture.

"Why!" She set her basket aside. "I'm a woman. If my father knew you were alone with me . . ."

"What's the matter with that?"

"I can't explain it if you don't know." Her voice still held an edge, but her eyes had softened. She took a step nearer William, her basket held before her, her shoulders swaying from side to side.

"When will you be old enough to marry?" he asked.

"What!" Outrage suffused her face with a crimson flush. "What's the matter with you? Are you some kind of red savage?"

"I am a Dutchman!" William said, leaping from the rock. His answer was nearly as sharp as her own comment, surprising Louise. But not daunting her.

"That's worse," she said with pert impudence. She turned her back on William and started away through the oaks, which glittered with golden sunlight.

"Wait." He followed her and was beside her in three strides, taking her arm at the elbow.

"Let go of my arm," she said in a frosty tone. His hand fell away obediently.

"I didn't come to make you angry at me."

She kept walking, her small feet crushing the leaves underfoot. She did not look at him. Her reddish curls bounced as she walked. Her chin was uptilted.

"I only came because I wanted to see you," William persisted. "Not to see Richard. You."

She stopped and turned to face him. "Why?"

He didn't answer her directly. "Why do you say it is worse to be Dutch?"

"I just wanted to hurt you," she answered with a shrug. "You frightened me and then you laughed at me."

"Then you have nothing against the Dutch?" he asked eagerly.

"No." The faintest of smiles escaped her, lighting William's world, causing his heart to step up its already rapid pace.

"Good." He sighed. "I was afraid you had."

She started on, walking more slowly now. Her hips swayed gently from side to side. She looked at the leaf-littered earth, at the sun-struck oaks.

"Why did you ask when I would be old enough to marry?" she said finally.

"Why . . ." William's bold composure deserted him. His tongue made odd clicking sounds. "No reason," he muttered finally.

"No?" She stopped, turned to face him, and smiled. Her lips parted and the sunlight through the oaks lit her hair with liquid fire.

"I only thought I would like a son with green eyes and hair like red gold," he said, surprising himself. His hand lifted and touched her curls, and she did not draw away, though he saw her breast rising and falling rapidly.

William's heart was racing; his blood throbbed through his veins. Suddenly it was all too much and he turned and nearly ran into the woods, losing himself in the mottled shadows, the sound of laughter ringing in his ears.

He sagged to a fallen oak log and sat there, his head spinning, cursing himself, thumping a hand against his forehead. Had he said too much, too little? How did these English people court, ask for a bride?

He remembered her laughter, and his ears turned red. But the longer he thought of it, the less it seemed that the laughter had been mocking. It was merry, sensual, and not at all derisive.

Finally he nodded, and with a huge grin, William Van der Veghe rose. He leaped wildly into the air once, clapping his hands together; then, still smiling, he turned and walked toward home, his eyes blind to all he saw, his heart floating six feet above him.

Very suddenly it came down to earth. He had emerged from the oak grove, and now, along the banks of the river, he saw them. William took a dozen quick steps backward, and there, pressed into the shadows of the oaks, he watched.

John Dawes had been correct. He was no longer alone. He was the first into the valley, but by no means the last. As William Van der Veghe watched from his sheltered position, sixteen wagons drawn up in a loose circle were being unloaded along the river.

He saw women and men, children, running gleefully along the river, oxen, horses, and something which was still an unusual sight—firearms. The men, most in tricornered hats, had pistols poked into their waistbands, and some carried long blunderbusses with flared snouts. *Donderbus*, thunder-gun, they had been christened by their inventor. The English had altered the word to "blunderbuss" after the weapon's tendency to misfire. But they did not misfire often enough to suit their victims. William had had an Oneida uncle who was killed by one of these fire-spewing weapons.

No doubt the weapons were improved greatly by now. He was interested in their weaponry and managed to pick out three weapons which looked more modern, different in design. These were long guns, with octagonal barrels, and they looked deadly; William doubted there was much blunder in these weapons. His father had scorned these guns, pointing out that they were useless in rain or hard weather. The powder had to be dry in the flash pan or the weapon did not fire.

But then, most wars were fought in good weather.

The guns fascinated him, but so did the people, their dress, their accouterments. Iron stoves and beautiful furniture. Barrels containing who-knew-what. These people had come to stay, that much was obvious. He saw the plowshares, the long two-man saws, the axes, and he knew they had come to build . . . and to fight for what they had built.

When he had seen enough, he sifted back into the woods and circled homeward. He still thought of Louise, but somehow the sight of these new arrivals had taken the excitement from thoughts of her.

They would return at night with full impact. Woman, soft, beautiful, teasing. Waves of long reddish-gold hair, tempting lips, haughty green eyes. He could not sleep, but tossed and turned, feeling the blood in his body eagerly answer the visions of his mind.

It was at the hour before dawn, when, exhausted from a restless night, he lay half-awake, haunted by Louise's inviting specter, that he saw it.

He was startled awake and sat for a long while, arms braced behind him, panting, staring at the dark cabin walls, his body bathed in perspiration. For he had seen her laughing, head tilted, lips parted to reveal straight, white teeth. With the suddenness of all nightmares it happened, and he watched as his vision was washed away.

A dark hole, a third eye, appeared in her forehead, and

from it blood streamed. Writhing blood-red worms crawled from the wound, and Louise's face went pale and still, like bleached leather. But there was time for her to laugh brokenly, to speak in a cracked voice: "I thought you were a Dutchman!"; and then she fell and he saw the arrowhead, white, barbed, finely chipped, protruding from her skull.

It was a winter of dark silence. Life went on as before, except that the clouds of vague apprehension, of unease, hovered over them, casting shadows across their souls. William was the most despondent, although they still did not guess the cause of his unhappiness; Sachim the most equable. She found she enjoyed the splendid isolation of the long winter. Their world during these months was very small, yet it suited her.

But the isolation was only illusion.

Across the valley, ten new houses stood in a box-shaped configuration, a miniature fortress. According to William, there were new settlers even farther south. And during the white hush of one winter morning, Sachim saw them.

Shawnee riders moving slowly northward, their shoulders hunched, their faces grim. The wind lifted their horses' tails and drifted the light fallen snow before them, screening them so that they appeared as ghostly images wrapped in furs, wearing their feathers, each man carrying weapons in his hand.

The hunting season was long past. These men belonged in their winter lodges, smoking, telling tales of the hunt and of the spirits, but they rode the long white land, and Sachim knew there could be only one solution to this riddle.

"What can we do?" Van der Veghe asked Crenna. "There will be trouble. It's obvious now. But we can't possibly move until spring, and even then, where can we go?" The tall Dutchman got to his feet and went to the fire. Standing, staring down into the flames, he looked older than his years. The firelight deepened the lines on his face, darkened the shadows. "It is my fault for not agreeing with you, for moving immediately."

"Then perhaps it is my fault, Peter, for bringing us here in the first place," Crenna said softly. She moved to her husband, and holding his shirt, she kissed him. "It is *not* our fault. We do not wish to fight, we meant to make trouble with no people."

"But trouble is surely coming." He ran an anguished hand through his hair. "After all that we have been through—"

"Shh!" She placed a finger to his lips, and her eyes, wide, dark, seeing into his very thoughts, smiled. "As you said, we can do nothing now. We have until spring, then, to decide what to do. When the snows have gone, we will decide. When there is a problem to be solved, I believe it should be done." She added logically, "But when there is nothing to be done, we gain nothing by worrying about it, Peter."

"No, you're right, as usual," he said, holding her, rubbing her shoulder through the shawl she wore. All the same, a man worried. Knowing that death drifted on the winter winds, a man worried.

She sighed and rubbed her arms. It was cold, and growing colder. It would snow again by nightfall. Cara looked to the skies above the long ranks of pines, confirming her guess. The thunderheads were stacked high and deep, dark threatening angels approaching mercilessly.

She should turn back toward the house before it hit, she knew. She was a good two miles from the cabin, and if the snows came, it might be difficult even to find her way. Yet she did not turn back; why, she did not know.

True, it was too hot, too stuffy in the winter house, and she longed for the fresh cold air, to feel it sucked into her lungs, stinging and nearly overwhelming, but above all, invigorating. She longed to stretch her legs, to move in long strides across the empty, snowbound land, until the act of walking itself became the act of existence, until her mind went nearly blank and large problems became small ones, small ones vastly distant.

At home her father hovered worriedly over them, looking drawn and pale, himself taking every excuse to go outside. The horses were looked at a dozen times a day. William prowled about like a caged thing, his thoughts apparently on the red-haired woman whom he had described so often and in such glowing terms that Cara thought she would scream in frustration if he began again.

Yet these small abrasive moments were not what drove her to walk on, penetrating farther into the forest. That was know-not-what, a compulsion which visited her at odd intervals. Know-not-what, which would sometimes cause Cara to rise and go out to the smokehouse to discover the weasels at the meat. It was know-not-what which held her back when the rattlesnake had somehow gotten into the corncrib.

It was know-not-what which now pushed her along, and it was as irresistible as the wild winds which swayed the tall pines towering over her.

She crossed the icy brook where William had killed his first deer, passed the broken cedar where her father had hung his propitiating basket—she shuddered involuntarily. He was still there somewhere, the strange one with one eye, the wolf killer, the winter hunter, the wild one. Somewhere. This she knew.

But now an even stronger impulse compelled her to continue on deeper into the forest while the snow-laden thunderheads loomed overhead, while the shrieking winds blew through the long stands of timber.

Instinctively she followed the brook, walking toward its source, the bubbling fountain where crystal-clear cold water gurgled up from the depths of the granite heart of the earth.

She shuddered, and it was not from the cold. Her eyes went to the left and then to the right, seeing only the deep, solemn ranks of pines. The wind was in her hair, pawing at her clothing. She wrapped her shawl more tightly around her and went on, walking through the deep snow as the wind, whispering in the trees, spoke to her.

Abruptly she stopped. She stood to mid-calf in snow. The forest was dark, the skies growing blacker. She shivered and her head turned northward, to her right, toward the deepest part of the forest. A sound, a whim, a desire? Whatever it was, it was gone in a moment, like vanished lightning. Cara walked on, fording the tiny brook, her heart hammering in the prison of her rib cage, demanding to be set free, to be allowed to soar into the clouded skies, to pass through the thunder-shackled clouds to the clear, bright heavens above, to soar toward Manitou's eye, to wing toward the Place Beyond, to tumble fearlessly earthward before swooping across the vast land, turning up at the last moment, crying exultantly, singing mad songs of revelation.

He was there.

She saw him sagged beside a jumbled stack of snow-frosted granite boulders, his face drawn taut with pain, his eyes dark and savage, his hands gripping the shattered leg. Blood oozed from between his dark fingers. He had wrapped a cloth around the wound, tied a rawhide tourniquet above the gaping wound, but it was no good. He was weak and the loss of blood blurred his vision, muddled his thoughts. Crimson stained the white snow. Thunder crackled overhead, and Cara came out from under the trees to confront him.

"Go away," he snarled.

"You're hurt."

"I *am* hurt, woman. I am hurt because of you." His words came from between tightly clenched teeth. Had he been a lesser man, he would have screamed out with pain. The agony the wound caused was etched on his handsome—too-handsome—features, but the Shawnee dream-man did not scream out. His black eyes burned like coals.

"You know who I am?" Cara asked, coming closer.

"I know. Mingoe woman. One with long braids." He might have smiled, but the expression was broken off by pain.

"Then you know I did not harm you, did not wish to."

"I know nothing," he snapped.

She approached him as one would approach an injured wolf. She could explain none of it. How could she tell him that she had known him intimately, for many years, that he was a man sent from out of her golden slumbers, out of her dreams, to become flesh, that he was, already, her man.

"Go away, Mingoe."

"I am Oneida," she said softly, taking another hesitant step forward.

"White."

"Yes. Half-white." She took another step, saw his hand clench on the haft of a bone-handled knife, clench until it turned white at the knuckles, and she was not sure if it was anger or pain, hatred or fear which caused it.

"I only want to help, not to hurt," Cara said. "You will die without help."

"Then let me die! Sooner that than be touched by white hands."

"I am not white!"

"Worse, daughter of a white dog and a Mingoe whore,"

Cara's face flushed to a burning crimson beneath the mahogany of her skin. She weighed the moment, and considered turning, leaving him to die in the snow. It was the pain which caused him to speak in this manner, she decided. He had been injured. As an injured dog will accept no help from a human hand, no matter how well-meaning, so he would accept no comfort. But he was not a dog, a wolf, a wild thing, but a man, and so she went forward.

"My father is a learned man, a priest, my mother was the great headwoman of her people, a council leader, a war leader."

He didn't answer. His eyes had a vague, glassy aspect. His head lolled on his neck. The sticky blood on his leg was deep purple and profuse. Lightning crackled once again overhead.

"You must let me help you . . ." She came near enough to bend down and touch his head, but her hand held itself back.

Then it no longer mattered. His hand unclenched, those dark eyes went cold, and he fell onto his side in the snow, lying still. Cara knelt down and touched his forehead. He was burning with fever.

Her lips pressed tightly together, she examined the wound in his leg. It still bled badly, although the cold had slowed the flow. There was a hole the size of an acorn, no larger, but the upper thigh was shattered, the bone broken, the muscle severed.

She got to her knees and tried to think. There was no doubt about it, he would die if left here. He might die anyway, a dream dead before she had been able to clutch it to her, to hold it, but this was no time for romantic notions, for girlish visions. It was a time when something had to be done.

The tourniquet he had placed on his leg above the wound was too loose and too low. She loosened it, watching anxiously as the flow of blood increased in response to the lessening pressure. She slid the tourniquet higher up the hard-muscled thigh of the warrior, amazed at the solidity of his flesh, the definition of muscles. But that was only a passing observation. She had no time to dwell on inconsequential matters; there was only time to work, and little enough of that.

She pushed all thoughts of the Shawnee as man, as dream, as symbol, from her mind and forced herself to perceive him only as a badly wounded *thing*. It was easier that way. And she was glad that he had lost consciousness; to have those accusing eyes boring into her as she worked would have been unnerving, perhaps unbearable.

She tightened the tourniquet with a twig and lashed it into place. Standing, she wiped back her dark hair and took a deep breath. Now what!

He could not remain here. Already the snow was beginning

to fall, already his body was taking on an unhealthy pale color. The wounded leg would not live long with the blood supply cut off, and the thought of having to sever the leg was sickening. This was a young, healthy, alive man. Still, it might come to that. Her own father did very well with one arm after Ta-Tando in his madness had attacked him and destroyed that arm.

Cara, who had always thought of herself as self-composed, now hesitated. It was life and death, and somehow more than that, if that were possible. Her own life, her own death, seemed bound up in this.

Take him home. There was no other answer. Both Crenna and Sachim knew more medicine than she did. Home was warmth, food, comfort. And if it came to amputation—she shuddered again—her mother had once done such a thing, on her own husband.

She fought back that thought. She imagined briefly the outrage that the young warrior with the dark eyes would feel if he awoke to find his leg gone. They might as well kill him—but Cara would not allow him to die, she would not allow him to be crippled!

Home. He must be transported. Now, before the storm grew worse, the cold winds, the snows increased, before the warmth of his body trickled out and was replaced by the all-embracing cold of endless night.

Using the warrior's knife, taken from his rigid hand, Cara cut two sapling poles, lashing them together hurriedly with the man's own discarded legging. It was a poor travois, but she had no illusions about her ability to carry the man two miles through deep snow.

He would have to be dragged along behind her on this poor litter, and even then it was a difficult journey, perhaps impossible, but she did not choose to admit such thoughts. She would have him home, in bed, his leg tended by her mother and aunt. She would watch him grow strong . . . Thunder rumbled and a web of bone-white lightning bridged the gray, twisting skies.

Cara rolled him onto the simple litter, and trying to ignore the ghastly appearance of his face, the cold weight of his body, she lifted the ends of the travois poles and began laboriously trudging downslope toward the house in the valley.

Thunder roared and rumbled, mocking her smallness, summoning the snow demons who swirled around Cara, blocking her way, blurring her vision as she stumbled on, dragging the man behind her. He might be dying . . . he might already be dead—but she shook those thoughts off.

She sang a little song her mother had taught her when she was three or four. She imagined spring, golden sunlight, green grass, crops rushing toward ripeness, imagined two people dancing across the long meadow, imagined the flourish of color brought by the flowers of spring, bluebells, black-eyed Susans, lilac. She imagined the song of bluebirds; and the snows fell.

She had walked for hours, struggling through the whirl and wash of the snow, she had walked for miles, across continents; still the cabin was not in sight. The snow and cold had invaded her body, turning her lungs to ice, her legs to frozen stone.

Cara gritted her teeth. The travois handles bit at her raw palms. She glanced behind her. He lay cold and still, and for a stark moment she thought . . . She turned her eyes away and walked on, the snow falling around in a gray-white froth.

It loomed up suddenly, dark, squat, reassuring. It was an island of refuge in a vast sea of white. She could smell woodsmoke from its fire. Cara dragged herself and her burden across the yard toward the cabin door. She squatted and let go of the handles of her litter, tried the latch string, and found that her numbed fingers would not obey her commands.

She pounded on the door then and called out, her voice oddly strained, cracked, overloud.

It opened almost instantly. Crenna stood there, backlighted by reddish flames. She could see her father peering curiously toward the door, William's puzzled face. And then she fell into her mother's arms.

"Cara!" Crenna held her daughter, felt her slack weight against her, the rising and falling of her breast. Crenna examined her with puzzled eyes, and then she glanced across her daughter's shoulder, saw the snow-covered bundle lying on litter poles, and the puzzlement vanished and was replaced by swift, competent action.

"William! I need your help. Sachim, will you heat tea for Cara?" She turned, still supporting her daughter, and sat her at the table. William had already crossed to the door, and his blue eyes turned to his mother when she returned.

"He's Shawnee," William said. "This means trouble for us. Why did she bring him?"

"If you don't know, your education has been mishandled, William," Crenna said peevishly. She had bent over the body and was now lifting it by the shoulders. She needed help. "William!"

"If he dies in here, Mother . . ." He broke off his argument. His mother's expression was stern, taut, brooking no objections. A man was hurt; they must help him.

Sighing mightily, William helped to lift the cold, inert body of the Shawnee warrior. His hair was frosted with snow, the wound on his thigh was bruised and bloody. Frozen purple blood caked his flesh.

Van der Vaghe guided them to a hastily made bed on the floor of the new room. He had two lighted candles in his hands, and he set them on the floor, one on either side of the wounded warrior's head, an arrangement which reminded him too much of the dead. A memory sprang into his mind. An uncle, name unrecalled, who had lain similarly in the dark foyer of their house for two days.

But the Shawnee was not dead. Still his soul lived in that ravaged body, and Crenna, pushing her sleeves up, went to work.

She cut away the tourniquet, and the unconscious man's face tightened with sensation. Blood began to flow immediately; color returned with a rush to the leg.

"Sachim?"

Sachim handed Crenna clean cloths, and herbal powder, a narrow-bladed skinning knife which had been passed through the flames of the hearth fire. All of it was done unbidden. These two had seen many wounded men in their time, and they knew what had to be done.

Crenna worked at the wound as Cara, face drawn, her upper lip curled back in an involuntary grimace, watched from the doorway. William stood by, arms folded, his expression slightly censorious.

There was blood flowing over Crenna's capable fingers, and it worried her. The body was a vessel, filled with fluid and blood, but it held only so much. So much, and then the empty vessel existed no more.

Still she had to probe, had to cut at the living flesh, the meat of this warrior's thigh. Cara saw her face, strained, bathed in concentration, and she watched it, waiting for a sign that all was right. She could not bear to watch her mother's hands or the shining sharp steel of the skinning knife.

"More cloths," Crenna muttered, and Sachim moved ghost-like from the room. The blood was pooled on the floor now; the candles flickered and wavered, hovering near death themselves.

Crenna worked carefully; she was near the artery which, if ruptured, would leak blood in a tide they could not stem. Then she felt the solid, floating weight of metal and she knew. Recovering the object was ticklish. It was wedged against the bone, nudging the artery, which pulsed heavily, but finally she did extract it, and she brought it from the wound into the light.

"A lead ball," Van der Veghe said. It was flattened on one side, perhaps from hitting the bone.

"Musket ball," William said, though no one paid any attention to him.

Crenna least of all. She was busy at her craft. The wound was sprinkled with herbal powder and then with simple flour, which would cause the blood to clot. She took the clean cloth Sachim had brought to her and tamped it gently into the wound, knowing that if the man were conscious, the pain of this alone would cause him to scream out, be he the bravest warrior that ever walked Manitou's earth. Fortunately the spirits had been kind to him, had flown his soul briefly skyward, and he felt none of it, although his entire body glistened with perspiration.

Finally Crenna wrapped the wound tightly, so tightly that they could hear the joints of her arms and hands creak as she strained against the bandaging. Knotting the bandage, she sat on the floor for a minute, catching her breath. Cara had not moved throughout the operation. She sagged against the door frame, seemingly ready to topple and fall. But she held herself together.

Now she asked, "Will he live?" Crenna could only shake her head. She did not know; it would be days, perhaps weeks, before they knew. Sometimes the evil blood spirits returned to gnaw on the leg they had coveted. Then the leg had to be cut away and burned to appease them. That, of course, did not assure that the man would live either. Much blood had been lost, and the body would mourn the dead leg; sometimes the grief would be strong enough that the body would wish to follow the leg to the Bright Land.

"We shall see," Crenna said finally. She rose, bloody, exhausted. She wiped back her hair and repeated, "We shall see in time."

She collected her materials with Sachim's help, and Van der Veghe washed the floor around the fallen Shawnee. Cara did not move. William walked past her, giving her an odd appraising glance, but she didn't respond to him. She felt the weight of her father's gentle hand on her shoulder.

Then they were all gone. She heard low voices in the main room, once William's harsh laugh, but she was aware of all of that only in some deep, distant compartment of her mind. She stood watching the Shawnee, all of her attention on his supine, motionless body.

The candles flickered beside him, their light casting changing, intersecting shadows across his bronze chest, a chest which lifted ever so slightly as he breathed. His face, one formed by Manitou to worry the women, seemed almost peaceful, and she had a sudden vivid memory of those black, black eyes. She half-expected his eyelids to flicker open, those eyes to fix their gaze upon her, but they did not. He slept. He slept and perhaps awaited death.

He would die unknown if death did come; he would not die unmourned.

"Come away, Cara, have something to eat, change your wet clothes."

She shook her head, and Crenna went away, leaving her daughter to her vigil.

"You understand, don't you, Father?" William was asking. He sat with his arms on the table, his hands spread expressively. "Mother?"

"No," Crenna said, settling into a chair by the fire. Her mind had been distracted and she had nearly, automatically, seated herself on the floor. A lifetime's habit. She smiled to herself. "I do not understand. The man is hurt. He may die."

"He was shot with a musket!"

"A musket?" Sachim turned toward them, her expression uncertain.

"A blunderbuss, Aunt Sachim. A new sort of weapon."

"Like the weapon which killed our brother, Manto?"

"Like that," William said indulgently. "What the weapon was is not important. What is important"—he leaned forward, blue eyes intent—"is that this Shawnee was shot by a white man."

"Yes." Van der Veghe nodded. He drummed on the table with his fingers. "Still . . ."

"You agree with them, Father?" William asked.

"Of course," Van der Veghe answered mildly. His son threw his hands into the air.

"What troubles you so, William?" Sachim asked softly.

"This—the man is Shawnee. We are living on their hunting grounds. Other white families have come. A white man shot the Shawnee. If they find him here, we will be blamed. If he dies, we will be judged the murderers. It stands to reason."

"Mercy stands to reason, William," Crenna said in her native tongue, annoying William, who had been conversing in Dutch.

"It can be misunderstood," William said. He rose suddenly. "Suppose this man dies. Suppose he is found near our home. What then?"

"I do not know," Crenna replied. "I only know that he is hurt; he must be helped as long as it is in our power."

"Father!" William turned to Van der Veghe in exasperation.

"I cannot agree with you, William. Not if you mean what I think you do."

"What does he want?" Sachim asked. She had lost the drift of the conversation. Her own Dutch was rudimentary.

"I believe," Van der Veghe said, "my son would like us to take this wounded man as far from the house as possible and leave him there."

"Yes!" William said, and Sachim recoiled from this violent response. "Get him out of here. The man is going to die. We'll die because of him. You don't bring a wounded wolf into the house."

"He is a man, William," Crenna pointed out. "I am disappointed," she added. "Whose son are you, William? Mine, Van der Veghe's? What you suggest is criminal."

"Mother—"

"Criminal. It reveals a lack of compassion, a flaw in your spirit, William. It hurts me to have you suggest such things."

"They will come," the boy answered, his voice taut with emotion, "and they will kill us!" He waved an arm at the adjoining room. His mouth was drawn down with emotion, the cords on his throat stood out distinctly. "If that man dies . . . we will die, Mother. And I do not care if the Shawnee dies . . . only *where*. Because . . . I care . . . for you."

"There can be no more discussion," Crenna said, and her voice, to Van der Veghe, was reminiscent of the tone she had used in the council lodges all those years ago when she had stood up before the tribal elders, those hard-bitten warriors and Oneida statesmen, and passed her final judgment.

William, his eyes narrowed, hurt, watched her and then shook his head. "No more," he agreed, but there was an underlying meaning to his words.

He said nothing else, but he picked up his fur coat, his snowshoes, his bow and arrows. They did not try to stop him as he dressed; he was too much a man now for that. Outside, it was snowing heavily, but he was not bothered by that. They did not ask where he was going; they knew that too.

Across the valley were his friends, his *people*. The white settlers; the woman. "No one has considered them," William said before leaving. His voice shook with anger. "They might be dead, mutilated. This Shawnee has been raiding. He might have killed the woman I love."

Then he was gone. There was a brief flurry of wind and snow as the cabin door opened and was pulled shut again, and then there was only silence, the snowflakes melting against the earth of the cabin floor.

"Tea?" Crenna rose and poured herself a cup of the elderberry tea. It was a moment before Van der Veghe nodded.

"You didn't drive him away, Crenna," her husband said.

"No."

"He is worried about his friends."

"I know that." She gave Peter Van der Veghe his tea and seated herself opposite him. His hand rested briefly on hers. "Are we losing him?" she asked.

"A parent loses them all."

"Not like this."

"No. But if he is wrong, he is wrong. We can't give in to him in a case like this. To please him, to avoid hurting his feelings. He can be no different from any other man at a time like this. If his ideas are opposed to ours, we must not give in."

"No." Crenna sipped her tea, found it too hot, and asked without looking up, "Are we right, Peter?"

"You know we are. There is a logic to Willliam's argument, a selfish logic, I suppose. A trait I do not admire, but one common enough, especially in the young. He sees danger—and he is right in that respect, Crenna. You do realize that?"

"I realize that." She paused. "Are we doing *right*?"

Sachim stood near them still, her shadow on the table, and softly, so softly, she said, "How can compassion ever be wrong?"

There was no answer to that, but as Crenna turned to look to the open doorway to the small room where Cara still stood her vigil, she was reminded of the tale of the spirit healer, Miko, he who had compassion for a wounded bear and healed it in his lodge. They lived together throughout the winter, until the spring brought strength to the bear and it departed. Miko had had compassion; the bear had none. It killed Miko and ate him. They were not always grateful, these savage things.

❁ 4 ❁

The eyes moved as Cara crossed the room. The candle burned low and the flame was reflected in those dark, dark eyes. Outside, the snow fell as it had for days, and now and then the muffled boom of thunder shook the solidly constructed log house. She crossed the room as she had a hundred times that week, each time expecting, hoping, that the black eyes of the Shawnee would open, would smile at her. Now that they were open, she wished that they would close again.

There was an anger in them, a cunning, a savagery. Where was the self-possessed youth who had ridden to their farm all those summers ago? Or was this what pain did to a man?

"I have to change your bandage again," she said, not looking at his face as she put the basin of water down. She had fallen into the habit of talking to him as he lay silently beneath her ministering hands. Now her voice broke off uneasily and she simply did her work. Those eyes wished for no communication.

It was difficult to clean the musket-ball wound because the leg was broken and splinted. The splint absolutely could not be removed, and it left little room to get at the wound, which still bled—bled more than it should have at this point in his convalescence.

She removed the old, scabbed bandage and felt him flinch.

Cara looked up, smiling. "I'm sorry, but it really has to be done every day, you know—"

His voice interrupted her harshly. "Why did you bring me here, woman! I told you to leave me alone."

"To die!" Cara answered sharply. His attitude angered her.

"I would not have died," he insisted, craning his neck to look up at her, his eyes fierce and confident.

"You would have bled to death. If not that, you would have frozen or starved."

"I have wintered out before."

"Not with a wound like this," she countered. Then she added quietly, "Or you wouldn't be alive now."

"Woman . . . !" he began to shout, but the pain or exhaustion cut him off. His head went back against the folded blanket beneath him, and he stared at the ceiling, the small muscles at the corner of his jaw working in exasperation.

"I'm sorry," Cara said with anger, "sorry that we saw fit to save your life. Sorry that we've tried to keep you warm and feed you." She yanked the last bit of old bandaging away too harshly and saw him tense with pain. "I'm sorry . . ."

"Why?"

"What did you say?"

"Why did you help me?" His voice now was strained. His eyes seemed to search hers, to run through her dark, loose hair and across her breasts. But he did not answer when she told him.

"Because you were hurt; because I was there to help."

She replaced the herbal powder and began winding the new bandage on the leg, lifting it gently as she went under and over tightly.

Tearing the cloth with her teeth, Cara knotted the ends of the bandage and sat back on her heels, watching his face in the dusky light.

"What is your name, what are you called?" she asked. There was no answer. His eyes closed and his head turned away. "Will you eat something? You must."

Again there was no answer. Cara rose, sucking in a deep, angry breath as she did so. She snatched up the basin, spilling some water. "Stubborn man."

She walked to the doorway, hesitated, and said, "I thought you were a fine, strong warrior. A man. You are a boy to lie and sulk in your doctors' home. I thought you were more than this."

She had turned again to go into the big room where the family now lay sleeping, warmed by the banked fire in the stone hearth, when she heard him say quietly: "Ousa. My name is Ousa."

Cara smiled. She did not turn back into the room or look at him, but she smiled and then said, "Good night, Ousa."

His temper was not much better the next morning, but his appetite was stronger. He drank down a bowl of Crenna's venison broth too quickly and demanded more.

"You can have no more, Ousa," Cara told him. "You know it is not wise. It's been a week since you've eaten. Your stomach is shrunken."

"More!" He thrust out the bowl, and as she shook her head, he threw the bowl across the room.

"No." Cara rose and picked up the bowl. "You must get well slowly. You cannot force bone to mend, flesh to heal. It must be slowly if you are to become truly strong again."

He had his head turned away, and Cara could see the tautness in his throat muscles, the gauntness of his cheeks. He was angry, angry because he could not rise, pick up his weapons and go into the forest, return home to family . . . and wife? That caused her pulse to quicken. Why wouldn't he be married, or at least have a chosen woman? Young, strong, handsome—there could be no lack of women. That idea, so obvious, so new, rested in her stomach like an irritating foreign substance maliciously scratching at her entrails.

She certainly had made no impression on him. He was as sullen and ungrateful as ever; she was his nurse, and a symbol of his present weakness, a weakness which seemed to humiliate him.

"I'll be back later with more broth."

Ousa did not answer, did not speak until she was nearly gone, and when he did speak his voice seemed softer, his eyes less turbulent. "What are you called?"

"Cara," she said, turning and smiling. "I am called Cara."

"Cara," he repeated musingly. Then he nodded, and his eyelids dropped wearily, hooding those compelling eyes. Cara stood there a moment longer, expecting—or hoping—that he would say something else, but in a minute it was obvious from the gentle rising and falling of his chest that he had gone to sleep again.

"How' is our injured warrior?" Crenna asked as Cara came back into the main room.

"His name is Ousa," Cara answered.

"And how is Ousa?" Crenna then asked, rephrasing the question. She had to smile at the distraction on her daughter's face as she went to the door, emptied the water basin, and returned.

"I think he is doing well now," Cara said, forcing her thoughts to the practical.

William had returned after walking through the storm to the Daweses' house to assure himself they were all right. He sat glaring into space, still violently unhappy with the Shawnee's presence.

"They killed three Englishmen," he had told them the day he returned. "Burned two houses. Stole two horses. The one in there"—he had nodded his head toward the small room—"was shot by a man named Parkinson as he tried to set fire to their house."

"The Daweses were not bothered?" his father had asked.

William's answer had been succinct. "Your Shawnee is still alive, isn't he?"

Crenna had been hurt by the brutal threat implicit in her son's words, but she understood. In her own land it had been law: if the tribe were injured, the enemy would be injured. If they killed three Oneida, four of them must die. If a maiden was stolen by the Algonquin, two Algonquin maidens must be stolen in answer. It was the law, a way of assuring the survival of the tribe. Any enemy must expect prompt and costly reprisal. Knowing that, few attempted to attack the powerful Iroquois tribe.

Those who had not survived—those other, lost tribes—had been the ones for whom peace was sought at any price. Let the enemy have a little of our hunting grounds. Let us not make war over the loss of Solitary Pine Tree's daughter, they may kill us all. And they did, slowly, a feather at a time, as in the tale of the goose and the weasel.

Crenna understood William, but this man, this Ousa, was in their own lodge, and that was different. He would not be harmed inside their house. Things were not done that way.

Now William glowered at his sister. "No sense hovering over him as you do, Cara. He'll make it or he won't."

"He *won't* make it if he is not tended properly."

"All the better," William muttered, but Cara heard him.

"He has the same right to life as your white friends!"

"Yes, except my white friends did not go raiding the Shawnee camp, did they? They did not go murdering and burning." William half-rose from his chair before his mother's cool eye caused him to sag back down and begin to eat his meal sullenly.

"He is our guest as long as he lives here," Crenna said, making it law. "After he goes, he is what he makes himself—friend or enemy."

"Do you think he would come back here and harm us?" Cara demanded of her brother. "After we have saved his life!"

"You know him better than I, Cara," William answered without looking up from his plate. "What do *you* think?" And to be truthful, she did not know what a man like Ousa might do. She knew nothing at all about him. Maybe he would return with his warriors one day; perhaps William was right. Her pride kept her from saying so, and as she turned away, her pride was nearly enough to stop the tears from flowing.

Foolish tears, damnable tears, a woman's curse. She went out into the cold bright day and began walking. Walking nowhere, trying to smudge the bright, clear thoughts which arced through her mind, thoughts of destruction, and of her own family's murder.

The walking did no good. The day was empty of comfort. When she returned home, she stood in Ousa's sickroom watching him, as if she could read his soul from the expression on his sleeping face. She could see nothing written there, and he did not speak.

After dark, when she returned again, he still slept, and she stayed close to him, wanting to feel the whisperings of his soul, to understand this man, to know that she had not brought death into her family's home the day she dragged this injured man out of the hills.

But the night was silent, his soul distant and quiet. She could only rise and go to her own bed, to sleep and to suffer the tormented dreams.

"Broth?"

Ousa's eyes seemed to smile, but it was only a brief, fragmented expression. "I would like some meat."

"Still too early for that, I'm afraid," Cara told him with a smile of her own.

"Always too early. Everything is too early with you, Cara," he responded, but there was no anger in his words.

"You're simply impatient. All sick people are impatient. Sometimes," she said, kneeling beside him, "they are so impatient that they hurt themselves in their attempts to hurry their healing."

"Yes." Ousa took a spoonful of the broth. Swallowing, he went on. "Perhaps they feel they are a burden to the living—these half-living who are the ill."

"Half-living! It is no shame to be ill. We all are. It is how one deals with illness which marks the man."

"I do not deal with it well," Ousa said. "My life is out there, you see." His arm lifted vaguely. "There is much to do. Much. Illness is a weight upon my soul."

"Then do as I say and grow healthy," Cara said, spooning another helping of broth into Ousa's mouth, which was now definitely—if most faintly—smiling.

It was two weeks before he could stand. By then he was thin and gaunt and unsteady in his movements. But he was young, and his strength would return quickly. Cara had made a crutch by cutting the crotched branch of a young willow and padding it with rags. Ousa came to the table that morning, his eyes flint-hard, flint-dark.

William got up from the table immediately, and with one sharp, challenging glance at Ousa, he was gone, snatching up a slab of broiled venison as he went. Ousa seemed more amused than offended.

"White Indian," he grunted. "I know that man."

He did not mean he had met William before, spoken to him. He meant that he knew by his actions, by the single piercing disparaging glance, he *knew* this man. Knew his heart, his intentions, his warrior's stance. Ousa had seen many like William. He knew instinctively that this one would fight if it came to that, knew that he was not soft, nor afraid. Possibly he could murder.

Ousa seated himself in the unfamiliar chair with some reluctance. In the end it seemed he gave in to this white custom simply because it would have been much more difficult for him to lower himself to the floor with his bad leg.

"How is your leg?" Van der Veghe asked. There was no answer from the scowling Ousa.

Crenna, holding back a remark which was on the tip of her tongue, served the young Shawnee tea, parched corn, and venison. She knew little of Shawnee ways, but among her people a man was at least polite—polite if he couldn't be friendly—in another's lodge.

Ousa ate greedily at first, and then his rebelling stomach forced him to stop. With one last sip of tea he rose, hobbling to his feet.

"Where are you going?" Cara asked, rising herself.

"Outside. There is no air to breathe in this . . ." He waved a hand, as if trying to grab an adequate adjective out of the air. "This house."

"It's snowing," Cara told him. "You'll need a blanket."

"I need nothing!" Ousa said darkly. Cara acted as if she had not heard the man. She went to her mother's trunk and took out a fine Onondaga blanket, one which had never been used, one which had been promised Cara when she married. Her parents said nothing as she returned and wrapped this blanket around Ousa's shoulders.

Cara seemed to realize suddenly the significance of what she had done, and she turned her eyes away. "Come on then," she said to Ousa.

"I mean to go out by myself."

"And how far will you go in the snow with that leg? Come along. I will support you."

Ousa shrugged her arm off, but when she replaced it, he accepted her help. Once, the barest beginnings of a smile appeared on his mouth, but it was gone before they reached the door.

Outside, it was blustery, slate-gray clouds drifting past in ragged procession, with occasional snow falling. William's tracks were impressed in the otherwise pristine meadow. On the bluffs behind the house, low clouds obscured the deep forest so that only the ragged dark heads of the pines were visible. From not far distant came the sound of the brook rushing toward the river.

Ousa at first tried to place no weight on Cara, but they hadn't gone far before he was forced to lean on her shoulder. Cara knew she should tell him that walking too far was unwise, but she was afraid of his contrariness, afraid that he would force himself to walk as far and as fast as possible to prove something to her. Was he always this sullen, she wondered, always so quick to take offense, and so perverse?

She supposed he considered himself to be in the enemy

camp. They had raided the white settlers; he had been shot. Therefore, in Ousa's mind at least, a state of war existed.

"Let's sit down," he said finally, and she nodded in silent agreement.

There was a large, nearly square gray boulder on the verge of the spruce forest, and they walked to it, pausing to sweep the snow from it before they sat. Ousa was panting heavily; he threw his head back to take a great draft of the cold air into his lungs. Then he sat, hands on knees, the blanket loose around his shoulders, looking out at the meadow and the hills beyond. Cara sat beside him silently, shivering a little as the clouds closed out the sky and the wind increased.

"You are a foolish woman," the Shawnee said suddenly. He was not looking at Cara. His eyes continued to scan the meadow.

"Foolish?"

"Yes. To heal me. To keep me warm. Your brother would not have done such a thing."

"You heard him!"

"No!" Ousa laughed. "I did not need to hear what he said about me. I know. He and I, we are the same. I am his enemy, why let me live?"

"But the rest of us," Cara said, her eyes sparking, "we are foolish to care for you?"

"Yes." He turned his head slowly toward her, and his eyes reflected inner amusement. "For you see, I am your enemy. I would destroy you. If it had not been for the Englishman with the musket gun, I would already have harmed you. Your house was on my list for destruction."

Cara gaped at him. Finally, after several false starts, she said, "You were going to come here? To destroy our house?"

"Oh, yes," he said easily, shifting his position slightly. "But then I was shot. My brother Shelokta would have taken charge of the war party." Ousa became more animated, his face glowing. Returning thoughts of battle seemed to stir him. "I don't know what happened after we became separated. Perhaps Shelokta suggested another target, perhaps we had too many wounded."

"You would think he would have come looking for you," Cara observed.

"Shelokta?" Ousa laughed. "No, not Shelokta. You should remember him, Cara—he rode with me the day we stopped to talk to your mother."

"That one," she said, recalling very well the youth with the crooked mouth and the broken nose, the one who had trampled down their corn out of sheer spitefulness.

"Yes," Ousa said knowingly. Cara turned her eyes to him, and he nodded as if at some private joke. "That is my brother Shelokta. There are many people who do not like him."

"I don't know him," Cara said, lifting her hands in a small, expressive gesture.

"But you saw him. His heart is written on his face. Yes, my brother, Shelokta . . ." Ousa's thoughts and voice trailed off into private regions.

Cara maintained her silence, although she had much to ask. She wished to know more about Shelokta and more about the war against the settlers in the valley. Was it even a war, or just a raid for horses? Would there be more attacks in the spring; would they return to attack her own house?

She wanted to ask much, but she kept silent. She did not want to speak of war to Ousa, to watch his eyes light up with fire, to hear his berating tone. Now he was at peace, empty of his warrior soul; he was only a man sitting quietly, musingly, as the gentle snow fell, and she was only a woman sitting beside him, her shoulder to his.

There were many walks after that day. Gradually Ousa discarded his crutch, gradually he could walk without leaning on Cara, gradually his strength returned. She could see it in the lean, hard muscle of his chest, of his shoulders. His face lost its gauntness. He moved like a big cat, sure, quick, silent.

Still he limped, but she knew that it was only a matter of time before he left. When his leg was well, when the snows ceased, then he would wander his own trail and she would not see him again.

Yet when he mentioned it, a panic seized her. She had never mentioned the dream, her many encounters with him under the wings of sleep, but she had always thought that he would *know* when he came, this man from out of the dream.

He did not even seem to care. "Soon, I think," Ousa said. They were in the spruce forest, where patches of snow still lay. He tested his leg, crouching down. "Yes," he said, nodding with satisfaction. He rubbed his leg with his hands. "Soon I shall leave. Poor Shelokta"—he laughed—"he will be crestfallen at my return. I imagine he has entrenched himself well in my absence."

"You are not ready," Cara murmured. Ousa looked down into her eyes, and said that he was. It was time; this was not his home, these were not his people. It was time.

"Your leg is not healed properly," Cara insisted. There was urgency in her voice, and Ousa seemed to pause, to reflect on that.

"It is healed. Shall I prove it to you, woman?"

Cara's brow furrowed. "Prove it?"

"Yes, come on." He took her hands and turned her. "Do you see the broken cedar? I will race you to that."

"You can't run," she protested. "If your leg is not healed properly . . ."

"But it is, Mingoe woman!" He laughed again, and there was a hint of derisiveness in his tone. "That is what I shall prove to you."

"No," Cara said, shaking her head slowly.

"Come on!" he challenged with what was almost boyish enthusiasm. "Race me, woman."

And then he was gone, loping easily across the snowfields, the shadows of the pines flickering across him. He was laughing, laughing as he ran, and Cara, lifting her skirt, took off at a run, sprinting after Ousa. Why, she could not have said, but it seemed urgent that she prove something to him, prove that she could outrun this Shawnee warrior.

Now he was running backward, waving his arm and laughing as she rushed after him, leaping a fallen limb, her legs striding smoothly. She was nearly to him when she heard him laugh again, make a pleased, sham sound of astonishment, and turn to run on for all he was worth.

Still he laughed, but Cara would not give in. She had her bunched skirt in her hands and she ran with all of the lithe strength that was in her while some mocking voice in the back of her mind scolded her for her foolishness.

Do you think you will keep him this way, woman?

The cedar was fifty yards away now, its long shadow nearly reaching them. They were head and head, and now Cara saw that Ousa's mockery, his amusement, had faded and his face was grim as he ran; he had something to prove as well.

It was a dead heat. Ousa reached the tree and pulled up, giving his leg a favoring limp as he struggled the last few paces to the tree. Cara stood by, winded. She was bent over at the waist, forcing air into her lungs. Ousa had his back against the tree, and his eyes, reflecting amusement, excitement, suddenly altered.

He pushed himself away from the tree and came to her, his moccasins tracking the pale blue-white snow. The scent of the cedar was rich in the chill air; a squirrel wrapped itself around the trunk of the cedar and climbed higher in a spiral ascent.

Cara's eyes were wide; her heart drummed like thunder. He was to her, and Ousa, the stern, was no longer smiling, no longer mocking. His arms slipped around her and his hand rested on the swale of her back, his fingertips touching the upward swell of her hips.

Her vision began to blur as his arms tightened around her, and her nostrils filled with the scent of him, warm from the race. His eyes, those black eyes, looked downward, and she felt the pressure of his fingertips on waist and shoulder increase, felt herself drawn to him, felt the rising and falling of his chest as their bodies met, her spine inadvertently arching; and then his mouth, searching, intimidating, was on hers. There was the pressure of his knee against her thigh, the hand gripping her shoulder, the grating of tooth against tooth, his breath against her throat, her mouth going slack, yielding to his persistent force.

He stepped back, but his arms did not fall away. He appraised her with softened eyes, measured her, smiled, and kissed her again, only it was no longer the same.

The desire was there; she could feel the close insistence of his pelvis, see the dark light in his eyes, feel the almost pleading touch of his lips on her throat as she stood, slack and ripe in his arms, her head thrown back, but it was not the same.

There had been a moment when all was right, magical, swirling, emphatic with their exultant proclamation of existence. Then Ousa had stepped away, he had formulated it, he had structured this next moment in his mind, and it could not be as rich and loving as that first urgent, unplanned kiss.

"Do you want me, Ousa?" she asked quietly, her own hands now resting on his shoulders, her eyes turned downward.

"Yes," he murmured. Something else was lost as he breathed the word into the dark, silky richness of her hair. His warm exhalations touched her cheek, her neck, her ear, inflaming deep needs, desires lain dormant since the night of the first dream.

His diction was blurred as he spoke, his body was tense

muscle and demanding heat. She could feel the flat, firm webs of muscle on his back beneath the buckskin shirt; but she could no longer feel the magnetism, the great upsurge of rightness, of longing in her own body.

"Do you want me, Ousa?" she repeated, and again he murmured an affirmative answer, turning her so that her weight was against the cedar as his hands slid across the swell of her hips, across her breasts, most tentatively, and then, when she did not deflect them, with frank, practiced caresses.

"I want you," he answered finally, and he must have felt the rigidity in her, the withdrawal. He went on eagerly. "I will build you your own lodge and I will come to you each night. I will see that you want for nothing—"

"What do you mean, Ousa?" Cara asked sharply, suddenly knowing what he did mean.

"What I have said. You will be my woman." He laughed and bent his head to kiss her again. Cara put her hands to his cheeks, not pushing him away, not drawing his head to her.

"What do you mean, Ousa?"

"I will keep you well. You will live well."

"As well as your wife?" Cara asked, cutting through the obscurity of his proposal.

"Every bit as well. If I should marry Tadona, she will have no more than you."

Tadona. The name, vague, meaningless, dropped like a stone into Cara's heart. There was a woman, then. What she had divined was the truth. He wanted her, this Ousa, he wanted her to live for him but not with him. Now the hands which framed Ousa's face dropped away.

"Go to her, then," Cara said.

"You are angry?" He dared a laugh. "Why? I am Kispkotha, of the warrior clan. I will be a leader of my people. I must marry a woman of position, a woman like Tadona. Surely you can understand that!"

"I am not Shawnee; I do not understand." Cara turned her back, crossed her arms beneath her breasts, and stared into the distances. *Foolish woman*. His hand rested on her shoulder as if to comfort her; then it fell away.

"You could not have thought . . .! That I would marry you!" His laugh was a humiliation. "I am Kispkotha. You are the daughter of white dog and a Mingoe!"

"I thought nothing," Cara lied. He tried to turn her, but she would not face him.

"It is impossible, Cara."

"Even if you wished it."

"Even if I did!" he said heatedly.

"But you do not?"

His response was oblique. "You cannot stay here. There will be war. Your home will be burned. You will be killed as well. Can't you see all of that?"

"I see nothing. I am a blind woman, it seems."

"Cara." His voice was softer now, and she let him turn her by the shoulders. He kissed her forehead, but the kiss seemed a mockery. "I am trying to do what is best for you."

"And for Ousa."

He was exasperated. His hands fell to his side and he shook his head. "I am offering you survival," he said, spacing his words emphatically. "A good life awaits you. Here you have nothing!"

"How stupid a woman is," Cara said to herself. She looked at his face, self-satisfied, confident. She shook her head. "Your leg is healed; go away."

"Cara?"

"That is what you wanted. Go away."

"You must understand! I am of the Kispkotha clan."

"And I am the daughter of Crenna, headwoman of the Oneida nation, and of Van der Veghe, the scientist. Not," she said quietly but with fervor, "some Shawnee warrior's concubine."

"One day you will wish you were!" he said with stark vehemence. Then he turned, his hand held up for a brief moment as if he would turn back and strike her. The hand lowered and Ousa stalked away, shaking his head. He lost himself in the dark woods, and Cara watched long after he was gone.

She did not notice the tears until she felt them chill her cheek, and then she wiped them away with anger. Spinning on her heel, she walked homeward. She had not gone far when she saw the footprints. Someone had watched; someone had heard.

She didn't have to look long at the tracks to know who it was that had left them. The Wild One. He who killed wolves and frightened young women.

Cara stopped and spun around, looking into the forest in the direction the tracks had taken. "You too!" she shouted angrily, her fists bunched. "You go home too! We don't want you! We want you no more than we want this injured Shawnee warrior.''

There was no answer but the ranting wind, and she did not turn toward the forest again to see the dark, crooked figure moving through the trees, staining the snow with his uneven shadow.

She returned to the house in a vile mood. Crenna could not draw her out, and decided wisely that Cara was suffering through a problem which she believed was unique, which could never have possibly been experienced by her elders.

Ousa burst into the house minutes later, the wind tossing his dark hair. He still limped slightly and he dragged his right leg across the room, coming to a halt before Van der Veghe, who had been filling his favorite pipe.

''I ask for your daughter, white man. I will trade you your safety for her. Give me the girl and I will go away. You will live. I take an oath the Shawnee will not return to harm you.''

Cara uttered a small, frustrated shriek. Crenna's head came around angrily, pride and disgust flashing in her eyes. Van der Veghe was the person who had been addressed, however, and he was the one who replied to Ousa.

''Go away, Ousa. Perhaps your customs are different from ours. We do not sell our daughters into slavery.'' Van der Veghe's voice was soft, but there was timbre in it. Ousa looked once into the Dutchman's pale eyes, and then, turning in a circle, he waved his arms in frustration.

''This family is mad. A white dog. A Mingoe woman. A crazy daughter. Do you want to die, white dog?'' he asked, leaning nearer to Van der Veghe. ''That is what will happen without Ousa's blessing on this mad family.''

''I do not wish to die,'' Peter Van der Veghe said calmly, rising to his feet. ''But my wife and I have lived with danger, we have lived with death. We have never lived without honor. Stay, Ousa, if you wish, if you are not well. If you cannot understand honor, then go.''

He said no more. Ousa looked into Crenna's dark proud eyes and then he shook his head. ''Honor—white dogs and Mingoes.''

''Go, it is best,'' Cara said, her voice small.

''Go!'' the Shawnee warrior flared up. ''I will go when I wish. I will go when I am well. What kind of people are you to speak of honor when you cast an injured man out into the snow!"

Then he was gone, the door banging behind him. Van der Veghe glanced at Crenna and offered her a thin smile, knowing, wise, yet apprehensive.

"Youth pursues life as if it were a hare," Sachim said. "As if it were not there, at every turn. As if *it* did not pursue us."

"He knows nothing," Cara said acidly. "He is not a man. He is himself a dog. He runs sniffing at the trees, lifting his leg, barking, and asking to be admired."

Then she was gone, marching out the front door, banging it behind her, and Crenna said quietly to Van der Veghe, "They are in love, husband. I will have to begin preparing their wedding gifts."

Van der Veghe looked dubiously at his wife, who wore the faintest of smiles. Crenna began humming softly as she rose and started digging through the trunks they had brought with them from the Hudson.

He shrugged, wondering at his wife's conclusions. If Cara could have heard her mother's speculative comment, she would have perhaps burst into tears of frustration. Ousa undoubtedly would have barked a mocking laugh, but Crenna seemed to have no doubts. Sachim nodded her head sagely and helped her sister as they dug through the trunks, taking out the finest blankets, the feathered cape with shell trim, and two beautiful black-glazed pots.

Van der Veghe watched them for a time, puffing on his pipe. Then, scratching his head, he rose, stretched, and went out to chop firewood and feed the horses.

The skies were clear but for a thin veil of clouds along the western horizon. Here and there green grass showed through the patchy snow. A flight of snow geese sketched a jagged V against the placid sky.

The horses were gone.

There were footprints in the snow. One man wearing moccasins, and the tracks of the two led horses. Van der Veghe threw down the pitchfork he was carrying and called back to the house. "Crenna. They've taken the horses!"

He did not know if she heard him or not. He took off at a long loping run across the snow. The tracks were still fresh. There was a chance of catching the man.

Without the horses, logs would have to be moved by hand, the wooden plow Van der Veghe had devised would have to be drawn by himself or the women. A hundred tasks would be made more difficult, and there was little hope of replacing the animals.

"They" had taken the horses, he had hollered to the house. There was only one man, but he supposed that in the back of his mind he had placed the blame immediately on a Shawnee war party.

Ousa. He almost halted as that thought came to him. Instinct told him that it had to be Ousa. One man who knew where the horses were. And, God! *Cara*. That had to be it; he had abducted the girl.

"Van der Veghe!" His name was barely recognizable, the accent was so heavy, but the lean runner who rushed out of the woods to join him was instantly identified. Ousa was running to join Van der Veghe, and his dark face was concerned.

"Is it Cara?" the Shawnee demanded as they ran side by side.

"I don't know." Van der Veghe pointed to the tracks. Ousa could not read much from them: the snow was melting, the tracks indistinct.

Together they ran along the brook, toward the timber. Van der Veghe was panting heavily, his lungs afire. Ousa grimaced; his leg was still bothering him despite his protestations to the contrary.

Then Van der Veghe saw the other tracks, and his heart swelled into a lump inside his throat. Ousa saw them simultaneously, and he breathed a profound Shawnee curse.

Here Cara's tracks—it had to be she—angled from out of the woods. Here she had rested, or been tied to a tree, for there were signs of someone having been seated at the base of the pine.

"Tied," Ousa said, breathing heavily. "Here, she struggles. Many marks."

Van der Veghe nodded his understanding, recognizing that Ousa felt it necessary to explain everything to the untrained white man. As they paused, nearly doubled over, fighting for breath, Van der Veghe looked back to see William running after them, his yellow hair flying. He was too far back to wait for, and so the two men plunged ahead.

"Shawnee?" Van der Veghe wanted to know. "Shawnee?"

Ousa could only shake his head; he did not know. He only

knew that a man had taken Cara, that they were mounted, and that the pursuers were afoot. Now, by the lengthened strides, Ousa could tell that Cara's captor had lifted the horses into a canter.

"Faster, we must run faster," Ousa said. He himself looked capable of no such thing. Van der Veghe, who was no longer a young man, was fighting age, which resisted his attempts to run on, let alone increase his speed.

Glancing once across his shoulder, he saw that William, young and fit, was gaining on both of them, running up the wooded, snow-dappled slopes like a bounding deer.

"That way." Ousa pointed a finger as he ran, and Van der Veghe frowned. The tracks of the horses veered left, but Ousa was pointing right. He trusted the Shawnee, he had to. There was no mistaking the concern etched into Ousa's face. This was not of his doing; he would not stop until exhaustion felled him.

Van der Veghe followed obediently, loosing a stride every twenty feet they ran, until eventually Ousa was far ahead, cresting the rocky knoll just as Van der Veghe started up.

"Father!" William was beside Van der Veghe now, and Peter, his abdomen knotted, his lungs cramped with lack of oxygen, could only point a finger toward the knoll. Let the young men go on; he could do no more.

William, eyes bright, bow and three arrows in his hand, took off at an even faster pace. Ousa was only a dark loping figure weaving his way through the forest. And ahead—if Ousa had not been mistaken in chosing his direction—were Cara and her captor.

But Ousa had not been wrong. The trail which had veered left, now circled right beyond a stack of snow-frosted, stark boulders. A dead pine tilted over the trail.

Ousa ran on. He heard the sounds behind him and looked back to see the white Indian, William as they called him, cresting the knoll, his face a mask of fury. Momentarily, with brief amusement, Ousa was glad it was not he who had taken the girl.

Then he saw them and he threw himself to the ground, lifting a hand as he fell to indicate to the trailing William that he had seen them.

He lay in the snow, watching, eyes dark, his hands empty, his heart filled with rage. Ousa's eyes were black and murderous.

Still he led her forward, and Cara could do nothing. He

had come out of the woods, his clawlike hands wrapping around her face and waist. He had dragged her to the pine and tied her there, stuffing a filthy cloth into her mouth so that she could not cry out.

Then he had gone away, the Lone One, the Wolf. He had returned with the horses and had thrown her on the back of the little bay, his single eye glassy and obscene.

Then with a jerk he had led the horses out, while Cara's gagged mouth formed silent screams, as she kicked and tried to leap from the horse's back. Once she had gotten from it, but he had thrown her up roughly again and lashed her ankles together beneath the horse's belly.

They rode on now at a faster pace, the horses' hooves kicking up spumes of snow, their nostrils blowing steam as they circled the knoll, the cool shadows of the pines draped over them.

The Wild One rode recklessly on, his eye revealing a madness, his face alternately cheerful and menacing. He turned constantly in the saddle to look at Cara, to let his eye linger on her. He scratched his cheek constantly with his damaged hand even as they rode at a gallop through the deep snow on the northern slope of the knoll.

She wanted to scream out her protest, to demand where she was being taken, what his purposes were, but the filthy, coarse rag in her mouth prevented it. Perhaps it was best; perhaps she would not want to know.

Her head lolled back; nausea was developing slowly in her stomach—the result of the combination of fear, the motion of the horse bucking through the snow, and the taste of the foul, mildewed rag in her mouth.

He came from off the jumble of rocks, a dark panther springing. Ousa hit the Wild One high on the shoulders and they toppled from the horse, which reared up and whickered in panic.

Ousa landed on top of the Wild One, and he tried for the throat, but his grappling hand was knocked away and the Wild One, exhibiting a strength extraordinary in a man of his years, gripped Ousa's arm at the elbow and rolled him over his hip.

But Ousa did not let go. Together they rolled down the long slope, snow dust billowing into the air as they fought for superiority.

The Wild One regained his balance first, and he came up in

a crouch, swinging out a moccasined foot, which caught Ousa on the throat. Ousa went down, clutching his own neck, and the one-eyed man threw himself on top of him, his knee slamming against Ousa's thigh as he tried for the groin.

Ousa rolled to one side, barely evaded a forked jab of the Wild One's fingers, which would have blinded him, and came to his feet.

They stood facing each other on a narrow ledge at the end of the long slope. Below them was another drop, more sheer, and at the bottom of that, black basaltic rock and death.

The Wild One smiled wolfishly. His hand slipped behind his back and reappeared with a knife, a long-bladed, evil-looking weapon. He held the knife low, blade turned up. His eye glittered as he moved toward Ousa, both hands in front of him. Ousa backed away, circling, looking for an opening, but there was none. The Wild One was many things, and he was a fighter to be reckoned with. He came in patiently, this one-eyed man with the long gray hair across his face. The knife flicked toward Ousa like a snake's tongue, and the Shawnee leaped back.

But he was not so quick as he had been before his leg had been wounded, and the knife came perilously close. The Wild One smiled; he knew. He knew that Ousa was injured. But he was not impatient, this specter in greasy buckskins. He was content to circle and feint, to probe. Ousa saw what the old man was doing, but he could not stop him from doing it.

Slowly he was being backed against the bluff, slowly cornered in the area where a rocky outcropping formed a natural buttress. There was nothing he could do about it. But Ousa preferred the offensive to the defensive, even if it cost him his life. The Wild One stood leering, knife cutting back and forth as he came forward.

The moment Ousa had been waiting for came suddenly. William appeared on the bluff above the two fighting men, and the Wild One's eye flickered that way. As his attention was distracted, Ousa lunged.

He hit the man low, just above the knees, and they went down in a heap. Ousa felt the stab of pain in his back as the Wild One struck out with the knife. The blade of his knife skidded off Ousa's scapula and found the ribs. The pain was excruciating, but the wound was not dangerous. Ousa had no time to think of the seriousness of it. He had no time for thought at all.

It was instinct which drove him now, instinct and the years of training for combat. He drove his forearm up savagely, catching the Wild One under the chin. He heard bone splinter, saw blood gush from the Wild One's mouth, felt the Wild One wriggle madly in his grasp, but he was no match for the younger man. Ousa again slammed his forearm into the Wild One's face, this time across the bridge of his nose, and as the older man cursed and struggled to unpin himself, Ousa managed to grip the Wild One's arm. He locked one hand behind the elbow, and falling back, managed to get a second grip on the wrist. The knife glittered in the sunlight, hovering over Ousa's head, but he had the man now and he had no intention of letting go.

He bent the arm back upon itself, tendons straining, the Wild One's pain-filled, bloody face next to his, his fetid breath in Ousa's nostrils, until with a terrible crack the arm gave at the elbow.

The Wild One howled lika an animal in mortal pain, and the knife dropped free. Ousa yanked the Wild One to his feet and tried to lock his forearm behind his neck, to shove up simultaneously on the point of his chin with the heel of his hand. He wanted to break this demon's neck, to leave the Wild One dead in the snow.

The Wild One went suddenly limp in Ousa's arms, but then he stiffened, throwing a knee at Ousa's groin. Ousa grunted, felt nausea rising in his throat, felt the Wild One, in a last desperate effort, drive his fist against Ousa's right wrist, and the hold broke.

Ousa fell back half a step and lunged again, but it was too late. The Wild One took two running strides, his broken arm flapping at his side, and then he leaped. Ousa clutched at him, felt the buckskin shirt slip through his fingers, and then the Wild One was gone.

Ousa walked to the edge of the precipice and saw the old man hit, bounce, cartwheel crazily through space, a spume of snow following him, and then be lost behind a third ledge.

He turned, bent over at the waist from pain and lack of oxygen, and started to climb the bluff. But Cara was there before he had begun his climb.

She had seen it all, her heart in her mouth, from the top of the bluff. Van der Veghe had reached them finally and had cut Cara free of her ties.

She leaped from the horse and fell. Her legs had gone dead from lack of circulation. She rose again, fell again into the snow. Impatient with her legs, she dragged herself to the rim of the bluff, and her mouth fell open soundlessly.

She could see the two men grappling, hear their grunts of effort. They were distant enough to make the tableau seem unreal, but they were flesh and blood; probably one of them would die. And one of them was Ousa!

There was nothing to be done, nothing at all. She got to her feet and stood, the wind washing over her, watching the grim struggle, and then, in moments which had seemed like hours, it was over. She saw the Wild One fall, saw Ousa turn, his eyes lifting to the bluff, and then Cara was down, sliding across the snow, tumbling, falling, landing roughly on the ledge, and she was to him.

His arms went around her and he held her, his black eyes caring, loving, and when he kissed her again, it was back. The magic, the intentness of that first kiss, with none of the cold calculation of the second. His embrace was tight, his lips gentle; his hands searched her shoulders, neck, and back as if to assure himself she was real, that she was unhurt.

He held her then, there on that empty, wind-washed ledge, and Cara knew that it was right, that this was the end of one dream—and the beginning of another.

❁ 5 ❁

The door to the cabin was open despite the chill, and they could see the moon on the snow, the deep ranks of pines, the high ridge, stark and square against the night sky.

Ousa's manner was nearly diffident. He spoke quietly and politely, as if the struggle with the Wild One had purged him of some virulent, degrading poison. He spoke neither to Crenna nor to Van der Veghe, but kept his eyes between them as they faced each other across the table, Cara standing a pace behind Ousa's chair, Sachim, silent and smiling, hovering in the background near the dully glowing hearth.

"You know what I wish to ask you. I wish to ask you for your daughter, Cara. I wish to marry her and take her with me," Ousa said.

"To be your wife?" Crenna asked incisively. "That must be understood."

"To be my wife," Ousa said with a touch of regret, a shading of shame. "Before, I acted like a fool. I believed my own myth, I came to you pridefully and was the fool."

"You are sure?" Van der Veghe asked. "You must be sure, Ousa. She is our only daughter. We must know she will be happy."

"I am sure." Ousa's reply came on the heels of the question. "I know this is the woman I want, the only woman."

"Cara?" It was Crenna who looked at her daughter's shadowed face. "You must be sure as well. You will be going to a strange land, among people with different customs. You will be alone."

"As you were when you went to my father?" Cara asked with warmth. "Yes, Mother. I am sure. I was sure before I ever saw this man, this Ousa. I was sure when he came to us that day with his father and uncle. I am sure now . . . I shall always be sure."

"Then there can be no objection," Crenna said, "none that you would heed."

"We must speak of the marriage price," Ousa said.

"All right," Van der Veghe replied. It would do no good for him to say that there was nothing they wanted but Cara's happiness, that any price named would be far too low for their only daughter. It was the way of Ousa's people, and it would achieve nothing to ignore what was proper in Ousa's mind. They wanted this to be a strong marriage; it was proper to accept a marriage price.

"I propose to give you six horses, Van der Veghe—"

"Ten," Crenna said quickly, surprising her husband. "No less than ten." Let the young man know how highly Cara was valued, she thought, assure yourself that this is no whim of youthful blood.

"Ten," he said without objection. "Six knives-"

"Twelve," Crenna again said, her face unreadable.

"Twelve knives . . ."

"And a pact of peace," Crenna suggested.

"You need none, Mother. You are my wife's family."

"A pact of peace. A wampum belt with the pact woven into it."

"There is no white blood in you, is there, Mother?" Ousa asked with a thin, respectful smile. "You shall have that. You shall have all of it. If I had a hundred times what you ask, I would give it to you gladly. For happiness." Cara stepped forward then and rested her hand on Ousa's shoulder.

They all noticed simultaneously the lessening of light. A silhouette in the doorway blocked out a portion of the reflected moon.

"William!"

"What is this?" he asked grimly. He stood tall and angular, blond hair loose around his shoulders, bow in his hand.

"Your sister and Ousa—"

"No!" There was no anger in his voice, but it was heavy and metallic. He came into the cabin, tilting his bow and quiver against the wall.

"It is not up to you to speak, William," his mother said sternly.

"Someone must speak. This man is Shawnee." His finger lifted accusingly. "This man is our enemy. This man murders people!"

"William!" Cara shouted.

"He does." William waved a hand at his sister. Now, as they all stared at William Van der Veghe, Cara was amazed at the hollow cheeks, the depths of his eyes, the tension in her brother's body and voice. The muscles of his throat stood out like braided rope, vanishing beneath his fur jacket into the lean shoulders.

"Why is he here?" William asked rhetorically. "Because he was wounded while committing crimes, while trying to kill simple farmers. We take him in, and he seduces my sister!"

"William!" Crenna said, rising. She was truly angry now, her eyes glowing with dark fire.

"It is true. May not a man speak the truth? A seduction of the mind if not the body."

"William—" It was Ousa who tried to speak, but William would not be interrupted, not now.

"You came and mocked my sister as she tried to heal you. When you were well, you mocked my parents by trying to buy her for your harlot. Now, seeing that you must try a different approach to get what you want, you come with this mocking proposal of a marriage!" William strode to the table and banged his fist down against the heavy planks. "No! Father? Mother? This criminal comes and wishes to take your daughter. Where? How will she live? You do not know what is in his heart!"

"But I do," Cara said. Her voice was soft, her eyes confident. "I know what is in this man's heart. It is love, William. I know what is in my own heart as well. Go, you have no business here. We know your thoughts now. Go, then, before you expose more of yourself."

William's jaw worked silently for a minute; then he wheeled and stalked out, knocking over a bowl as he did. They saw him walk out onto the snow, a dark, angry figure in the moonlight. Van der Veghe began to apologize.

"Say nothing," Ousa begged him. "I know the man's feelings. He is right, perhaps. I came and I was arrogant, I was a fool. How is he to know the changes Cara has wrought in me? I hold no rancor. I understand the man." Ousa lifted the corners of his mouth in a bare smile. "I think William and I are very much alike. More than he would ever admit."

There was nothing more to say. The Shawnee would have their daughter and she would have him, and so the marriage was agreed to, sealed as Ousa stretched his hands across the table to grasp theirs, his left resting over that of Crenna, dark and capable, and that of Van der Veghe, pale and hard.

They sat talking for half the night. Ousa told them about his village, about the people who lived there, their frailties and quirks. They drank tea, and when it got colder they prodded the fire into life and closed the door, listening as Ousa, with excitement in his eyes, related the kind of life he and Cara would have—youthful dreams, but at that moment they all believed it.

Later they spoke of the Wild One. Van der Veghe showed him the arrow they had taken from the wolf that winter's night, and Ousa, turning it in his dark, powerful hands, nodded. "It is his. I do not know his real name. It was he we sought the day we first rode through your valley."

"He lived with you?" Cara asked.

"For a time." Ousa winced slightly. "He was found by my cousin, Windstalker, half-dead, along the upper river. A man as white as bleached bones, with no more meat on him than a skeleton. My cousin brought him back to the village, and he recovered. He was silent, eating if we brought him food, going without if we did not. No one spoke to him; it was not permitted. But we watched him. Sullen, sunken, and shriveled. Watched him crouch in the shadows and watch us with his dog eye.

"Then he began to put on his weight again. He was not a heavy man ever, but now there was growing muscle. His hair, which had been dark, now turned gray."

Van der Veghe interrupted. "How did you keep him, Ousa?"

The Shawnee shrugged and inhaled slowly. "He was kept penned. A wild one, a white one, one with a glittering eye. It was the way to keep him. It was the law."

"I see." He and Crenna exchanged a glance. "Hawk."

"Hawk?" Ousa frowned and looked from Crenna to Van der Veghe and back.

"Another man we once knew who was imprisoned. One for whom the law was wrong. One who became a man only by breaking the law in the end."

"Yes," Ousa said thoughtfully. "I can understand that. I can see how it might be. But the Shawnee law was meant to protect us, and its purpose was served by keeping the Wild One isolated."

"What happened?" Cara asked. She was interested in the background of this wild man, he who had saved her mother and then threatened Cara herself. She could envision that dark angry eye, imagine him squatting for day after day in some pen like a caged animal, his gray hair hanging across his face.

"He was wily, he was always a sly one. One night, after we had kept him for almost a year, he broke free. He killed a man who happened upon him. He took this man's weapons and stole a horse. And then he ran. But first," Ousa said, his dark eyes lifting to theirs, "he slipped into a lodge and raped a young girl. It was a savage act, perhaps not so sexual as retributory." He shrugged.

"He was mad."

"Yes," Ousa agreed. "And who knows if he had always been so or if we made him mad ourselves. I suspect he always had been that way. You could see it in his eye. Why was he here? Where had he come from? Who was he? No one knew. I doubt," Ousa said after some hesitation, "that the Wild One himself knew any longer."

"He saved my life," Crenna said quietly.

"I know." The Shawnee looked at her. "But what he had given, he may have taken away. What would he have done to Cara?"

"Well," Van der Veghe said expansively, trying to lighten the ominous mood which had settled over them all, "now he is dead—poor savage man—and we are alive, in health, and have a marriage to celebrate."

"Yes," Ousa agreed readily, although he wondered. He had seen the man fall, but that was all he had seen. The Wild One might be dead, but perhaps he was not. Perhaps they would never know; with any luck, they would not.

Crenna poured them warm elderberry tea, and their thoughts

veered away from the Dark One toward the happy days which were to follow.

And they would be happy—Cara knew that. She vowed to make them happy ones; she vowed to make Ousa happy. He was the man she had always known he would be. His hatred had been shed like a snake's skin, his truculence had fallen away. He spoke softly, yet there was great strength in him. At times his vision was narrow, and yet he was open to new ideas. And he loved her—what else could matter?

Her heart flowered and pulsed with anticipation. Her eyes filled with hot tears at the thought of leaving her parents, but she would come home to visit—Ousa had agreed that it was a good idea through the early years. Then how could there be sadness?

But it was there. A sadness which was mingled with surging joy, which flooded her heart with a thousand nameless emotions, which flooded her eyes with tears. She could not sleep; her joy was too deep. But she could laugh, she could anticipate, she could love. This was no mistake; all of time, all of the spirits, the Great Manitou himself, had planned this long since. And she had read their plans in the night stars, had sensed them, had traded knowledge for dreams, and now the dreams would be bartered back. Now it would be fulfilled.

They left on the third day following. The sun had broken through, and the morning glittered with reflected sunlight. The small patches of snow beneath the trees were brilliant mirrors spotted at intervals across the wilderness. Magpies chirped in raucous chorus from the pines.

They stood together, Crenna, Sachim, and Van der Veghe, and Cara hugged them each in turn, clinging longest to her mother, who looked down into her face, the memories of past years, of nursing babes and tottering children, lighting her eyes with sadness, with the joy of completion, for that was what marriage, what the upbringing of children was all about, was it not? The fulfillment, the maturity. Yet you do not let go easily. Crenna hugged her again, and Cara, looking up, felt a tear flow from her eye.

"I am sorry to be foolish, Mother."

"Only those with souls of ice do not cry. This," she said, touching the tear, lifting it from Cara's cheek with her finger, "proves that you love, that you feel."

And then, suddenly it seemed, they were gone, riding the two borrowed horses eastward, the scent of pines heavy in the crisp morning air, the sun bright and hard in a clear sky, and the man she had chosen, he who had chosen her, was beside her. Ousa reached out and touched her hand, smiling, and she returned the smile, looking at him through the blur of her tears.

They saw William finally. He had not been at the house for the marriage, for the leave-taking. He sat on a rocky outcropping, legs crossed, eyes fixed not on them but on the distance. Cara lifted a hand, but William did not respond. He looked anywhere but at them, even when they passed under his nose.

William wore the solemnness of a child; in fact, Cara realized, he was a child then. A child who is angry but still wishes to be loved.

She waved a hand again, again received no response, and she smiled. They were out of sight, fortunately, before the laughing fit overtook her.

"He does say good-bye in odd ways," Ousa said. Then he too was laughing. Cara laughed until her sides ached. Not so much at William as at the foibles of all people. At the solemn man-child who would perch on a rock, not wanting to miss saying good-bye, determined not to say any such thing, as if it were an accident he had come to be there. Cara thought: Don't we all do such things? And still she laughed, laughed until her shoulders shook.

Ousa, grinning widely, had drawn up his horse. They were into the pines now, on the far side of the ridge, where a grassy valley, warmed by the sun, was sheltered from the wind by the surrounding forest.

"What is it?" Cara asked. Her laughter came intermittently, breaking up her attempts to speak. "What is it . . . Ousa?" Now she had begun to hiccup. His hand rested on her thigh, and his eyes met hers. "Oh . . ."

She laughed, hiccuped, began to cry, and then he helped her from the horse and they stood, arms around each other. Ousa kissed her gently on the lips, and she hiccuped. He walked with her away from the horses and they lay down in the sun-warmed grass, its scent rich and pervasive. Above them the wind whispered through the pines. Beyond this sheltered valley was the wilderness, extending for thousands of miles, primitive, empty, vastly beautiful.

Cara was no longer hiccuping, no longer laughing. He laid her back gently and sat above her, propped up on one arm. His look was intent, affectionate. He tilted his head to one side and then the other. Then he bent low and kissed her again, and Cara's arms went around his neck, holding on to him, her heart racing.

His hair was sun-warmed, his body taut and close. His hand ran across her thigh, and she felt her own body grow slack, heavy. Sitting up, she slipped out of her dress, turning her head, unable to look into his eyes just now.

The sun beamed down, caressing her body as Ousa's hands ran lightly across her abdomen, breasts, and shoulders in amazement. When he leaned down again to kiss her, to hold her in those strong, protective arms, she realized with shock and then with growing delight that he was naked. Naked and warm and close in the tall spring grass, and she laughed. She laughed again, a joyous, exultant expression as she ran her hands across his broad back, through his long glossy hair, as he rested his cheek against her breast, and then Ousa too laughed.

"There is so much pleasure in you, Cara," he said.

"It is pleasure you have sown," she said. Her lips touched his ear.

"Then I mean to sow more, much more."

They did not move for a long, long while. Cara grew used to having his body, hard, muscular, so masculine, next to hers. Her hands explored him, gingerly at first and then with growing confidence. Finally she looked up at him, seeing his face dark against the bright backglow of the sun, seeing the strange, hungry slackness of his face, the tenderness there.

"My husband," she said half-questioningly, and then she hugged him tightly, drawing him down against her, feeling his chest flatten her swelling breasts, feeling his long, hard thighs against hers. Her head lolled, heavy, sleepy on her neck. Her hand caressed the strong column of muscle which was her husband. Her body seemed to become sweeter, riper. She was aware of his deep, warm exhalations as they intertwined. She saw concentration on Ousa's face, felt the quivering of his hands, and she was pleased, pleased as he came to her and became her husband, pleased as the dream took on a substance, a reality beyond any anticipation.

They lay in a tangle of contentment, their conversation drowsy and fragmented as the sun drifted past. They touched each other in wonder, in pleasurable amazement, learning. She no longer laughed, but she felt like she should; she felt she should shout, leap up, dance around in crazy, exultant joy.

He was her man and she had awakened from a long dream to find life.

They rode southward for three days, stopping frequently to eat, to water the horses, to love, to lie quietly in forest or shaded glen, to talk, to learn about each other, and Cara disliked none of what she learned. All of the stiffness, the latent savagery, was gone, and she felt some pride in that, as if she had removed those darker aspects of the man, like a healer who had removed a poisonous growth and healed him.

He was bright, eager, laughing, tender. But they did not mention war.

On the fourth day they saw the Shawnee village. It was larger than Cara had expected. Nearly a hundred lodges of bark over pole frames rested in the forest clearing. Smoke rose lazily into the skies, and there was the sound of dogs barking, the shout of an excited boy.

"Now, my husband, now I am worried," Cara said as they sat their horses atop the low wooded rise, looking toward the river where the village stood.

"Now?" He laughed. Leaning over, he drew her to him. "Now you are home. Nothing can harm you ever again. Now you are my wife."

"One more day?" She looked at him, wanting him to understand. "Can we have one more day, Ousa?"

He looked into her eyes for a long while before slowly nodding, and she hugged him tightly, nearly falling from the back of the patient bay.

For one more day, then, there would be lazy, slow loving; for one more day she would be Oneida. Tomorrow a new world would begin; with the coming of dawn, Cara would be Shawnee. For one last day she was to be only woman, Ousa only man. They were tribeless wanderers, as rootless as First Man and First Woman, whom the Great Manitou had nurtured in his nest.

The day passed quickly, and evening came, cool and pleasant. She slept beside Ousa, beneath their new blankets, gifts from Crenna. The stars passed in slow parade, timeless, silent, and aloof. Cara felt her husband shift, felt the weight of his thigh across hers. She smiled and stroked his hair.

Then, with the stars still beaming down, she fell asleep. She awoke sometime after midnight, shaken and trembling. There had been a dream.

Long, bony fingers stretching through the holes in the vast, dark sky. Flames advancing in curtains, writhing and altering until they became fiery snakes, each striking with a startling, snapping sound like the crackle of lightning.

There were people spread across a vast plain, and Cara knew they were dead. Knew the snakes or the flames had struck them down. One of them, she knew, although she could not see his face, was Ousa, and she had awakened with a sob, a silent scream in her throat.

Her heart was hammering against her ribs. Her eyes opened wide, searching the skies, but there was nothing but the same placid stars, eternal, mocking, and she shivered, holding Ousa more tightly.

She did not sleep again that night, but only lay close to her man, holding him tightly, awaiting the Shawnee dawn.

When it came, it was a brilliant dawning. Red arrows pierced the low clouds to the east. The clouds themselves were violet, edged with gold. Doves winged low overhead, heading for their feeding grounds, cutting sharp, darting silhouettes against the flame of dawning.

When Ousa rose, it was with a smile. His contentment was rich and complete, and when he turned to her in the morning light, he wrapped himself around her and enveloped her briefly in his own joy.

The apprehension returned sharply when they tied their bundles onto the horses' backs and began walking toward the Shawnee village. There was still dew on the grass; smoke from the morning fires lifted in wind-wrought curlicues into the pale sky.

They stopped on the forest verge, and Ousa turned to her, his hand on her shoulder, his eyes on hers. "This is our home, I am your husband. There is nothing to be afraid of."

"Of course not," Cara said with a laugh which rang false even to her own ears. He smiled, winked, and squeezed her shoulder. Then he turned and led the way forward. Suddenly they were into the village and there was a wild chorus of welcome. Children ran shrieking toward them, a pack of dogs yapping at their heels. Women cried out, and the men came from their lodges, some carrying their breakfast in their hands.

"Ousa! It is Ousa!"

Dark faces broke into sudden grins. There were impromptu dances, shouts of welcome, people crowding around. Dark eyes examined Cara and then returned, brightening, to Ousa.

It was a revelation. She had known he was a chieftain, a man of importance, but the entire village seemed to turn out, the village seemed to embrace him, to hug him, to fit itself to him, to wrap around Ousa and welcome him.

Cara felt awkward and displaced. She knew no one. Milling dark faces lit with excitement as they looked at Ousa, darkened again as they examined Cara. She felt small and useless. Ousa was too distracted with greetings and the cacophony of voices to give Cara any attention.

There was a press of bodies, a jabber of voices, and Ousa was physically cut off from her, carried away in a mass of bodies as Cara stood beside her horse watching.

Two especially excited young men came racing from the river; they laughed as they ran, and reaching the mob of welcomers, they simply hurled themselves forward. They reached Ousa, who hugged them and lifted them from the ground, one in each arm, his head thrown back joyously.

It was then that Cara saw the other one.

The dark one, the man with the crooked face. It was Shelokta, and he stood alone near the entrance to one of the lodges, a blanket over one shoulder, his chest draped with shell necklaces, his arm hung with bracelets.

He stood watching the scene for a long minute. When a man came walking past, Shelokta grabbed his arm, and nodding toward the crowd, he asked a question. The warrior shook his head and walked on. Shelokta's hand remained open, raised as if he still held the other man's arm.

Cara, fascinated, watched Shelokta. His eyes were dark and poisonous. His crooked mouth was twisted into an expression of dark hatred. His entire body went rigid and then began to tremble. He spit on the ground, threw back his head, and then seemed to regain control. His body slackened and he shook his head as if trying to work a kink out of his neck. He stood expressionlessly then, but he had not managed to convey amiability to his eyes. They still brooded, dark and cutting. Abruptly his gaze shifted to Cara.

Their eyes met, and Shelokta frowned, not quite remembering her. Then he did, and his lower lip was pushed out in a sort of dirty, knowing smile. He spit again, quite deliberately, and then just as deliberately turned his eyes away.

Ousa had broken free of the mob of welcomers, although many of them trailed after him, cheering, and he walked to where Cara stood, her thoughts still on the cold, crooked Shelokta.

"Here!" she heard Ousa shouting. "Here is the war prize I have brought with me." He laughed and came to Cara, his arms going around her waist. He was beaming, basking in the warm welcome of his tribesmen, excited and jubilant, man-proud of his new wife.

He lifted her and spun her around, laughing all the while, unaware that the smiling faces of his welcomers had turned dark. He set her down on her feet, dizzy and flushed.

"Cara!" he shouted. "And these," Ousa went on, grabbing by the necks the two young men Cara had seen earlier, dragging them to him, "are my brothers Tak and Kalthipsa. The fat one is Tak." He laughed and pinched the extra skin around the waist of Tak playfully. Tak frowned and opened his mouth in complaint, yet it was obvious that it was all brotherly foolishness, that he was bothered not in the least by Ousa's description of him. Kalthipsa seemed slightly more serious, but merriment danced in his eyes too; boyish likability smiled up at Cara from a face which would one day be as handsome as Ousa's.

"Welcome, brother," the intruding voice said.

Ousa turned. He still held Tak in a playful neck lock. Now, however, he let him go, gripping his younger brother's shoulder as he faced Shelokta.

"Shelokta."

The crowd of Shawnee shifted like the tides. Some drifted away, others surged closer, expectantly.

"I thought you had been killed."

"You did not come looking for me, Shelokta. Perhaps you were overanxious." Ousa smiled, but there was no humor in it. Cara looked at the two brothers, sensing the tension between them.

"I do not understand you, brother. You were war leader. Of course we looked for you." Shelokta's pretense of innocence was sheer, his tone was a theatrical one, its sarcasm thinly veiled by a slightly mournful expression. Ousa read him plainly enough, as did Tak and Kalthipsa.

Shelokta rested a hand on Ousa's shoulder and gave him a squeeze which might have been interpreted from a distance as affection, but which transparently was not. It was an unveiled threat.

"And what bitch is this, Ousa?" Shelokta asked, his eyes flickering to Cara.

Ousa tensed, his fist balling up, and Cara touched his arm, trying to restrain him. She saw him nod, saw his fist unclench. "This is my wife, Cara," he said, his breathy words coming fiercely from between clenched teeth.

"Wife?" Shelokta stared for a minute at Cara, sucking in his lower lip; then he threw back his head and roared with laughter. "Fine, Ousa. Brother. I am happy. You have brought me a gift, then! I am happy for you, you fool of a man."

Then Shelokta, still smiling, turned away. Ousa's eyes were raking his back, but Cara held him still, keeping him back. "What did he mean?" she asked. Ousa seemed not to hear her. The crowd had thinned now, and Ousa shooed most of the rest of them away. A face on the perimeter of the mob had caught his eye, and he turned to Cara.

"I must see her."

"Her?" Then Cara too saw the woman, slim in the hips, full-breasted, with mocking eyes. *Tadona.* No one had to tell her who the Shawnee woman was. Her scathing eyes were fixed on Cara.

Ousa, her Ousa, had gone to war one night and had not returned. Ousa, her Ousa, had been killed, or so they had told her. But he had not died, he had returned with a woman. Tadona and Ousa had been engaged; now he had brought back a Mingoe woman. His wife! All of this could be read in Tadona's eyes.

"I'll be back . . . I must," Ousa said, holding Cara's fingers.

"Yes." She nodded. She could see how it was. The woman must be spoken to.

Ousa walked away, and suddenly Cara was alone in an alien camp. Only Ousa's two younger brothers remained. Tak sucked at the knuckle of his thumb and smiled shyly, his round face amiable. Kalthipsa seemed worried.

"What did he mean?" Cara asked. "What did Shelokta mean when he said, 'You have brought me a gift'?"

Tak, who had been staring with open interest at Cara, now shifted his eyes away. It was the lean, slightly buck-toothed Kalthipsa who answered.

"Why, it is simple. How can Ousa lead his people? He has

come back with *you*. A humiliation. You have no rank, you are not even Shawnee. He has given up a good marriage for you . . ." Kalthipsa fell silent suddenly. He did not appear embarrassed, only compromised.

"Yes," Tak said. "He had degraded himself. Who will vote for Ousa in the council lodge? Who can respect a man so foolish as to marry . . ." Tak *did* look embarrassed.

"It is a great advantage for Shelokta," Kalthipsa said, rescuing his brother. "Ousa's judgment will be questioned because of you."

"I see." Cara nodded slowly, listening to Ousa's younger brothers with only half a mind. Her eyes, her thoughts, were with Ousa and Tadona.

She had seen him go up to her, seen her brittle smile and wooden shrug, seen him stretch out a hand which never quite reached her shoulder. His back and neck were quite expressive as he spoke to her, just out of Cara's hearing. She could see Tadona's eyes, hard, angry, search her and then fall away, see the tight lines around the beautiful Shawnee woman's mouth.

Then they turned away, and Cara saw them walking toward the river, Ousa still explaining something, and Cara felt her first painful twinge of jealousy.

Tak and Kalthipsa were jabbering about something, too rapidly for Cara to follow. The Algonquin tongue, which she had from her mother, was very similar to that spoken by the Shawnee. Communication with Ousa and his tribesmen had been easy, but if they spoke too quickly or fell into cant, to local dialect, Cara could not follow them.

She stood there in the middle of the empty clearing, the bright morning sun falling on her shoulders, feeling quite alone and empty. Her husband was gone with his Shawnee woman; the crowd had withdrawn. These two young men spoke in light tones she could not quite understand, in a manner which caused her to believe they were speaking about her. She began to understand how her father must have felt among the Oneida; she began to understand why her family had been uneasy about her coming to the Shawnee nation.

A stranger, an unwelcome woman in a land where anyone, anything not of the nation, was an enemy. She heard the bay horse blow, heard it shift its feet. And then the wizened man in the striped blanket came to where she stood with Tak and Kalthipsa.

goe woman." He said it not without warmth, but with a sort of questioning tone. Then he halted, looked her up and down, and smiled. "I am Turtle Back."

"I remember you well, Father," Cara said to Ousa's father.

"Father!" He laughed in the cracked voice of the very old. He looked her up and down once more, smiled gleefully and asked, "Are you with child?"

Cara flushed. "I do not know, Father. But if I am, his name shall also be Turtle Back."

Turtle Back chuckled happily. He put his withered arms around Cara and hugged her. "Where is my son, that foolish boy to leave such a woman? Never mind, come with me, Mingoe woman, come with me and drink tea, smoke the pipe with a foolish old man." His eyes, sparkling with devilment, shuttled to his sons' faces. "Lazy boys, go catch some fish for our larder. Hunt, grow strong, bring back strong, broad-hipped women like this one, fit to bear many children for an old man's pleasure!"

The boys ran off then, Tak taking a flying leap as if afraid of his father's hand, and Turtle Back laughed out loud, saying, "He is the joker in the family. A fine son. A fine, lazy, fat boy!

"You," he said, lifting his white eyebrows, "now I know you! The woman from the white man's farm. The daughter of the Oneida woman."

"Yes, Father Turtle Back."

"You see!" he said with apparent delight. "My son Ousa has an eye. I saw you that once, and I thought: There is a fine woman with broad hips and good breasts, good for childbearing, one with a good temper—I saw it in your eyes—good for raising boy children, good for laughing in bed with, not like this other one with the pinched face. . . . I speak wrongly. If my brother Stone Wolf heard me, he would laugh and say Turtle Back is an old fool. Ousa is to be war leader, clan leader, perhaps supreme chief. To marry such as you is dangerous to him. It crushes his chances; but I am an old fool. I would rather see happy smiles on my son's face in the mornings, see fat happy babies nursing at good, ripe breasts. And so I am a fool. . . ."

Turtle Back put his bony hand around Cara's shoulder and smiled again. "Come, daughter, let us have tea and bannock. Let us talk and discuss how we can get us a baby son."

She went along with her father-in-law, finding his welcome

odd but warm. Food was served by an older woman, not Turtle Back's wife, obviously, perhaps a sister, Cara thought. She was not introduced.

The tea was sycamore, pale, pink, mild. It lifted her spirits a little; still Cara was beginning to be upset with Ousa. He was gone for a long time, and the memory of the handsome Tadona remained in her mind, taunting her.

Cara and Turtle Back spoke for fifteen minutes, mostly about the necessity of having male children—Cara was unable to divert him from that single subject. When the door opened a crack and then suddenly burst wide, a patch of light spilling across the blanket-covered earthen floor of Turtle Back's lodge, Cara turned eagerly, expecting to see Ousa.

It was Shelokta. He stood in the doorway, his hips canted, his arms folded, eyes amused, and then, at Turtle Back's beckon, he came into the lodge. He did not seat himself, however.

"What do you think of my daughter?" Turtle Back asked, his mouth splitting into a grin which revealed a missing tooth. At the same time, a gnarled, leathery hand rested on Cara's wrist.

"I think winter madness took my brother," Shelokta said. He crouched down and stared at Cara in a way which was almost insulting.

"Why?" Turtle Back was still smiling. "I like her. I think she is a fine Mingoe woman."

"She is a woman—that is enough for you. She will breed."

"You do not give me respect, Shelokta," Turtle Back said, wagging his head heavily. With a shaky hand he poured more tea for himself from the basket pot.

Shelokta simply stared at his father. He was still crouching, the backs of his hands resting on the rug. "I do not mind the woman," he said. "Where is Ousa?"

The question was directed at Cara. She could only shake her head. "Speaking with one of his friends, I think."

"Tadona!" Shelokta laughed. He seemed to have already known just where Ousa was. Then he said to Turtle Back, "There must be a council meeting."

"Why?"

"Because Ousa is back. He was war leader; now I am. There must be no confusion among the Kata Shawnee as to who is their leader."

"We need no leader now. There is no war. The council

meeting can wait," Turtle Back said. He turned his face back to Cara and smiled with private pleasure.

"You are growing old, Turtle Back," Shelokta said harshly to his father. Turtle Back hardly seemed to mind.

"Yes, yes. It takes no eyes to see that. So, I am old?" One bare shoulder lifted in a weak shrug. "So let me think on what concerns me."

"I will have a council meeting," Shelokta said, rising. Then, with a last contemptuous glance at Cara, he stalked from the lodge, a briefly silhouetted figure against the brilliant glare of sunlight off the river.

"This council," Cara said, "will they try to take Ousa's power from him?"

"Why do you worry about things like that?" Again he patted her hand. "Just worry about having a son."

"I am worried about Ousa. He is my husband. It is his right to be chief of the Kispkotha, war leader of the Kata Shawnee, is it not?"

"It is what he was born to." Turtle Back frowned. He let go of Cara's wrist and told her, "My son is no fool. He has made his choice; I decided not to mention it, but to speak of the good that would come of this marriage."

"You mean he cannot be war leader."

"He has degraded himself in the eyes of the men who matter, the council."

"By marrying me?"

"Yes, of course," Turtle Back said, lifting a white eyebrow. "I thought you knew that."

"I did . . . I think I did. Ousa said something."

"But he chose you," Turtle Back said, leaning back, his hands on his bony knees. "And so let us think about the good things that may come of his choice. I do not dwell on the dark things—I learned that long ago. To dwell on the dark things is to summon them to you, to give them strength, and in time they will pull a man down."

Cara listened with only half her attention. A *dark thing*. She was a dark thing. Good only for childbearing. A young, promising leader had foolishly married a dark thing, and so he would lose status. They would live forever on the fringes of Shawnee society. And how long would it be before Ousa blamed her for this marriage, despised her for it? She would not allow that to happen! But what was there to do?

The worst of it, perhaps, was that now, with the arrival of

English settlers, now when the Shawnee needed an intelligent, stable leader, they would lose Ousa and have the savage Shelokta in the position of power.

The light again fell across the floor of the lodge, and looking up again, Cara saw her man standing there. He smiled, but there were reservations in his eyes, or seemed to be—would she always feel that there were reservations to his love now? She shook off that dark thought and smiled up at him. Ousa crossed the lodge to sit beside Cara.

He gave his hands to his father, and Turtle Back took them in his own hands—hands gnarled and twisted, hands with prominent knuckles and even more prominent dark purple veins standing in relief. Hands which had hunted, fought, held his own babies.

"Father. How do you like my fine woman, my wife?"

"I like her very much, Ousa, very much indeed," he said, but again Cara had the impression that there were things unspoken between them. Thoughts of Cara, of the son who had, out of winter madness, married a Mingoe, an outsider, a classless woman and brought her home, effectively ruining his promising career.

Neither man would speak of it, even when Cara slanted the conversation in that direction. She felt oddly frustrated and a little angry; at home matters of importance had been discussed in front of the children. Van der Veghe felt they had the right to know.

Here the two Shawnee men spoke only of trivial matters, although much of it was interesting, some amusing. Tak had encountered a bear near the river. A woman, Thekastoka, had produced triplets after being blessed by the shaman, whose name was Sa-Miwok. Ousa's aunt, Meniimo—it was she who had served Turtle Back and Cara tea—had been visited by a night spirit who advised her to take the crow as her totem, and Meniimo, who had always been in the Turtle clan, was having a religious dilemma.

Cara heard it all with half a mind. She sensed, or thought she sensed, unease in Ousa. That was the trouble—she only *thought* he was unhappy, vaguely uneasy. She would continue to have these suspicions, to feel guilty. She even thought, wildly, once of returning home, leaving him to the life he had been born to.

Yet all of these thoughts, these fears, faded away with the sunlight, and after nightfall when the two retired to Meniimo's house and they lay down together, the warmth of the night stimulating the warmth of their bodies, their flesh meeting in soft reassurance, when she slept in his arms, feeling his naked strength, his mind and body at ease, the worries seemed to have drained away from her, to have been taken from her in some mysterious way by his ministrations.

He slept, his face untroubled. The lines of his face were blurred and smoothed by sleep, by physical satisfaction, and he was a child in her arms. She studied the contours of his face, the line of his jaw, the hollows of his cheeks, the long-lashed, peacefully closed eyes, the raven-black hair, a strand of which bisected one cheek, the hard, rounded muscle of his shoulder, the flat, slabbed muscle of his bare chest, and she felt no concern, no worry. This was how it was meant to be.

Tribal allegiance, the quest for power, the prideful strivings, were distant from his dreams. She wished suddenly, eagerly, that she was with child, that it would be a son, and the image of Ousa. Let the world go by. Let them have their vicious political struggles, let them scheme and fight. They would be apart from it, First Man and First Woman.

Then, moments before she fell asleep, the worries returned. Would a life like that be enough for Ousa? Would the sunlight sustain their peace as the whispering night did?

She yawned, surprised to find that she had exhausted herself with worrying, exhausted herself to the point where she was no longer able to sustain a complicated thought, and she let her mind fall back into familiar soft recesses where it consoled itself with images of green grass and flowered fields as it had since childhood.

She was there suddenly, face up to the sun, spread-eagled against the grass, and she noticed with amusement and with the satisfaction of dreams that white, soft-petaled flowers were growing from her flesh. She lay still, not wanting to disturb their growth. She lay still and let them take nourishment from her flesh as she took hers from the warmly beaming sun.

Beyond the field was the river, silver and clear. Trees swayed gently in the wind, their wind-ruffled leaves making a pleasant rustling sound.

Cara saw her then. She came from the trees, from out of the river. She was naked; water-heavy hair hung from her scalp. Her legs were long, slightly bowed. Her eyes were dark jewels glittering with fire. In her hand was the knife. It was curved oddly, the blade slightly twisted. The metal was silver, inlaid with some yellow metal. If Cara strained hard enough, she could read the inscription the yellow metal formed.

No, that was not true—she could make out some meaning, some sense of the inscriptions, but the final solution eluded her. She would read half of the pictographs, and while groping for the meaning of the second half, the first, elusive and misty, would flit out of her mind.

There was no meaning to it, she decided. The meaning was in the blade itself, and she felt her heart begin to protest within the bony cage of her breast. She felt it flutter and lift to a racing, surging pace.

She lay still, the flowers turning smiling faces to her, black eyes framed in soft white petals, their little song filling the summer meadow. And over her hovered the woman with the knife, and then she could read the meaning of the inscriptions quite clearly. The message was simple. *Death to dark things.*

Cara's eyes flickered open in the night. She saw the familiar bark roof of the lodge, the pole framework, the dark, sleeping bulk of Ousa . . . and the woman hovering over them.

Cara rolled from her bed, her mouth opening in a soundless shriek, and the knife flashed past her face. Again her dreams had summoned reality, and this reality was deadly and cold, insane.

Cara staggered backward, felt her foot tangle in the bedding, and she fell away just as the knife slashed out again. She landed roughly on her back. She saw the woman in silhouette, blurred and menacing, seeming large and powerful, saw the knife lift again.

Then Ousa was from his bed. He was a panther attacking, and he shouted, "Cara!" again and again, his voice rising. The attacking woman turned to strike out at him, but she was too slow.

Ousa had her arm, and he crimped it behind her back, the knife long, menacing between her shoulder blades. He forced the wrist higher, and then, with ease, he folded the hand in on itself and the knife dropped free.

Angrily then he spun Tadona around and slapped her face with the flat of his hand, sending her sprawling. Cara could only watch. Her mouth opened in protest, but she was unsure if she managed to call out or not. The only audible sound was the screaming, the crazed ranting of Tadona.

Cara heard the sounds of rushing feet, saw the curtained doorway admit four people, Turtle Back among them, saw Tadona rise and fall again, stumbling over her own feet in her mad anxiety.

Ousa lifted her by her dress front, and Cara saw his hand lift, saw by the light of a torch carried by one of the men in the doorway, his face drawn taut, his teeth exposed in an involuntary grimace, saw Tadona's eyes at once turbulent and pleading.

Then slowly Ousa's hand lowered and he threw her back. Tadona hit the wall so hard that the sound of her breath rushing out was audible across the lodge.

Then Ousa went to Cara, helping her to her feet, hugging her tightly. It was a long moment before Ousa realized they were naked and that the lodge was filled with half a dozen Shawnee, male and female.

He flipped a blanket around his loins and held a second blanket out for Cara to wrap herself in. Then he turned, his eyes smoldering. "Take this woman from me," he said, his voice trembling, his finger leveled at Tadona. "Take her before she is no more, before she is a dead woman."

It was Shelokta who came forward, Shelokta who crouched, and smiling filthily, assisted Tadona to her feet. Tadona looked at Ousa one last time, her eyes slashing, her mouth bitter and harsh, her head held proudly, her hair in a wild tangle.

"Keep her, then!" she spat. "You are not a man. No longer, Ousa. You are nothing!"

And then she was gone, Shelokta dragging her from the room as she hurled invective at Ousa and Cara, as she wriggled and kicked out wildly.

"Fool! You fool, you have thrown it away . . . for *this*. Fool, Ousa! To waste your life, to waste your love, to waste it all . . . for what?"

"Get her out of here!" Ousa said. His voice was calm, hollow. His chest rose and fell heavily. When they were gone, he remained where he had been standing, looking at the door; then, with a massive shrug which seemed to slide the weight from his shoulders, he turned to Cara and took her in his arms.

She could feel the tension in him, the weakness in her own

knees. The darkness no longer seemed comforting, sheltering. It was a deadly enemy. Strange leather-winged creatures hid in the corners of the room; women with knives prowled outside.

"She will go," Ousa said. "I will not have the woman in this camp."

"You don't have to do that—I am not a child," Cara said, feeling very much like a child at that moment.

"I won't have you hurt. I won't have you threatened. I won't have you treated badly." Ousa held her at arm's length as if studying her, although it was so dark in the lodge that Cara could not see his face. Then his arms closed around her again and her cheek was against his chest. She could hear the slowing beat of his heart.

He led her to bed then and they lay quietly side by side, Ousa's arms behind his neck as he stared at the roof of the lodge. She did not know how long he lay awake or what his thoughts were, but she knew his mind was troubled, troubled by more than the mad attack of the jealous Tadona.

Daylight summoned Cara out of the lodge and into a world of unreality. She recognized none of the faces in the village. She knew no one. No one spoke; curious—hostile?—glances were cast her way by the women on their way to work, tanning hides, weaving, basketmaking, planting.

Ousa had been gone when she awakened, and now she stood in a strange land, uneasy among a strange people. She wanted to shout: I am Shawnee too!

But she was not. She was Mingoe. Classless. The destruction of a good man. *I'm making too much of this,* she decided, throwing back her head to take a deep breath of the crisp morning air.

Tak was walking past, in his hand strips of rawhide of the length needed for making snares.

"Hello, Tak."

The youngest brother of Ousa turned his face to her. Smiling, the heavyset youth came to her. "Have you seen Ousa?" she asked.

Tak shook his head, his eyes wondering. Hadn't this new wife seen her husband this morning? Cara looked around the camp, which covered almost a hundred acres along the river. There were a few scattered oaks, but the land was mostly flat, mostly clear. She should have seen Ousa if he were here.

Perhaps he was in his father's lodge—but that was where Tak had come from.

"Are you setting snares?" she asked Tak.

"Yes," he answered with pleasure and with some surprise. Hesitantly he asked. "Would you like to come along?"

"I would," Cara said. After all, Ousa was not here. What else was there to do? Why not get acquainted with Ousa's brothers? "If you'll let me get something to eat first."

"You don't have to worry about that, sister," Tak said. He showed her a bag slung over his shoulder. "I have plenty. Pemmican, bannock cakes, smoked fish." He flushed slightly. "I do not go without food. It's foolish, don't you agree?"

Cara laughed. "I do agree. I would be happy to share your food, if I may."

"Of course, sister," he answered, his engaging smile splitting his dark elliptical face.

They walked slowly through the village, Cara's eyes darting here and there, watching the women at their work, the children at play, the small knot of men gathered around a roan horse. But there was no sign of Ousa.

Down the river, among the shelter of the great oaks, stood a large building. Smoke rose from the hole in its roof. Tak said, "That is the council lodge."

"Is that where Ousa is?"

Tak only shrugged. He might have known, but he gave no indication of it. Instead he told Cara, "We have to cross upstream a little ways. That is deep water."

"All right." She nodded, allowing her thoughts to drift. There was a small ford upriver where a sandbar curled near the far shore. Tak led her across, struggling against the swift current. The water eventually reached their waists, its cold weight persistent and briefly treacherous.

On the far side, wild fern grew down to the river's edge. Tak wound his way through the heavy tangle of vine and blackthorn beyond that, and soon they were in pine and cedar forest. The sunlight beamed through the canopy of the trees, striking the ground at intervals, leaving pools of molten gold.

Tak indicated a rabbit run, a trail worn by the feet of rabbits that habitually used the same path time after time, generation after generation, to reach the river's edge.

Tak found a likely spot and knelt down to set his snare, bending a pine sapling, weighting it, forming a loop with his rawhide thong. Cara watched him work, smiling to herself at his intense concentration, at the tongue which thrust itself from Tak's wide mouth as he worked. Tak was a man, but for most of his life he had been a boy, and the boyishness was there, appealing and innocent.

His muscles were blurred by the layer of fat beneath his copper skin. His hair hung limp and dark across his cheek.

Satisfied, he rose and moved on toward another rabbit run. On the way, he showed Cara a bee tree, and a deadfall trap he had set for porcupines. This was only a log propped up on another, which was fixed into a notch. There was a bit of parched corn for bait, tied into a pouch, which allowed the porcupine to smell the corn but not get at it. If the porcupine tugged at the bag, the log would fall, killing or holding it. Tak explained the flavor and desirability of porcupine liver with great relish.

"Sweet and healthful. It must be taken raw," he said. "There is no better meat. And Aunt Meniimo is always happy to get porcupine quills."

The quills would be used for needles; also they could be flattened and used to decorate moccasins and capes. But it was obvious that Tak's primary objective was the liver.

The sun rose higher, but the day grew no warmer deep in the forest. Cara, leaving Tak briefly to his tasks, walked among the towering columns of the trees, listening to the birdsong in the pines, watching the lazy streams of dust floating on the sunbeams.

She found a tangle of wild roses, deep purple, just coming to bud, discovered a thin, crystalline waterfall beyond them. She stood for a moment watching as the water misted into the air, casting rainbows.

The feeling came over her gradually, creeping up her spine. Cara turned around suddenly. There had been someone there. She knew it, was certain, although her eyes could detect nothing but the tangle of vines and roses, the silence of the virgin forest.

She knew. That subtle sense which had been a part of her since childhood, which was as reliable as her hearing, as her vision, had been alerted, and she knew someone had been watching her.

Only Tak, she told herself. But why would Tak choose to watch her from the underbrush? He had only to walk up to her. He was not a guileful youth, one given to odd conduct—or so she thought.

If not Tak, then who? The answer seemed to be Tadona, and that sent a second shudder through her. Cara crouched down and picked up a fist-sized rock. If it was Tadona, she would not find her murderous task simple. Cara did not fear the woman; she only wondered at the jealousy which seemed extreme. Perhaps she did not understand all that had gone before. Now, boldly, Cara took a step forward.

"Tadona," she called out as she went on. "Tadona, I want to talk to you." The forest answered with vast silence. "Tadona! Let us speak. I am Ousa's wife—I am sorry if you wished to marry him, but I am his wife now. Come out here, vent your hatred. Let us speak."

Silence. Nothing but the silence, unbroken by any sound but the soughing of the wind in the pine boughs, the musical sound of the waterfall at her back. She felt foolish standing there, stone in hand, but someone had been there. There was no mistaking the prodding insistence of her subtler senses.

"Tadona?"

She was at the verge of the undergrowth, her feet moving silently across the pine-needle-strewn earth. Still nothing. Had she been mistaken?

Then he was there. A dark, crooked figure with one eye. *The Wild one*. He watched her from the undergrowth, the looping shadows cast by the roses crosshatching his face with basket-weave gray bands.

Cara took one quick backward step and lifted the stone, and in that instant the man was gone. Simultaneously she realized that it was not the Wild One at all. Her mind had searched for a plausible solution to the appearance of this apparition and had provided her with that answer. Yet it was not he.

This man was an Indian of middle years; the right half of his face had been smeared and grayed with ash. His left eye had been circled with ash, giving him that suggestion of having only one eye.

But it had not been the Wild One. Who, then?

Cara, who had backed away automatically, now took a slow, deep breath and went forward, toward the tangle of brush. But he was gone. She could see where he had been standing; the pine needles and fallen leaves were crushed down there. But he had made no footprints when he left.

She sagged against the earth, squatting as she looked into the forest. What was her life to be? Why was she haunted by these apparitions? They were real men, and not a form of madness, but they were apparitions all the same. They seemed to watch, to know, these silent, dark men. They *knew* . . . what?

Sighing, Cara got to her feet and walked back toward where she had last seen Tak. He met her with a smile, holding up a large porcupine by a rawhide string tied to its tail.

"A large one," Cara said.

"Yes, and . . ." He sensed her uninterest, her unease. "What has happened?"

"There was someone in the forest, spying on me."

"Tadona?" he asked with concern.

"No, not Tadona." Cara described the man.

"Oh, that's only Sa-Miwok," Tak said, a grin of relief spreading across his stolid features.

"Si-Miwok?"

"The shaman. He was probably gathering herbs."

"He was watching me," Cara insisted.

"Yes?" Tak scratched his head. The porcupine, quills extended, still hung from his hand. "Perhaps he was only curious."

"Perhaps."

"If Tadona has not paid him to place a spell on you." Tak frowned again at that idea. He brightened immediately. "But Sa-Miwok does not like Tadona. I know this, although the shaman has never said a word against her. When she comes near, his eyes go gray, like storm clouds."

They started back toward the river and the village beyond. "Why would he be watching me?" Cara wondered out loud.

"He simply saw a strange woman and wondered who she was," Tak suggested.

It was logical. Probably Tak was right, but somehow Cara didn't think so. The man had been there for some time, watching her. He had run away instead of coming forward to question her. Run away—it was more like a smoky wraith vanishing in the wind!

The river was quicksilver in the afternoon sunlight. Smoke still rose from the council lodge. Reaching Meniimo's house, where they would stay until Ousa could build their wedding lodge, she found her husband still absent.

She seated herself on a blanket and stared at the open doorway, giving in briefly to her darker emotions. She recalled her own house, mother and father, Aunt Sachim. She looked around her at the empty, unfamiliar lodge, recalling the wooden expressions on the faces of people she had met here in the Shawnee village. The terrible image of a wild-eyed Tadona flared up in memory. She saw the man with the ash-covered face, Sa-Miwok, lurking in the tangle of vines. Where was Ousa!

She sagged and gave in to the emotions for a moment. Self-pity began to lift its head. Her hands rested inertly on her lap. Her head hung.

Then, abruptly, Cara got hold of herself. *This is not me,* she scolded. I am Cara, the daughter of the Oneida headwoman, Crenna. I am Manitou's daughter. A few shadows have passed over me, that is all.

She lifted her head and took a deep breath, ashamed of her passing mood. She was young, strong, just married to a man she loved deeply. She was in a new place, that was all; it took time to adapt.

Would she let a jealous, frantic woman and a lurking little man ruin her happiness? She wiped her hair back and stood. When Ousa came, he would be hungry. She would visit Turtle Back and ask for food to prepare for her husband. She smiled with fond anticipation: Ousa's father, at least, would be happy to see her.

And Ousa—he would return. The day might have been shadowed, but the night would be brilliant with the lights of love, with the beaming smile of this Shawnee warrior, warm with his embrace, and what did the rest of it matter?

6

"No." Shelokta's face was veiled by the thin screen of smoke which rose from the calumet as he took three ceremonial puffs and handed the pipe to his left, to Stone Wolf, his uncle.

Ousa sat staring at his brother with barely concealed rage. "Say what you want, it is not a council matter, but a family matter."

"It is a council matter. It is a family matter. I am the head of both," Shelokta said firmly. He smiled crookedly at his brother.

"You have assumed the position, Shelokta," Ousa reminded him, "but you are not lawfully the head of either the family or the Kispkotha clam. I am elder brother. I am Kispkotha head. I am family leader."

"Such was your position, Ousa. But you were away the long winter." Kispkotha shook his head with mock regret, and Ousa wondered if any of them were fooled by the fatuous gesture.

"Father?" Ousa looked to Turtle Back, who despite the heated exchange, seemed to be sleepy and distracted.

"It is a family matter," Turtle Back said slowly. "I do not know why you bring it up in council, Shelokta."

"It bears on tribal affairs." Shelokta pointed a finger at

Ousa and said, "Ousa has shown himself to be without judgment."

"That can be debated later," Ousa said impatiently. "For now I have asked for ten horses to give to my father-in-law. That is the bargain I struck—"

"When you didn't have ten horses!" Shelokta said.

"Shelokta"—the speaker was a tall, broad-shouldered warrior named River Bird—"do not waste the council's time with personal affairs, please." He looked wearily at Turtle Back and at Ousa, a small shake of his head revealing his displeasure.

"I have said this bears on tribal affairs, River Bird," Shelokta said emphatically.

"I do not see how. Your brother needs more horses for his marriage gift. Honor demands that you help him, that the debt be paid."

"Who has ever given ten horses for a marriage price!" Shelokta demanded. There were fewer than thirty horses in the Kata Shawnee camp. They were still rare and very valuable. "Who has ever paid one knife for a Mingoe? You see, River Bird," Shelokta went on, leaning closer, the dull light of the council fire glossing his features, painting him with flickering shadows, "this reveals a man without judgment, and *that* is where it bears on tribal affairs.

"My brother marries a Mingoe, discrediting himself. You know a man married to such should, by rights, have no status at all. It is only through kindness that Ousa sits among us now. A man marries a Mingoe," Shelokta went on, his eyes intent as he looked at the gathered council, "and promises twice the wedding price anyone has ever given! That reveals his judgment in treaty making. A man promises a Mingoe woman and her white-dog husband a peace belt. This reveals the man! They are our enemies—he is white! Yet Ousa has promised them a wampum treaty."

"Give him the horses," the thick-chested brave, Owl Eyes, said wearily, "and let us get on with business. It is late."

"I fail to see your point, Shelokta," River Bird said.

"I see it!" This was the old sachem, Ta-sho-haka. "Who can trust Ousa's judgment? He does not conduct himself thoughtfully."

Someone else muttered agreement, and Shelokta smiled thinly.

"One-third of our horses gone for a marriage price," Ta-sho-haka said. He looked at Ousa with shadowed eyes. He had a prominent brow which overhung his eyes. The firelight completed the illusion that Ta-sho-haka had no eyes at all. "It is crippling to our war efforts."

"This can be debated at another time," River Bird said. "Let us hear no more about the Mingoe woman and the marriage price for now. It is a family matter. When Ousa made his promises, he thought he was war leader of the Kata Shawnee." He looked again at Shelokta. "He could not know that his brother had returned to say Ousa was dead and that Shelokta himself had been made war leader.

"I say Ousa is still war leader."

Ta-sho-haka shook his head and muttered something unintelligible. He was not the only one who disagreed.

"I say so too," Owl Eyes put in. "What has Ousa done to be removed from his position? We thought he was dead. He obviously is not." He nodded at Ousa, who had been sitting silently, listening, determining who was with him. Outside of Owl Eyes and River Bird, no man had spoken up for him. If it came to a vote, there would be only two white stones placed into the basket. The rest would be black, as black as Shelokta's eyes. Ousa glanced again at his brother, seeing the smug satisfaction there.

Finally, the hour being late, the council adjourned itself. The final vote for war leader of the Kata Shawnee would be held at another time, when everyone had had time to think upon it.

"Remember," Shelokta said in parting, "I have been leading us well. We have lost no warriors."

There was a secretive look about Shelokta, as if he were bursting to let everyone in on a great secret and could not. He confirmed this when he added mysteriously, "Soon I shall reveal how all of the English can be driven from our land. Soon I shall reveal how the Kata Shawnee can become a wealthy people. Under my leadership," he added, as if that were an obvious condition of this future wealth and power.

"What is he talking about?" Ousa asked River Bird as they stood together with Owl Eyes outside the council hut, watching darkness settle, the shadows envelop the village, the late sun cast an orange glow across the high clouds.

"Who knows?" Owl Eyes shrugged.

"He is up to something," River Bird said thoughtfully. "Remember, Owl Eyes, the month he was absent. It was no hunting trip."

"An alliance with the greater Shawnee nation?" Ousa asked.

"Perhaps with the Miami," River Bird said. The big man was frowning, his expression gloomy in the gathering darkness. "We shall have to wait and see."

"He has the old warriors in his war bag," Owl Eyes said. "I can see that. Some of the younger as well. Ta-sho-haka behaves as if he were supreme chief himself."

"But what is behind this!" Ousa asked. "I know Shelokta wants power. I know he wants to discredit my judgment to achieve that. Why? What is this wealth he speaks of?"

"The plunder to be gained by defeating the English?" Owl Eyes suggested dubiously.

"It seems he means more than that. He has a grand scheme—or so it appears."

"I think," River Bird said, his voice tight and grim, "that perhaps it would be better for all of us if during the next raid it was Shelokta who did not return."

The suggestion was shocking, even to Ousa. "Do I understand you, River Bird?"

"I think you do. Where is Shelokta leading us? We need a man with stability as war leader. You, Ousa, and not your brother."

"This is not over, River Bird." Ousa put a hand on the big man's shoulder. "Speak to the other members of the council. I'm sure that is what Shelokta is doing even now. Convince them that my brother is unstable."

"They do not care about that; they care about victory and wealth. That is what Shelokta is promising them," Owl Eyes said.

"Victory!" Ousa managed to laugh. "Do they think we can fail to achieve victory over these Englishmen! There are but a handful."

"There were. Since you have been away, Ousa, a hundred more have moved into the upper valley. Their leaders have encouraged it. They have built a town with a stockade around it."

"A fortified town? Here?"

"Yes. They come. They will continue to come."

Ousa felt anger flare up. What right had these people to build villages on their hunting grounds? "It cannot be allowed," he said.

"No. But the war must be handled intelligently. Shelokta's

promises are all very well, but we need you, Ousa." River Bird's voice was sincere, and it encouraged Ousa. "If only," he added with a sigh, "you had not brought home this Mingoe woman."

They parted with that, and Ousa walked homeward, feeling anger against his friend. That River Bird, loyal as he was, could be influenced by Ousa's choice of a bride indicated how strongly the point weighed in the minds of those who were already opposed to him.

His anger with River Bird faded as Ousa remembered with shame his own initial prejudice toward Cara and her family. If they could know her as he did, truly know her . . . They would, but perhaps by then it would be too late.

What did he care! The emotion surged up and broke over Ousa like a gigantic wave. He felt momentarily unburdened. What did he care about Shelokta and his manipulations, about the power structure of the tribe?

He had a new bride. He was welcome in the arms of the tribe. His father was a good man, warm and generous.

He did care.

First, he supposed, pride caused him to oppose Shelokta. It was habitual. He had been trained to be war leader. He had been brought up to believe that the responsibility was his. He had been told that he was chosen by the Manitou.

Second, more important, Ousa knew that the times which were approaching meant trouble. The white man did not fight wars as they did. A spring foray, a winter retreat to their comfortable lodges, where all was forgotten. He fought only to win, and to win meant the annihilation of the enemy. The fate of a people was to be in the hands of an ambitious, greedy, unstable leader. Shelokta.

Unless he could be unseated. The weight of responsibility returned and rested heavily on Ousa's shoulders as he approached the lodge of Meniimo. Ousa could smile as he saw the bundle of crow feathers knotted to the lintel of the doorway. Meniimo had converted to that totem, apparently, surviving her religious ordeal.

He swung wide the blanket draped across the entranceway, and all thoughts of the outside world immediately took wing and flew away: she was there, beautiful, patient, loving.

Cara looked up and then rose. She did not hold her arms out to Ousa. She simply watched him as he came to her, his movements graceful and fluid.

Then his arms were around her and his lips met hers. There was no more thought of the one-eyed shaman, of the loneliness of the Shawnee camp. There was only his reality, warm, strong, tender. She felt his need as well, the need to shut the world out of their lives, to be alone, content with each other.

Then Ousa's mood seemed to change. He smiled down at her, tenderly brushing her hair with the palm of his hand. His smile was wistful. His body was still warm with the need for her, but the world had returned. She could sense it, and so she offered him reality.

"Are you hungry?"

"I am," he said with forced joviality. "Can you cook too, woman?"

"You shall have to be the judge of that, my husband," she said, her words lightly challenging.

Ousa tasted the corn soup, puckered his lips, and made an astonished sound. "It's true—the Mingoe woman can cook." He smiled, but there was a weariness in the smile.

Cara got to her knees beside him. "What is it, Ousa?"

"What? I don't understand you." He hugged her playfully, but there was a rigidity, a note of pretense in the gesture.

"There is trouble."

"Trouble!" Ousa laughed. "You, beautiful maiden," he said, turning Cara, drawing her to him so that she lay across his lap, her face up toward his, "you are my only trouble."

He kissed her and let his hand rest on her thigh. His eyes were bright, his smile nearly sincere.

"That is what I mean, Ousa. I am your only trouble."

"My only joy," he said, bending to kiss her forehead.

"How long will you continue to treat me as a child? I can see that something is wrong, that all is not well."

"What can be wrong?" His eyes drifted away from hers.

"See!" She jabbed a finger into his ribs and he smiled. "I must know, Ousa. If we are to be as one . . . if this is to be a marriage."

"It is only Shelokta," he said, simplifying things greatly. He went on to explain what had been discussed in the council lodge—and what had not been discussed. "He is up to something else. He is using you as an excuse to discredit me. But I do not know why. Something is written in the winds, but I cannot read the signs."

"Ask yourself what he wants," Cara suggested.

"I have done that. He wants absolute power, wealth."

"And the way to those goals is through war." Cara lifted a hand and touched Ousa's cheek. He seemed not to notice.

"Yes. But if I were war leader, it would be no different. I too would drive the white man from our land."

"Then you would be a powerful man, wealthy. Does Shelokta's jealousy prod him?" Cara asked.

"Possibly." Ousa considered this. Shelokta had been a jealous youth. Ousa, without false pride, knew that he had been the stronger child, the more handsome, the swifter, the better with arms. And he had been firstborn, favored by his father and mother.

Shelokta had been a bitter child. Perhaps because Ousa was favored. But the deeper his bitterness, the more Ousa was loved. You could not blame Turtle Back or their mother for that. You could not, perhaps, blame Shelokta. It was the way it had been, and the bitterness had never dissolved; it had taken root and grown over the years into an angry, tangled vine.

"There seems to be more to it. The man has a plan of some sort. No one seems to know what it is. I can't puzzle it out. I only know that it is for Shelokta's benefit and not for the good of the tribe. That is what worries me."

"And it is my fault." Cara stared into the firelight, watching the twisting fibers of red and gold.

"How can it be your fault!" Ousa laughed, hugging her, turning her chin so that her eyes met his once again.

"Is it?"

Ousa hesitated a moment too long. "No, of course not, Cara. You imagine too much."

"But they are using me to discredit you."

"No." Ousa was not a good liar, Cara noticed with both unease and distant, objective pleasure. He did not like to lie; yet now he was doing just that.

"Eat your meal," she said, managing a smile. She sat up and watched as Ousa with false enthusiasm hunched over his bowl.

The council met again the next day, and Ousa knew before he entered the lodge what would happen. River Bird was standing outside, waiting for him, and when he saw Ousa he shook his head slightly, just enough to convey the information.

Oddly, at that moment, Ousa felt nothing. He had been prepared to feel anger, to berate and curse his brother. Now he felt only a cold emptiness. They did not want him; fine—let them have Shelokta. What did he care?

The council took many hours to make it official. They spoke first of the war, for there would be war. The English continued to come. There were a hundred families along the Ohio River, a smaller colony near the Kanawha. Those people must be driven out, or a hundred more families would come, a thousand—who knew?

There was no disagreement among the council members, no voice to speak for peace. Peace meant giving their land to the English. There could be no thought of it.

Abruptly Shelokta suggested they vote on war leader, since it was a time of war. Ousa, looking around the circle of men who sat on the floor of the council hut, knew beforehand what the result would be.

Owl Eyes spoke for Ousa nevertheless. "He is the eldest son of Turtle Back and should be Kispkotha chief. Such was Ousa's position. Then he went to fight a battle." Owl Eyes moved his arm, his flat palm describing the going away. His two hands met. "There was a confrontation with the English, and Ousa was wounded." Owl Eyes's hands continued to sign the story. "Now, then, his brother comes back and says he is dead. What can be done? The next son of Turtle Back must become Kispkotha chief. So it is done.

"But Ousa has come home! He was not dead. How can we treat him as if he is dead? We make of him a ghost who never returned from battle. A wandering spirit. It is a wrong thing."

The speech was to no avail. The vote was taken quickly. Some of those present did not glance at Ousa, let alone meet his eyes. *Why?* Ousa knew Shelokta's motives. What were the motives of the men who stubbornly supported Shelokta?

Ousa knew then—he had given them something. Given or promised something to the warrior leaders. *What*? He watched them with growing discouragement. These men had fought beside him; he had grown up with them. They knew Shelokta well enough to know his erratic mind. Yet they voted for Ousa's brother.

When it was done, there were only four votes for Ousa. Turtle Back, Stone Wolf, River Bird, and Owl Eyes had spoken for Ousa. Four men out of thirty. That was the number of Ousa's friends in the council.

"You shall of course be a subchief, Ousa," Shelokta said in a way which was openly insulting, inviting Ousa to pridefully reject the offer and sever himself from the core of leaders.

"I accept, naturally," Ousa said.

"I have spoken to Turtle Back," Shelokta went on. His crooked smile spread across his dark face. "I have decided the wedding price should be paid. It is a matter of family honor, of tribal honor."

And with those few words Shelokta indicated that he now was head of the family as well as head of the Kispkotha war clan. *He* had decided. Ousa looked at Turtle Back and then rose, walking from the council lodge into the open air, the scent of tobacco and cedar-bark smoke following him.

A ghost. Shelokta had killed him with his lie, had assumed power while he was absent. No matter what he now did, he would remain a ghost. The older brother who was killed in battle last autumn. Sly was Shelokta. Sly and devious. A ghost among us. Ousa walked to the river, stripped off his leggings and breechclout, and dived in, swimming hard, his arms knifing through the blue water, his legs kicking strongly. He swam to the far side and drew himself up onto the bank, where he sat naked in the sun, his arms looped around his knees, feeling the warm sun on his back. He watched the river flow, fighting back the emotions which rose in him. Not anger, nor red hatred, but subtler emotions which verged on despair. He was anathema, he had been ostracized like a mad one. How had it happened? He had gone away whole and returned to become . . . a ghost among them.

He should have hated Shelokta for it, but you cannot hate a wolf for being what it is. He felt only puzzled and somehow less confident, even less a man. He had thought his footing to be solid rock, and yet it had crumbled away, shifted like sand beneath his feet.

Ousa stood and sucked in deep breaths, feeling the caress of warm sunlight on his body. He tried to shake off the mood. He plunged into the river again, swimming until his legs ached, until his lungs burned, and then he dragged himself up onto the bank near the village, where the great oaks grew. He was exhausted, but it had done nothing, nothing at all to silence the mocking small voices inside.

"Father Turtle Back?"

Turtle Back looked up from his bowl and broke into a shapeless grin. "Come in, Daughter Cara. Come in."

''Finish your meal,'' she begged him.

''It is tasteless. Weevils seem to have found the corn, and Meniimo does not even notice. My sister spends all of her time communing with Crow.'' He chuckled dryly. ''But you, Cara, what brings you to my lodge? You cannot have come just to honor an old man, when you have a strong young husband to make you laugh in bed.''

''I have come to ask you something.''

''Oh? There is something you need, Cara? Something I can help you with. What is it, daughter? What is it you wish?''

''Status.''

Turtle Back placed his bowl aside, wiping his fingers on his breechclout. He looked at Cara with bright eyes. The scores of crosshatched lines on his face, lines carved by the many winters, by squinting into many summer suns, seemed to deepen. He nodded slowly. ''I see.''

''There must be a way,'' she said, getting to her knees, taking Turtle Back's hand. ''I do not know the Shawnee. I do not know what to do. I only know that my husband has been scorned because of me, that he and I will never be anything if I have no status. Please, Father Turtle Back, what can be done?''

''Have you spoken to Ousa?'' the old man wanted to know.

''He laughs at me. He says it does not matter; we have each other.''

''He is right.''

''No. He is changing, Father Turtle Back, already changing because of what has happened. Where is his spirit? They have stripped him of his pride. Now he suffers it, but in time he will grow bitter. Will he blame me?''

''No.'' Turtle Back patted her hand. ''Not Ousa.''

''And what of his son?''

''His son?'' Turtle Back's face brightened, and then his eyes narrowed.

''Yes, you understand me. Ousa's son, your grandson, who should by all that is right become Kispkotha clan chief, will be nothing. Perhaps he too shall become bitter. Perhaps he will blame his mother—this Mingoe woman who could not leave the Shawnee warrior alone to lead his own life.''

''You have thought much upon this.'' Turtle Back shifted and picked up his pipe, holding it before him for a moment before he began filling it. ''I seldom smoke except for the ceremony," he said, as if speaking to himself. Now he did smoke, however, using a brand from his small fire to light the pipe. The mixture in the bowl was willow and tobacco. Cara sat back on her heels, allowing the man a few satisfying puffs.

"It is only pride, Cara," Turtle Back said finally. "Pride which makes you wish to alter what cannot be altered."

"Yes, Father," Cara agreed. "It is pride, but what is wrong with pride? Not false pride, boastfulness, sham pride, but a knowing pride, a confident pride. A warrior needs that, does he not? A woman too requires pride."

"Yes, yes," Turtle Back said, suddenly appearing harried, "but when there is nothing to be done . . ."

"There is generally something," Cara prodded.

Sighing, Turtle Back put his pipe aside. Still smoke rose, forming itself into tangled blue strands above Turtle Back's head. "There might be one way. Only one for a woman like you to attain status. But I could not advise it."

"Why?"

"It is difficult, and expensive."

"How difficult, how expensive?" Cara demanded.

"Wait, child, wait," Turtle Back said, reading the eagerness in her eyes. He held up a hand. "It is only a chance. It is not up to me at all, nor up to you."

"Turtle Back, Father!" Cara said pleadingly. "What is it you are speaking of?"

"I speak of shamanism." Turtle Back spoke in a whisper, as if it were a dire secret. "I speak of becoming a shaman woman. But . . ." He shrugged. "I cannot say it is worth it. I only know that it takes many years, that the price of the instruction is very high, that there have been no women to attain that position in my lifetime among the Kata Shawnee, that it is not up to us at all whether it could even be begun."

"It is up to Sa-Miwok." Cara sat back again, her hands on her knees, her legs folded under her.

"Yes," Turtle Back replied, mildly surprised that Cara knew about Sa-Miwok. "You have not spoken to him?"

"No." Not spoken to him, but she had observed the shaman. He was the watcher, the ashen-faced ghost, the mysterious eye. And what did Sa-Miwok want that day? Why was he watching?

"I think a person must have the gift of the spirits to follow that trail, Cara."

"Perhaps I have," she replied.

"So?" Turtle Back's lower lip thrust out in surprise. "You . . . have seen visions?"

"Not visions. But there are times . . . when I have *known*."

"Ah!" Turtle Back waved a negligent hand. "There are times when all of us have such knowledge. In battle sometimes a warrior knows that the arrow is in flight, knows that the Yuchi with the war club is behind him."

"Then perhaps it is nothing to recommend me," Cara answered.

"Perhaps not." Turtle Back grinned. "But you mean to find out."

"Yes, Father, I mean to find out. I mean to speak with Sa-Miwok and find out." She rose then, taking Turtle Back's gnarled hand again in farewell. "Thank you for speaking with me."

Cara had turned and started toward the open door of the lodge before Turtle Back, half-rising, called out: "But, daughter, what of this son? You spoke of a son. Is there to be one?"

She stopped in the doorway and turned back toward him. Her smile was faint, her eyes deep. "We shall see, Father Turtle Back. Soon we shall see."

Then Cara was gone. Turtle Back, his expression of barely subdued joy pursing his lips, lighting his eyes, whispered, "Ah!" and then, chuckling, he relighted his pipe and sat on his rug, his old eyes distant and bright. "Ah!"

Kalthipsa was outside his father's lodge. The young buck-toothed man was finishing the needlework which had occupied him all morning. Now as Cara stood silently by, Kalthipsa, using a porcupine-quill needle and deer-gut thread, finished sewing the decorative wolf-hair fringe on his new quiver.

"Hello." Ousa's brother looked up at Cara, squinting into the sunlight. "I have not seen Ousa."

"That is not what I wanted to ask you, Kalthipsa," Cara said, squatting down to examine the quiver, making small noises of admiration over the article, which was in fact made beautifully. Beadwork representing the Thunderbird and a fallen wolf decorated the quiver. Cara blew on the wolf fur, smiled, and handed it back to Kalthipsa.

She looked into his eyes. "Where is Sa-Miwok?"

"Sa-Miwok?" Kalthipsa seemed on the verge of laughter.

"One never knows where to find our shaman." His eyes brightened with sudden enthusiasm. "Are you going to pay him to curse Shelokta!"

"No!" Cara had to laugh. "Though perhaps that is not a bad idea."

"He is evil, my brother."

"And Ousa?"

Kalthipsa looked as if he had been stung. "Ousa is a great warrior, a friend."

"Yes. I think so too." Cara smiled again, and Kalthipsa nodded, seeming to accept her smile, to accept her as Tak did. "Why do you want to see Sa-Miwok?"

"I cannot tell you now," Cara said. "You do know where to find him, don't you?"

"No. I can only tell you where his lodge is. I cannot tell you if Sa-Miwok is there. Sometimes he is gone for days. The Great Manitou takes him away. As an eagle he comes, and then Sa-Miwok flies across the world, sees all, and returns exhausted. Other times he speaks to the river spirits or the forest manitous. There is much to occupy a shaman."

"Yes. But will you show me his lodge? Perhaps he is there."

"He may be there, but he may not see you. He may not wish to speak to you."

"I will ask him," Cara said.

Kalthipsa shrugged as if, trying to explain something to a child, he had failed. "If you walk along the river and see a great gray stone streaked with white and shaped like Dzhe Manitou's thumb, you will see a trail leading through the oaks and up toward the wooded bluffs. If you follow that trail, you will find the lodge of the shaman, Sa-Miwok."

Cara thanked the boy and left, walking from the tumult of the village, leaving behind the yapping dogs, the dust clouds which rose from the heels of the playing children, the shouts exchanged by neighboring women.

The river, glimpsed through the great dark oaks, seemed silver and placid. Far downstream three small boys were diving from a snag into the water. Their yellow pup sat on the snag, head cocked to one side, watching curiously.

The oaks were dark, communal, ancient. Cara walked southward along the riverbank, passing no one. She had no idea what Dzhe Manitou's thumb looked like, but she found a gray granite boulder which was streaked with white in a starburst pattern. Behind the boulder was the beginning of a trail which led up through the willow brush and rhododendrons now just coming into flower, spattering the hillside with white and purple.

The hillside path was in the shade. Tangled roots grew out of the bank, which had been washed out by the previous winter's rain. There a gray squirrel no larger than the palm of Cara's hand had taken shelter, and it looked at her with bright eyes for a moment before with a nervous twitch of its tail it rushed for the base of the great white oak tree upslope.

The trail wound higher into the hills, surprising Cara, who had expected to find the shaman's lodge nearer the camp. She was breathing hard after fifteen minutes of climbing, half of this up a trail which went as close to straight up as any path she had ever seen. Sa-Miwok must be in amazing condition for a man of his years if he traveled this way every day.

But then, maybe the Eagle Manitou clutched him in its talons and flew him up.

Cara was smiling at that idea still when she topped the rise, where blackberries grew, and found the gray lodge. The bark used for the walls was old. The roof swayed. A sun emblem in scarlet had been painted above the entranceway, but now the emblem was chipped and peeling.

Smoke rose from a hole in the roof. It was oddly scented, smelling of herbs Cara could not immediately identify. She heard a drum beat three times and then stop.

Then she was before the lodge, hesitating. The whole idea seemed suddenly foolish. What was to be gained by coming here? In all likelihood the man was a charlatan; perhaps he would not even see her.

She stood there a moment, the wind shifting her hair. She started to go, but something kept her there. There was a hope. A thin hope, a feeble hope, an outlandish one, perhaps. But there, in the lodge, behind the red-and-yellow-striped blanket which hung across the entranceway, was a hope, a way to assure a better, happier life for herself, for Ousa, for their unborn children.

"Will you stand out there until you wither, until the wind blows your dust away, woman?"

Cara's head snapped up. The reedy, high-pitched voice came from within the lodge, but there was no way anyone inside could have seen her—unless there was a chink in the bark walls. That, she decided, looking them over again, was entirely possible.

She could hardly turn around now, and so, tossing her hair back, straightening herself with resolve. she walked to the lodge entrance and rapped on the entranceway frame.

"May I come in?" There was no answer. She stood smelling the sweet, overpowering incenselike smoke which was heavy in the lodge. "May. . . ?" She took a last breath of the clear outside air and drew the blanket aside, entering the lodge.

She could see nothing at all upon entering. The room was deep in shadow. A vague whitish mass was to her left, veiled by smoke. All else was dark and invisible.

"Here, here!" the reedy voice piped again, and Cara hesitantly started that way. She tripped over some unseen obstacle, and the voice broke into a cackle.

Cara squinted angrily into the darkness. The smoke was nearly overpowering. "Sa-Miwok?" she asked. "Are you Sa-Miwok?"

"Yes, yes. Come closer, blind one. Can't you see old Sa-Miwok?"

And then she could. Vaguely. He was a darker shadow against the background of shadow. She stood blinking, the smoke stinging her eyes. Gradually her vision improved and she could make out the narrow birdlike figure of a man, naked but for his breechclout, sitting cross-legged on a mat of reeds. Before him were two bowls. From one of these, smoke still rose. There were six sticks of different colors at his right hand.

"Well, you took a long while to come. Did you lose your way, Mingoe woman?" he asked with another dry cackle.

"No. How did you know I was coming?" Cara asked. Looking back toward the wall, she could see no crack, no way for the shaman to have known there was anyone outside, let alone identify the person.

"I summoned you," he said. "Those I summon always come. They must." He picked up the smaller of the bowls and dipped his fingers into it. Then he sprinkled a liquid—plain water, Cara thought—on his back and bare chest.

Cara went nearer still. Now she could see that Sa-Miwok had tattoos covering most of his upper body and thighs. These were totem signs and prayers. Other tattoos—which, she did not know—were to commemorate sacred events, like the passing of a comet. The tattoos were made by cutting the flesh and rubbing ash or mud into the wounds.

"I received no summons," Cara said, inching still closer.

Sa-Miwok continued to sprinkle his chest, shoulders, and back with water. As he did this, he chanted under his breath, making what were scarcely more than grunts as he rhythmically worked.

He stopped abruptly. "I summoned you in the forest, Mingoe woman. You saw me, and I gave you the thought. It was a time before the worm of the thought came from the seed. You thought it was your idea, but it was mine, mine planted in your brain."

Cara started to smile, thought better of it, and asked, "Then you know why I am here."

"Why are you here?"

That's what I thought, you old faker. Cara crouched down, her clasped hands resting on the floor between her feet. She was five feet away from the old man now. Finished with his obscure ablutions, he pushed the bowl to one side and looked up with bright, curious eyes, as bright and shining as the eyes of the small squirrel she had encountered on her way to the shaman's hut. No sooner had her mind made that odd connection than the shaman burst into laughter again.

He held his knees and rocked back and forth gleefully.

"Why are you here, Mingoe woman?" Sa-Miwok repeated. Cara found herself fascinated by the tattoos now, and it was a moment, as she studied the mystic representations, before she realized he had spoken again.

There was something in the air. That smoke—it fogged the mind, overpowering one's thoughts. Cara blinked and finally replied, "I wish to become a shaman."

"You?"

"Yes."

"A woman?"

"Yes."

"A Mingoe?"

"Yes," Cara said with irritability.

Sa-Miwok was smiling. They looked at each other closely, Cara with some perplexity, the old shaman with a distant, unreadable, almost smug expression.

"Look, will you answer me, Sa-Miwok? I have come to see you out of desperation. My request is sincere. I came expecting almost any response but your amusement. I do not mean to offend you, but my heart is heavy; I am in no mood to appreciate your jokes."

"Jokes!" Sa-Miwok seemed genuinely offended. "I do not joke, Mingoe woman. I am not the one who approaches the subject with insincerity. It is you who come to me, you who make me aware of your insincerity. I think perhaps it is you who make jokes."

"Me!" Cara laughed. She shook her head heavily. Was there no communicating with this little man?

"You." Sa-Miwok was no longer smiling. "I am shaman. I am a man who walks with the spirits, who learns the omens, who travels a holy way, who instructs the tribe in rightness, who attempts to pacify the gods, who wishes to lie in the Great Manitou's arms, who burns offerings and recites the prayers of our people . . . Wait! It is I who fast, who suffer, who mortify the flesh. I, Mingoe woman! I am sincere in my occupation, in my dedication.

"It is you," he said ominously, "who come to me seeking to use my office for political purposes, to lift yourself above the ordinary, to do for your husband—don't deny it, I know these things!—you who come with insincerity in your heart. How could you hope to be shaman! To come mocking, with only your own benefit in mind?"

It was a long moment before Cara could bring herself to answer. He was right; he saw through her. "I have made a mistake," she said.

"Yes."

"You are right in everything you say. I did not come to learn your path, but to make my own path easier." She started to rise. "I beg your pardon, Sa-Miwok."

"Stop. Where are you going now, foolish Mingoe woman?"

She looked at him with curiosity. "Back to my husband's lodge, where I belong."

"Perhaps you belong here."

"What?" She took a slow breath. Was this man insane?

"I said, perhaps you belong here. Why have you come? Perhaps you do not know why. You only think you know. I told you that I planted the seed of thought in your mind. Why? Because *I know you*. You have come to the right door, but with the wrong motive."

"What are you saying, Sa-Miwok? Please, I am too weary for riddles."

"I am saying that you may be the one I am looking for.

You may be a shaman. I sense it in you. You walk close to the spirits. But not close enough." His hands described this. "You walk a parallel path. It is as if you are on one side of the river and the knowledge you seek on the other bank. You must swim the river—I am the one who can teach you how to do that."

"You would be willing. . . ?" Cara was incredulous.

"I would be willing to begin; you must be willing to finish."

"All that you said before . . ." She shook her head. The smoke seemed to have settled there; she could understand none of this.

"I said it because it was the truth, because it needed to be said."

"I won't be able to forget why I came here, Sa-Miwok. I won't be able to put concern for my husband, for status, aside."

"No." Sa-Miwok shook his head. "But in time it will become secondary, or will if you are the right one. Once I had another motive for becoming shaman. I cannot now recall what it was," he said, breaking again into his cackling laugh.

Sa-Miwok rose and crossed the room. He swung open the blanket across the doorway, and thick, liquid sunlight painted a bright rectangle on the earthen floor of his lodge.

He looked even thinner surrounded by light. He was a bony silhouette, his head wagging from side to side as he chanted something under his breath.

"So . . . nine horses, nine years."

"Pardon me?" Cara had risen. This caught her unawares.

"You must pay for instruction. A horse a year, Mingoe woman. Nine horses."

"Nine years!" Would it take so long?

"Nine years' testing time. After that I will not be your teacher and you will not be my student. Then we will continue together. Your studies will not be ended any more than mine are. There is no end to the learning. I do not know the gods any more than a dog understands its master, any more than the flea knows the dog. I know only what is revealed. We are forever infants to the great spirits. A man says, 'I do not understand how the spirits could let this happen. I do not know why Manitou would do this.' Of course he does not!" Sa-Miwok laughed outrageously. "A man who presumes to know them so well is a fool. The dog does not know its master."

"I do not have nine horses, Sa-Miwok," Cara said.

"You need only one for now," he reminded her. One horse and one desire. "You are the one, Cara," he said. Astonishingly he came to her and put a scrawny arm around her shoulders. "I approached you in this way so that you would understand what I expect. I do not want a woman who uses me, but one whom the gods can use. It must be so. If it is not"—he shrugged—"it will cost you a horse. For you will come seeking me, and I will not be here. There will be a skull on the floor, and it will have the coyote sign on it. The sign of insincerity. Then you will know that you must go home and trouble Sa-Miwok no more."

Cara was out the door and to the head of the path, Sa-Miwok watching her from the doorway, before realization hit her, breaking through her melancholy with its bright message: He has accepted you!

On his own terms, to be sure, but she had been accepted! Cara had not really expected it. Deep inside, she had thought the idea folly. There was no reason for her to expect a man she did not know to take her under his wing. Oddly, she supposed she had half-expected Sa-Miwok to see through her, to know it was not a spiritual need which called her.

Nine horses! She looked back toward the lodge, saw Sa-Miwok grinning as if he was listening to her thoughts. She waved a hand, lifted her skirts, and started toward the path. She was nearly away before his last words, distant, shrill, reached her ears: "Tell Turtle Back that it is to be a man-child!"

Then he began laughing again, and Cara could only stand and stare. He knew that she was with child, too. It was time to tell Ousa before the entire tribe knew. A man-child. He could not know. She told herself Sa-Miwok could not know, but she believed he did. She believed he actually did know!

Then, skirts held high, Cara rushed down the path, her feet flying, her heart light. She stopped abruptly, forcing herself to slow. There was a child growing within her. If Sa-Miwok had planted his seed, there was another man who had also done so.

The day seemed bright, the river danced before her eyes like a thousand mirrors. The village—it seemed suddenly like home, a welcome place where the people she knew lived.

Turtle Back, Meniimo, fussy old thing, Tak and Kalthipsa. Ousa. She hurried on, glancing once more at the glittering river.

She found him in the darkened hut, gathering articles together. Ousa's face was glum; the fire was gone out of his eyes. He had painted himself with an odd symbol. A death's-head and a half-moon.

"Ousa. Husband!"

She went to him, and he turned slowly. His eyes were lifeless, and Cara winced. But she had news which would put the fire back into those black, black eyes.

"I have been visiting with Sa-Miwok."

"Oh?" He selected ten arrows from the dozens which rested in an oversized wooden quiver in the corner of the hut. These he placed into his deerskin quiver.

"He has accepted me. I am going to become shaman!"

"Fine," he said.

"Ousa?" Cara put her hand on his shoulder. She smiled up at him, and he kissed her distractedly. "Ousa, I am going to be shaman. We will have status again. Your wife will no longer be an outcast."

"Good. It is good," Ousa replied.

"Ousa . . ." It somehow hadn't penetrated before. Her happy thoughts had blocked it out. Now she saw what Ousa was doing. "There is a battle?"

"There is. I am subchief. There will be an attack on the British settlement."

"Subchief! But, Ousa, tell them I am not casteless now! They must let you become sachem."

"It is decided." He shrugged.

"Because of me?"

"Because of Shelokta," he said with bitter rancor. He smiled at her then, a smile meant to be reassuring, but one which left his eyes clouded.

"You shall have your rightful position again, Ousa," she said.

"Yes. Of course."

"There is other news," Cara went on. "I am going to have a baby. Sa-Miwok says it will be a son."

Ousa's expression was tender. He dropped his quiver and held her, simply held her. He did not speak, he did not move. Finally when he did draw back his eyes were softened. "I am happy. I feel proud. Proud of us for having been able to do such a thing." Then he laughed, and for a minute he was the old Ousa, proud, strong, cheerful.

Then that mood passed. His hand slid from her shoulder, and as he gathered up his weapons and war bag, the melancholy returned. "It is within the hour that we leave," he told Cara without looking at her. "You see . . . I have painted myself."

"You will be careful. Strong and skilled, Ousa," Cara said, knowing nothing else to say. "*We* will be awaiting your return."

"I will be careful. Don't let that rascal Sa-Miwok talk you into tattooing yourself, Cara," he responded with a short-lived laugh.

"No! No, I will not." She hugged him again and was only then aware of someone standing in the doorway behind her. It was a tall, thick warrior who had painted his chest similarly to Ousa's.

"It is time," the tall man said.

"So soon?" Cara felt something tug at her heart.

"This is my friend River Bird, Cara. He is your friend too. If I am ever . . . not here, River Bird will give you what you need. He will take care of you."

"It is time," River Bird repeated.

"All right." Ousa picked up his war bag and paused before his wife. "Now I must go. It will not be long. A week perhaps. Tak and Kalthipsa will take your marriage price to your family. I thought you might go with them if it would please you. Visit your mother for a day or two."

"Yes, I will," Cara said. She did not cling to Ousa, but her eyes gripped him. There was so much they had not spoken of. She wondered suddenly if they could speak of the deeper problems, the hidden emotions. What did that mysterious paint mean? Then, before she could say anything else, he was gone. Ousa followed the big man, River Bird, from the lodge, and Cara was left in dark loneliness.

She started toward the entranceway and then halted, her hand rising and falling in a futile gesture. There would be war; always there would be war. A hundred times he would go out that doorway. He was Kispkotha, of the warrior clan. In ancient times the tribe had been divided into clans by the elders. The Peckuwe to deal with priestly matters, the Kispkotha to fight, to protect the tribe, to assure the people of survival. If there were no warriors, there would be no tribe, no Kata

Shawnee at all. For there were always powerful enemies, people who wanted their land, their women, their wealth. There always would be, and so there would always be war.

Cara stood alone in the dark lodge. She turned in a tight circle, impelled by frustration. She threw back her head and opened her mouth, barely containing the scream which built in her throat.

Calming, she walked to the entranceway and watched as the warriors gathered. Shelokta, on a paint pony, sat imperiously, arms folded, watching his men. Ousa stood to one side, and beside him was River Bird. They were joined by a dozen other men, each with his body painted in imitation of Ousa's.

Cara leaned her hand against the doorframe, her forehead against her hand. What was that sign? Why were these men wearing it? She would ask Turtle Back or Sa-Miwok what it meant, that death's-head and half-moon. She thought she knew, thought somewhere someone had told her that it was the ghost sign. But why would Ousa wear the ghost sign? And the others.

Then there was no time for thinking on it. At a signal from Shelokta, the raiding party moved out, two hundred strong walking and riding northward, toward the enemy's camp, into endless battle, and Cara was left alone. Alone with her new ambitions, with her worries, with the new, growing life within her womb.

7

The day was cool and bright; shifting soft clouds bulged against a deep blue sky. Cara rode homeward; beside her were Tak and Kalthipsa. The rest of the horses were strung out behind them on two long tethers. All were fine-looking animals, glossy and sleek. Turtle Back would use no culls. None of the animals had been broken completely. The Shawnee preferred a bit of wildness in their horses; it showed that a strong spirit lived within the animal. And so these pulled at the tether, kicked up their heels, and wandered as much as Tak and Kalthipsa would allow.

The two youths had been sullen when the journey began. Instead of being allowed to fight beside their brothers against the English, they had been given the job of escorting a woman to her home.

Gradually, however, their natural high spirits had returned, and now they seemed content to ride the long valley, talking and laughing.

Cara didn't understand all their jokes, and she felt sure there was a lot going on behind her back. But the boys were not deliberately excluding her; they had accepted her as a sister, or so she thought.

Thoughts of Sa-Miwok, of the baby, concern for Ousa's safety, rode with Cara, and her own mood was flat and introspective. Once she asked Tak, "What of the paint Ousa and River Bird were wearing? What did that mean?"

"The society," Tak said, obviously enthusiastic. "I mean to join it when they will have me." He shifted on his horse until he was riding sideways across the animal's back, his hand gripping the horse's mane.

"What society?" Cara had to ask.

"Did he not tell you? Perhaps a woman is not supposed to know. But you are Ousa's wife; I will tell you. Kalthipsa!" Tak pointed out a chestnut horse which had started chewing on the tether, and Kalthipsa rode to take care of that problem, rapping the horse smartly on the muzzle. Cara waited patiently.

"It is called the Ghost Society," Tak said, returning his attention to Cara finally. "They have their secret ways. The society is Ousa's invention."

"When did he invent it?" Cara asked. She had never heard Ousa mention it; and why *Ghost Society*?

"Just now," Tak said.

"You mean today . . . yesterday? When?"

"I don't know. Just now." He shrugged. When his horse set a hoof down hard, the soft fat under Tak's burnished skin jiggled. It did so just as he shrugged now, making the gesture massive.

"You say they have secrets. Do you know what they are?" Cara asked with concern. She also felt a little angry. Why hadn't Ousa said anything?

"Oh, yes," Tak said, waving a hand, "but I cannot tell you, if Ousa has not."

"He does not know," Kalthipsa called. "Admit it, Tak!"

"I know some," he said with less confidence. "I will be in the society one day."

But it was obvious Tak knew no more. Cara let the matter drop. They were far enough north now that she recognized the landfalls, the contour of the river, and her heart began to beat more quickly, expectantly.

She had not been away long, but the changes in her life had been dramatic, making it seem as if she had. Tadona's attempt on her life, the strange encounter with Sa-Miwok, the very act of becoming a man's wife all seemed to cut her off from home and the life she had known before becoming Shawnee.

Cara thought that and smiled. She had become Shawnee.

Now she felt that she was a part of the tribe, that she would die Shawnee.

The thin blade of smoke rose into the jumbled skies, and Cara's heart skipped a beat. She glanced at Tak and saw him smiling. Her eagerness was that obvious.

"Perhaps we should not go with you," Kalthipsa said then. "We can wait along the river."

"You are *family,* Kalthipsa," she said with emotion. Kalthipsa shrugged. Perhaps he did not think much of being in the same family as a Mingoe and a white dog. He said nothing, nodding his head.

They came out of the oaks along the river, and Cara saw the tilled field, the familiar low house, the bluffs beyond the house . . . and a woman rushing toward her. Cara leaped from the horse's back and ran to her mother, meeting her with a hug and a cry of joy which was half a sob.

"Cara."

Crenna kissed her daughter's hair, her forehead, her mouth, then turned with Cara to look at the two young Shawnee who sat wooden-faced on the horses drawn up behind them.

"Oh, look at you now!" Cara said in exasperation. "Smile, won't you! Get down and meet my mother."

They would not until Crenna, walking closer to them, arms folded, smiled up at Tak and said, "I believe I see a hungry Shawnee warrior. Come into my poor lodge and eat."

A half-smile played on Crenna's lips, and then, as Tak grinned, her own smile blossomed.

She patted his hand, a gesture he did not deny her. Cara stood beside her mother now, her hand on her shoulder. "This is Tak, Mother. And Kalthipsa."

"Ousa spoke of you warmly," Crenna said, and at the mention of their brother's name, they seemed to loosen up. "Now, come to the house and eat. We are family."

Tak slid from the horse's back, and Kalthipsa eventually followed. Leading the string of ponies toward the house, they saw the other woman, small and frail, dressed in bleached buckskins, standing before the door.

Cara took off at a run, and they saw the two women embrace, saw the small one pet Cara's hair, saw her large luminous eyes pore over Cara. And then the white man appeared in the doorway.

Tak stopped dead, nearly staggering. He had never seen a

white man in his life—with the exception of the Wild One—and this one had yellow hair! There was gray woven into the yellow, but it was definitely yellow. He had blue eyes flanking a thin, straight nose. Tak simply gaped as Cara went to the white man, who had but one arm, and held him tightly.

"Come along, now," Crenna said, beckoning to the Shawnee youths. "Let us eat and smoke. This is Van der Veghe, my husband, a brave warrior."

Kalthipsa looked dubiously at Van der Veghe, but he nodded, following Crenna into the house, Tak at his heels. Both men looked uncomfortable, but Tak was pacified by venison, duck, and corn pudding. Kalthipsa ate as well, but not with such a show of appetite. Cara had only blackberry tea, and as they sat drinking it, she told all that had happened to her.

Van der Veghe frowned heavily when she told of Tadona and the attack. "Is the woman still around?" he wanted to know.

"I have not seen her. Tak?"

Tak shrugged. Kalthipsa said he had not seen her either.

Crenna asked after Ousa, and Cara told them he was out raiding. Crenna and Van der Veghe exchanged a glance. The subject was quickly dropped.

"I would like to have one of the horses we have brought," Cara said. Then she explained why, telling about finding herself classless in the Shawnee camp, of her visit to Sa-Miwok.

Sachim, who sat in the corner silently listening, watched Cara with intense interest. "You have chosen correctly," she said when Cara was finished. "The shaman is right. You have the gift. I have always said so."

"But nine years," Van der Veghe exclaimed. "Is it worth that?"

"What shall I be doing for nine years, Father?" Cara asked. She answered her own question immediately. "I hope to live for nine more years. If I do nothing, do not study, then I shall simply be nine years older. If I remain with Sa-Miwok for those nine years, I may become shaman. Either way, the nine years have passed."

"That's so," Van der Veghe conceded. "Of course you may have the horse. With luck, natural increase will provide the other eight horses for your fee. I saw a fine stallion out there."

Kalthipsa lit up at that. "The red horse? Yes, he is a fine big stallion!" The Shawnee fell silent again, as if ashamed of having spoken.

"Shall we take a look at him?" Van der Veghe asked, getting up from the table. There was no way for Kalthipsa to refuse politely, and so he went out with Van der Veghe.

"He will return a friend," Crenna said. "All men become friends with Van der Veghe."

"Where is William?" Cara asked abruptly.

It was a moment before Crenna answered. "He lives at the settlement now, Cara. Soon I expect he will marry Louise Dawes."

"But if he's there now . . ." Cara blurted out. That was where Ousa was undoubtedly going. Cara fell silent, biting her lip as she looked from Crenna to Tak, who had pretended not to hear and was still engrossed in his meal. "We could go there . . ." No, they could not go there. To interfere with the Shawnee war plan could be disastrous for Ousa. There was nothing to be done, nothing at all.

"Futile," Cara said to herself. "All so futile." No one answered her. There was nothing to be done, nothing to say. War would go on. Once it is in motion, those who would stop it are already too late.

"Crenna?" Van de Veghe was in the doorway. Across his arm was the wampum-belt treaty which was a sign of friendship between the Shawnee and the Van der Veghes, not to be violated under penalty of death. "Where should we put this? How beautifully it's made. Look at the purple beads . . ."

"It is a beautiful *wampumpeak*," Crenna said, using the full word, which means "string of white shell beads." She took it and examined it, knowing that it was very valuable. The clam shells it was made from were not easily obtained in Ohio. There was much purple in it—the more valuable of the shells—but chiefly it was white, signifying peace and friendship.

"I think on that wall, Peter, away from the fire. The smoke might damage it. "You must thank your people, Tak, Kalthipsa, Cara," Crenna said, including her daughter in the Shawnee cortege. "This wampum is a sign not only of eternal friendship but of the linking of our families, and that makes it very valuable and dear to us indeed."

"We cannot let these young men go home without gifts,"

Van der Veghe put in. He had hung the wampum belt on the wall and now stood admiring it.

"No, of course not," Crenna said. "What shall they have?"

"I have no use for twelve knives. Ousa has given us twelve knives. These young men must each have one. And a horse apiece—any but the red stallion," the Dutchman said. Tak and Kalthipsa were both beaming. For a man their age to have his own horse was unprecedented, although they had heard that it was not uncommon among the western tribes.

Their gratitude was evident. Their faces shone. "And do take food with you, Tak," Crenna encouraged.

"What he has eaten will last him ten days." His brother laughed.

"Come," Van der Veghe said, placing his arm familiarly around Kalthipsa's shoulder, a gesture the young Shawnee accepted. "Let us look at the horses again. Now I shall see which ones you praised out of politeness and which you truly favored."

Tak went along with them, his cheeks still bulging with food, and when the women were left alone, Crenna, standing before her daughter, hands on her shoulders, asked, "Are you happy with your Shawnee man, Cara?"

"I am happy," Cara replied without hesitation. "There are problems, but they are not between Ousa and myself. Then"—she shrugged—"there are always problems while we live, are there not?"

"Always. But I wish you a little time with only small problems."

"Mother . . ."—Cara hesitated—"there is a child within me."

Sachim nearly leaped to her feet, clapping her hands with joy. Crenna was more subdued. She simply hugged her daughter, holding her tightly, feeling that unique emotion which is a part of knowing that life continues, that one generation proceeds from the last, that hopefully progress is made toward happiness, toward knowledge with each new life; with this was mingled the sadness which comes from knowing that this sort of progress is not always made, that life continues to carry with it identical sadness, frustration, and confusion, that it seems we are incapable of learning from previous error, from the success of another generation, that each step must be taken anew, that old knowledge is useless to new intelligences.

"Bless you, bless the baby," Crenna said, and then she had to turn away. "I am too old to cry."

They stayed the night, Tak and Kalthipsa sleeping in the river grove. Cara had her old corner, and she lay awake trying to recapture the old feeling of belonging, of security, that she had always felt sleeping in her parents' home, but it was gone. It was a sad realization, but she did not belong here anymore. It was as if, leaving, she had left the old Cara behind. She could not return and crawl into the sheath of soul which had been Cara, the girl. It was over.

She had intended to stay another day, but with the morning Cara felt that she had to go. She was Shawnee; the village beyond the river was her home.

Cara, Tak, and Kalthipsa were ready after a large breakfast, and they sat their horses, saying their farewells. The two young Shawnee were perched proudly on their ponies. They sat with their backs rigid, their eyes straight ahead. Cara imagined they were not so sorry now that they had been forced to accompany her home, but she said nothing like that to them. She simply smiled, waved to Van der Veghe, Crenna, and Sachim, who stood watching her, waving back until they were vanished into the trees. The day was cool and bright, and Cara, feeling only slightly ashamed of the emotion, knew that she was glad they had departed. Ahead lay home—home, where Ousa would soon be returning, where the rest of her life awaited her.

"Where's Van der Veghe!" the man in the faded blue uniform called down from the stockade wall. The settler nearest the wall took off at a trot, searching for the Dutchman. He found him with Richard Dawes at the Baxter kitchen window. The settler, whose name was Granger, a tall red-bearded man out of Connecticut and Dover, had expected to find Van der Veghe and Dawes together—they were inseparable . . . except when Louise Dawes was near. Then Van der Veghe saw no one else. Louise Dawes was too spicy, too saucy for Granger's taste, but then, he supposed some liked them that way.

"Van der Veghe!"

William, a cup of tea in his hand, turned toward Granger. "What is it?"

"The captain wants you. I think he's spotted something."

William put his cup down on the sill of the Baxters' kitchen window, and snatching up his musket, he dog-trotted back to where Captain James Compton, Ohio Irregulars, stood along the rampart, his spyglass in his hands.

William climbed the pole ladder and eased up beside Compton, who turned grimly toward him. Compton, a man of middle years with green eyes and a drooping military mustache, pointed toward the river flats. "There's something moving down along the bottoms, Van der Veghe."

William lifted the spyglass to his eye and turned the eyepiece, focusing the telescope. "Where?"

"Near the twin oaks, back among the willows."

"I don't see anything now," William said after a minute's slow search.

"I'm sure of it. I think we should prepare for an assault from that quadrant." Compton tugged thoughtfully at his mustache, and took back the telescope.

William shrugged. "They'll not come across the flats, Captain. There's too much open ground."

"Dammit, I tell you I saw something!"

"A diversion, perhaps," William said. "If you like, I'll go out and have a look."

"Out there?" Compton was aghast.

"Out there. That was my backyard as a boy, Captain. They'll not come up on me easily."

"William." It was Richard Dawes. He stood at the foot of the ladder, squinting into the sunlight. "Don't go out there."

William laughed. "They'll not see me, Richard. You should know that."

Richard remembered a hundred boyhood games of hide and seek—those games had always been a humiliation to him. William was the smoke on the wind in the woods, soundless, swift. Still, this was a different matter. There were armed men out there who wished to kill them.

The Dawes house had been attacked the night before, and burned to the ground. Fortunately Compton had come upon the battle, and the Shawnee had retreated. Now John and Martha Dawes—both shaken up, John with his head badly wounded—lay in the Baxter house, tended by Louise.

"I'm going out," William said. "But if they attack, Captain, it won't come from the flats. More likely from out of the brush to the east."

"There's not cover enough there for a rabbit," Compton said. He still hadn't gotten used to this wilderness fighting, to this enemy which was all shadow and paint, who struck and then was gone.

"There's cover enough for a Shawnee," William Van der Veghe replied, looking eastward himself. "We're starting to lose the sun. I'd strengthen the eastern wall, sir."

Having said that, William winked and leaped from the low parapet, landing agilely. He handed his musket to Richard Dawes, who continued to watch him with concern.

"You'll need a weapon."

"I'll take my arrows," William told him.

"William?" William Van der Veghe turned to find Louise rushing toward him. She wore blue gingham, the neckline of the dress cut lower than seemed decent. She lifted her skirts as she ran to him, her green eyes flashing. "What are you doing? Mr. Baxter said you were going out there."

"I am. Don't worry about it. It's safe. I don't think there are any Shawnee toward the river anyway. The captain"—he nodded his head toward Compton—"wants to be sure."

"Then let him go out!" Louise said loudly enough for Compton to hear.

"It's my sort of job, Louise."

"Dangerous, you mean," she said impatiently. William didn't answer. He kissed her on top of the head and walked off. Louise's eyes followed him. Finally she stamped her foot and made a loud disgusted sound. "He'll die. One day he'll die."

"How's Father?" Richard asked, putting his arm around his sister's waist.

"It's not good, Richard. Mother's babbling on . . . it's enough to drive a person crazy. Why did we stay here? Leave it to the Indians! We ought to just go. They'd let us."

"Would they?" Richard looked to the east, where William expected the attack to originate. "I'm not so sure they would. Not now."

"Dawes!"

"Yes, sir?" Richard looked up to the parapet where Compton stood. "Captain," they called him, although he had no official rank. There were no regular British forces in Ohio as yet. The settlers who were there, forced to band together for protection, had simply voted themselves a leader. Compton had been a career soldier in His Majesty's grenadiers. All but John Dawes had voted for Compton to assume command, since there obviously needed to be someone in charge if there was to be any effective organization.

Richard liked the man no more than his father did. Arrogant, dull-witted, he had assumed his rank as if accepting the crown.

"I want you to pull those people off the eastern stockade and bring them around to the west end."

Richard glanced westward. "Sir, I thought Van der Veghe said—"

"Damn Van der Veghe! Which side is he on, anyway? His mother's an Indian, isn't she?"

"Not Shawnee," Richard objected.

"I don't intend to stand here arguing. You swore an oath to accept my leadership, Dawes. Do I have to remind you of that each time I give you an order?"

"No." Richard's expressive mouth turned down at the corners, his lips slightly compressed. "I'll get the word over there."

"On the double."

"Yes, Captain. On the double." Richard turned away before he said what was on his mind. It helped nothing to tell Compton what an ass he was making of himself. "Get on back to the house, Louise," he said. His sister started to argue, out of habit—it was one of Louise's great joys in life to debate every point until, worn and wearied, her opponent simply gave in to her. "Or get a musket," he added.

"All right." Her reply was unusually meek. Her glance was challenging, however, as she lifted her skirts again and started back toward the house, and again Richard wondered how William ever meant to tame that woman. Many men would try to beat it out of her—Richard doubted even that would work with Louise. She was her own woman, which would have been admirable had she common sense to go along with the dedication to her own rightness.

Then Richard was off at a trot, passing between the Baxter and Chamliss houses to the ragged stockade wall. "Captain wants the western wall reinforced!" Dawes called up to the bald, short-tempered Chamliss, who was in charge of this squad.

"All right. Six of you stay here," Chamliss commanded. "Everyone else, down the ladders. We're moving."

* * *

It was silent and still along the river. The only sound was the breeze stirring the leaves of the oaks. William Van der Veghe lay beside a mossy boulder, peering into the reddish light of the dying sun. It was still warm. Perspiration trickled down the back of his neck. He had to wipe it out of his eyes—a slow, cautious movement like all other movements he had made since slipping out of the stockaded town.

He had seen nothing. There were no moccasin tracks, nothing at all to indicate anyone had been moving around along the river. Still, a cautious man who had learned the importance of remaining still while hunting, he held his position, letting only his eyes move, listening for the small telltale sounds.

Nothing. He had been downriver half a mile, and then, circling far east, he had come back to the river at a point a mile or so north of his present position. He was now determined to wait until dark before slipping back into the stockade. He had a grim thought, and he smiled. As edgy and unskilled as most of those people were, he'd be lucky if they didn't shoot him on sight.

A swarm of gnats, attracted by William's body heat, clustered around his face, delving into ears and clouding his vision with their persistent cloud. He wished he dared light his pipe to smoke them away. He didn't.

Compton, he decided, had been seeing bogeys along the river. He hadn't thought the old soldier was imaginative enough for that. William sighed, blew out a stream of breath which separated him from the gnats just long enough for him to inhale, and sighed again.

The sun was low now, its face red and harsh above the pines to the east of the stockade. The trees, black before its brilliance, stood in deep stolid ranks. He let his vision shift to the willow brush which spotted the flats to the east of the stockade. Suddenly he froze, his body going rigid, his attention so fully engrossed that he was no longer aware of the swarm of annoying gnats.

"A moving shadow," he told himself. No, tricks of the eye. The sun was a fierce, glaring ball of crimson. Nothing. It was only that he expected—sooner or later, today or tomorrow, the day after—to see something from that direction. He remained unmoving against the hard earth, smelling the river, the pungent scents of the underbrush.

Nothing. And then the sun erupted with fire and sound. Sundown was another word for death. He saw the clumps of brush come to life, heard the first bellow of a musket, saw a puff of smoke, a rushing Shawnee reach the base of the stockade wall, a man topple from the rampart, an arrow through his chest; a fierce war cry followed by hundreds of others shook the stillness of the Ohio dusk.

William was up and running before he knew it, before he had time to consider the folly of showing himself, of rushing an armed stockade from out of the darkness in buckskins while a hostile force was attacking. Before he had time to stop and curse Captain Compton for the fool he was. For William could see now that there was practically no support on the eastern perimeter.

He could see swarming Shawnee appearing above the jagged line of the parapet; saw one hit and fall, another leap to the ground out of his line of vision.

Louise. Red anger, as bright as the last fireball of the dying sun, flared up in his mind, and he ran on, his bow and arrows tightly gripped.

He splashed across the river, achieved the far bank, and ran on as the muskets popped and the war cries continued to pierce the dusk.

A Shawnee warrior loomed up suddenly before him, a man with odd paint on his chest—a half-moon and a death's-head. William dived low, rolled to one side, and came up in a sitting position, his arrow already notched. As the Shawnee, shouting an unintelligible, ululating oath, sprang at him, his war club raised to crush William's skull, he let the arrow fly, and it flew true.

The Shawnee twisted sideways in the air, slapped at the arrow embedded in his chest, and sprawled on the earth, his leg twitching.

William was on his feet and running again before the Shawnee stopped moving. The stockaded town cut a dark, bulky silhouette against the purpling sky. He could see nothing of the battle within, but he could see the confusion along the western parapet as the settlers tried to scramble down from the wall in the face of the enemy and reinforce the eastern perimeter, which had caved in under the first wave of the attack.

They were dark, indistinguishable forms, antlike, frantic.

Then, as William ran nearer, he could make out the faces. Men unskilled, untrained in combat, facing death for the first time, their eyes wide with terror. One man was killed and thrown over the sharp palings.

It was only then that the obvious struck home: he had no way of getting into the stockade! William rushed on thoughtlessly. Louise was in there, Richard, John and Martha Dawes, a dozen others he knew intimately now. Perhaps he could do nothing, but he would try. He hit the main gate, pounding on it with his fists, yelling to be heard above the din of shrieks and gunshots. It was impossible.

A Shawnee appeared around the corner of the stockade, and William, alert for this possibility, sent an arrow into the man's heart before he could react.

The last thing they expected was to find a white man outside the stockade, and in that light, for only a moment, his buckskin-clad figure must be taken for that of a Shawnee. He could not rely on that, however.

The smoke of burned powder lay like a pall across the town. Using that and the settling darkness to cover his movement, William worked his way toward the eastern wall, twice passing within feet of Shawnee warriors who, not expecting to see a white man, did not see him.

The smoke was heavy and acrid. William wondered if Compton had fired his prized cannon. He could not recall hearing the deep-throated roar of the thunder-gun, but it seemed likely that it had been fired. And too low. The eastern wall had exploded into jackstraws. The Shawnee, storming it, had been repulsed the first time, but now the assault was renewing itself.

The haze of darkness and the gunsmoke blurred the action. William saw a body here, a man there, appearing like drifting specters through the warfog. It grew only thicker as he stumbled toward his goal—the gaping hole in the eastern wall. Then he saw the first bright flags of flame. Crimson and gold, they sparked skyward, adding to the smoky darkness.

William found a Shawnee in his path. The man had been staring upward at the fired stockade walls, but some sense had caused him to whirl, war club raised. William leaped forward, buried his knife to the hilt in the warrior's abdomen, and pressed his body to the Shawnee's as the man died, his warm blood spilling across William's hand.

Then, with a quick look around, William sprinted for the wall, where the Shawnee were falling back in confusion. He saw raised hands, heard warning voices, and then the cannon exploded again. Six men were hurled from the parapet, flung like rag dolls. A wave of heat washed over William, and his eardrums were rattled by the thunder of exploding gunpowder.

Before the Shawnee could reorganize themselves, William leaped to the wall, clambered up over the broken bodies and shattered logs, and was into the compound.

He came face to face with Emil Baxter, who swung the muzzle of his musket around sharply. His eyes were glazed, his hair hung in his eyes. He had not removed the ramrod from his musket barrel, and had he pulled the trigger, he would have skewered William with it in a deadly fashion. At the last moment, however, he recognized William and lowered his weapon. Baxter staggered back and leaned his back against the side of his house—his seemed to be the only one which had not been fired by the raiding Shawnee.

"Where's Louise?" William demanded. Baxter simply stared at him. "Louise Dawes!" He shook Baxter by the shoulders.

"They killed my wife," was all he said.

William looked eastward, through the smoke and darkness. Would they come in again or wait until light? There was no way of knowing for sure. He looked for someone who had landed on his feet, and finding Reg Chamliss, he told him, "Let's drag some of this timber back and set up a barricade, Reg. If they come again, they'll certainly try to breach the wall here again. Withdraw fifty feet or so and fort up. You can lay the timbers between the Baxter house and the smokeshed. Leave enough litter out there to slow them up if they do come."

"All right. Sounds practical to me," Chamliss agreed. He was a man with an evil temper, but just now he was meek and accepting. William found out later that both of his young sons had been clubbed to death.

"Where's Compton, anyway?"

"I don't know," Chamliss said with a shrug. "Blair, MacDonald! Give me a hand with these timbers."

William strode through the camp. There were still a few bodies which relatives and friends had not covered or carried away. Flames rose brightly from the house where John and Martha Dawes had lain injured, and it was there that he found

Louise. She stood, arms folded, her face burnished by the flames. No tears fell; her mouth formed a perfectly straight line.

William slipped his arm around her shoulders, and she jumped. "In there?" he asked, and she nodded.

They stood together watching the flames. There was no attempt made to put the fire out. They were cut off from the river, and what water they had would be needed for drinking. Nor was there any hope of entering the house at this stage. Sheets of flame rose skyward, writhing, snapping, and snarling. Anyone in the house would already have been dead from the smoke.

They stood together; there was nothing else to do.

"I'm frightened," Louise admitted. Her words were barely audible. William bent his head nearer. The heat was terrific, and the roof of the house suddenly collapsed, sending brilliant splinters of light higher into the sky as the logs caved in. "I want to get married. Now. Tonight," Louise said. "I want you to marry me, William."

"All right." His hand was still around her shoulders; now it dropped free to hang at his side. He squinted into the flames. "All right, Louise. We'll be married tonight."

Ta-sho-haka touched his shoulder, and Shelokta turned to him angrily. He was weary. His shoulder had been injured breaching the stockade. They had lost too many men and achieved too little. Shelokta had been sitting brooding, staring into the fire. There must be victory, and it must be brilliant victory. Otherwise the mantle of power might be returned to Ousa—something Shelokta would not tolerate! Now and then he glanced at the men who sat together in a dark knot across the camp—Ousa and his followers. There were few of them, but that did little to ease Shelokta's mind. What did they want? What were they planning with this secret society of theirs? Ta-sho-haka had interrupted these black, brooding thoughts.

"What is it?"

"A friend." Ta-sho-haka inclined his head toward the pines behind the camp.

Shelokta lifted an eyebrow curiously but said nothing. He rose, throwing his blanket around his shoulders, wincing as the wounded arm complained with a stab of pain. Ta-sho-haka took his place by the fire, and Shelokta walked among the sleeping and quietly talking warriors toward the pine woods, not moving hastily, pausing to speak to a man here and there.

Once into the concealing darkness of the pines, he hurried on. The half-moon cast searching beams through the tall black trees. Shelokta stopped once and squatted, listening, but no one was following him.

He saw the dark outline of a horse, saw it lift its head in curiosity, and Shelokta frowned. He walked forward, his mouth twisted cynically.

"I was not expecting you. I thought . . ."

"I know," Tadona said. "But I wanted to see. You promised it, and it has not been done."

She was near, and Shelokta was aware of her varnished beauty, of the animal eyes, the sleek movements, the catlike essence of Tadona. He pushed aside thoughts of her as a woman.

"Ousa is always with me."

"You don't have to do it yourself," Tadona said, taunting him as if he were a fool. Shelokta's fist clenched. "Find some excuse, send a party of men out."

"I don't—"

"We agreed that the Van der Veghes must be destroyed," Tadona said, cutting off his objection.

"I said I would think on it, Tadona," Shelokta said wearily.

"Think on it until Ousa cuts your legs from under you!" Tadona hissed.

"He hasn't the strength."

"What do you think the Ghost Society has been formed to do? Can you not guess, Shelokta!" She laughed mockingly, in a whispery, private way.

"Yes, I suppose that is the reason for its existence," Shelokta said. "To oppose me."

"There can be no other reason." Tadona touched his arm. The wind in the trees caused a bough to creak somewhere. She looked around sharply, those cat eyes dancing.

"It's nothing," Shelokta said. He felt Tadona's hand drop away.

"You have given in to Ousa," Tadona continued, her words accusing, harsh. "You have let this white dog live on our hunting grounds. There are others who will not like this."

"I know, I know," Shelokta said impatiently. "I don't like it either. I didn't want to give them the wampum belt."

"But you allowed it."

"There was no choice at the time."

"Now there is, Shelokta."

Shelokta nodded. He looked at the woman, seeing the depths of her hatred. She only wanted to hurt Ousa's woman, if possible to drive a wedge between Ousa the Shawnee and Cara the Mingoe. But she had logic on her side.

"It will be seen that Ousa cannot even protect his own family," Tadona insisted. "It will be seen that Shelokta always wins. No one will be able to prove that Shelokta was the one who caused the death of the Van der Veghes, but everyone will know—they will know that you cannot be opposed. It will weaken the Ghost Society, Shelokta. Perhaps it will ruin it. If those men know that you will be always victorious."

Shelokta stared at her. *I thought I knew how to hate,* he thought. Her eyes positively glittered. She was tense with excitement. What, he wondered, did Tadona hope to gain out of this? Did she think Ousa would ever come back to her now, no matter what? No—he realized it suddenly—she only wished to humiliate Ousa, to shatter him, to grind him into the earth. Defeat was not enough; it must be humiliation, complete and abject.

"How can it be done?" Shelokta asked, wondering what gave this woman her strength. He knew one thing: he did not ever want Tadona opposed to him.

She smiled for the first time, a brilliant moonlit smile which brought out her sensuality. It was a force which had lain latent until that moment, but, Shelokta conjectured, maybe he had felt it all along, had been captured by it. Her earth spirit, the spirit of the bed, had always been strong. Yet in Tadona it was completely at her bidding, under control at all times. It made her less than human.

"What is your plan?" she asked.

"At the moment? To return to the fortified town."

"No. That will not do. You must travel north to raid the settlements on the Ohio. You need not explain yourself to your men, but you may suggest that it is better to attack a second unprepared village rather than return to one which is alerted and ready."

Shelokta felt irritation growing. Now the woman would explain tactics to him. Even then, however, he had to admit that her war plan—if it were authentic—made sense. What was to be gained by attacking the fortified town again? He waited expectantly, piqued and fascinated. It was then, perhaps, that he decided he would marry Tadona. What a wildcat she must be!

"The wounded will be sent back to the village. Say it is too far for them to travel. You will not need so many men anyway. In the north the settlements are smaller. Take a trusted man aside and instruct him. Tell him the Van der Veghes must be destroyed."

"They will not like it. The wampum belt . . ." The penalty was death for any who violated that treaty.

"What does it matter what they like! Tell them that you will see them die if they do not carry out your orders. Tell them that Cara is a witch, her family evil. Tell them anything. They will not be caught—who will survive to say who did this?" At that she smiled with wicked enjoyment.

"I do not know . . ." Shelokta objected. Doubtful shadows had begun to drift through his mind. The woman was mad with vengeance.

"Come. There is one more thing I have to show you, my Shelokta, my sachem, my war leader." She enunciated each word clearly, maliciously. Shelokta felt like refusing her, but curiosity beckoned, and he followed her to her waiting horse.

"What is this?" He watched as she untied a small bundle from her horse's back, and then his eyes opened appreciatively as the package fell to the earth and spilled out its contents. "White clothes." Shelokta knelt down and lifted them piece by piece—trousers, coats, shirts. "Where did you. . . ?" he started to ask, but he knew perfectly well where she had gotten the clothes.

"If your men are seen . . ." Tadona picked up a tricornered hat, tucked her hair under it, and laughed out loud. "It is the whites themselves who did it. Come out of anger to kill the two Indian women who live in the house. Van der Veghe himself was killed trying to protect his squaws."

Shelokta stood, shaking his head. The woman was a flawless work of evil. She made no mistakes. Her revenge was cold and ruthless. No wild-eyed passion for Tadona. She had had her moment the night she burst into Ousa's wedding house to kill his bride. Now she was calculating, hard as flint, savage.

Shelokta rose, took one step toward her, and wrapped his arms around her, his hands on her hips, pressing himself against her. If she dared to laugh that mocking laugh, he thought he would kill her, but she did not. She was inflamed by her own dark emotions, excited by the thought of blood and fire, and she came to him eagerly, letting Shelokta hold her, kiss her, lay her down on the earth while the moon shone through the black pines.

8

"What was that?" Crenna lifted her head. She was busy sewing beads onto the buckskin shirt she had been making for William. William, whom they seldom saw, whose eyes had grown moody and distant. William, whom she loved deeply.

Van der Veghe, beside the fire, stretched his arms overhead and yawned. "I heard nothing."

"The horses, I think," Sachim said.

"Oh?" Van der Veghe rose and put his pipe carefully on the mantel. "The stallion, no doubt. The red horse is a wild thing."

"I think we shall have many foals in the spring," Crenna said in agreement.

"Still . . ." Van der Veghe sighed. There had been a bear around lately. "I'll have a look." He walked past Crenna, shouldering into his jacket, and on some impulse he stopped, patted her hand, and went out.

Van der Veghe looked toward the horses, glanced once at the silver half-moon floating through the deep velvet sky, and then it happened. They came up from out of the shadows, and he saw the war club lifted. He thrust out his arm, trying to fend off the blow, but it was useless. The club snapped his forearm, and its heavy stone head slammed into Van der Veghe's skull.

He was falling, and there were others on him now, beating him ferociously. He saw their faces—grim, emotionless. He saw the moon whirl away. He thought he screamed; maybe he did. Something buzzed in his ears, some reminiscent, awful echo.

He had time to regret many things before the pain became a fire surging through his brain, before his heart finally gave up its protesting thumping.

Crenna, he thought. *She is all I will miss.*

Sachim bolted from her chair. Crenna sat motionless for a moment, the horrible scream echoing through the room freezing her with horror. Then she was to her feet.

"Peter! Peter!" She raced toward the door, but Sachim had reached it first. She slid the bolt and stood with her back pressed against it.

"No, Crenna!"

"Let me out! Stand away, are you mad?"

She tried to yank her sister aside. The scream still hung in the air, fading now eerily. Sachim would not be moved. For a moment their hands dueled as Crenna clawed at the door.

"Sachim!"

"Stay in here. Do not go out! There's nothing you can do."

"I don't know that!" Crenna's face was a mask of grief. Her eyes were too wide, her mouth open. A vein in her forehead throbbed violently.

"I know it." Sachim looked at her sister, her eyes dark and nearly fierce. "I know it, Crenna. There is nothing you can do."

"Let me—" Crenna's plea was interrupted by the pounding at the door. Sachim drew away as many bodies slammed into the planks. The door shuddered on its hinges, and Crenna, backing into the far corner, wrapped her fingers around Van der Veghe's ax.

They watched as the door was struck again and again. The jolting caused bits of their sod roof to drift down from the ceiling to lie against the floor.

The door was struck again and again. It seemed that a hundred men were battering it with stones. A splinter, deep and long, was torn loose.

Three shots rang out in rapid succession, and the beating on the door halted abruptly. Crenna, still holding the ax in both hands, took a half-step forward. Her eyes met Sachim's questioningly.

It was silent. The storm had struck, battering their home, and then as quickly dissipated. "Are they out there?" Crenna whispered. Sachim shrugged an answer. She crept nearer to the shuttered window, hoping to see something through the gaps in the shutter planking.

She saw nothing but the moon and the dark, formless thing sprawled on the moon-frosted grass. She closed her eyes tightly and turned away from the window.

Then they heard the sounds of rushing feet, and Sachim's head turned again toward the door. Her hands, despite herself, had begun shaking. There was the faint smell of smoke from somewhere, the shouting of excited voices, and then one voice lifted above the rest.

"Mother!" The excited rapping on the door began again. "Mother!"

"It's William." Sachim looked at Crenna, who stood still in the center of the room, the ax in her hand, her eyes vacant. Sachim slid the heavy bolt and opened the door.

William stood there with a dozen other armed men. "William . . ." Crenna walked toward him, letting the ax fall from her hand. He stuck out his arms, but she brushed past him, going outside, passing through the knot of men as if they were not there.

She went to where he lay, to where it lay. Broken, crushed, lifeless. All that had been Peter Van der Veghe. She got to her knees and threw back her head as if she would shriek, yell, curse. She did none of these. As they watched, she slowly bent her face to his bloody chest and lay there, holding him, perhaps whispering, for they saw her lips move, but no one heard a word.

William had to turn away.

A dozen more men came striding toward the house from the piny bluffs. "See anything?" Richard Dawes called out.

"Lost 'em. Who in hell you figure them for, William?"

William didn't answer. He looked neither at the men nor at the dark crumpled form of the mourning woman.

"Can't fathom it," Chamliss said, removing his hat to wipe his forehead. "They were white men. I saw them clear by the moonlight."

"They were Shawnee," William said, his voice distant. "Look at the footprints. They were all wearing moccasins."

"Shawnee? Why the getups?" Chamliss wondered out loud.

William failed to answer him again. *We had a treaty,* he thought. We had a treaty with the bastard. Yet Ousa had not honored it. He had proven himself to be a man without honor, and on this night, a coward. *I'll find you, Ousa.* I'll find you and cut your heart out.

"William?" Richard Dawes was beside him, had apparently been there for some time. "Are you all right?" William nodded. "I'm sorry." He rested his hand foolishly on William's shoulder.

"Yes."

William walked to where his mother knelt over the crushed thing which had been Peter Van der Veghe. Some of the men had gone around to the back of the house to where the Shawnee had tried to start a fire.

"Mother . . . ?" She did not look up at him. William could see one eye, but it was a lifeless thing, a dull gleaming object like wet stone in the moonlight. Her jaw was slack. He touched her hand, but she did not respond.

"William . . ."

He rose and turned to see Sachim standing there, her hair loose and drifting in the light breeze. "It is better if you just go. You can do no more."

He started to object but didn't. He felt like shouting, like ranting, cursing, like smashing something. He didn't. He simply nodded, and without looking back, turned on his heel and started walking down the long valley, his heart cold and heavy in his chest.

After a minute the other men followed him, and Sachim, arms folded, stood, watching them go. An owl called from the pine woods, and Sachim wiped away the hot tear which tracked down her cheek.

She turned toward Crenna. Her sister had not moved. Her body lay as lifelessly as Peter Van der Veghe's, buckled at knees and waist, head slack on her neck, her cheek against his chest where the blood was drying into a purple crust.

Crenna looked but did not see; Sachim did not know where her sister was, but she was not there in front of this roughly constructed log house in which a family had lived, had grown, had laughed together. She was not there, where the only man she had loved her life long lay against the bitter earth.

Perhaps she roamed the long hillsides with her young Peter Van der Veghe, rolling in the long grass and meadow flowers as the sun flickered through the oaks. Perhaps she sat with him beside a silver, quick-running stream, speaking in loving tones to him, her head on his knees. Sachim did not know—she only knew that wherever Crenna had gone, Sachim could not go.

Sachim could not help her to mourn, for Crenna would not let him die. She could not comfort Crenna, for Crenna was not here. Sachim looked to the stars, finding them blurred and distant. She looked to the dark house, knew she could not go into it again, and then she began walking, going up to where the piny bluffs shut out the stars and the night and memory.

Sachim slept without resting. The night was a tangle of taunting spirits, mocking voices, cold eyes, loud, thudding heartbeats, anxious faces, and twisted hands.

The sunlight was welcome. She rose and rubbed her eyes, looking down through the pines toward the house, hoping . . . But it had been no terrible vision; the dream was over.

Crenna still lay with the body. In the daylight it was a horrible-looking thing, this crushed object which had once been a man. They had attacked him vengefully, madly.

"Crenna." Sachim stood over her sister, whose eyes had been closed. They now flickered open. The emptiness remained. "Crenna, it must be done. Rise. It is wrong to continue this."

"Let us sleep awhile longer," Crenna said.

Sachim crouched down, her hands on her lap. "Crenna. It must be done."

"Let me sleep with my husband, this fine laughing Dutchman, for a time," Crenna said. Her lips barely moved as she spoke. Her cheek was bloodstained, her eyes lifeless.

"Crenna!" Sachim shrieked the name. She had never used such a tone in her entire gentle life. Now she did, and she reached over to shake Crenna's arm. "We must send him to his gods. We must bury him according to his custom."

"Bury him!" Crenna sat up immediately. "You cannot bury him. I will not give him to his gods! He is mine." She clutched her breasts and hissed vehemently: "Mine!"

It was then that she came apart. She collapsed against the earth, and her body was torn by convulsive sobs. Sachim let her cry, her own eyes lifted to the long meadow where the wind turned the grass silver in the sunlight. She looked again at her sister, who now, finally, nodded and allowed Sachim to help her to her feet.

"I shall make breakfast," Crenna said. She did not look again at the body. She walked stiffly toward the empty house, her head erect, her shoulders rigid. Sachim herself dug the grave beneath a massive white oak, and when it was time, she went to Crenna.

"There is a task to be done, Crenna."

"I must make breakfast for William and Peter," Crenna said, although she was doing nothing of the sort. She was sitting staring at the cold ashes in the fireplace as if there were flames there, as if they fascinated her with their hidden messages.

"Crenna . . ." Sachim said gently.

"If there is a task, have Cara help you or do it yourself," Crenna said with some sharpness. Sachim nodded. Biting her lip, she turned and went out. She dragged Peter Van der Veghe to the grave and rolled him into it, covering him again without looking at what lay there.

Finished, she stood over him, the wind chilling her body. She did not know what ceremonies, what words would please Van der Veghe's gods, and so she simply whispered to the Great Manitou, "He was a good man who loved us well."

Again Sachim slept out. Spending the night in the house was unbearable. Crenna would not be touched, would not be comforted. She would not speak except for a bit of nonsense now and then, and once when Sachim had least expected it, she had said quite lucidly: "I do not want to be here. You know that, my sister. I do not want to be in a world where there is no Peter Van der Veghe. My children do not need me, and so I pray that the spirits will come and take me. I pray to die, and I think that soon they shall have pity on me and I shall die. Together we shall see what lies beyond the sky. It is right."

Those were the last lucid words Sachim heard her say. There were a few broken fragments of speech now and again. Meaningless syllables, words in three languages jumbled together. But she was going. She wished it, and so she would go. It was the way of their people; Sachim could do nothing but watch and wait.

She lived for ten days, growing gaunt and more lifeless

with each of the ten. On the last, at sunset she looked at Sachim with those horrible hollow eyes, seemed to smile, and then her fleshless head bobbed in a confident nod and Crenna was no more.

Sachim placed her on her bed, dressed her in her feathered cape that she had worn as headwoman of the Oneida nation, placed her white moccasins on her feet, and went out of the house.

The fire was slow getting started, but then, as Sachim watched, the eaves caught and the red fire curled skyward, smoke rushing toward the stars.

It burned for hours, sending up fountains of golden sparks. And when it was done, there was only the heat, the sad heap of ashes, and the slender woman standing alone in the wide valley.

Sachim took only a single blanket. She would forage for what food she needed. They were gone, the two she had loved most in this world, and she wanted no world without them. She wanted no human companionship, no loveless communion. She would return to her spirits to be alone with them as she had been before these two made the human world warm for her, before they had welcomed her into their home.

She stood only a moment longer, and then, with no objective in mind, with no destination, she simply turned and merged with the wilderness shadows, becoming, as she had always been, a substanceless spirit wandering the earth.

Her heart leaped with joy. He was there, laughing, unhurt, strong. He crossed the camp, emerging from the crowd of exultant returning warriors.

Ousa came to her in the twilight, and his arms were strong around her, his lips eager and searching. Cara kissed him again, the flat of her hand resting on his chest. He seemed more than healthy; he seemed whole. She had worried about him being injured, vaguely about his death, but her deepest concern had been for his spirit. He had gone away heavy in heart, grim, unwell. Now he was her man again, strong, confident, smiling.

Those black, black eyes, how they laughed as he hoisted her in his arms and swung her around.

"Woman, my woman, my Cara. I did not know how much a man could miss his woman."

"It was only a week," she said. Her heart fluttered with

the excitement of several mingled emotions. Joy at seeing him, joy at seeing him well, the joy that her body felt in being close to his, in anticipation of the soft night ahead of them. "Come in, my Ousa, husband, and eat."

With their arms wound around each other, they entered the house. Outside, all was pandemonium. The bonfires had been lighted; already the victory drums had begun their urgent message. Triumph was in the air. Triumph brightened the faces of the warriors.

Ousa stripped off his shirt and leggings and sat on the blanket eating as Cara washed his back and shoulders, chest and arms, with a damp cloth, pausing frequently to give him loving hugs, to touch him.

Perhaps men had died, but they would not speak of that tonight. Those Shawnee who died in battle would not be mentioned by name until tomorrow. Tonight belonged to celebration.

Cara continued to wash his body. The movement of the rough cloth across the hard muscles of Ousa's body, the slight efforts her back and hips had to make to perform this task, were all vaguely sensual.

She stopped, kissed his neck, and received a brilliant smile in response. "More food?" she asked, her lips close to his ear.

"More of you, woman," Ousa said, turning, falling backward, dragging her down with him.

"Ousa?" the voice interrupted.

Their eyes went to the doorway, where the big-shouldered warrior River Bird stood, his hooded eyes amused.

"What is it?" Ousa asked, obviously irritated.

"There is a council meeting."

"Tonight?"

"Yes, tonight. Now."

"For what purpose?" Ousa asked. He sat up, his hand on his wife's shoulder.

"You shall see. It is important." Then River Bird was gone, and Ousa, frowning, stared at the empty doorway.

"Why tonight?" he asked of no one.

"Must you go?" Cara asked. Her fingers tangled themselves in Ousa's hair. "Yes, I know you must. Why weren't you told before?"

"I don't know. Shelokta obviously did not want me there. That is reason enough to go."

He began dressing slowly, his eyes thoughtful. Something which had not yet been made apparent was going on. Shelokta was too confident, too distant, too secretive.

Cara first saw the thin figure in their doorway. She smiled a welcome, and Sa-Miwok entered, crossing first to the bowl of venison stew which Ousa had left. He squatted down and began eating with three eager fingers, saying nothing.

"What brings you here, Sa-Miwok?" Ousa asked indulgently. The old shaman's head swiveled around on his birdlike neck.

"I have come for my sister, my student," Sa-Miwok said.

"Then my wife managed to obtain a horse for you?"

Sa-Miwok chuckled with enjoyment. "Yes, yes, I have the horse."

"What is it?" Cara asked, her voice lowered. She squatted beside Sa-Miwok, who motioned with his fingers for the bowl to be refilled. Cara smiled, glanced at Ousa, who was dressing in his best white elkskin clothes, and went to refill the bowl.

When she returned, Sa-Miwok said, "There is a council. I shall attend. It is my right as shaman. My apprentice shall accompany me. That too is my right."

"You wish me to attend the council meeting, Father Sa-Miwok?" Cara had to ask.

"Of course!" He paused and then grinned slyly. "Although I am certain that neither of you wishes to go so much as you would like to go to bed to laugh."

"What is the point in this, Sa-Miwok?" Ousa asked. "Why take my wife with us?"

"With me, not with you," Sa-Miwok replied. "Perhaps to let them see her. Perhaps to make sure she is informed. Perhaps to make them know that she is not a woman to be trifled with. Perhaps to irritate Shelokta the proud."

"Perhaps all of those," Ousa said, and Sa-Miwok laughed, his head bobbing on his neck.

"Perhaps."

The smile had passed from Ousa's lips. Now finished dressing, he stood watching the shaman methodically, leisurely finish his bowl of food.

"What is the purpose of this council meeting to which no one is invited?" Ousa asked the shaman.

If Sa-Miwok knew, he would not admit it. "We shall

see," he said, burping with satisfaction, "we shall see now, Ousa."

Outside, the victory celebration was in full swing; the drums played riotously as jubilant men danced before the huge bonfires, their shadows undulating across the fire-tinted earth. River Bird had been waiting outside, and he fell in beside them with a curious glance at Cara.

They walked toward the great oaks along the river, the sounds of the celebration, the brilliant glaring firelight fading as they entered deep shadows and followed the path toward the council hut.

They could see firelight in the windows of the hut, see a man, possibly Ta-sho-haka, go in, and then Ousa halted sharply, his arms flung out to halt the others.

River Bird grunted and whispered a curse. A man stood by the four strange horses, a blue cap perched on his head. He was short, slender—and white as snow.

"What is this!" Ousa demanded, walking forward. "What audacity is this?"

Cara looked worriedly at her husband, recognizing the anger in his eyes.

Sa-Miwok, amazingly, chuckled and touched Cara's arm. "Surprises all night," he said.

"Who are you!" Ousa walked deliberately to the white man, keeping his hand on the haft of the knife at his waist. The man turned to him, his forehead furrowing. He looked mildly surprised, but hardly fearful. He answered Ousa in a tongue which Cara did not know, shrugged, and turned his eyes away.

Ousa was ready to put hands on the man when the blanket hung across the entrance to the council lodge swung open and a voice called out, "Leave him, Ousa. He is our guest."

It was Stone Wolf who had spoken, and Ousa looked at his uncle in amazement.

"Yes," Stone Wolf said, "I know what you are thinking. But when men are our guests, it is wrong to lift a hand against them. Come inside and see more."

Ousa, turning his back deliberately on the white man, looked to River Bird to enlighten him. The big man only shrugged. "Let us enter."

Ousa went first, throwing the blanket aside to enter the smoky lodge, River Bird behind him, Sa-Miwok and Cara trailing. Cara stood blinking as they came into the council lodge. The smoke was from many pipes and from the fire which seemed not to warm the room nor illuminate it much.

There was light enough to see outrage on Shelokta's face, however, as he saw his brother advancing, as he looked beyond Ousa to see Cara standing in the doorway.

"What is this, Ousa!" Shelokta demanded, coming to his feet.

"What is *this*?" Ousa responded. His finger jabbed at the three white men who sat at the head of the blanket, flanking Shelokta. A wooden trunk rested in the center of the blanket.

"This is council!" Shelokta said loudly. Then, modulating his anger: "Not a war council, but a treaty council. A war chief has no business here. You were not invited."

"He has the right." The voice was Stone Wolf's. Shelokta's head spun toward his uncle, who was just now seating himself again beside Turtle Back.

"What right?"

It was Turtle Back who said, "He is the former clan chief. As I am. He was not retired in disgrace. He has the right."

Shelokta took a deep slow breath; they could see the taut fury in his face. The cords of his throat stood out rigidly. "That one has no right to be here." He pointed at River Bird, who turned and went immediately out. "And the woman! He brings his wife!"

"Ousa did not bring her, she is with me," Sa-Miwok said. "The woman is my associate shaman. *We* have the right to go where we please, Shelokta."

Sa-Miwok's voice was singsong, nearly merry, but there was an undertone of strength, perhaps even threat to it. Shelokta muttered something about "fools" and seated himself again, not glancing again at Ousa as he seated himself, nor at Sa-Miwok, who crouched down in the far corner where the shadows hid him.

Cara followed Sa-Miwok's example. It was a time while they smoked, passed the pipe to the three white men all of whom wore odd clothes of a similar cut, dark blue with metal buttons, and who sported white wigs which made Cara want to burst out laughing, but finally Shelokta began to speak.

"These men are our friends," he began. At that statement Ousa's head snapped up and he appeared on the verge of speaking, but he maintained his silence. "These men are

French. They have traveled a long way to the camp of the Kata Shawnee to see us, to offer us help, and to bring gifts.

"They come from a man named Duquesne, a mighty soldier sent from across the sea by the French chief to help us repulse the Englishmen, to chase the Englishmen back to their own land."

Cara noticed that at least one of the Frenchmen seemed to be able to follow Shelokta's speech. He nodded with satisfaction and whispered to the man on his left, the tall one with the white hair above his lip.

"What do *they* want?" Ousa asked angrily, no longer able to contain himself.

"They want to beat the English. Across the sea there is a great war between the French and English. There was a war farther east"—Shelokta's flat hand gestured eastward—"between the French and English. The French want only to crush the English. The French did not bring people to live on our land. They wish to trade, to make allies with us, to drive back the English."

"They have no settlers?" Stone Wolf asked.

"No. Only soldiers to protect their trading posts from the English." Shelokta leaned farther forward, his eyes glittering in the firelight. Cara wished she had listened more closely to her mother's descriptions of the French and English war along the Hudson, the war which had driven them from their land. She only knew that both sides had used the Iroquois, the Algonquin, that the Indian had gained nothing from the conflict in the end.

Ousa seemed to sense all of that without knowing what had gone before. His face was like carved wood. Except for the eyes, which were alive with anger.

"The French do not want our land. It is the English who do. The French wish to trade with us." Shelokta flipped open the lid of the trunk which rested on the floor before him. "This is what they bring as a peace offering, but there are many more trade goods. For two beaver pelts, this can be bought." Shelokta brought out a steel skinning knife with a bone handle. "For three beaver pelts or one fox pelt, this can be bought." He showed them a copper pot. "For one fox pelt." He held a string of brightly colored beads up for them to see. Each item, he threw into a pile to hold the eyes of the gathered chiefs. "This is not all."

Shelokta lifted a hand, and Ta-sho-haka, who had been standing near the door, went out. In a moment he was back, and in his arms were four muskets. There was a murmur of approval. All of them had seen the wonder of these weapons at close range. All of them had coveted a white weapon. The only one so far captured had not worked; perhaps it had been broken, perhaps they did not know how to use it properly.

Cara glanced at Ousa, who seemed fascinated despite himself. Sa-Miwok was squatting beside Cara, his arms wrapped around his legs, his birdlike head thrust far forward, his eyes glittering. What he thought was unfathomable.

"Come outside," Shelokta invited, snatching a weapon from Ta-sho-haka's arms. The Frenchmen exchanged a pleased glance. The Shawnee, excited by this gift that still inspired amazement, followed like pups at Shelokta's heels.

"Very bad," Sa-Miwok muttered. He said no more. Cara rose with the shaman, and they trooped outside to where Shelokta was preparing the musket. He used a powder horn to measure out a precise amount of black sand, inserted a patch of what seemed to be cloth and then a small metal ball like a smooth river stone. Each step was followed by the tamping of the material with a slender rod.

Shelokta seemed to be practiced in this, and Cara wondered where the Shawnee chief had learned. Finished, Shelokta smiled at those surrounding him. He poured a little powder into a pan at the side of the weapon, near the curved projection which stood out like a single ear.

Then, placing the weapon to his shoulder, he turned around in a slow circle, peering down the barrel. The Shawnee yipped and dodged aside. Shelokta trained the weapon on the Frenchmen, and they produced strained smiles.

Shelokta laughed, turned around, and fixed his eye on the trunk of a small birch tree. He hesitated a moment and then pulled the trigger. The musket exploded with a force which turned Shelokta half-around, and the tree was blown to splinters, sagging to the earth as the smoke filled the clearing and the roar of the gun echoed in their ears.

Shelokta held the gun high, laughing wildly, performing a brief dance. The Shawnee shouted with delight and crowded around to examine the weapon. Ousa turned away, looked once at Cara, and then shook his head.

"Now!" Shelokta yelled above the uproar. "One more gift. One more gift from our good friends the French."

Shelokta looked at the Frenchman who understood their tongue, and the man nodded. He said something to the man holding the horses. The soldier disappeared, and returned in a minute rolling a barrel along the ground. The Shawnee parted to let him pass through.

The barrel was set up on end, and Shelokta walked to it, his face shining with glory. With his war club he knocked the head off the cask, and as the puzzled faces around him watched, he dipped his drinking bowl into the liquid which filled the cask.

Then, picking out a splinter, Shelokta drank deeply from the bowl, handing it to the man beside him, Ta-sho-haka, who eyed it dubiously. He smelled it, and his nostrils filled with fire. His face wrinkled with repugnance and he tried to hand the bowl back to Shelokta. Shelokta, laughing, pushed it back. "There is magic in the liquid, my people. The French call it rum. If a man drinks of this, he becomes happy. He can fly, run across the skies, visit the spirits of his ancestors. Do you think I lie? Why are you looking at me like that, Stone Wolf? Drink deeply, drink deeply. This is a bond of alliance."

One of the Frenchmen, sensing the unease, stepped forward and dipped into the casket with a metal cup he had produced. He stepped back, threw back his head, and drained the cup, wiping his mouth with satisfaction when he was done. Shelokta patted him on the shoulder, borrowed the cup, and himself drank again.

Ta-sho-haka, feeling shamed, placed the bowl to his lips and drank. He gasped, holding his throat, but when Shelokta encouraged him again, he drank it until the bowl was empty.

Grinning, Ta-sho-haka handed the bowl to Tamava. The young warrior dipped into the cask and drank, nearly gagging once, it seemed. Cara stood at Sa-Miwok's side, watching, wondering.

"They drink their magic," she said.

"They drink their death," the shaman said under his breath.

Ousa did not take a drink, but even Turtle Back had decided to try it. By the time the cup had gone around twice, the men were flushed and happy, obviously enjoying themselves. Ta-sho-haka stood with his arm slung around the Frenchman's shoulder, a musket in his hand.

The Frenchman touched the musket, mimed something, and handed Ta-sho-haka a powder flask. With a little help he had the musket loaded in a few minutes, and pointing it skyward, Ta-sho-haka touched off the powder, sending a roar of delight through the crowd.

By the time Sa-Miwok touched Cara's shoulder and nodded his head, the sachems of the Kata Shawnee were dancing like children in front of the council hut. The French, minus their wigs, which three braves now wore, danced with them. At intervals a musket was discharged. There was a contest to see who could shoot the moon, and a bonfire blazed up precariously close to the dancers.

Cara turned with the shaman and walked slowly back upriver toward the village. They were still in the oaks when the sounds of the muskets began to be overshadowed by the distant thunder of an approaching storm. Lightning flashed, streaking the skies with quicksilver.

Sa-Miwok nodded, looking to the skies and then back toward the council hut. "It is fitting," he said. Then he touched Cara's shoulder in farewell and turned toward home. Cara watched him go, feeling the gusting wind at her back, the first few cold drops of rain sifting through the canopy of the oaks.

"What did he say?" Ousa wanted to know. He was dour, as dark as the onrushing storm clouds.

"He said that the omen was a fitting one," Cara replied.

Ousa looked to the closing skies, to the lightning-streaked clouds, and he nodded.

"Ousa, what will you do?"

"What can be done? Shelokta has allied us with the French. He has worked it all out well. Bringing guns and gifts, bringing this rum to fill their bellies and cloud their minds. There is nothing to be done. The debate has been won by rum."

"But you cannot accept that," Cara said. She knew her man too well to believe he would simply bow under. They remained in the oak grove, watching the rain slant down, dimpling the river.

"I do not. *All* of the whites must go. All of them. The French have not come to plow the land, but only to trade. Fine. The French give us gifts. The French wish us to kill the English. How long can this alliance last? How long before there are French settlers, how long before Shelokta is giving them our land?''

His face was turned up to the rain, glossed by it, lighted intermittently by the bursts of lightning across the slate-gray sky.

''He had it all planned long ago, didn't he?'' Cara asked. ''He only waited for the proper time. When you were wounded, he moved ahead with it. Ousa,'' she said, turning to face him, ''I know nothing of these things, of war and treaties, but I know it is bad. I know that these Frenchmen wish to use the Shawnee. I know that Shelokta is trying to accumulate wealth and power. If I can see this, won't the others?''

''They will not see it on this night,'' Ousa said bitterly. He looked again toward the council hut, hearing the discharge of another weapon. ''They are children, accepting gifts, and before the Frenchmen leave, they will have wampum treaties, promises, loyalty bought with gifts. And Shelokta knows it all—curse the man, my brother, my sachem!—he knows it all. He thinks he is clever, that he is using the French. He believes that if it must be, he can crush them as he crushed the valley settlers. Perhaps,'' Ousa said slowly, shaking his head, ''he is right . . . perhaps.''

''I don't believe it, nor do you,'' Cara said.

''No. I do not believe it.'' He looked at the skies, smiled weakly at Cara, and told her, ''The rain is slackening; let us go home.''

They walked from the trees and crossed the empty village. They had nearly reached their own lodge when Meniimo appeared. Ousa's aunt came toward them, and then from behind her back she produced a bundle of crow feathers.

''Meniimo?''

Meniimo held the feathers high, shaking them over Cara's head, chanting something Cara did not understand. Then, with a half-guilty glance at Ousa, she was gone, scurrying through the night, her heavy hips rolling as she ran.

Cara's first impulse was to laugh, but looking at Ousa's face, she saw that there was some import to this which she did not understand.

''Ousa?''

He stood looking after his aunt until the darkness and the rain swallowed her up.

''Ousa, what was that about?''

"Nothing," he said, his voice light without achieving sincerity. "An old woman's foolishness. That is all."

Later they lay in bed, the rain falling down gently to patter against the roof of the lodge, their furs around them, the soothing rumble of distant thunder punctuating the constant murmuring of the rain. It was a gentle time, warmth and love surrounding them, and yet Cara felt the tension in the air, a tension which had nothing do with the storm and the night.

"He will destroy us," Ousa said finally. His voice was a whisper. Cara opened one lazy eye and rested her hand on his bare chest. "He will destroy us. I know this."

"If you see it, others will. They will strip him of his rank."

"Will they? Greed lights their eyes. At a time when we should be building healthy alliances with our Shawnee brothers, with the Miami and Wyandot, standing firm, driving the invaders out of the valley, my brother flirts with other white men who wish us harm."

"Ousa," Cara said slowly, "have you ever thought that perhaps Shelokta is sincere? That he wishes to do what is right for the tribe?"

"Yes." His voice was quiet and distant. "He is my brother—I have given him the courtesy of considering that. But it is not true, Cara." Ousa's head turned toward hers. Lightly he kissed her lips and then her nose. "He is a madman, but a clever one. Sincerity is not among my brother's attributes."

"Then what can you do?"

"For now?" He shook his head slightly. "Nothing. I shall fight at his side as long as he *is* serving the interests of the tribe. As long as we are making war against the invaders. But there will come a time . . . Shelokta wants me at his side no more than I wish to be there, but this is no time to split the tribe. There are too many wolves in the forest."

They were silent then. Cara snuggled closer, sliding her knee up over Ousa's thigh, resting her head on his chest, clinging to him as the gentle rain fell and the night passed by.

They had a few days then, happy days when she fished with Ousa along the river, when they swam together in the seclusion of a sun-silvered pond, and lay in the new grass talking, sharing the quiet moments, the sunshine, all that was good in Manitou's universe.

Yet it lasted only a month. Then the war drums, impatient

with their idleness, began the ancient chant. A council of war was held, and Cara knew it was coming, knew he would go again, knew the wars would continue endlessly, and she began to hate it all. War, Shelokta, his French allies, the English—especially the English, who had come to tilt this happy land on its side and cause her joy to slide away.

She was sharp with Tak, injuring his pride when he happily announced, "The next battle, I shall ride with the men. Shelokta has promised it!"

"Has he also promised Kalthipsa an early death?" Cara had responded.

"There is too much white in you," Tak answered angrily, "or perhaps too much woman. I am Kispkotha, a warrior." He thumped his own chest. His eyes were serious, peering out of a moon face. "Without warriors, Cara, there is no peace. Not even a moment's peace. There is only destruction, the death of the tribe. And the tribe is *all*, it must be all or we are only lonely wanderers, easy prey for those who would destroy us."

"I'm sorry," Cara told him. "I truly am sorry. You brought your joy to me and I snubbed you. It is only . . ." She looked to where the war ponies were being painted, medicine bags knotted into their manes. "I do not want my husband to die, or anyone I love to be hurt. That," she said, smiling, placing her hands on Tak's heavy shoulders, "includes you, my brother."

"Too much woman," Tak said, but he laughed as he said it.

"Perhaps. . . . Tak," she asked as they walked toward the lodge where Ousa even now was preparing his war bag, "Meniimo has been watching me oddly. She no longer speaks to me, but I catch her peering at me from shadows, from behind trees. Once she shook a bundle of crow feathers at me. Have I offended her in some way?"

Tak licked his lips. "What did Ousa tell you?" His eyes lifted to Ousa's lodge.

"Ousa said she was a silly old woman."

"Yes, that is all she is."

"Still, she must have a reason."

Tak hesitated and shrugged massively. "Perhaps."

"Tak?" Cara stopped and took his hands, drawing him to one side, under the lightning-blackened sycamore tree which grew beside the lodge. Her eyes searched his. "I want to know."

He looked behind him, touched his tongue to his lips again, and said, "She thinks you are a witch. She was trying to cast a spell on you."

Cara's head was cocked to one side. She stood with a hand on her hip, half-smiling, so that her upper teeth, straight, white, uniform, showed. "A witch!" It was the last thing she had expected to hear. "But why, Tak?"

"Why?" Tak faltered. He was obviously uncomfortable.

"Tell me, Tak. You don't also think it, do you?"

"No." There was too much hesitation before he answered. "It's only that the women have heard it. They were told that it is so. It is just . . . your father was a white dog, some say a sorcerer. How, they ask, did you make Ousa fall in love with you? Ousa despises all whites, he mistrusts Mingoes. He was a sachem! He had a good marriage prepared for himself, with Tadona. That would have strengthened him; Tadona is high Peckuwe—of the priestly clan. Instead, he brings you to our camp. It is the act of a madman."

"Tak!"

"Wait." He held up a broad palm. "Then you are adopted by Sa-Miwok. How is this possible? You are a classless woman, a Mingoe. No woman has been shaman since my grandfather's grandfather's time. You have only just come, and yet you beguile Sa-Miwok into accepting you as his apprentice. Such a thing is not possible."

"Except for a witch."

"That is what they say."

"Tak," Cara said thoughtfully, "someone must have started this rumor among the women. Who could it have been?"

"I do not know, Cara."

"No? Where is Tadona, Tak?"

The youth seemed to cave in slightly. He managed to recover quickly. He beamed a smile. "They say she is gone."

"But is she?"

"I think . . ." His voice had dropped to an indistinct mutter. "I think perhaps not."

"That is what I think," Cara responded, her eyes losing their amiability. She managed a smile for Tak, however. "Thank you for telling me, Tak."

"I should not have." He shook his head worriedly. "After the other thing, they are afraid of your wrath."

"The other thing?" A slow, cold premonition was creeping up Cara's spine. She felt her heart rate quicken, felt her lungs empty out. She put a hand on Tak's shoulder. "What thing, Tak?"

"The other . . . I cannot tell you! I thought you knew."

"Knew what!"

"I should not say."

"I'm not a witch, I'm your sister! Tak!"

"Your parents, Cara. Your parents are dead. The Englishmen killed them because they were Indians, because they were sorcerers."

Tak continued to speak, but Cara did not hear him. Her feet were stones, her arms distant, wooden. Her eyes did not focus properly. She seemed unable to catch her breath. She turned toward the lodge, passing people whose faces were only blurs.

"Cara!" Ousa looked up from his packing to smile with delight. His smile was washed away by deep concern. "What is it?" He stood and went to her, wrapping his arms around her, finding her rigid, distant. "Cara? What has happened?"

"Did you know?" she asked, her lips barely moving. "Did you know, Ousa, and not tell me?" Her voice rose sharply.

"Cara." He shook her by the shoulders. "How can I answer you if I do not know what you are talking about?"

"I am talking about my parents being murdered!" she said with violence. She felt anger flooding her, replacing the cold unreality of moments ago. Anger, directionless, futile. Then it too was gone and she simply clung to Ousa, letting her tears wash down his chest.

"I did not know," he said, his hands moving comfortingly over her back. "I did not know. Who?" he asked suddenly, tilting her chin up to look into those tear-blurred eyes. "Who did it?"

"The English."

"But why? William is in their camp!"

"And I am in yours," Cara reminded him. She drew away, knuckling her eyes. "Two decent people who harmed no one ever. Who came here . . ."—her voice broke off into a sobbing, hysterical laugh—"looking for peace."

"Are you sure of this?" Ousa asked. "Sure that they are dead? Perhaps it is someone trying to hurt you."

"Do you think. . . ?" She lifted her eyes to his again. Faint, fleet hope flickered in her eyes and then was snuffed out. She did know. Somehow she did. She had known in the moment Tak spoke that it had happened; perhaps the knowledge had been lingering, suppressed in the back of her mind, in the farthest reaches of her soul.

"I will ask. I will look into it," Ousa promised. What he found out was very little. The Van der Veghes were dead. A passing Shawnee runner, a man named Kiima, had seen it. A party of Englishmen had set upon Van der Veghe and beat him to death. Then they had tried to fire the house and the woman, Crenna, trying to stop them, had been killed. Kiima swore it was the truth, and another warrior, the one called Fox Eyes, had passed recently on a hunting trip and seen the house in ashes. The fields were overgrown. The horses had been taken or broken free. No one lived in that valley now.

No one lived. And the others were going out to die. Cara watched them mount and ride out to war, the Ghost Society men together, Shelokta, proud and haughty at their head, a new French musket in his hands.

No one lived. The village became empty. The women looked at Cara as if she were a ghost now. Tak and Kalthipsa had gone hunting, full of high spirits as they anticipated the next battle, the one they would be allowed to join.

No one lived. Cara spoke to no one. She wandered the deep woods, watched the long sinuous river wind its way to the distant sea, imagined towns burning, men dying, imagined a small, sad heap of ashes in a distant valley, imagined a man and his wife lying cold in the earth.

Two entities made life bearable at that time, bearable when she was snubbed by the women, when old Meniimo would rush out of hidden places to shake bundles of crow feathers in her face, when her husband was riding to war, when her parents lay dead.

There was Sa-Miwok, who continued to teach her, who only smiled his vagrant, sly smile when Cara's attention wavered, when she became distant and morose. He was capable of comfort, that scrawny old tattooed man.

Second, there was the child. The man-child which grew stronger, which caused her belly to swell, who kicked and thumped and twisted inside of her, anxious to be out in the world, to run and play in the sunshine, to swim in the silver river, to laugh, to leap. He was her greatest consolation.

9

He was born when the stars were bright in a distant sky, when his father, Ousa, the warrior, was far to the north, fighting the men who would take his birthright, the land, from his hands, when the crickets sang along the riverbanks, when there was no woman to help her, when the great god Manitou declared that the time for birthing had come, that the fruit of Cara's womb was ripe.

He had the night wind for his birthing song; he was cleansed in the cold, dark river with only the crickets and the frogs to chant joyously to the god Manitou. His mother was there alone, panting as she walked heavily, painfully to the river's edge, feeling the night breeze cool the perspiration on her brow, feeling her insides, heavy and distorted, ache, her breasts swell with anticipation.

There she knelt and washed him until he cried out with the shock of it. There he was wrapped in a dry new blanket and lifted to her breast to take his first nourishment, to establish his first bond with Mother, to warm slowly as Cara's heart slowed its pacing. There she lay back, and with a blanket around them both, fell into a deep restorative sleep as the stars peered down and the cricket song continued in jubilant chorus.

His name was Kokii, and he was dark, sturdy of limb, sound of lung, with a mop of dark flyaway hair and black,

black eyes. He was a laughing baby who rode on his mother's back to the lodge of Sa-Miwok and played quietly while Cara learned to read the sticks, to tell the smoke, to understand the stars and the whisperings of the wind spirit.

He was his father's joy, but his father could not remain at home long. There was war and fire to the north. The British had brought their soldiers to the interior, and the war had changed. It was no longer a matter of driving out a few settlers; the red-coated army had come to fight. They were clumsy, stupid, lining their men up like trees in a forest to be cut down, but they were learning, and there were many of them.

It was at Point Pleasant, as the British called it, on the Ohio, that Ousa was wounded again. He lost two fingers and had a gash cut into his cheek by a musket ball which nearly killed him.

His wounds healed well, but he was forced to remain home for a time. He was there when Cara's first daughter was born. Her name was Shanna, a chubby, giggling baby who was spoiled by her father beyond endurance. Kokii was a doting older brother, trying futilely to cope with the girl's crawling exuberance, her odd appetite, her penchant for thrusting tiny fingers into noses and eyes.

The war ran on, and it seemed there would never be an end to it. There was a British general named Compton, who had raided Duquesne's fort on the northern lake at the place the French called Presq'isle with such deliberate savagery that the French began to call him Mad Compton.

Still Cara studied. She had her children—the second daughter, Lychma, was born the following spring, so pale and blue-eyed that she caused the witch tales to surface again—she had Sa-Miwok. They had cut her off from the tribe, but she suffered it. She had her man and her babies, her studies and the friendly voices of her spirits to comfort her.

With sadness she watched Lychma grow, an absolutely beautiful baby whose eyes insistently remained a sky blue. Dutch eyes peering with curiosity and sadness out of a dark face at a world which did not quite accept her.

The days were clear, but the nights chill. Always there was war talk. "So . . ." Cara watched the bonfire, the dancing men, noticing Tak and Kalthipsa, "it continues."

Ousa, beside her, his arm around her shoulders, nodded. "It continues. The English do not fight as we do. There is no respite, there is no truce at hunting time. Nothing stops them but winter snow. By then," Ousa said, squinting at the skies, "it will be too late to hunt and bring winter provisions home."

"What does Shelokta intend to do?"

"Shelokta intends to be fed by the French," Ousa said bitterly. He looked across the camp. All had changed. The men who danced now danced not with the joy the spirits put into the heart of a warrior, but wildly, their hearts lifted, their faces brightened by French rum. Shelokta had enriched the tribe, but much had been lost.

"The trail leads downward," Ousa said wearily.

Cara nodded. A warrior wearing a French coat lay drunk beside their lodge. The lodges of many people were gray with age, badly in need of repair.

"He has made them wealthy," Cara said. "Wealthy and yet as poor as any Indian has ever been. Where do the pots come from, the knives, the muskets?"

Ousa did not answer. At first their trade goods had come from pelts. Who had the time to trap these days? Now it was the land itself which was traded.

There had been violent exchanges between Ousa and Shelokta. Shelokta had signed away a million acres to the French. This was a debt, Shelokta said, which had to be paid.

"A debt for fools!" Ousa had exploded. "We pay for rum with our hunting land. It is *the land* which we are fighting for, Shelokta! Now we have given it away."

"To our friends." Shelokta's eyes had been rum-bright on that night. Looking around the council blanket, Ousa saw none who agreed with him. But then, they were all drunk. Stone Wolf lay comatose in the corner. Turtle Back, who continually interrupted to ask after his grandson, wavered as he tried to sit erectly.

"Our friends! They may as well be our enemies, Shelokta! They are slowly taking the land, slowly taking our minds, the strength of our young warriors' bodies."

"What would we do without them!" Shelokta rose now, still holding his cup of rum. "The British are here with soldiers and muskets! Where would we be if I had not signed an alliance with the French? Dead, all dead in our lodges."

Ousa looked slowly around him and said quietly, "We are all dead now, Shelokta. All dead."

There were no more councils. There was no more bargaining. "It is time," Ousa said. "We are no longer Kata Shawnee—those of us who are Ghost Society. It is time for us to make our own war."

"Against the French, the English, and Shelokta?" Cara asked.

"If we must."

"It is death!" Cara said.

"This is death," Ousa responded. Her eyes followed his own to the crackling bonfire where men danced madly, drinking rum as they staggered and chanted, their voices heavy and slurred. "To win is to lose. To defeat the English is to become slaves to the French."

Cara was silent. As they watched, Shelokta appeared, Tadona at his side—the woman was no longer kept hidden. Ousa's threats were ignored. Shelokta was sachem, was king, was Manitou.

Shelokta wore a French coat, tailored to fit him. He wore many beads of brass and of glass. He carried a musket in one hand, a cup of rum in the other. He had forty horses in the long valley behind his new lodge. He was a warrior chief, a fool, a destroyer of the Kata Shawnee.

Ousa turned away, unable to watch. Cara stood fascinated. He walked among them and was hailed, bowed to, clapped on the shoulder. Honored and admired, he moved through the crowd.

"The fool." The voice was Ousa's and the tone was so terribly bitter that Cara was startled. "No more, Shelokta. No more."

Ousa left her then, and she stood motionless, watching the mad celebration. With the dawn there would be another battle, more bloodletting, all in the cause of the French, the enemy. But they seemed not to see it, any of them. Tadona's eyes met those of Cara across the fire-bright clearing, and there was challenge, mockery, evil in those eyes.

She had done it. Tadona had blackened Cara's reputation, destroyed Ousa, gained Shelokta's confidence. Cara wondered who it was who guided the tribe's fortunes—that strutting sachem, Shelokta, or the tall, vicious woman who walked at his side.

When she could stand no more of it, Cara turned and walked slowly into the shadows of the great oaks. She found the stone called Dzhe Manitou's Thumb and followed the trail which wound into the hills beyond.

The night was still, the stars peaceful and bright, the wind whispering against her cheek. Sa-Miwok was not about. His lodge was empty and cold, smelling of dead fire. Cara had not expected him to be there; in a way, she was relieved that he was not.

She did not wish to speak, to be seen. Not by the human eyes of the shaman, Sa-Miwok. She had come to this place where the spirits hovered to speak to them, to learn, to know, to inquire. Outside, the world was in turmoil. The storm which was seeping toward the Kata Shawnee was still an empty whirlwind, but in time it would gather force, in time it would be the wind of destruction, in time it would remove the Shawnee from the land, and there would be not a trace left of them except in the faulty dry memory of their enemies.

This Cara knew. What she did not know was what must be done, how to hold these forces at bay, how to preserve her way of life, to hold back the wall of destruction which advanced so mercilessly. Must Ousa die, must the children be torn apart by the Wind, made slaves of the white man? Those were her questions, questions without answers unless the spirits could guide her, unless the breath of Manitou could carry a single inspiring word to her. Ousa spoke strongly, and his body, his will, was strong. But he hadn't the real strength needed to break Shelokta's grip on the tribal throat. This too she knew, although she would never say that to Ousa, who was proud, who was angry and defiant and needed support, not criticism, no matter how well meant.

Cara stripped off her dress and threw it to one side. She lit the lantern, which was a wick of hemp in bear fat. It cast a dim, wavering light around the interior of the shaman's hut. A skull winked at her from its niche across the room—the skull of the last truly magic shaman, the giant Sha-no-Halsa, who lived in the Grandfather times. He who had eaten bannock with Manitou, he who had soared above the earth on the back of the Eagle Manitou, he who had bested the great beasts, Talking Heads, Stone Giants, those who had come to devour the Kata Shawnee.

Cara cast the sticks and she read them. There were five sticks. Each red on two sides, white on the others—bone and blood, spirit and flesh. The reading was favorable. The sticks read: *It is the time*.

Sitting back on her heels, Cara closed her eyes. Her hands rested on her bare thighs. Her hair, long and loose, lay draped across her shoulders; the flickering candle burned low. She was not practiced in such things, but her need was so great that she hoped the spirits would talk to her. *It is the time.*

The time to destroy the evil of Shelokta, the cunning of Tadona, the machinations of the French, the grasping greed of the English.

Against them stood Ousa, the Ghost Society, and a young woman.

Cara was silent, expectant, calm. There was suddenly a warmth within her breast, like an explosion of liquid pleasure spreading through her veins. It washed over her, rippled along her skin; her mouth went slack, her eyes rolled back beneath closed lids; her eyelids fluttered, her skin seemed to be alive with a thousand pinpricks. A faint, breathy exhalation escaped her lips.

The room seemed to expand and contract; a breath of wind unlike any wind Cara had felt brushed against her cheek. The air filled with streamers of light. She could see the candle flame wavering, see a ribbon of light come from it, purple edged with pale yellow. It seemed to brush her cheek, to wind upon itself, to form a maze, a net of color and texture.

She seemed to rise, to be wrapped in peaceful arms, to be lost in a velvety net, a muzzy, deep length of cloth which undulated, shutting out the candlelight, becoming a thousand tentacles scraping at her mind, demanding that she . . . *what*? Live, die, rush into combat, watch her heart be torn from her, swim vast jewellike seas, take to dark wings and soar. . . .

She knew. She smiled in peaceful meditation. She knew and she sat motionless against the faded blanket in the hut of Sa-Miwok. She knew and she smiled, looking into the black, unblinking eyes of the ancient shaman, Sha-no-Halsa. It was what must be done. There was no promise that it would be enough. But it must be.

Cara felt no elation; but there was a certainty, a knowledge that she was right, that she had been given strength enough; that we all have been given strength enough to attempt what must be done, if only we will.

She found herself outside the hut, not knowing how she had gotten there. The stars were the same; the pale silver disk of the moon beyond the oaks was as it had been. The river ran; but it was different. Different because she was a woman—she had been a girl too long, a girl who watched life and prayed that it would change when it would not, not without her doing what she could, not without her being what she could be, not without her finding strength and bringing that strength to the cause which was right.

She looked down at herself, laughed as she realized she was still naked in the night, and she stretched her arms toward the heavens, an unspoken prayer rising from her thoughts.

Later, after dressing, putting out the candle, placing the sticks back into the clay pot where Sa-Miwok kept them, she walked the winding path homeward.

It is so simple—always so simple, she thought. To be what you are is all that is required. That and the knowledge that what you do is just.

Nothing could be simpler; but the gap between thought and execution is vast. It must be bridged; it must be done.

She stood in the shadows, watching the flame-lit dancers continue the war celebration. With sorrow she watched them, seeing them as children celebrating their own end, the end of the time of the Shawnee.

Tak stumbled across the clearing, wearing his warrior's feather proudly. In his hand was a pot of rum. Tak had taken to the stuff too readily. His eyes were no longer alert, never bright, but only overbright in the evenings when he had his fill of the rum.

Tak reached a small oak just outside the circle of light, and leaning against it, he was sick. Cara felt ill as well. A fine young man, a brave one, one with a deeply ingrained sense of humor, an innocent turned into this stumbling wretch by his brother Shelokta.

And still the man would stand up in council and proclaim his love of his people, still he would presume to lead them, and they—like children—would follow him to the death.

Unless someone intervened.

Who was there? Ousa had tried, but they would not listen. His Ghost Society was a small organization. There were, it seemed, many more who preferred Shelokta's rum and guns, beads and finery, to Ousa's ideals.

Cara slipped into the lodge and undressed in the darkness. Approaching the bed, she saw that the baby, Lychma, was awake. Her eyes peered up at Cara, but she did not make a sound. Cara lay down, moving next to Ousa, who slept peacefully. Lychma crawled up on her, and Cara gave the baby a kiss. Shanna slept between Cara and Ousa; Kokii lay on the other side in his father's arms.

The night was peaceful and warm; they were surrounded by love. If there were only no world outside the lodge—but the drums thumped on, voices were raised in wild celebration. And beyond the firelight, somewhere in the darkness, destruction waited.

She told Ousa about it at dawn when they alone were awake. The babies slept in a contented jumble.

"You can't mean it!" was Ousa's reaction.

"The sticks said: *It is time*."

Ousa nodded, still frowning. A man does not ignore the omens and signs. "Still, Cara, it seems dangerous."

"But if it works?"

"If it did work," Ousa said, running his fingers through his hair, "it would be very good indeed. Logic has never swayed them, certainly. Maybe . . ." His voice and thoughts drifted away.

"Well?" she asked brightly, bending to peer up into her husband's worried eyes.

He laughed. "I hate tricks and deception, but it may be what we need. We have to loose this hold Shelokta has on the warriors, that is certain. If you think it might work, maybe it is indeed time."

"They have given me the name; let me live up to it."

"I hate it," Ousa said, "in that it blackens you."

"Does it? They have told me I am a witch—very well, let them have their witch. Let them have the magic they wish. They know I am shaman, they believe I am probably a witch. Let us use their beliefs."

"How would it be done?" Ousa asked dubiously. He was fascinated but unconvinced.

"With a little flash and a little thunder, but mostly by speaking, I hope. All I want to do, Ousa, is to get their attention long enough for them to be told the truth. You have told them time and again, but your words are shed like water. As you say, reason does not appeal to them. So, let them have their witch. We have nothing to lose."

"If you are sure," Ousa said, putting his arms around Cara's waist. "If the signs were right, if the spirits will it—who am I to speak against it? But you must be careful, Cara, promise that."

"Of course." She smiled with a confidence she did not

feel. The gesture seemed futile in a way. To lure the men from Shelokta would not be simple. What caused her to believe she could do it? Still, it must be tried, and so she would try it, for Ousa, for the tribe. For her people.

They planned it for the night of the full moon, two nights away. Cara made her preparations and stayed out of sight in the lodge. Ousa spoke to the Ghost Society men, and in a secret meeting they pledged their support.

Shelokta began to send out small raiding parties without official councils of war. They went out drunk and returned drunk, nearly falling from their horses. Ousa had to turn away in disgust. What sort of war was this? What sort of warriors? Where was the honor, the dignity of the Kispkotha?

Shelokta paraded around in silk jackets, wearing red and yellow plumes in his hair. He wore a pair of white shoes with buckles on them until they hurt his feet so badly he could not walk in them any longer. He had taken to carrying pistols with him—the first any of them had seen. He would pull them from the waistband of his leggings and discharge them at the slightest excuse.

The French came frequently, and many payments passed between the whites and Shelokta. Shelokta's wealth was becoming legend.

The moon seemed to rise slowly on the second night. It roused itself lethargically, first painting a thin, promising ribbon of light on the narrow bands of sheer clouds which clung to the eastern horizon. Finally, hesitantly, it peered over the skyline and rose lazily, flattened at one end, into the cool skies, lighting the world.

The Shawnee camp was flooded with its pale orange light. The trees stood in stark relief against the background of moonlight. There was no celebration on this night, no bonfire burned in the clearing, and the sudden activity was made more dramatic by the darkness and silence which had held the camp.

The drums came first. Dozens of them, beating an unfamiliar cadence which approached the war drumming, lifting the heart to a swift responsive rhythm, but did not quite reach the proper, familiar stridence.

Tak, who had been sleeping on his side beneath the sycamore, sat up, heavy with drink, to rub his eyes and peer at the intruders. Ghost Society men came forward, naked but for breechclouts. They wore the familiar moon and skull paint.

Some had their legs outlined with white, representing the bones of a skeleton. They thumped the muffled drums with sticks muted with rabbit fur.

Across the clearing, men and women emerged from their lodges, squinting into the moonlight, peering at the dark, slowly marching Ghost Society men.

"What is this? A religious ceremony?" the warrior Tamava asked.

Tak could only shrug. He got heavily to his feet, watching as the Ghost Society men moved slowly into the clearing, forming a circle. The drums continued their strange, hypnotic beat, and Tak found that the sound jarred his rum-saturated brain. He stared dumbly at the Ghost Society, wondering what was happening.

He saw her suddenly, and he stepped back involuntarily, astonished. He knew it for Cara—it had to be Cara, and yet it was not, could not have been.

She wore a feathered cape unlike any Tak had ever seen, and her face was painted. Half red, half black; one black eye peered out from the red side of her face, seeming to fix Tak with an accusing glare. Protruding white fangs had been painted around her mouth. Her arms were painted with snake symbols; around her ankles and wrists were circlets of fur and bone.

She moved in time to the drumming, her head thrown back, her feet gliding across the earth; and then, to Tak's astonishment, there was an explosion beside Cara. White smoke rose into the air, and then black smoke, but there was no gun at hand, and the smoke did not smell like gunpowder.

Tak walked slowly forward himself, drawn by the drumming, the magnetism of the apparition. From the corner of his eye he saw Shelokta come rushing into the clearing, bare-chested, his face suffused with anger, but Tak paid no attention to his brother.

It was the woman who held his attention, the woman and the drums, slow, methodical, compelling. The faces of the Ghost Society dancers, their features blackened with paint, drifted past him eerily, and Tak felt his muscles tense, felt his spine go cold as if it were made of ice. He did not like this; and yet he was drawn to it. He glanced nervously around the perimeter of the clearing, expecting . . . what? They were summoning some spirit, some ghost or demon, some Force which Tak did not understand.

Again there was a flash of light, a puff of smoke, and Tak turned his face away, burying his head in his hands. When he looked back, his heart slowing, he realized he was in a crowd. Others shouldered against him, asking him questions he could not understand. A woman screamed. The Ghost Society dancers moved on, their shadows bent and wavering. The moon was a huge orange globe backlighting the strange procession.

Suddenly it stopped.

It stopped and Tak felt as if his feet had been pulled out from under him, felt that he would tumble forward, fall on his face. Was it the rum? Or was there even now a spirit force weaving its way through the throng of Kata Shawnee, touching them with icy fingers, probing their hearts?

"Kata! Kata Shawnee. People of the forest, Manitou's Children, sturdy warriors, lost ones!"

The voice was Cara's—or it came from the mouth of the woman Tak took to be Cara. The words were powerful, strident, accusing.

"You are marked by sin! You are betraying yourselves, your tribe, your Manitou!"

There was a strange rumbling chorus of assent, which Tak finally realized was coming from the throats of the Ghost Society men.

Cara was standing on something, had to be, since she towered over the warriors, but Tak could remember nothing having been there for her to perch on. He didn't have time to ponder things like that. Cara's speech continued, her voice strong, authoritative.

"You are a shame! You have taken an enemy to your hearts. You have taken the poisoned water from his well and bloated your bellies with it, contaminated your minds and your souls. You will not listen to the truth when it is spoken. You care only for beads and rum, for guns. Where is your pride! There is no man," she said, bending slightly forward, spacing her words for emphasis, "who can live without honor, without the dignity which is his birthright. Dignity! That which places you above the beast, who thinks only of his own gratification. Who is a creature of appetite. You have minds but do not use them; you have souls but you bury them beneath layers of filth, saying, 'I am satisfied, my belly is full, my mind is stunned with poison waters!' Men!" Tak had never heard the word spoken so contemptuously. It caused him to turn his eyes downward.

"You are not men any longer. You are ceremony dolls with which the French play their games."

"And who are you!" a voice demanded. To Tak it was incredible that anyone could have interrupted the woman. Her voice held him in its sway; and he was not alone. Glancing around him, he saw shamefaced warriors, reflective eyes, men suddenly sobered.

Cara answered the intrusive voice. "I am the one who has been sent, I am the one who comes before destruction, I am the eyes of Manitou, I am the voice of the wind, I am the fire, the truth, the one called Witch who knows the spirits, the shaman who speaks with the sad-eyed Manitou, she who sees you, Shelokta! She who knows you."

There was a press of bodies against Tak's back; he hardly noticed. Someone suddenly called out fervently: "Lead us!"

The musket shot rang out, explosive and fierce. Tak saw the muzzle flash, saw Cara thrown backward as if a great hand had yanked her away, saw the Ghost Society men milling in confusion, heard Ousa's animal roar.

"There is magic! There is witchery!" the voice screamed.

Tadona stood, musket in hand, staring haughtily at them. She was still undressed, having risen from her bed to witness this. She stood, lithe and confident, supercilious, beautiful, her eyes challenging them, her head thrown slightly back, her teeth showing in amusement.

"There is magic. Here!" She held the musket overhead and threw the weapon into the crowd of warriors, striking one man in the head with the butt.

"There!" Tadona, like some naked avenging spirit, pointed toward where Cara lay, where the Ghost Society men huddled over her. "There is the Mingoe's magic. There," she said, pointing at the musket, "is that of Shelokta. Judge which is stronger."

Then she turned and sedately walked away. Tak's head swiveled at the clamor before him. Men were thrown aside, and Tak saw Ousa clawing his way past the warriors, his eyes seething with fury.

"Where is she! Where is she!"

But Tadona was gone. There was nothing left but the odd after-silence. The moon beamed down, golden now and placid. Cara lay sprawled against the earth. The warriors were drifting away. And Shelokta stood, hands on hips, his lip curled back, his eyes on Ousa, who could only stand staring into the forest beyond the camp. He turned, kicking angrily at the musket which lay on the ground. Then Tak watched as his brother returned to where Cara lay.

He crouched, scooped her up in his arms, and walked through the subdued crowd to his lodge. Tak followed, feeling suddenly sober, suddenly guilty.

Ousa's arms supported her. Cara knew something had happened, but what? Had Manitou struck her down for daring to use his authority? She opened her eyes and saw Ousa's strained face, saw the stars high overhead, the pale face of the moon. She thought she spoke, thought Ousa smiled and murmured something comforting, but she was not sure of that.

There was a terrible fiery pain in her chest. The stars blurred, spun madly and merged before they exploded in a burst of color and sound.

When she again opened her eyes, the familiar face of Sa-Miwok was hovering over hers. He had taken her dress off and was applying something to her shoulder.

"Hurt?" he asked with a smile.

She thought she answered him. Ousa stood in the background, his face merging with the shadows and then becoming starkly clear. He held the two girls, and Kokii was tugging impatiently at his leggings. He still wore his paint, although it was smeared badly.

"Is she . . . ?" Ousa asked, although his voice was distant, as if it came through a long hollow log. She saw Sa-Miwok, rising on distorted limbs, his hands bony and gnarled, nod.

". . . Young and sturdy. But such foolishness." Sa-Miwok laughed. His voice was a distant crackling, like flames in the forest. Ousa was not smiling at all.

Her shoulder was on fire. Someone had placed heavy stones on her chest, tring to stifle her heart's beating. Something was wrong, for it was light outside, and she knew very well it should be dark.

Ousa was sitting beside her; the children were gone. He held her hand and there was sadness in his eyes. She reached over with her other hand and patted his wrist. At that he brightened.

"What happened?" she managed to ask, although her mouth felt dry and stiff.

"Tadona shot you."

"Such magic," she said, laughing briefly, although it hurt. "Such a witch! They will not believe that of me again." She squeezed Ousa's hand and told him, "I'm sorry, my husband. It was a failure."

"Don't apologize to me, Cara, for doing what was noble and right." He bent his head and kissed her. "Don't apologize to me for anything. You have never done a wrong thing. You are beautiful and brave"—he stroked her hair and smiled—"and magnificent. For a witch."

Cara was slow in healing. Once the fever came over her and Sa-Miwok had to burn herbs and dance to chase the demons away. Tak came to see her as she was sitting up in bed, propped up on a bundle of furs, Lychma crawling over her legs.

"Cara?"

"Come in, Tak. I am pleased to see you. What is it?" she asked, her eyes narrowing, noticing that he had come for a purpose other than to visit the sick.

His eyes shifted about the room uneasily. Finally, squatting near Cara without looking at her, he said, "I have come to tell you that I am Ghost Society."

"Tak!" Cara said with delight, "it is right. I am happy for you and for Ousa."

"Yes." Tak smiled weakly. Lychma was near him, and he picked her up, sitting the baby on his knee. He looked into her smiling blue eyes with wonder. "It was your speech which brought me to myself, Cara," he went on. "Wait—I know it sounds foolish. Others mock you now, mock the Ghost Society. When I saw you lying on the ground, when I knew you had done this for Ousa, for us, I saw myself as well. Saw what I had become."

"And so, we are together again, a family."

"Without Kalthipsa, I'm afraid," Tak said.

"He will come around."

"Perhaps." He sighed and placed Lychma on the floor. "Tadona is gone, this time for good. She knows what Ousa will do if he sees her."

"If only we could drive Shelokta off so easily."

"I'd gladly let him shoot me if he would go," Tak said, not with venom, but with humor. Tak was not a man to become angry often, and it was difficult for his cheerful disposition to support anger for long.

When he was gone, Cara, hugging the baby, who slept now, tiny fists clenched, eyelids fluttering, stared at the roof of the lodge. At least, she thought, I have accomplished that much. One man weaned from Shelokta. One brother. Her shoulder ached and she plunged into the solace of sleep, suffering through a series of disconnected, vague dreams.

She was awakened by Ousa, grim-faced, tense. He held his war bag in his hand. She stretched out her arms toward him, yawning sleepily. Then she became aware of his mood. She sat up too rapidly, bringing a jolt of pain to her shoulder. "What is it?"

"Trouble. The English."

"Attacking!" That was unthinkable, or had been. The war had kept the settlers on the defensive, with the Shawnee able to raid and withdraw as they pleased.

Ousa nodded a response. "English soldiers. I don't know which way they're moving, but they were seen ten miles east, across the river. The settlers, it seems, have grown tired of us." The smile was rueful, the eyes showing no amusement. "I don't think they can find our camp," Ousa said, trying to reassure Cara. "Shelokta has been told to attack, and so he will."

Cara nodded her comprehension. Attacking armed soldiers was a new experience for Kata Shawnee. Heretofore it had been the quick raids, the swift withdrawal, the burning settlers' houses writing smoky messages of warning against the sky.

Ousa was ready now, and he kissed her only once before, shouldering his bag, he turned to go. Cara saw briefly, through the open doorway, the gathered men. There seemed to be confusion in the clamor. The blanket closed again, and she was left in dark silence, feeling useless and alone and more than a little frightened.

The Creek woman entered the lodge and busied herself straightening Cara's bed, preparing the noon meal. Her name was Dava, and she was a distant cousin of Ousa's. She was a pleasant, squat woman with high-arched eyebrows and pouting, heavy lips. "The men," Dava said, "they have battle shirts."

"Yes, Dava," Cara said, repressing a smile.

The Creek, distantly related to the Shawnee, spoke a dialect which struck the Kata ear pleasantly, although Dava's idioms were difficult to fathom at times.

Dava scooped up Shanna and placed her on her broad hip as if she were the child's mother, and Shanna did not object in the least. She rode about on the Creek woman's hip, laughing from time to time. Cara laid her head back, feeling weary again, angry with her body, which gave her so little support these days. Yet her wound, despite its nagging insistence, did not occupy her mind any more than the soft humming of the Creek woman, which seemed equally distant and unimportant just now.

Her thoughts traveled with Ousa, and she wished, not for the first time, that she could ride with him, sleep out nights with him, be not torn away from him each time the war drums sounded . . . and it seemed they sounded with insistent frequency these days.

Despite Shelokta's strutting and boasting, Cara knew, they all knew, that they had lost men, and many of them these last months. Cara could only wait, could only sleep, hoping that the dreams which taunted her were the worst of it, that she would not awake to find her nightmares had become reality.

"One mile, maybe less." The Dutchman, his hair blowing in the wind, jabbed a thumb back across his shoulder and steadied his sidestepping roan horse.

"Ousa?" the young lieutenant asked. Excitement lighted his eyes. There was a five-hundred-pound reward for the capture of or for the scalp of Ousa, the Kata Shawnee war chief. There was that, and, Lieutenant Hightower reflected, the certainty of promotion.

It was the man before him who had given a name to the Shawnee leader, who had condemned him. Van der Veghe knew the Shawnee well—his sister was married to Ousa, the butcher who commanded the tribe called Kata Shawnee, and William Van der Veghe hated the man with a savagery. Ousa had killed his mother and father.

"I didn't see Ousa," Van der Veghe said.

Hightower knew that Van der Veghe regretted that; and he wondered what would happen when he finally did. Van der Veghe was a cool one, yet lurking in his eyes was an almost animal light, a hatred so deep that Van der Veghe was careful not to let it show.

Hightower looked back at his scarlet-coated, white-trousered company and then returned his gaze to Van der Veghe. "What do you recommend?"

"Recommend?" William Van der Veghe seemed ready to burst into laughter. "Attack, Lieutenant, always attack. These people have had their way long enough. They make war with impunity, knowing that the settlers don't dare leave their homes to mount an assault. We have no such tethers."

Van der Veghe's expression was horrible, wolfish. Hightower looked to his sergeant major, a big-shouldered Welshman named Reid. The sergeant major's face was expressionless behind a huge sand-colored mustache.

"It's a trap out there," Hightower said almost to himself. He looked at the oak forest, rife with holly, at the long, cloud-shaded riverbed. "This isn't my kind of fighting, Van der Veghe. Dammit, it scares me!"

"Scares me too, sir. What scares me more is the idea that the Shawnee can run back here after slaughtering our people and know we won't come after them. It builds confidence in them, breeds contempt."

"Can we flank the Shawnee?" Hightower wanted to know. The Indians were mostly mounted; his men were infantry. They had mobility, a knowledge of the terrain, and were little inferior in terms of weaponry. Hightower thought little of this plan of Compton's—pursuing the Shawnee to their stronghold. Van der Veghe himself had spoken against it, but now, so near that he could sense the presence of the Shawnee, he seemed overcome by battle lust. The Dutchman actually twitched with animal excitement.

"We can strike their village," Van der Veghe answered finally. "They've circled wide, wanting to flank *us*. They've left their home ground open."

Hightower considered it uncertainly. Van der Veghe was staring at him with excitement lighting his eyes. The lieutenant supposed he might be as anxious if the Indians had killed his own parents; yet he was not willing to risk the company under his command, his career, on Van der Veghe's suggestions.

"We'll stand in the woods and meet them if they come to us. If they run, well and good. They'll at least know we are here."

William didn't like the scheme. He doubted the Shawnee would engage them on those terms. It was not the Indian way. He would have preferred to strike at the Kata village, burn the lodges and destroy the food stores, cut off the Shawnee and force them to fight. But the British had not taken him on to make command decisions. He acquiesced.

"There's a hillrise yonder, wooded, but with a good field of fire, sir." William indicated the spot he had in mind. "If they want us, they'll find us, but we'll have fair cover."

Hightower nodded agreement and passed the order to his sergeant major. The company, their faces pale and uneasy, marched forward, taking positions on the wooded hillrise. Hightower, forming ranks with whispered commands, noticed that his guide was absent, and he cursed slowly.

"Reid!" the lieutenant hissed.

"Sir?"

"The guide. Van der Veghe. Where in hell is he?"

The sergeant major had no answer. The Dutchman was unpredictable, as they had been warned. He was a savage himself, or so Compton believed. Now he was gone, leaving the young lieutenant perched on this godforsaken hill in this godforsaken wilderness with an approaching war party working its slow way toward them.

Hightower cursed again, eyed his company, his first command, and slapping his hand angrily against his thigh, turned again southward, peering into the smoky distances, where the low fog wove its way through the oak and maple forest, where the Kata Shawnee, silent as the fog, crept toward his position.

"Load," he said in as quiet a command as has ever been given in the British army.

It was still. The fog was settling. The tops of the trees were cut off by the curling smokelike wraiths along the river bottom. The river itself, narrow and gray between extended sandy banks, trickled past.

William held his position behind the skinned oak log for long minutes, listening. Water dripped from the trees around him and spattered against the earth. A lone crow drifted, cawing, through the forest, eyes bright.

Nothing else moved, although there must have been a hundred Kata Shawnee out there.

William crept forward, moving up the hillslope opposite, scrambling through the tangle of fog-damp brush. He knew the Shawnee were near, perhaps within a few hundred yards of his position, but they would not be expecting a lone man, would not be alert to his presence.

The British, as they had already discovered, were given to mass formations, to defensive wilderness fighting. The Shawnee had grown careless.

William saw the figure—dark gray against the lighter gray of the fog—and he pressed himself to the earth, his cheek against the damp grass. He peered through the network of runners the tangled blackberry vine spread before his eyes, seeing the Shawnee—this one armed with bow and arrows—creep downslope toward the ravine.

Van der Veghe did not move. He was not the one.

His heart felt amazingly light; he was at ease in the wilderness, curiously unafraid of death, which hovered over every man in this valley. His mind was fixed on his single purpose—Ousa.

He was here, must be, and it was Ousa that William Van der Veghe sought, Ousa that he would find, kill. He would rip his heart from his chest, this bastard Shawnee who had seduced his sister, murdered his parents while they were under the protection of the wampum.

He had attempted to disguise his warriors as white men, but the attempt was clumsy. It only revealed the duplicity of the man Ousa. There were others who hunted the Shawnee warlord now, seeking the five-hundred-pound reward the colonial governor was offering for Ousa's capture or scalp.

But the others were chasing ghosts. Men unaccustomed to the wilds, they would fail; perhaps they wished to fail—to face Ousa was to face death. He was a fighting man; William would give him that. He was also a devil.

A musket shot sounded behind him, from the hillrise. An undisciplined British soldier? A sniping Shawnee? It creased the silence of the fog-shrouded day with a note of immediacy. Someone would be dying. Perhaps many.

William crept forward again, staying on his belly. The grass was heavy and damp. He froze in position again. A dozen Shawnee, summoned by the musket shot, were racing down the hillslope, swift as deer, silent as the wind. William watched them go past his place of concealment. The man he wanted was not there.

Now the battle had burst into life. A volley of twenty muskets sounded loudly, the rolling echo sweeping across the valley. Answering scattered shots from Shawnee guns popped intermittently, nearer to William.

He was creeping forward again, eyes alert, hands drawing

him upward, his right clenching the bow he still preferred over the musket for its silence, reliability, and quickness. If a musket took a competent soldier a full minute to reload, William could fit a second arrow within moments after having fired his first.

William stopped suddenly, his heart pumping furiously, his eyes alert and cold, his muscles bunched. The warrior had come from out of the forest and was now easing down the slope. He seemed to be alone, vulnerable. It was Ousa.

William slid his bow into a comfortable position before him, changed his mind, placed the bow aside, and unsheathed his knife. Slipping back into the deeper brush, moving cautiously so that there was not the faintest whisper of sound, he moved down the slope himself toward the point where two water-cut gullies intersected.

Concealing himself, he waited, the knife in his hand gripped so tightly that his knuckles were an ivory white. Ousa was moving cautiously down the slope, almost as if he expected something to happen, yet William was sure he could not have been seen, could not have been heard. There was a moment's gap in the fog, and sunlight splashed itself across the green of the hillside. It lasted only a heartbeat, and then the gray cat's paws of fog reached toward them again, shutting out the sun, bringing the damp, comforting darkness.

William slowly raised himself to a crouch, his free hand on the earth before him, his knife in front of his chest. He peered through the fog-drenched hair which hung in his eyes. He could feel his lips draw back in an involuntary grimace, feel the surging of his blood, the joy which filled his brain.

One more step. The shadowy figure moved nearer, becoming distinct from the surrounding gray. A musket was fired distantly. The crow still circled, complaining loudly.

William sprang from the gully. He hit Ousa full tilt, his shoulder burying itself in the Shawnee's chest. He raised his knife to strike, but Ousa blocked the downward stroke with his forearm, kicked out, and then they were rolling into the gully in a tangle of limbs, Ousa's dark eyes flickering with recognition, William breathing curses into the Shawnee's ear.

They rolled through space for a fragment of a spinning second and then thudded to the sodden earth. William gasped, felt his knife wrenched from his hand, felt the jagged pain of broken bone in his wrist.

Ousa, catlike, deadly, had landed on top of him and now had his hands on William's throat.

"William, stop it! There is no need—" Ousa's voice broke off painfully. William had gripped two of his fingers and was prying them back. Ousa had to give way, and he tried to come to his feet to fend off the savage attack.

William, still flat on his back, kicked out with both feet, catching Ousa painfully on the knee, and the Indian staggered and fell. He rolled farther down the gully and came up roughly against a jumble of boulders, William pursuing him all the way, his wet yellow hair flying, his blue eyes alive with hatred.

The Dutchman had scooped up a rock somewhere, and he intended to bash in Ousa's head with it. Ousa rolled, heard rock click against rock, spun and kicked out himself, trying for William's groin.

Then the two men were locked together, Ousa's hands on William's wrists, their chests pressed together, their faces so close that Ousa could feel William's breath on his cheek. The fog swirled past; the distant muskets barked intermittently.

"William! What is this? Stop. I am your brother!"

"Brother!" William's shout was hoarse, strained, mocking. There was a ferocity in his blue eyes that Ousa had never seen in a human being. The man had a broken wrist, and the pressure Ousa was applying to the arm should have been enough to send him to his knees in anguish, but he fought on madly, kicking, clawing. He panted over and over, "You killed them! You killed them!"

The man was out of his senses, and he fought with the fury of the insane. Ousa was fully conscious of the circumstances, however. Not only did he have this madman to contend with, but there was a battle going on. At any moment a British soldier could come to William's rescue. The possibility was also strong that the Shawnee, rushing to the battle site, would find William and kill him before Ousa could stop it.

The fight had to be ended before one of them died. Ousa hooked his foot behind William's heel and pushed hard, his hands against William's chest. The Dutchman went down, and Ousa, falling on him, clubbed him with the side of his fist. Blood streamed from William's mouth, but none of the fight had gone out of him.

Regretfully Ousa hit him again, until William's head sagged

back against the sodden earth. Ousa, panting, picked William up by his shirtfront and threw him back.

From the corner of his eye he saw the men approaching through the fog, and he pressed his body beside William's, hoping that the white man would not cry out. He was semiconscious now, his head rolling from side to side. Ousa clamped his hand over William's mouth and watched as the shadowy figures above them slipped by. Shawnee. Four of them, and now Ousa saw that William was alert, that his eyes followed the stalking warriors and then returned questioningly to Ousa's face.

Long minutes later Ousa removed his hand, gesturing for William to remain still, quiet. There were others out there in the fog. William wasn't to be stifled.

"You killed them!" he said, too loudly, "you ki—" The heel of Ousa's hand was jammed against the point of William's chin and William's head was pressed back against the earth, his mouth clamped shut by the pressure. He wriggled frantically, until Ousa raised his free hand threateningly.

"Listen," Ousa hissed in his ear. "I don't know what you are talking about. When I let go, you will tell me quietly, calmly. All right?"

William's eyes glowered, but he slowly nodded his head—as much as that was possible with Ousa's hand still holding his jaw. Ousa, lying flat beside William as the battle on the hill intensified, let go and waited expectantly.

"Tell me."

"I'm talking about my mother and father," William said. He was having difficulty keeping himself under control. "You came and murdered them. No matter that they were kind to you, that you married their daughter, that you had given them your oath and a treaty belt."

Ousa could feel William's body quivering with emotion beneath him. The eyes were deeply malignant.

"I don't know what you are talking about," Ousa said. "Your parents were killed by whites. One of my warriors saw it."

"I'll bet he did," William said acidly. "I saw it too, Ousa. The tail end of it. I was there!"

"Then you know I was not."

"I know nothing of the kind. We came up there and ran off a bunch of men. They had already killed my father. My mother . . . died later. Grief, I suppose." William had to blink the tears away. "Those men were Indians. They were Shawnee! Dressed up in white men's clothes."

"But, William, how do you—?"

"They all wore moccasins. There aren't any white men unknown to us in this valley who could have been there. They killed my father with war clubs," William said, bitterly ticking off his reasons.

Ousa was silent. Yes, the whites could have worn moccasins. To blame the Shawnee? Why, when they were dressed in their own clothes? And then to kill with war clubs—no, it was the truth: they had to be Shawnee. Ousa's eyes went hard as he remembered again the kindness of Van der Veghe and Crenna, the gentleness of those people, the wampum belt, the promises.

"You are right, William," he said, slowly lifting his hand which had rested near William's throat. "They had to be Shawnee. But I want you to believe this—it was not me. It was no one I sent. I would not have broken my word; I would not have hurt them. For what reason, William? For what reason would I have done it?"

This time it was William who was stumped for an answer. There was no logical reason. William was tenacious: "You are responsible. You are Kispkotha chief. You are the war leader."

"No, William. I have not been since I returned to the tribe. I am not chief, it is my brother Shelokta."

"Your brother!" This news was obviously startling to William. "I guess they've laid their bounty on the wrong head," he said, managing a grim smile.

"What bounty . . .?" Ousa's voice broke off. There were three men moving toward them through the cottony fog. He waited until they had passed before asking again.

"After Corbettville, General Compton put a price on your head. He wants you dead, Ousa. That slaughter was inhuman."

"Wait, wait!" Ousa put a hand to his forehead. "What slaughter?"

"Corbettville lived only three months. A man named Harry Corbett started it with his own family and those of his brothers. A dozen friends came with them."

"Where was this?"

"South fork of the Elk just before it comes into the Kanawha. The Shawnee hit them three months back. They hit them fast, killed Corbett and two others in the first attack, captured the women and children and locked them in a grain shed. Then . . ." William's eyes were glazed with loathing. "They got themselves good and drunk and began torturing them. Cut off the fingers and toes of little children. Raped the women—they butchered them, Ousa! Don't tell me you did not know."

"I did not," Ousa said. But now he did, now he knew. "It is Shelokta. Shelokta and his rum."

"It brought the army in, Ousa. There'll be more." As if to underscore that, the muskets on the hill opened fire in a long, pealing fusillade. "There were some people in the government who sided with the Shawnee—don't look at me like that, it's true—they believed the Indian had the right to his land, that the English had enough land east of the valley. This has torn it all, Ousa. They're after you. They're out to destroy the Shawnee nation—and they don't know Kata from Shibeloh. All the Shawnee will be involved. The valley will run red, Ousa. That's what's been done."

Ousa seemed not to be listening to him. His eyes stared into the distance as if his vision could cut through the lurking fog. Another volley of shots sounded, and Ousa sat up, his head turning that way. "I must be going."

William did not answer. Perhaps he did not believe what Ousa had told him, perhaps he still believed Ousa had ordered his parents killed. If he did, there would be no convincing him otherwise. Ousa's mind was occupied with other thoughts. What William said was true, Shelokta had brought war upon them, war such as they had never seen. There would be red-coated warriors in the valley, more of them and more. One man's dreams of glory had brought the storm of destruction drifting westward.

Yet another volley of musket fire brought Ousa to his feet. He remained in a crouch for a minute, looking at William, who had not moved; then with a last glance back, he was gone, moving like a ghost through the relentless river fog.

There was a battle that day, a battle in which neither side gained a victory. The British held the hill the day long, picking off the occasional careless Indian who revealed himself. The infrequent sortie on the Indians' part did nothing to dislodge the soldiers, but produced a few compensating casualties on the British side.

The river fog lifted at sunset, first forming gilded ribbons among the oaks, and with the dissipation the Shawnee were forced to withdraw or leave themselves open targets.

The homeward-straggling war party was in high spirits. It had been a good fight. They had stood up to the redcoats. They had drawn blood. At the home camp there was warm food and warm rum waiting. They would sleep long and deeply.

Only Ousa was silent, only Ousa was worried. They had fought a skirmish. It meant nothing. The fact was, whether any of his warriors knew it or not, they were now branded outlaw. They had become vermin in the eyes of the enemy, and the enemy was now dedicated to the annihilation of the Shawnee.

The home camp, familiar and lighted brightly by campfires, was strangely desolate to Ousa's eyes. With a warrior's eyes he measured it and found it sadly lacking. It was indefensible—they had never considered the possibility of having to defend it against British attack. Their numbers had been far superior. It was unimaginable that the settlers would ever attempt a counterattack. Suddenly the idea was not so preposterous.

There was little comfort in these thoughts, little in the welcoming Shawnee's cheers, the spontaneous dancing.

She was comfort, the only comfort. She waited for him and he walked to her wearily, realizing how much he loved her, his Mingoe woman, she who had nearly been killed trying to help a people who had shunned her. She came to him and wrapped her arms around him, smiling up at him with lips which met his briefly, and for a moment it was almost enough to chase the storm clouds away. Cara.

10

He was warm and strong beside her, and the night was peaceful. The children were piled against them, their soft, innocent snores touching. Cara should have slept easily, but she could not. The dream had come again, and she had wandered through it with the scent of blood in her nostrils, the cries of the wretched in her ears, the heat of warfire scorching her flesh. She awoke to find peace, and yet she knew that the peace was as ephemeral as the terror of the dream, that real terror was abroad in the world of waking. It lay, an unhatched, evil egg awaiting the moment. The night was warm, yet she shivered and drew nearer to Ousa, studying him by the faint starlight which filtered into the lodge.

She loved him dearly. Her heart ached for him when he was gone. She wondered how she could live without him; and yet she knew he was a warrior. A man born to combat.

In other times, perhaps, things were different. Then a warrior, proud and strong, cold-eyed, was due a long and honored life. Those times, perhaps, had gone.

What had happened? It angered her briefly. She clenched her fists until her nails bit into her palms. Their life together was happy. Ousa was a loving husband, a gentle father—yet just outside of their lodge entrance the world grew dark and stormy. The weight of the world was crushing Ousa, and if she was not careful, it would crush her as well.

Vague, tangled thoughts, guilty emotions, drifted through the night and settled around her. She wondered if she were to blame for all of this, for Ousa's disgrace and depressions. A *witch*. The thought, ludicrous as it was, did not bring a smile to Cara's lips, but only uneasiness to her heart.

She lay awake the rest of the night, and not even the close comforting strength of Ousa could drive away the barbed, persistent disquiet.

"It was Shelokta who killed them . . . or had it done. I don't know when or how, but it was my brother." Ousa's eyes lifted to hers, seemed unable to hold her gaze, and turned down again.

"Why!" the question was a breathy, incredulous expression.

Ousa shrugged heavily, rubbing a hand over his bare shoulder, where a deep purple bruise had blossomed. "To hurt you. To hurt me through you. To convince others that the English are savages. A hundred answers. But we shall never know unless Shelokta tells us." He paused, his thoughts going to the mocking face of Tadona, wondering. He shook memory of her away.

"How do you know this?" Cara asked.

He told her briefly of his meeting with William. Her eyes were open wide. "He might have killed you," she said, aghast and stunned.

"He tried," Ousa said quietly. "It's a wonder he didn't. Your brother is a strong man, a cunning fighter. I thought no man could come up on me silently, but William did it. Fortunately for me, I broke his wrist before he could finish me."

Cara simply stared. William and Ousa. And what if either of them had been killed? "He told you about Shelokta?"

"No. He told me that Shawnee had done it. Told me how he knew, and then I saw it all, saw the grotesque hand of my brother in this business. There was more, Cara." He took her hand and slowly told her about the massacre at Corbettville, about the strengthening of resolve the British leadership had experienced, about the price which had been placed on his head.

"But why you?"

"To their knowledge, I was war chief."

"William!"

"Yes," Ousa confirmed, "he must have given them my name. No other white knows anything about us."

"But you have explained it to him."

"I . . . tried. I do not know if he believed me."

Cara rose. Her gestures were short and choppy as she paced the lodge. She and Ousa were alone this morning; Dava, the Creek woman, had taken the children out to play near the river. "If the British are determined to drive us out, the war will come. Does Shelokta understand the British? Does he know that there will be no lengthy council meetings, no runners sent from tribe to tribe, no conferences, no waiting for good weather? Does he know they will come with cannon and cavalry and infantry *and do what they have come to do?*"

"I don't think so." Ousa too rose. He stood, arms dangling, staring at nothing. "But the French certainly do. The French welcome it. A war between the Kata Shawnee and the British. They do not care who wins. Only that casualties are inflicted upon the British. My brother does not understand any of this, and he will not listen."

"Then . . ."

"There is the Ghost Society."

"It is not enough, Ousa, unless you mean to make war upon your own brother."

Ousa nodded, recognizing the truth of Cara's observation. "It is not enough," he said.

"Withdraw."

"Withdraw?" He looked blankly at her. "What do you mean, Cara?"

"In a few months it will be time to travel to the winter camp in the south. Why not go there now?"

"And leave this land to the British? How could we return?"

"I don't know." She ran a harried hand through her hair. "I wasn't thinking. What will we do then?"

"I don't know . . . The Ghost Society . . . No," he said in irritation, "that's no good. To start a war within the tribe is madness."

"And what if it is the only way, my Ousa?" Cara asked, but Ousa did not answer. Perhaps he did not want to reply.

Later, after dressing and eating, they walked down to the river. The wind was cool, and it seemed the river must be cold, but the children, under Dava's watchful eye, were enjoying a swim. Kokii was a little otter, and his father's eyes lighted with pride as he watched his son dive from the snag, swim back to the shore, and clamber up the water-polished boulders. Shanna was nearly as adept. She was younger and hadn't Kokii's speed, but her strokes were effortless, strong.

Lychma, who was only three, had to be content with splashing in the water near the bank where Dava sat. The sunlight on the water was pleasant. The patterned shade of the oaks was cast upon the river. Distantly loons called.

"Swim with us, Father!" Kokii called from the far bank, waving his hand invitingly. Shanna took up her brother's cry, and Lychma started babbling gleefully.

"Shall we swim?" Cara asked. It seemed inviting. She would swim until she was weary, laugh with the children, and forget all.

Ousa touched her arm. "Not now. Look."

She turned toward the camp, shielding her eyes with her hand. Cara saw them too: four men on horses, wearing blue French uniforms.

"Now what?" she muttered.

"I don't know, but I'd better find out." Ousa started away, and Cara fell in behind him. "He won't like your being there."

"Nor you," Cara reminded him.

"No. I don't think he likes me being alive," Ousa said quite earnestly.

Cara was shocked enough to halt and stare at Ousa. "But he wouldn't . . . ?" she asked excitedly, hurrying after him. "Not your own brother."

"I don't think it would bother my brother Shelokta in the least, Cara. I think he would have killed me by now if it weren't for my friends." He squeezed Cara's shoulder. "Or perhaps he fears my witchwife!"

"He should," Cara said without a smile. "If he tries to hurt you, he had better fear me."

Ousa smiled, touched by her sincerity. "Nothing will happen," he said, convincing neither of them.

Ta-sho-haka, Shelokta's lieutenant, was at the entrance to the council hut, and he tried briefly to block Ousa's way, but the expression on the warrior's face, his solid shoulders and massive chest, made it a fleeting attempt.

Ousa ducked the lintel and swept into the room, Cara fast on his heels.

Shelokta, who was sitting, joking with the Frenchmen, looked up. The smile froze on his face as he saw his brother and Cara. "What do you want?" he demanded.

"To discover why these men are here."

"And the woman?"

"She is shaman."

"Not yet. She hasn't finished her studies."

"We won't argue small points, Shelokta. She is here. I am here. My question is, why are these Frenchmen here?"

Shelokta was trying hard to form his face into a mask of unconcern, but his smile was a travesty. His crooked mouth seemed to sneer of its own volition. "It is personal business—these are my friends."

"Then welcome them in your own lodge. Since they have come to the council lodge, I assumed it was a tribal matter."

"Are these the men who poison our people, Shelokta?" Cara asked, looking deliberately at the French. "Are these the people who come to ask our warriors to become butchers, to slaughter women and children?"

One of the Frenchmen blanched slightly, the interpreter.

Shelokta's expression froze on his face. It was a moment before he could remember to become angry.

"What business is it of yours, woman? What standing have you? How do you dare to speak?"

"I dare to speak for the good of the people, Shelokta," Cara went on. Shelokta seemed outraged that Ousa did not silence his wife. Far from it, the former sachem stood nodding his head in admiration.

"A woman speaks for you now, Ousa!" Shelokta mocked.

"My wife can speak for me at any time, Shelokta. And do a better job of it than I. But you have not answered the questions."

"What questions?"

"We wish to know about Corbettville," Ousa said, taking three paces forward, aware of the eyes of the Frenchmen on him, of the unsubtle presence of Ta-sho-haka, musket in hand, behind him. "We want to know about the murder of the Van der Veghes. Was that the idea of your French masters too?"

"I do not know what you are speaking of. I do not know

why you are attacking my friends. I do not know why you are accusing me of crimes.''

Ousa had to admire his brother's coolness. He never faltered, never so much as twitched; but then, he supposed that a man without conscience would not have many qualms about bald lies.

The French, on the other hand, looked uncertain, slightly uneasy. Who was this mad Shawnee who burst in here with accusing eyes? Who was the woman?

''You!'' Ousa had turned to the Frenchman who spoke their tongue. ''What is your name?''

He hesitated before answering, ''Jacques . . .''

''Is this your chief?'' He nodded at the mustached man.

''This is Captain LaFerriere, the commandant of the garrison at Venago, second in charge to Baron Dieskau, the commander of the French North American Company.''

The interpreter puffed up a little as he delivered this answer, his nervousness disappearing. Ousa let Cara respond.

''We do not know who Captain LaFerriere is, nor need to. We have no place known as 'Venago' in our valley. We do not know or care who Baron Dieskau is. My husband, interpreter, asked you a simple question: Is this man your chief?''

''Yes,'' Jacques replied after blinking his eyes in annoyance or bafflement.

''Then I wish to speak to him. Be so kind as to translate, interpreter Jacques. Tell this man''—Ousa looked directly into the cobalt-blue eyes of Captain LaFerriere who showed no discomposure—''that if I see him again in my camp, he will be killed. Tell him that any Frenchman in this camp—''

''Wait a minute!'' Shelokta, shaking with rage, sprang to his feet. ''He is going nowhere. By what authority do you threaten my guests, Ousa?''

''With the authority of a man who possesses a bow and arrow, brother.'' Ousa promised him, ''If I see them again, I shall kill them. Go,'' he said, spinning on LaFerriere again. Take your rum.'' Ousa stalked to the trunk in the corner, to Shelokta's treasure chest. ''Take your . . . beads!'' He threw them across the room to land in a tangle. ''Take your blankets, your knives . . .''

Shelokta moved without warning. He leaped at Ousa, and Ousa caught only the flicker of a shadow on the wall. He ducked low automatically, twisted aside enough to dodge the down-plunging knife blade of the maddened Shelokta, and managed to drive his knee up as Shelokta sprang against him.

Shelokta jackknifed at the stomach where Ousa's knee had caught him, but he was determined. Wild-eyed and panting, he got to his knees and then his feet, the knife still in hand. Ousa stood waiting. Suddenly he kicked out, his foot catching Shelokta's elbow.

Spinning then, Ousa came in and slammed a fist into Shelokta's neck just below the ear. Shelokta went down and stayed there.

Cara had not been idle. At the first leaping attack, Ta-sho-haka, standing in the doorway, had brought his musket to his shoulder, and Cara had flung herself at him, her mind going red with rage. It couldn't have been called an attack—it was more of a lurching, frenzied act of desperation. But it was enough.

Ta-sho-haka, his eyes intent on the struggling men, his musket barrel wavering as he waited for an open shot, was hardly expecting the woman to throw herself on him. Cara's shoulder hit Ta-sho-haka's chin, her arm unintentionally knocked the musket from the Shawnee's hands, and they went to the floor in a heap.

That was the way Ousa found them, and he stood there, hands on hips, laughing with delight for a moment before helping Cara to her feet.

"Now you are a warrior too, my Cara! What would I do without you!" As he spoke, he picked up the sullen Ta-sho-haka's musket, reversed it, and showing it to Ta-sho-haka, he now added, "Go before I do what you would have done. You have chosen the wrong side, Ta-sho-haka. You have made an animal of yourself."

Ta-sho-haka, his face stiff with suppressed rage, threw back the blanket hanging over the lodge entrance and went out. Shelokta, moaning, was stirring in the corner. The French still stood gaping at the Shawnee.

"Go," Ousa said softly to them. "My warning is serious. Do not return. Go home, tell your leader that the French will have to fight their own battles from here forward."

Without a word the French, glaring coldly at Ousa, left. Ousa and Cara followed them out, watched them mount, and stood side by side as the French rode insouciantly through the Shawnee camp, maintaining their diginity.

"I have never fired a musket," Cara said, and Ousa saw

the smile playing at the corners of her lips. He handed her the weapon.

Aiming above the heads of the French, she pulled the trigger, and the gun exploded in her hands. The Frenchmen dug spurs into their horses' flanks and were gone in seconds, bending low across the withers, flagging their horses with their hats. Wigs askew, they vanished into the timber beyond the camp.

"Well?"

Ousa, looking down at his wife, said soberly, "You have much to learn about muskets."

Cara rubbed her shoulder, which felt as if it might be broken; then, throwing the musket away, she let Ousa tug her upright. Suddenly she was laughing, and the laughter, shot through with nervousness, was infectious. Ousa laughed too, shaking his head. The laughter died away as quickly as it had begun.

Shelokta stood in the doorway of the council lodge, leaning heavily against the frame. His hand lifted, and a finger pointed accusingly at each of them before his hand dropped again and he turned, reentering the lodge. He had said nothing, but the meaning of his gesture was clear.

"And now, my Ousa?" Cara asked.

He shook his head. *Now?* "We have torn the tribe apart," he said as they began walking homeward. "This is the end of it. Shelokta must go his way; we must go ours."

"Can you do that, Ousa? Can you leave your people to Shelokta? Think. If you go, who will there be to speak against his madness? Who will there be to protect them from their own folly?"

"I have thought of all that, Cara. Yet if I do stay . . . He means to kill us now, you know."

"Yes," she said simply.

"But I forgot!" Ousa hugged her. "All I need do is give you a musket. Who would dare come against us then! And if you have no musket, you simply hurl yourself at them and beat them to the ground."

He smiled again, and she answered him with her own smile, yet in moments they were both silent, both expressionless. Ousa was worried deeply. These were his people. His brother would drive them to their deaths. He could not leave, and yet to stay was to risk his own life and those of his family.

"We will stay," he announced. "For now. We will stay and

speak to them again. They must be made to see what is happening here."

The speaking seemed to have no effect. Cara spoke in public, with fire and emotion, but they did not listen to this wild Mingoe woman.

Ousa spoke in council, meeting the same objections.

"The British will mass and drive us from this land if we continue to fight."

"And if we do not fight?" Stone Wolf asked.

"I do not know."

"Yet you have driven away an ally who made us stronger. You have deprived us of our source of muskets and powder."

"It may be," he told his uncle privately, "that I shall have to leave, to split the tribe. Will you be with us, Uncle?"

"No." At Ousa's surprised expression, he explained. "Nor will many others. You ask us to go with you. Why? Because a redcoat army will come—you tell us this, I do not know that it is so. If the army does come, Ousa, who is it more advantageous to be with? The man who has no muskets, the man who has no allies, the man who has no numbers of warriors, or the other—he who has all of these?"

Ousa discussed Stone Wolf's observation with Cara. "It means that Shelokta still has contacts with the French," she pointed out. "Stone Wolf as much as admitted that."

"And so nothing has been accomplished, nothing at all," he said. He lay flat on his back, staring up at the darkness.

"Perhaps we are only foolish, my husband. Perhaps . . . it would be better if we went away. You and I, the children. Perhaps nothing can be done here."

Long minutes passed before Ousa answered. When he spoke, it was formally, his voice deep and carefully cadenced—his council voice, sounding odd and alien in their own bed, their lodge, in the still of night.

"I was born to be sachem. I was schooled to be war leader. The Kispkotha clan chief. I was taught that only the tribe mattered, only the survival of the people. I was taught that to lay down my life so that the tribe might survive was a noble end.

"Once I, Ousa, went into battle and was wounded. I was in bed the winter long, and when I returned I was only a ghost. My brother had taken my place as sachem. I had no more strength, I had no more duty. But honor! I still have honor, my Cara, I still have the obligation. I still must do what can be done for the tribe. Do you understand?"

"Yes," Cara said. "Yes, I do understand." To leave served their own purposes, to walk into the deep wilderness and raise the children away from this turmoil. But it was the tribe Ousa considered. Always the tribe. To walk away from them, to desert them, could only destroy his honor. "And so we will stay. For now"—she sighed—"we shall stay."

It was on the third night following that conversation, a still cold night when the stars hung blurred and frozen in a black, moonless sky, that Cara awoke, her mind fogged by sleep, yet alert with premonition.

What? Her heart was racing uncontrollably. Wild thoughts cluttered her mind, colliding, dissipating, reapproaching. Tadona with a knife; dark spirits; Shelokta, musket in hand; a raging panther . . . *what?*

There was nothing in the lodge, and yet her heart pounded so loudly that it seemed she could hear it. Foolishness. She told herself it was foolishness, and lay down again, but sleep was impossible in this state.

She rose and walked to the lodge entrance, peering toward the sky, inhaling deeply, trying to quiet her nerves. She had half-turned away from the entranceway before she saw it. She froze, terror washing over her.

It was only a pale glow against the eastern sky, but she knew instantly what it was by the subtle scent which drifted through the night air. A scent so indistinct and innocent that only her deeper senses, those beneath and beyond logic, had recognized the danger implicit in it as she slept.

She raced to the bed, shook Ousa awake, and whispered, "They've fired the forest."

He rubbed his eyes sleepily, sitting up. "What?" he asked heavily; but by then it had sunk in and his eyes came instantly alert.

He rushed to the entranceway, blinked, and slowly cursed. The glow in the skies was distinctly red, ominous. He turned to tell Cara to wake the children, but she had already done that and was rapidly dressing them. His eyes returned to the sky. Only the thin line along the horizon was colored. The rest of the world was black. The pines beyond the camp verge were clearly silhouetted now, backlighted by crimson, deep, bloody. The glow of intense red was creeping into the blackness of the sky. The wind was in Ousa's face. The illusion was of dawn at midnight, for it was midnight. Midnight, and the glow was fire, fire in the wilderness woods.

"I've got to wake them up," Ousa said. Cara looked around. She was tugging a shirt over a sleepy Kokii's head. She nodded her understanding. There was no telling how quickly the fire would advance through the forest. The wind was increasing, and already the gusts of wind which touched Ousa's cheek seemed heated.

He snatched up his blanket and went out into the night. Suddenly there was no need to awaken anybody. There was a distant, muffled explosion and then a low, indefinable sound like a deep, soughing exhalation.

Before Ousa could identify the sound, the cannonball crashed into the lodge beside his own, that of the warrior Tamava, and the lodge exploded in a shower of timber and bark, Tamava and his family rushing from the lodge, his wife naked and bloody, clutching a child to her breast.

The second cannonball fell within seconds, a third chasing it across the skies. "Cara!" Ousa leaned into the lodge, shouted to his wife, and saw her scoop up Shanna and Lychma, saw Kokii, his eyes wide, arms spread in terror, rush to him. Ousa snatched up his son and rushed out into the confused panic of the Shawnee camp.

Cara was behind him, a daughter in each arm. The sky seemed to be breaking, to be on fire itself as a dozen cannonballs, lofted through the air, impacted into the sleeping Shawnee camp. Cara heard a distant scream and then the booming of cannon once more. The fire seemed to have leaped forward through the dark woods. Waves of flames rose brilliantly against the sky, playing in the upper reaches of the pines, the smoke now rolling toward them as the wind increased.

"South!" It was Ousa at her shoulder, and she nodded, thinking of a dozen items she would like to have had, might have rushed back into the lodge to recover. But she had the children in her arms, Lychma crying steadily, fearfully now, clutching at her dress, and she knew that she had nothing which meant more than the children.

She followed Ousa across the camp. The panic, the confusion, was complete. Still cannonballs fell on the camp, and the flames of the forest fire, stretching skyward in long wavering tongues, crackled and popped as they rushed toward the camp.

Men and women scurried everywhere. A child, somehow

left in the center of the camp, sat against the earth and screamed. Cara started that way, saw the mother rush to it and scoop it up, saw the fear in the Shawnee woman's eyes, and rushed on.

Ousa had paused to wait for her, and she ran to him, passing dozens of armed warriors who ran naked through the night toward the fire, as if they would force the flames back with their muskets.

Shelokta, his face flame-bright, seemed hardly to see them as they passed him. Tak had appeared from somewhere, and Dava, her face blank with sleep.

They ran on until Ousa halted suddenly, pointed to the south, and told them, "They've fired it on this side too."

Cara looked around, seeing the panic, the people rushing in every direction, like confused ants on a summer anthill. "The river!" she gasped. "We must go to the river."

"Yes," Ousa agreed. "The river!"

Kalthipsa, his face puffy with rum, his movements confused, passed them, and Ousa grabbed his brother by the arm, swinging him around.

"Kalthipsa! The river."

"Shelokta . . ." He looked dumbly toward the camp, which was already threatened by encroaching flames, at the flattened lodges, at the dead strewn about the clearing, and he nodded. "Yes! The river."

"Turtle Back!" Cara gripped Ousa's arm and pointed. Ousa's father was wandering toward the camp. He staggered as he moved, his arms stretched out in confusion. His face was blackened, and glancing toward Turtle Back's lodge, Cara saw that it had been hit by cannon fire.

Dava, holding Shanna now, had Lychma too thrust into her arms. "The river!" Cara said brusquely. Kokii was clinging to Tak's knee, and Cara glanced at him as she raced to help Ousa, who was running toward his father. She had taken only three steps before the tall pine, sheathed in flames, toppled, and with agonized eyes she saw the tree fall heavily to the earth, engulfing Turtle Back in flames.

"Ousa!" She grabbed at his arms. He was still fighting his way toward the tree. "You can do nothing! You can do nothing!"

Ousa shook her off and shook her away again as she leaped onto his back, smoke stinging her eyes, burning her nostrils. He stopped suddenly and stood staring at the tree, watching the crackling flames dance and weave as they devoured the pine.

"He's gone." He said that softly, then seemed to come to himself. He turned, grabbing Cara's hand, and they raced for the river, appalled at the speed with which the fire was spreading. It had leaped the river upstream and swept across the Shawnee camp, the flames passing from treetop to treetop like some hideous, destructive message changing hands.

A pine fell, and then another, touching all with fire as they slumped defeated to the earth, the loud popping of their trunks like near cannon.

They made the river by rushing through a corridor of flame-lit trees. Cara ran bent over, holding Lychma protectively against her breast. Hot cinders rained down upon them, gray ash sifted through the night; trees lit up like columns of flame, burning with unimaginable swiftness.

"We're almost there!" she heard Ousa calling above the roar of the night, and then they were, plunging into the black river waters just ahead of another toppling tree. The night was awash with flame. The river mirrored the fire. Long, distorted bands of cold flame stretched from bank to bank, as if the river itself were afire.

They waded almost to midstream and stood there, only their heads and shoulders above the surface. Smoke curled across the river. Debris floated downstream, some of it still burning above the waterline.

The cannon seemed to have stopped firing, but they couldn't be sure of that; the forest fire roared with hot intensity, making even speech impossible.

They saw people along the banks plunging into the river. Fire clung to one warrior's back like a devouring beast, and his screams sounded shrilly for a single moment.

They passed the night in that way. At first standing in the crimson-and-black river, later perched on a snag, thoroughly chilled, the children in their arms, their eyes watching the haunted scene before them.

Morning found the fire still burning in spots. The blaze of the blood-red sun dulled the light cast by the fire but accentuated the blackened ruin of the forest. Pines stood like gaunt blackened giants along the riverbank. The river ran darkly, stained with ash.

Cara felt empty, cold, and bitter. She expected Ousa to share her bitterness, but he did not.

"We have burned their homes, and so they have come to burn ours"—he smiled ruefully—"and done a complete job of it."

The people of the village were gathering now on the west bank of the river, and they waded ashore to join them. The ground was still hot; the trees still sputtered with flame. People were searching the ashes of their smoking lodges. Now and then a wail could be heard.

"What now?" Cara asked.

"Now I think we shall travel to our winter camp," he said dryly.

But Shelokta was having none of that. He was mad with rage, although Cara suspected it was more because his possessions had been lost in the fire than for any other reason.

"We will retaliate!" He said it not once but a dozen times, a hundred times, as he stalked his ruined camp. He passed Ousa without speaking. "They shall see a slaughter such as they have never dreamed."

"To what end, Shelokta?" Ousa asked, but his brother did not respond. "I am a ghost again," Ousa muttered to Cara.

Shelokta was already working on his braves, lashing them with words, stirring them into a fighting rage. Someone had managed to save a few jugs of rum, and they drank that, sitting in the middle of an ash-strewn clearing, their families, dirty and exhausted, standing around them.

"Ousa . . ." Cara saw the determined light in her husband's eyes, and she touched his hand as he started forward. "Perhaps now is not the time."

"It is the time, while this is fresh in their memories. You know it is."

"Yes," she admitted, "I know it is."

"Men! Warriors! My people!" Ousa mounted a fallen tree and held his hands up. "Listen to me, please listen."

They turned weary eyes to him, eyes which peered dully out of blackened faces. "What is it, Ousa?" someone asked tiredly.

"This cannot go on. This war which has no honor in it. My brother says we must fight, we must die. But what are we fighting for!" He bent toward them, his fists clenched. "What? For the glory of the French!" He laughed harshly. "To continue is to die for no cause at all."

"What are you saying?" Tamava asked.

"I am saying this war must end."

"Ousa the peacemaker!" someone said harshly.

"Coward."

"I am not a coward—you know that, Wishosk. Nor do I love the whites. But the time has come when I can find no honor in this war, when I can foresee our defeat, when I know that the British will return, and return, and return . . ."

"Then we shall fight them again," Shelokta said. His back was to Ousa, his hands on his hips, his head thrust forward. "Despite the advice of cowards."

"And when winter comes and there is no hunting, when the larders have been burned?" Ousa went on passionately. "Let us retire to our winter camp. At least agree to that. There we can discuss what should be done."

But there was no convincing them, not on that morning when their hearts burned with the lust for revenge, when they sat abjectly among the ash and ruins, when the rum burned hotly in their veins, when Shelokta urged them on.

He saw that, and he knew the time had come. Ousa spoke once more, with finality. "I am going. I will not fight for the French. The Ghost Society cannot support this madness. Those who wish to come with us, let us be going. Those who wish to stay and die for the French, for the sake of a few beads—let them stay. I pity you, for you cannot see what your leaders are doing."

There was scarcely a response to that. A brief grumbling, a disparagingly waved hand, and then all was as before. Wearily Ousa stepped down and walked to Cara, who watched him with luminous, sad eyes.

"It is done." He held her so tightly that she could not speak for a moment.

"It is for the best, perhaps, my husband."

"Perhaps." He looked back toward the camp, at the warriors and their wives, at the children and sooty dogs. "I feel as if I am a traitor, I feel that I am deserting them when they need me."

"And what could be done here, Ousa?" Cara asked, using her thumb to wipe a bit of ash from Ousa's eyebrow.

"I do not know. But if there is anything . . . Come," he said, turning abruptly, "let us honor my father, Turtle Back."

There was little ceremony. Turtle Back had been crushed and burned by the flaming tree which fell upon him. He was buried near the river, and Cara whispered, "You have your grandson now, Turtle Back. Watch over him from the sky."

Stone Wolf caught Ousa just as the ceremony was completed. "He was a good brother to me. He was a strong warrior, a clever hunter, your father. He was not always old," he added thoughtfully. "Ousa . . . I wish to speak to you."

"Yes, Uncle?"

"It is this." Stone Wolf looked around, seeing nothing beyond the rows of blackened trees. "You have asked us to come with you. You have asked us to abandon our war leader, ignore the commands of the Kispkotha clan leader."

"I know that what I asked is difficult, but Shelokta will destroy you. This I know."

"I do not know it," Stone Wolf replied. The old man touched his brow with fingertips in an uncertain gesture. "What I have come to ask is this—what do you offer, Ousa? You see how it is."

"I don't understand." Ousa shook his head. "What I offer is new leadership."

"Yes, but, Ousa, how is a man to know what this leadership can do? It is this way: if there is war, as I have said, then a man must stand with the strongest sachem. If there is peace, perhaps a man might wish for peace, perhaps many of us do, but who among us can promise peace? Can you, Ousa? That is what the elder chiefs wish to know. You have not told us this."

"I see," Ousa said slowly, turning it over in his mind. "And if I could?"

"I do not know. For myself, I believe I would rather live under treaty, live with an honorable peace—it would have to be honorable, I would give the white man nothing—than die in a useless war. I believe I am not alone," he said, in a way which made it quite clear that Stone Wolf had discussed it with the elders already. "But we would have to have assurances, Ousa. Are you the man who brings an honorable peace?"

"This is a new thought, Stone Wolf. I am a blind man sometimes. I do not know," he said very slowly. "Perhaps. Perhaps it could be negotiated. I have heard that some of the British did not want this war, that they believed the whites had enough land east of the valley."

"I will tell you why that might be so," Stone Wolf said. "This costs them dearly. They must have soldiers here, and many of them. They must build forts. They would prefer to turn their guns on the French—this is what I think. This is what makes me hope. I know you have a white brother, Ousa. I had hoped you had touched on the problem of peace."

"I haven't. I am a warrior, not a peacemaker. Or I was," Ousa said, again sinking into thoughtful consideration. "But perhaps I shall become a peacemaker!"

"If an honorable peace could be made . . . We are too old to fight, too old to die for land which Shelokta has already sold to the French. Let the British drive the French away, let us reclaim our hunting grounds. Tell them that, Ousa. Tell the British that." Then, patting his nephew's shoulder lightly, Stone Wolf, seeming quite old and burdened, walked away, shuffling through the deep ashes. Ousa stood for a long moment, watching after him.

"Well?" Cara was beside him, her nose and cheek smudged with ash.

"It is a new thought. Ousa, a peacemaker!" He laughed.

"But there is logic to what Stone Wolf says."

"Yes. It has been much discussed—that is evident. The elders would agree to such a peace."

"You do not like the idea, Ousa?" she asked, reading his expression.

"Our people have never sued for peace. And I . . . I am Kispkotha. Why would I be peacemaker, going on my knees to the British?"

"For the tribe, Ousa," Cara said softly, and his eyes met hers. "You have spoken of honor, of the people who must survive. You have spoken of honor—to preserve their way of life is an honorable task. They do not ask you to lay down your bow and crawl to the British. They would not accept such a treaty. They want only an honorable way out of Shelokta's mad war. For them"—her hand swept away, toward the ruined village—"for them. That is enough, is it not, to make of Ousa a peacemaker?"

He didn't answer for a long while. The wind, playing in the treetops drifted ash down in a gray snow. Finally Ousa replied. "I do not speak English."

"No."

"I hesitate to leave you alone with Shelokta."

"I know that."

"There is a bounty on my head, Cara. If I am seen and

identified, I shall never have the chance to speak to this Compton or anyone else."

Cara smiled slowly. "I know that too, Ousa, my husband."

"Then *you* will go."

"Yes. I will go. It is what I had in mind all along." She stood near to him, her arms around his waist, smiling up into that darkly handsome face. "Perhaps I am better suited to make peace than my warrior husband. So fierce." She kissed his chest. "So proud."

"Cara . . . if this does not work, the tribe will be split. We must take our friends and leave this land, never to return. Shelokta will make his war, and in time I believe the British will destroy him and all that follow. If you cannot make this peace, Cara, there will be no more Kata Shawnee."

"We cannot allow it to happen. We will not."

"No." He paused. "Seek them out, Cara. Talk to them. Explain what we must have . . . but, Cara, do not promise them our pride, our dignity. I shall surrender that to no man, for no cause. Make sure that the English know that. For that, Ousa would fight to the death."

۞ 11 ۞

Morning was clear, bright, cold. A few thin, uncertain clouds drifted southward, casting footprints of shadow against the earth. The grass was long and deep in the valley, and there were oxen grazing on it. Smoke rose into the morning skies from the settlers' houses which huddled behind the stockade walls. As Cara came nearer, she could smell bread baking, could see two blond children playing some sort of game in the center of a dusty clearing.

The Indian woman stood for a long while on the grassy knoll, arms folded beneath her breasts, studying the town, the people who seemed at this distance so little different from the Shawnee. Children played, the women went about their household work, cooking or tending the gardens. The men were out hunting, some of them, or building new lodges. From here, where she could see no faces, hear no voices, the activities seemed familiar, eerily so, and she wondered:

What was it wars were fought for? All of those who fought wished only for peace, all of those who died wished only to live. They went out grim-faced and angry to kill their brothers—to kill themselves—and in the end there was only destruction, death, which no one had wished for. But war, as Ousa had told her, was reality, and once it became real, took on substance and malice, it had to be dealt with as reality. All that could be done then was to assure yourself that it was not your family which lost a husband, a grandfather, a child. Once war began its prowling, once it had emerged from its dark egg, there was no ignoring it, and they were only fools who turned their eyes and said: "I see no war, there can be no war."

She started down the long slope, the wind fresh in her face, carrying the sweet scent of grass, the pungent odor of woodsmoke. Approaching the stockade, she noticed how similar it was to the descriptions her mother used to give of the fortified Iroquois towns she had grown up in, and she wondered how much William had had to do with designing this white town.

There was a small gate on the riverside, and Cara stood near it for a time, trying to make up her mind. People went in and out, a dozen while she waited, but she was not bothered or approached, although a few harshly curious glances were cast her way.

Finally she made her decision, and she entered the gate. There were armed men on either side of it, and one of them, heavy-shouldered, heavy-lipped, started toward her.

"Got a squaw here, Brinegar," she heard him say. "Hey, squaw woman! What do you want?"

"She Shawnee?" the other man asked excitedly. "She Shawnee, Early! God, if she is, I swear I'll kill her, woman or not."

"Settle down. She's not ready for the killing yet—God, look at her, Early, she's finely built, ain't she?" He was standing directly in front of Cara now, his eyes grating over her. Cara kept her face expressionless. These men were stupid and, she guessed, cowardly. What was William thinking of, associating himself with people like this?

Then, sharply, Shelokta intruded into her thoughts, and she realized that her mind had been following an Indian prejudice. All peoples have their fools, their misfits, their truth-seekers, their cowards, their warriors.

"You be Shawnee, woman?" the man asked in an exaggeratedly slow speech. "You be Shawnee squaw come look for man?" He grinned at his friend and winked.

Cara couldn't restrain the impulse to answer him in what he seemed to believe was an Indian speech pattern. "I come look for brother mine."

"Oh!" He winked again at his friend. "Squaw woman come look for brother. What his name, Squaw?"

"His name," she said distinctly, "is William Van der Veghe. Do you know where I can find him?"

"Van der . . . *Christ*," he breathed. "He's not here right now. Over there's his house. I b'lieve his wife's in. Right that way, ma'am."

Cara, still expressionless, crossed the clearing, and the man named Early said, "See, you damned fool. Van der Veghe's sister. If he'd been around . . . well, you wouldn't want to tangle with that mad Dutchman. Mebbe you'll learn one day, Brinegar. Maybe one day."

"Yeah. Maybe one day," Brinegar mused. He watched the slender figure of the woman and shook his head.

Cara found the door to the small, sturdy house and knocked on it, and within seconds it was flung open.

"Dora, I've been . . . Oh! You're not . . . I was expecting someone else. Who are you?"

Cara looked at the red-haired woman, beautiful with green eyes, straight nose, and broad mouth, with only a certain harshness of character which now had begun to score lines around her mouth and eyes to keep her from being truly, astonishingly perfect.

"Louise?" At Louise Van der Veghe's hesitant nod, Cara said, "I am William's sister. I am Cara."

"Cara." Louise's answer was toneless. She placed a hand on her hip, waved her free hand, and said, "Come in if you like. William's not here."

"Do you know where he is? It is important that I find him."

"Where he is?" Louise smiled humorlessly. "I couldn't say. Somewhere out there. Killing Indians. Or trying to. One day he won't come back, I expect. He could be dead now." She shrugged. "I don't know where he is."

"Then I will not disturb you," Cara responded, still hesitating at the threshold.

"You're not upsetting me," Louise said, "if that's what you think. Come in and have some tea."

"Thank you," Cara replied. "If I may. The wind is cold."

"Yes. Sit down," Louise said, gesturing toward the puncheon table to her right. Ahead a huge kettle boiled over a hearthfire. Above the mantelpiece were muskets and Indian hatchets, crossed significantly. Louise read her eyes. "Trophies. My man's trophies. He goes out for months and brings back . . . things like that. It's a wonder he doesn't bring scalps."

"He is a warrior," Cara said, seating herself at the table.

"And little damned else!"

The shy face peered around the corner of the wall, and Cara smiled brightly.

"His name is James," Louise said, nodding toward the child, a bright-eyed boy of four or five. "My husband decided I needed something to occupy me while he was out warring. I got that."

James had flaxen hair cut square across the eyes, and a small impish mouth. "He is a beautiful boy," Cara said. "You must love him very much."

"Yeah." Louise's eyebrows drew together. She placed a cup of tea in a pewter mug before Cara. "He's all right." She patted the approaching child's head and smiled tightly. She sighed. "He's all right."

"Is your brother well?" Cara asked after tasting the tea, which was hot, far too strong.

"Richard is fine. He's army now. War—it's all these men know."

"It seems necessary to them."

"They love it!" Louise said, throwing her head back, slapping her hand on the table. "You've got a soldier husband too, don't you?" Cara nodded. "I'll tell you, they love it. Out tramping around, playing with their guns. Keeps them away from us."

Cara made no answer. She sipped her tea. "You do not know where William might be?"

"He could be at the fort. Fort Necessity, that is. It's upriver. I'll draw you a map if you can't find it. No"—Louise laughed—"you can find it, just follow the men."

Cara smiled, feeling awkward and embarrassed.

She turned then to go, sparing a last smile for the boy. Louise watched her from the doorway for a long while, her head against the doorframe, the boy hanging on to her skirt.

She was an unhappy woman, Louise. Unhappy, or perhaps just weary. Weary of the fighting—Cara could understand that, and she tried not to judge Louise too harshly. She had lost her mother and father to the fighting; and it seemed she had lost her husband to it, in another sense.

William had always been a wanderer—a fiddle-foot, her

own father had called him. It was not an easy task to try locking him within four walls. She lifted a hand in farewell, but Louise simply stared after her. The boy, however, raised a chubby arm and took three steps forward, watching after the Indian woman.

It was four days to Fort Necessity on the Monongahela, and might have been more except for a party of homeward-bound settlers who let her ride for a time on their wagon gate. This family, all of them religious people, named Lucas, had had enough of the warfare and declared that they would not fight to own land which belonged to someone else.

The skies were lowering before she reached Necessity, and now and then a few flakes of snow drifted downward; winter's promise was on the wind, icy, biting.

The gate guards wore red tunics and high peaked caps. She asked for William Van der Veghe and was told to wait at the gate. Cara turned her back to the wind and watched the low clouds shadow and envelop the forest, watched the Monongahela, swollen by upriver rains, flow southward, a white-stippled gray mass of slowly plodding water.

"Cara!" The voice was surprised, familiar. She turned to find her brother before her. Tall, blond, lean, and competent-looking, he now carried a jagged scar on his left cheek.

"You are looking well, William," she said formally, and then she threw her arms around him, feeling his astonishment in the rigidity of his body.

"Cara . . ." He loosened up now, hugged her tightly, briefly, and kissed her forehead. "What are you doing here, sister?" he asked in the tongue of the Oneida people. "Is . . .?"

"Ousa is alive and well," she said, anticipating his question. "Despite the bounty on his head."

"Ours or the French?" William asked as they walked into the busy fort, his arm around her waist.

Cara halted suddenly. "What did you say?"

"The French have outlawed Ousa—don't look at me like that, it's true. On this, all the whites seem to agree. Ousa is a mad dog who must be hunted down."

"It can't be . . ." She broke off. It could be, and probably was. Why not? Ousa had threatened French officers with death.

"I can show you a document we captured . . ."

"No, never mind. It is true, I know that."

"Why are you here, Cara?" William asked. Cara was

aware of the activity around them, the caissons, the wheeled cannon being moved somewhere. Across the parade ground a party of new recruits, uniformless, being coached through some rudimentary drill.

"I want to speak to Compton, William. I want you to be with me. Your English is much better than mine."

"But why?"

"On Ousa's behalf, I wish to discuss peace," she answered.

"Are you serious?" William peered at her as if it were not possible. She simply nodded. "Of course," he said. "Of course. I hope something can be done. I have seen too much . . ." His thoughts drifted away, then returned with a snap. "I'll talk to his orderly right away."

"William. I saw your son."

"James!" His eyes brightened immediately. "Now, there's a boy for you, eh?"

"He is that. Louise looked well."

"Yes." The answer was definitely subdued. "You must have seen how it is, if you spoke to her."

"How it is?" Cara said. They were nearing a row of low buildings. Uniformed men stood at attention along the plank walk, bayoneted muskets in their hands.

"With Louise. She isn't happy, and I know it. But that will change. I'm bringing them to the fort to stay with me. Soon. It will all change."

The words lacked much confidence; they seemed more a distant hope than a statement of fact.

William looked up. "Here we are." He stepped up onto the plank walk, followed by Cara. "I'll see if he can talk to you now."

With a smile and a fleeting look of puzzlement, as if he were amazed to find she was actually there still, he nodded and went into the log building. Cara stood, hands clasped, watching the guards, whose eyes were straight ahead, whose spines were rigid, who gleamed with brass buttons. These were professional men, she thought, unlike the rabble in some of these frontier units.

William's head appeared around the corner and he waved a beckoning hand. Cara walked past the motionless guards and entered a low-ceilinged, undecorated room. A red-faced, mustached man sat behind a desk made of halved logs.

William touched her arm. "In here," he said, leading her toward an inner room.

There was a window in this room, and before it stood a man of middle height, his hands clasped behind him, drooping mustache partly concealing a weak mouth. His eyes were green and cold. There were heavy dark pouches beneath them. His hair, full and long, was shot through with gray. He had begun to develop a paunch. This, then, was the feared Mad Compton. He stood observing Cara as if she were an interesting specimen of some rare species.

"Sit if you like," he said, speaking slowly. Cara took a chair, although she would have preferred to stand. William leaned against the log wall behind her.

"Well, William tells me you have something to say concerning your husband, Ousa." Compton's eyes were alert. He perched on a corner of his desk, his mustache twitching in an expression which Cara supposed was meant to be a smile.

"Ousa," Cara began, "is tired of the fighting. His brother Shelokta is now war leader—"

"Not Ousa?" Compton interrupted.

"No, not Ousa." Cara shook her head. She glanced at William for help, but he smiled—her English seemed adequate to him. "His brother does not wish to quit the fighting. His brother is an agent of the French."

"Don't I know it," Compton said. "Look, what do the French say about Ousa's attitude?" He leaned far forward, eyes lighting coldly.

"They do not know, except that Ousa warned them away from our camp."

"Did, did he? Good, good. Teach those bastards something."

Cara frowned. Was Compton interested in the Shawnee problem or only in the French?

"Go on, Cara," William urged softly.

"Certain high-ranking Shawnee have come to Ousa, asking him if he can give them certain . . ."

"Guarantees?" William provided.

"Yes, guarantees."

"I don't understand what you're getting at," Compton said.

"No?" Cara sucked in her lower lip and shrugged. "Very well, it is like this. The tribe will accept Ousa as leader, will follow him, will agree to sign a peace treaty with the British if the British will give Ousa assurances that it will be an honorable peace, that it will cost the Shawnee no land and none of their freedom."

"Their land, I understood, was sold to the French."

"Some of it, despite Ousa's disapproval."

"Would the Shawnee fight the French with us?" Compton asked. A punctuating fist slammed against the desktop. Cara stared at him for a moment, amazed at the fire in his eyes.

"No," she said. "Ousa would not lead his people against the French. There is no benefit in it."

"Young woman," Compton said, rising, "there *is* some benefit in it. The French are going to lose the American interior as they lost the seaboard. They will be driven into Canada, and those who are on the side of the French will lose all they have."

"Ousa is not on the side of the French."

"No, of course not." Compton paced the floor briefly. "Then what is our situation?" he asked rhetorically. "The Shawnee stand in the enemy camp. Ousa believes the majority of the Kata Shawnee will side with him if he offers assurances of an honorable peace. Then, by all means! By all means we can offer that. Peace. Pardon for Ousa." Compton spread his arms magnanimously. "This is to everyone's benefit. I see no problem at all."

Cara hesitated. "Can you give me a letter?"

"A letter?" Compton's eyebrows raised. "Can Ousa read English?"

"No. But if you will write a letter, William can read it to me. I will tell Ousa what it promises."

"You understand I cannot sign an official treaty with you," Compton pointed out. "It must be with Ousa."

"Yes, I understand that. I would simply like a letter which says to Ousa: 'We will speak under a truce. We do not wish your land, your freedom. We wish only to stop this war between our people.' "

"Of course," Compton agreed immediately. He sat to his desk, took out a piece of heavy parchment and a pen. "You do not think he would agree to fight the French with us?"

"No."

"But he might be willing to listen to arguments in favor of doing just that."

"I could not say. You must speak to Ousa. You understand—he is risking much just to come here. If he is seen conspiring with the British, it could mean death. He will be seen by some as a traitor to his people."

"Yes," Compton said absently, still scratching away at his message. "Damn, will this cut the legs from under Duquesne!"

Cara glanced at her brother. William's eyes were cold. He shook his head slightly. His arms remained folded.

"There!" Compton rose, blowing on the ink to dry it. "This is a letter of safe conduct to Ousa. William will read it to you, of course. I only want to speak to Ousa—there's nothing at all for him to worry about. If he comes over . . . well"—Compton shrugged—"it will be better for all of us. I'm glad you came, Cara. Very glad."

Cara took the letter and rolled it up. Then with a bow to Compton she walked from the office, William on her heels. Outside, the afternoon had grown dark. Light snow swirled down, filming the parade ground.

"Well?" Cara handed William the letter, and he scanned it quickly, handing it back to her.

"It gives Ousa temporary immunity. It is a letter of passage, allowing him to travel to the fort and speak to Compton. Compton promises to discuss a settlement with the Kata Shawnee."

"That is all?"

"That is all he could promise at this stage, I would think," William said. He turned up his collar. The snow was beginning to fall steadily. The soldiers on parade had fallen out and were rushing toward the warm log barracks on the south side of the fort.

"Yes," Cara said, "I suppose he could promise no more; but what do you think, William? Can Compton be trusted?"

"I think so," he replied after a long pause.

"You do not seem sure."

"I'm not. Look, Cara, I'll tell you how I view this man, but understand—I do not like him, I'm prejudiced against him. I don't like him because I think he's incompetent, because I believe him to be a strutting cock, because I think, beneath it all, he may be a coward."

"All right," Cara said slowly.

"I think," William said, "the man is serious in his offer to speak with Ousa. I can't see what he would gain by harming your husband. Compton is for himself first, for the British army second, but there is nothing to be gained here by betraying Ousa. If . . ."—William chopped the edge of one hand against the palm of the other—"if Ousa does come in,

Compton will undoubtedly try to persuade him to fight against the French.

"Let me explain if I can. Compton was an enlisted man in England years ago. He fought on the continent against the Spanish and against the Turks . . ." Cara was staring at him blankly. "He has fought in many wars, but he did not gain much strength. He retired and came to America. Here he was chosen leader by the settlers and given an honorary rank. Now he calls himself 'general,' although he has no official standing. But he is ambitious. He has been promised a regular-army rank of colonel if he can bring this war to a successful conclusion. There's a pension to go along with that rank, and a bonus, but knowing Compton, I think he wants only the recognition. A recognition he feels is long overdue.

"He's nearly desperate to defeat the French, Cara."

"And you, William?"

"What about me?" he asked, his jaw tightening.

"Why are you so desperate a man?"

"Do you see me that way?" He turned his head half away.

"Yes. Your wife does. I do."

"I don't like them, Cara. I don't like them at all."

"The French?"

"The damned Shawnee!"

"William," Cara said softly, "I am Shawnee."

"You're not. No more than I'm English." There was a long silence when they said nothing, but only watched the snow, which now gathered and fell earthward in thick curtains. "The Shawnee," William went on finally, "came into the valley and killed my mother and my father. They killed many others who wanted only to live in peace."

"Not Ousa!"

"They killed many children, tortured them. They killed women, they destroyed families, and all the hopes of those families. For nothing at all, Cara. For nothing."

"Can you not forgive, William?" she asked gently, touching his shoulder, turning him. "We all must forgive at times. This side you fight for—they too have done wrong."

"I have seen no infants murdered. They have not killed my parents. And yours," he said sharply.

"If Ousa does come in . . ."

"I shall not harm him," William said quickly. "He has our assurance. I shall stand by it. He is your husband," he added after a long pause. "As little as I like it, he is your husband."

"He did not do it, William. He did not order it done."

There was no response. He stood gazing into the snowstorm. Cara drew her blanket tighter around her shoulders and said, "Good-bye, William." Then she kissed his cheek, astonishing her brother, it seemed, and she stepped from the plank walk, the letter from Compton clutched in her hand.

"Wait!" William stepped down. "It's hard weather. Take a horse from me. I have many."

"William—"

"You can't walk that far," he said, abruptly cutting off whatever else she meant to say. "This way to the paddock. I have a long-legged roan gelding which might suit you."

Half an hour later she was mounted on the roan, riding through the gate into the swirling snow, and William was still standing there, still watching, his thoughts mysterious, hidden behind the stony expression in his blue eyes.

Cara lifted her hand, but the gesture was not answered. She could do nothing else, and so she turned the big roan southward, and as the snowstorm faded the dark bulk of the fort, she rode on, the rough parchment roll tucked inside her dress giving her little comfort against the gathering storm.

It was three days to the camp, through snow and sleet. Occasionally the sun burst free of its tethering clouds and spattered the snowfields with brilliant sunlight, but for the most part the trip was dreary and cold, the rivers fringed with ice, the game hidden in winter burrows and caves, the trees gray and lifeless. Winter had come. Winter, and the Shawnee still clung to their summer camp, to the warm promises of the French, their faces growing bitter and stormy as the days shortened and the dark season entrenched itself in the snowbound skies.

It was snowing heavily when she reached the Shawnee camp. The people were living in small makeshift lodges. Several had made tipis, like their western cousins, fashioning them of ancient hides. The pines circling the camp still smelled of ash, although they were clothed in white. Thunder rumbled deep in the throat of the god Hinu.

She saw only a few people, and these stared at her with empty eyes, perhaps blaming Cara for their state; they should long ago have traveled southward to their winter camp.

Cara was trembling with the cold, her clothing soaked

through. The roan was weary and chilled. Then she saw Ousa, and her heart exploded with warmth and joy. He had her in his arms and inside the lodge, and the children were around her, tugging at her skirt, shouting eagerly, simultaneously.

"What happened?" Ousa asked immediately. "How did it go? Did you see Compton?"

"I saw him." She withdrew the crushed parchment roll from her dress. "He sends this."

"What is it?" Ousa opened it and stared at it suspiciously. "What do the figures say?"

"It is an invitation to visit Compton and discuss peace. It is a promise of safe passage."

"And you trust him, Cara?"

She hesitated. So much depended on her answer. "I do not know, Ousa. He spoke little of peace, much of making war on the French. He wants you to join the British."

"It is impossible."

"I told him that."

"His heart, Cara," Ousa said, still holding the parchment, looking into her eyes. "What is in his heart?"

"I cannot answer you, Ousa."

"You had no impressions?"

"I had many. Tangled impressions of greed, of honesty, of untruth, of ambition." She shrugged. "I do not know."

"Will he kill me?"

"I do not know."

Ousa nodded. He walked to the fire, crouched down, and stared at the letter from Compton as if by staring at it long enough, hard enough, the message and the man behind the message might become clear to him.

"Will he make peace!" Ousa did not look at Cara. He simply stared at the parchment.

"William thinks so. William believes he will, if it will leave him free to war against the French."

"You saw your brother?" Ousa's eyes lifted.

"Yes."

"That is good."

Cara had seated herself near the fire. Lychma was clinging to her neck, Shanna holding on to her sleeve, while Kokii, trying to look as grim as his father, stood to one side, the firelight playing on his soft dark hair.

"I must go, Cara. If I do not go, then it is all lost. The war will continue endlessly. A few of us might withdraw, go southward or to the west, but we would never be able to return home. I must go if we are to continue as we have. If the bloodshed is to stop."

"Yes," Cara said. She looked across the fire at her husband, seeing for the first time the lines care had etched into his dark face. "It must be that way."

"Tomorrow." Ousa looked toward the entranceway. His eyes seemed to penetrate the distance. "I must go tomorrow. Delay can only mean death for others of us."

The snow was a howling wash out of the north. Lightning formed exquisite bridges across the skies, striking low and frequently. The wind lifted the fallen snow and hurled it against their faces, yet Kalthipsa was hardly aware of it.

He lay in the frozen ditch beside the settlement. Flexing his fingers, which were stiff and lifeless, he grinned. Ta-shohaka, beside him, grinned in return.

They were both warm, filled with the magic water, the rum which brought strength and visions and fervor. Shelokta had given it liberally the night before.

"My brother," he had said, placing his hands with what seemed genuine fondness on Kalthipsa's shoulders, "this must be done. It must be a terrible thing."

"I do not understand," Kalthipsa had said. He had been slightly wobbly as Shelokta drew his hands away. There were spirits in the fire, made visible to Kalthipsa by the rum which raced through his brain, seeping behind his eyes, and he stared at the flames for a long while, not hearing Shelokta's words until his brother slapped him.

"Kalthipsa! It must be terrible, do you understand?"

"Terrible," Kalthipsa had repeated dully.

"Do you understand why?" Shelokta had demanded.

"No. Give me the rum, Shelokta." Shelokta had, and he watched as Kalthipsa took another drink, a drink which caused his eyes to water, his stomach to burn and nearly turn over.

"You must listen, Kalthipsa!" Shelokta shook him roughly again, shook him until his head snapped back and forth on a neck which seemed suddenly devoid of muscle. "Ousa has gone to the British. Ousa wishes to destroy us. We cannot allow this to happen."

"No," Kalthipsa answered lamely. He wished Shelokta would just be quiet.

"If Ousa makes peace with the British, we will be executed. You and I, all who fought for the French. The French say this must be terrible; I say it. It must be so terrible that the British will sign no peace. Now do you understand!"

"Yes, Shelokta," Kalthipsa replied, just so that his brother would quit shaking him, yelling at him. "Whatever you say. I think I want another drink, and then I want to sleep."

"Yes. Have the drink, Kalthipsa. And do not forget. It must be terrible. We must ruin Ousa in the British eyes."

And so Kalthipsa found himself lying in this ditch on this winter morning as the snow floated down from white skies. He was warm with the rum, excited by it. Shelokta's words kept running through his mind. *Terrible; it must be terrible.*

Kalthipsa's eyes lifted to study the settlement again. It was small, unprotected. They were within a mile of Fort Necessity itself, and trusted this proximity for protection against hostile raids. There were no stockade walls, no men standing guard. Only nine log houses, the people in them warming themselves by their fires.

Kalthipsa slid down the bank, out of sight, and lifting his hidden jug, he drank deeply, then deeply again, until his brain started to whirl, his ears to buzz. The sickness which had taunted him half the morning was passing now, and the elation returned, the battle joy, the strength of the spirit which hid in the rum bottle.

He corked the jug, crawled back up the slope, and unlimbered his bow. Nodding to the man nearest him, Tamava, he moved out, a silent specter through the wash of concealing snow.

The snow was heavy and Kalthipsa was guided by only his nose at times. The nose which smelled the woodsmoke and guided him unerringly toward the log houses.

He looked to one side, but he could see no one. He did not have to see them to know they were there, an avenging army, an army which fought for its life. *It must be terrible.*

The first house emerged from the snow so suddenly that Kalthipsa nearly threw himself to the ground in surprise. He smiled, recognizing that the rum had tricked him. The rum had made the expected seem to be astonishing. The rum spirit was mocking him, toying with him.

Kalthipsa crawled nearer, catching a glimpse, a fleeting one, of Wishosk creeping across the snow, his hatchet in hand. Kalthipsa was suddenly there. Simply, without challenge. He found himself beside the wall of the first house, and he turned, crouching down, leaning his shoulder against the rough bark of the cabin wall as he waited for the others to position themselves. He gave them several minutes, and then, with the rum demons prodding him, with Shelokta's words echoing in his mind, he moved.

Tamava was at the front door by now; Wishosk, he had seen, was at the only window. Kalthipsa placed his bow down, and slowly, the snow covering his movements, he climbed the wall, gripping the eaves with numbed fingers, swinging up onto the sod roof.

The snow lay across the roof; the wind slapped him in the face with cold contempt. Kalthipsa crept forward as softly as possible, knowing that sod might trickle down between the logs and give him away.

Eventually he reached the stone chimney. He stood there for a time, watching the snow fall. It formed intricate patterns, swirling and drifting with each gust of wind. If a man watched it closely enough, he could read the patterns. . . . Kalthipsa shook his head. How long had he been standing there? He turned his attention to the chimney.

It must be terrible.

Kalthipsa put his shoulder to the stone chimney, and the stone gave, tumbling down into the fire below. Smoke and soot billowed up instantly, and Kalthipsa heard someone coughing in the house. He crept toward the front of the house, going to his belly against the roof.

The door opened and he saw the top of a man's head, saw an arm uplifted while the man shouted something back into the house.

Kalthipsa leaped. As he jumped, he saw Tamava come around the corner of the house, heard a woman scream, the distant rumble of thunder. And then his feet collided with the white man's shoulders, driving him facefirst into the snow. Kalthipsa lifted his war ax and started to strike. . . . *It must be terrible.*

Tamava was by him and into the house. The woman's hysterical screaming continued. A child was crying in panicked confusion. Kalthipsa closed his eyes, and there, kneeling in the snow, the white man beneath him, he asked for guidance, but he heard only the whip and roar of the wind, the whirring of rum in his head.

Kalthipsa lifted the man's head and slowly, deliberately cut his throat. *It must be terrible*. He heard a woman scream from far away, heard a war whoop. He cut off the white man's ear, held it in his palm for a moment, fascinated by it, then threw it away. He took the nose next, and then the eyes.

"Kalthipsa!"

The voice was far distant, impersonal. He listened to the spirits now, and not to the cries of humans. Let them fight their own spirits! "Kalthipsa!" A hand was on his shoulder, and he slapped it away. Kalthipsa saw that his own hands and arms were bloody, and he watched as the blood trickled off his fingertips, staining the snow.

"Kalthipsa, they come!" the voice said. The hand again touched his shoulder, and Kalthipsa, angered, spun around to face the man. It was Tamava, or a ghost pretending to be Tamava. You could take no chances—it might be a white demon.

"Go away." Kalthipsa's voice was a low growl.

"Kalthipsa, do you not know me?"

Kalthipsa threw back his head and laughed, and at that, the demon, knowing that Kalthipsa had recognized him for what he was, ran away.

"It must be terrible," Kalthipsa reminded himself. He took his knife, slit open the white man's coat, and began to flay the skin from his back, working swiftly, exposing white ribs and red meat.

"You bastard!" The voice was a long, drawn-out howl. Kalthipsa turned, saw the white solider, saw the butt of the musket lash out, felt it strike his face, and then he heard nothing else, felt nothing else but the cold snow beneath him, above him, around him, slipping down his gullet to freeze and torment his innards, to chill the fire of the rum.

When he awakened again, it was dark and a heavy man stood over him. He thought at first it was Tak, and he lifted his head.

"Brother. I dreamed—" A boot lashed out at Kalthipsa's head and he fell back, his face on fire. He had heard cheekbone crack, and now the blood trickled out of his eye socket, burning his face with red liquid fire.

The big man came nearer, although Kalthipsa, asleep in that void between pain and awareness, did not know it. He was a big man indeed, larger than Tak. His shoulders were rounded and soft-appearing when he was undressed, but that was illusion. He was an ox of a man, a smith for twenty years. Now, without encouragement, he lifted his boot and smashed it into the Shawnee's face, tearing his nose open, jarring teeth back into his throat.

"That's enough, for God's sake!" the young lieutenant said, grabbing Chambers by the arm.

"Is it? You didn't see what the bastards did to the Lytle family, sir."

"No, I didn't. And I don't want to see it reenacted here," Lieutenant Richard Dawes said icily.

Chambers hesitated as if he would smash his boot against the Indian's face again and the lieutenant be damned, but he did not. He turned and stalked heavily away, seating himself on the flour barrel in the corner of the storeroom.

Richard Dawes blew out his breath slowly, looked down at the battered Shawnee and across the room to the three chained Indians who sat glaring at him.

The door slammed open and Compton entered, his face cast in deep shadow by the faint lantern light. He walked directly to Dawes, ignored the lieutenant's salute, and stared down at the bloody body lying against the earthen floor.

"These the ones?"

Before Dawes could answer, Chambers spoke up: "Them's the bastards, sir."

Compton grunted. He stepped contemptuously across the man at his feet and stood before the three captured Shawnee. They appeared uninjured except for a few facial bruises. He stood there for a long minute, hands behind his back. Then one of them, a hatchet-faced warrior with paint smeared across his forehead, spit deliberately and accurately onto the shiny toe of Compton's boot.

Compton froze. He stared down at his boot and then lifted his green eyes to the Shawnee. The man, damn him, mocked Compton with a dirty smile.

Compton spun on his heel. "Very well, Lieutenant Dawes. That will be all." More distantly he added, "These are our new allies, are they? And I am expected to trust the Shawnee?"

"Sir, I thought Cara explained that Ousa is not war leader. This isn't his work, then."

"No? Then he has no control over his people at all, does he, Dawes? Then he is nothing, no one to be negotiating with."

"I thought—"

"It can't be both ways, Dawes! Dammit, either he's responsible or he is a powerless pretender. You are dismissed, sir."

"General . . ." Richard spun angrily on his heel and walked up the stepladder-style wooden steps from the underground storeroom. He wished to hell that William Van der Veghe was here, but William had gone to bring Louise and young James to the fort. This was rotten. It stank. He knew Compton, knew that gleam in his eye. It was impossible to blame the men for the savagery they felt, but again, if there was to be a right side and a wrong side to this war at all, one must at least have moral qualms. Compton had none. Men like Chambers had none. The savages had none.

Dawes came out into the open air, closing the half-log door behind him. He looked skyward and out across the snowbound nightscape.

You had to have some sort of moral ideals. You *had* to have. Otherwise . . . What was this? Two savage panthers taking turns mauling one another, excited by the smell of blood, worked into a fever pitch by battle. All pagan, degenerate. . . . The scream split the night, and Richard Dawes walked quickly away across the snowy parade ground.

An eye for an eye . . . But where does such thinking end? He paused. What was that? There were three men standing in the shadows near an isolated building which had been designed as the outhouse before sanitary conscience had relocated it outside the gate and away from the river.

Frowning, Richard Dawes moved that way.

"Sir." The corporal came to attention, saluted, and then stood, appearing oddly hostile, between Dawes and the building.

"Have you prisoners in there, Corporal Fox?" Dawes asked, looking toward the tiny log structure.

"No, sir."

"Then what?" Dawes demanded.

"Nothing much, sir," the corporal replied. "Trade goods, I understand."

"Trade goods?" Dawes frowned. "Whose?"

"They belong to the general, sir. They're trade goods, that's all I know."

"Then I'll have a look," Richard said, starting forward.

"No, sir!" The corporal practically lunged at Richard Dawes. "Please, sir. You don't want to do that."

"Why not?" Richard asked with a laugh, and then the

corporal told him and he stopped laughing. His face went rigid and he asked, "Are you sure?"

"Damned sure, sir, if you'll excuse the expression. That's what it is."

"I see." There was nothing more Dawes could do. He looked once again, with deep repugnance, at the solitary structure. Then he shook his head.

Retracing his steps, he was forced to pass near the store-room, and the cry of inhuman pain rose up to meet the falling snow and, frozen by it, fall away to silence. Richard Dawes, feeling very young and very old and weary at once, walked to the officers' quarters, and slamming the door behind him, threw himself down on the bed, his anger lifting his heart to an awkward, thumping cadence.

It's very simple, he told himself. Very simple indeed, Richard Dawes. Close your eyes, close your ears. It's war, you damned fool! What do you expect, bluebells and auld lang syne?

But this . . .

He closed his eyes, astonished to feel the warm tears there, and he slept, somehow slept.

"Wake up, Richard! I've brought your sister to us. She's setting up in the officers' wives' cottages."

Richard Dawes lifted his head slowly. It was a full half-minute before he could make out with certainty the features of William Van der Veghe, the wild Dutchman.

Suddenly Dawes sat up rigidly, his eyes wide, his hands on William's shirt. "It's wrong, William. Dead wrong. Even you—the way you feel about them—you'd agree with me."

"Are you awake?" William asked with a smile. Gently he removed Richard Dawes's hands from his buckskin shirt. "Awake or still dreaming? I can't make sense out of you."

"You can't!" Dawes laughed. "Nor I you, perhaps. Nor . . . Compton: do you understand that?"

William frowned, stood up, and walked to the doorway, watching the pale skies as Richard sat up on the edge of his bed and, head in hands, said, "Sorry, William. I was half-asleep. Now I'm fully awake, and it's even worse."

"What are you talking about?" Van der Veghe asked.

"Ousa. I'm talking about Ousa, William. They're going to kill him, my friend. They're going to kill him and all of the Kata Shawnee. . . . My God!" Richard sat up straight, rubbing his eyes. Orange light was creeping under the door. "It's morning!"

William Van der Veghe was standing, hand shoved down behind the waistband of his trousers, staring at Dawes as if he were crazy.

"Have you been hitting the bottle, Richard?" William asked—half-seriously, it seemed.

"No. Listen, William. It's Compton. He's going to kill Ousa, going to kill all of the Kata Shawnee if he can."

"If he can, I suppose so. This is war. But there's a chance now that it's all going to be ended."

"You don't understand, William." Richard crossed the room, opened the door to look out at the peaceful scene beyond the fort: sunrise on new snow, white-clad pines following the river southward. "Last night they brought in some captive Shawnee. They were beating them, torturing them worse than the Shawnee had done at the Corners."

"The Corners?" William leaned against a plank table, folding his arms. "They hit that? When?"

"Last night!"

"What about the truce?" William privately cursed; his lips went tight. There had been no official truce, of course, but the Shawnee had been sending out those feelers. . . .

"That's the hell of it. The folks at the Corners were feeling secure because of these rumors. They didn't even have a watch out. Shawnee came in, hit them hard, murdered three people—one man, one woman, one child. It was the way they did it . . ." Dawes swallowed hard, dryly. "There was a lot of torture involved, William."

"But are they sure they're Kata?"

"Ought to be. One of them was Ousa's brother."

"How do they know!"

"One of the Shawnee prisoners spoke enough French to say that—Compton is not entirely uneducated, you know."

"Christ!"

"Exactly." Richard Dawes paced the room. "You've got to talk to him, William. He's got a weapon out there he hasn't used yet." Richard's voice lowered. "I found out about it. I don't know how long he's had them, but he's got . . . blankets. Look there," Richard told him, nodding across the parade to the small building where two soldiers stood guard.

"Richard . . ."

"I'm all right, dammit. I know I sound crazy, but I'm not, William. Do you know what's inside that building?"

"Blankets, you said; a weapon."

"Yes. Compton was going to use them—gifts to the Kata Shawnee." Richard Dawes's narrow face was agonized. "Those blankets are infected with smallpox."

"Jesus!" William rubbed his jaw, started to ask if Richard was certain, realized he was, and then closed his eyes tightly.

"That's not a weapon of war, William. It's not a soldier's way, a gentleman's. . . . Maybe I'm wrong, maybe I glamorize all of this myself. But, by God, the man's a criminal!"

"I wonder when, how, he was going to do it." William fell into thoughtful silence. Richard was right—that was no weapon of war, it was a butcher's thought. Smallpox would spread among the Kata like wildfire, killing eighty percent of them, men, women, children. It would be especially tough on the old, the very young: the noncombatants. He placed his hat on his head and turned toward the door again.

"What are you going to do?"

"Talk to him. I'm going to talk to the man, Richard."

"He won't listen."

"He will listen, Richard, believe me." He put his hands on his old friend's shoulders. "I'll make him listen. I wear no uniform, I'll say what I like." They were standing together on the plank walk now, and Richard heard a voice calling to them. He looked toward the "cottages," as they were called, actually a series of tiny barked log cabins along the south wall, to see Louise waving an arm.

"I told her I was just coming over to fetch you," William explained. "Talk to her, will you?"

"Of course, but . . ." Then William was gone, striding across the snow and mud of the parade ground toward the commanding officer's quarters. Glancing back, he saw Louise, hands on hips, staring after him, the fury on her face evident even from this distance. William's mouth tightened and then relaxed.

"I want to see the general, Gus."

General Compton's orderly looked up in mild surprise. He was shining a pair of knee boots to a glossy sheen. "He's not here, Mister Van der Veghe."

"At his office? So early."

"I couldn't say, sir. I wasn't told."

William nodded to the orderly and went out, trudging

across the frozen earth to the headquarters building. Richard, he noticed from the corner of his eyes, had reached Louise and was now trying to placate her. She was upset, and probably had a right to be. They had traveled all night through bad weather, and no sooner had they reached the fort than he had taken off. That was the trouble with their marriage, as she so often told him—he was simply never there. Her hurt feelings would have to wait this time.

Stamping into the orderly room, he found Sergeant Major Reid sipping a cup of tea. The Welshman glanced up, put down his tin cup, and asked, "Help you, Mister Van der Veghe?"

"Where's the general?"

"He's not in, sir."

William, who could already see that—the inner-office door stood open—ran his tongue around the inside of his teeth, staring coldly at Reid. He liked the big Welshman, but Reid was concealing something now. And he would never get it out of him; the man was a soldier through and through.

"It is important, Reid."

"Yes, sir."

"I need to know where he is."

Reid touched his huge drooping mustache and shook his head. "I can't tell you, sir, without disobeying an order."

"Maybe," William said, leaning across Reid's desk, his knuckles on the hard, rough wood, "it is time we all thought about our orders, about just how lawful they are, about the man who is giving them to us."

"I really don't understand you, sir," Reid said in his gravelly voice. His gray eyes were calm.

"Let your corporal watch the orderly room."

"Why would I do that, sir?"

"I want to see the storeroom behind the armory. I would like you to show it to me."

Reid stared at him, asking no questions. Finally he shrugged his heavy shoulders and rose, putting on his cap. "Coleridge, you're in charge."

The slender corporal in the corner lifted his eyes briefly and nodded. "Let's go," Reid said. He had a key ring in his hand.

Reid had not asked any questions. He was a soldier; it wasn't his place to ask too many questions. William Van der Veghe had impressed him with his intentness. Something important was going on, and Reid wanted to know what it was. It cost him nothing to walk over to the armory storeroom.

The armory was of stone, the only such building on the post. It was a moment before Reid found the proper key and swung open the heavy door. The two men entered and walked past the kegs of gunpowder, the muskets, and gleaming new bayonets to the door which led to the basement, which was used for extra storage now.

Reid plucked a candle from the niche in the wall, lit it, and lifting the heavy door, led the way down the ladder. He had gotten only halfway when he stopped, cursed slowly, profusely, and turned back toward Van der Veghe, his face pale and gray. "What in hell happened? Why. . . .?"

William prodded the man and they both stepped down to the floor of the cellar. The men, or what were once men, lay sprawled against the floor, purple blood caked on their flesh and staining the floor. It was cold in the cellar. The arms of the Indians were frozen into awkward positions.

"They went at them, didn't they?" Reid asked. His voice was indistinct as he held the candle overhead, dimly illuminating the tortured Shawnee, all dead, all mutilated. "An Englishman did this," Reid said, as if the idea were so incredible as to be beyond the realm of possibility.

"An officer and a gentleman," William said tightly. He took the candle from Reid and went nearer, crouching down. These men had suffered, suffered for no reason other than their torturer enjoyed inflicting pain.

"All right, where is he, Reid?"

"A runner came in this morning early," Reid said without hesitation, "a Shawnee with a message from Ousa, requesting a meeting. Apparently he didn't want to come into the fort. They arranged to meet somewhere else."

"Where!"

"I couldn't say, sir. The general didn't tell me."

"No, I guess he wouldn't." William slammed the side of his fist against the stone wall of the cellar. Ousa would prefer not to come into the fort. Where would they meet? Where! It was obvious to William now that Compton had no thought of making peace with the Shawnee. Why make peace, why trust them, when he could simply slaughter them?

"How many people did he take with him, Reid?"

"A full squad, sir."

"Which direction did they take."

"South by west, Mr. Van der Veghe." Reid was still staring at the bodies, still appearing gray and sickened.

"All right—what about the blankets?"

"Sir?" Reid lifted his eyebrows in obvious surprise. "How did you know about that?"

"About what?"

"The general ordered half of those blankets transferred to a caisson. They took them with them. Gifts, I supposed, for Ousa."

"Gifts." William could only shake his head. Compton was taking no chances. What exactly was going through the man's mind, he did not know. But he could guess. He planned on killing Ousa, still perceiving him as the war leader of the Kata. If the opportunity did not present itself—if Ousa, for example, appeared with a strong contingent of warriors—then the second plan would be put into motion. The gifts of infected blankets along with assurances of peaceful intentions would pass between them. That would be Compton's way. Who could ever blame him with any assurance? The Indians had suffered a plague of smallpox. Such things happened.

"There are blankets left out there?" Van der Veghe asked.

"The blankets?" Reid looked stunned and confused now. "Yes. But why do you . . .?"

Then there was no one to question. William Van der Veghe was up the ladder and out of the armory, leaving Reid to contemplate the tortured bodies of the Shawnee, to wonder about the blankets, about this mad Dutchman.

"William!" The call was faint but clear in the cold, still air. He did not look back to see what Louise wanted. Just now she was intrusive. His eyes were fixed on the small outbuilding ahead of him, on the two scarlet-coated guards who watched his purposeful approach dubiously.

"Good morning, Mr. Van der Veghe," the tall man, a corporal named Travis, said.

" 'Morning, Travis." Van der Veghe moved to them and then past them, fishing from his shirt the buckskin pouch which held his steel and flint.

"Sir?" Travis was hovering over him as he knelt beside the building. "Sir, you're not allowed near here."

"No?"

"No, sir. General's orders."

"Do you know why that is?" William had his steel and

flint out. He was raking together a small pile of bark, stripping the slender dry fibers from the inside.

"Sir, you cannot . . . What are you about?"

"I said, do you know what you are guarding, Travis? Do you know what you are risking by standing next to this building?"

"Sir?" Travis was torn between duty and curiosity. Damn the civilian scout! He was striking steel to that flint. "I'll be forced to shoot." The musket came around. Travis' eyes narrowed reproachfully.

"Pox!" Van der Veghe said, not looking up. He struck steel to flint again, crouched low, and puffed on the smoldering tinder. "Pox, Travis. Did you see the men remove some of these blankets this morning? Did you see how they handled them? Seemed odd, did it, Travis?"

Travis muddled through his recollections, recalling how they had handled the blankets with poles, how the general had stood aside, arms folded, faint amusement in his eyes.

"It can't be . . ." But it could be, and Travis knew it. He knew also how the general would have used the pox-infected blankets, and it was logical, in character. He hesitated, balancing the weights of duty and the disgust which now welled up inside him, for he had no doubt at all that Van der Veghe was telling the truth.

"Tea!" Travis said suddenly. The man with him, a red-eyed Irishman who had been listening silently, nodded. Together then the two soldiers walked away as the thin tendrils of smoke rising from William's tinder turned magically to feathery flame and then caught hungrily. William, squatting on his heels, added loose bits of bark and scrap wood, watching as the fire built, as it licked the walls of the shed and finally caught its grip on the eaves, burning with a crackling, wind-bent eagerness.

He stepped back, aware of the men rushing toward him, of the low clouds building again to the north, of the distant figure of Louise, disgusted, not understanding, of the flames which licked at the rough log building, snapping and darting, chewing away at the wood, at his career and reputation.

He had to fall back again. The building now burned brightly, casting fiery shadows against the snow of the parade ground. The interior had begun to go, and the noxious smoke rose skyward.

William spun on his heel and walked away from the roar of

the flames. Ahead of him he saw Richard Dawes, standing ankle-deep in snow. Behind him was Louise, holding a curious James in her arms. James's eyes were bright. A stubby finger pointed excitedly at the fire; then his face brightened still more as he recognized his father. Louise's face was far from bright.

"What in hell are you doing, William! What! Your career . . . such as it is. If the army doesn't support us, what are we to do? You are nothing but a soldier. Where will we live!" Her dismay was deep. William supposed she had the right to feel that way. He tried to explain.

"I don't care about that! I don't care about a damned Indian. You never did either, except to wish them dead. Well, you're going to get your wish, aren't you? Ousa will die, or maybe Compton. What's the difference, you hate them both. Hate seems to be your strongest emotion, William. I've never seen anyone hate so long or so hard to the exclusion of other, more human emotions."

"Louise—"

"Well, it's true, isn't it! Why are you looking at me like that?" James was clinging to her skirts, and she gripped his arm tightly. "Richard? Why are you looking at me! It's the truth, isn't it? What do either of you care if every Shawnee in Ohio dies! It's what you've both been working for for years! I don't understand you, I don't."

Suddenly the green eyes filled with tears. William stepped forward to hold her, and she slapped his face twice, leaving red imprints. He halted, his arms still held before him. James had begun to cry.

"Louise—" Richard Dawes began, but she cut him off sharply.

"Death and destruction and disease . . ." Her voice broke now. "I despise this wilderness, and all of you *warriors*. You left me alone to go out and kill—now you want to leave me alone to go out and save the life of the man you've described endlessly, bitterly, as a savage killer!"

"I was wrong, perhaps—" William started to say, but Louise was listening to none of it.

"I had to sit there, I had to lie in bed and listen to the poison leaking out of you, to your hatred, which infected everything around you. I had to sleep alone while you went hunting, killing.

"I thought you were sincere this time, William. I thought

if you brought us to the fort we could be together, as you promised. I thought you would be with your son. We haven't even unpacked!'' she said, her voice rising to a hysterical shriek. ''If you go . . .'' Her finger lowered threateningly. ''If you go now, William Van der Veghe, do not return. There won't be anything at all here for you to come back to.''

He said nothing. He bent and kissed James on the head, feeling the small chubby fingers touch his cheek. Then he straightened, exchanged a glance with Richard Dawes, and turning, walked toward the paddock.

''Going out, Mr. Van der Veghe?'' the stableman asked.

William only nodded, adjusting the cheek strap on his horse's bridle before slipping the bit between the chestnut's teeth.

''It's going to snow,'' the man persisted, scratching his armpit. ''Going to blow good and heavy. Me, I'm glad to be cozied up here with the horses.''

And it was snowing even before William reached the front gate. Snowing, the wind snapping the pine boughs. The tracks of General Compton's party would be obliterated within an hour. William heeled his chestnut gelding forward, following the already blurred tracks toward the river.

Somewhere ahead there was a madman plotting an assassination, and if he succeeded, he would be destroying the last hope for peace in the Ohio Valley.

12

The storm was a howling, colossal beast rampaging across the world from out of the north, darkening skies, hurling tons of stinging, biting snow earthward to stun the fragile warm-blooded creatures which dared challenge its might by existing in this winter Armageddon.

William Van der Veghe had long ago lost the tracks Compton's party had imprinted across the snow, and he rode on blindly, shoulders hunched against the cold and wind, eyes frozen, mustache hung with tiny icicles, hair hoary and stiff with ice.

He rode on, oblivious of the discomfort, heated by the rage within him.

He glanced up, seeing nothing but the downward-slanting snow, the dark mass of the unyielding forest. This was a fool's mission. Perhaps Louise was right about him after all. That caused a momentary pang of regret.

What had she done to deserve this? But what had the Shawnee done? In the topsy-turvy world he now traversed, a world where direction was impossible to ascertain, where there was no life but the life of the stampeding north wind, he grew uncertain. He was a warrior—fighting what? Whom? He had hated Ousa, but Ousa had done no more than he. They were, in fact, closer than brothers beneath the skin.

He had fought for Compton, half-knowing that the man was a fool, a coward, malicious. He had left his wife alone, allowed his son to grow up without a father. For what?

Van der Veghe was no longer certain of anything. The snow fell. He could be in a valley, atop a mountain, riding across the snow-heavy clouds for all he knew. The world was white, powerful, unrelenting, and quite unforgiving.

He was certain of only one thing—Ousa must not be murdered. He thought broodingly of Cara, tried to imagine her face, grief-stricken, accusing. He hurried his reluctant chestnut forward. If only someone had known where this meeting was to be held! Ousa, cautious and clever, had arranged to meet Compton away from the fort. Perhaps he had feared arrest.

He had fallen into Compton's scheme. Compton, convinced perhaps that the Shawnee was lying, that he intended to continue the savage raids such as that at the Corners, driven by the wish for revenge, by his own ambitions, would destroy Ousa. Failing that, he would achieve still worse goals. If Ousa, for example, had brought many men with him, too many for Compton to massacre, he would genially sign a peace treaty and send Ousa away with the peace gifts—the infected blankets.

The thought of it made William sick, and he heeled his exhausted horse again, spurring it forward through the deep, swirling snow, riding blindly to avert disaster.

If only someone had known . . . But of course there was someone who knew where the meeting was to be held, where Ousa was! Cara. William squinted against the snowstorm, picking out the river winding through the snow-draped countryside. He might not be able to find the rendezvous point, but he could certainly find the Shawnee camp.

He urged the weary horse on. He was impatient with the weather and himself, with the plodding animal beneath him. He was wasting time, and there was nothing to be done about it. He followed the river southward, the horse up to its knees in new snow.

Impossible. The whole thing was impossible, and he was slowly realizing it. All he had done was waste his career. He was a traitor! That thought seeped slowly into his consciousness. He had destroyed His Majesty King George's property. He had run to give advice and military information to the enemy. All of that seemed to matter little. . . . His thoughts were on the red-haired woman, on those disappointed green eyes. No, not disappointed; it had gone beyond that. To despair and malice. What Louise had said, she meant. He would have no wife to go back to. And no son. That wrenched William's heart, and he tossed the thought aside, refusing to look back at it.

The snow cleared briefly, like an opening drapery, and in that gap he saw the Shawnee village. What there was of it. Tattered, surrounded by burned forest, makeshift and rudimentary. He winced.

Oddly, only now did he think of what sort of welcome he could expect here. He walked the chestnut horse forward, eyes alert. There should have been guards out, but he had seen none. Everyone seemed to be inside, inside the flimsy tipis, the half-burned lodges.

It was eerie, still. Perhaps no one was there at all. But smoke wriggled from the vents in the lodge roofs, torn into shreds by the gusting wind.

He turned in his saddle, looking across the camp. He could hardly go from lodge to lodge. He was likely to end up with a hatchet buried in his head. Then, remarkably, he saw her. She stood in the entranceway to a lodge, staring at her brother as if, in some way he did not understand, she had expected him, had known he would come.

She held a small child in her arms, and as it caught sight of Van der Veghe, she buried her face in the hollow of her mother's shoulder.

William swung down, started to go forward, and staggered badly, so that he had to cling to the chestnut's neck for a moment while the dizziness cleared. He was exhausted and hadn't realized it. The horse stood miserably, head bowed. The snow had begun again.

"William?" Cara watched him, obviously puzzled. There was anxiety in her eyes. She knew that something had gone wrong. Perhaps in the way she had always known small things.

William made it to the lodge and was shown inside. A chunky woman sat playing some sort of game with a boy and another girl. The boy, seeing William, leaped up and ran for a pint-sized bow, until his mother said something stern and scolding to him.

Cara gave him warm tea—sycamore, he thought—and let

him rub his arms for a minute. "It's Ousa," William finally said. "Is he gone?"

Cara nodded her head, staring at her brother, whose lips were blue with cold. Water dripped from his sodden buckskins, from his buffalo coat. Terror thumped away in her heart. *Ousa*. "What is it?" she demanded impatiently. William seemed ready to fall asleep on his feet.

"I couldn't find him. I knew you'd know where he's gone. Compton means to kill him, Cara."

Cara placed Lychma down beside Dava and reached for her coat. It was a trap! She had warned Ousa, but he had simply smiled and said, "Perhaps it is. But it is not much to risk for the sake of the tribe."

"Please, Ousa, take men with you."

"No." He had dressed slowly, putting on his ceremonial clothes. "If it is a risk, why take others with me to be slaughtered? If it is a true peace, it needs only me to accept the treaty."

Then he had kissed her and gone, and she had watched his back, feeling the tears beginning to well up, knowing . . . She thrust her arms into her coat, missing the left sleeve twice in her impatience.

William started toward the door with her, and she said sharply, "You must stay. In your condition, you'll only slow me down."

"Cara . . ."

"Your horse is weary, you are exhausted. Stay, William. What can you do? If you are seen, you shall be killed too."

He would have argued with her, but she was already gone. Cara was right; he knew that she was. He gave in and sagged to the floor of the lodge, the three children staring at him with incredulity. He hardly noticed. He sipped his tea and sat, dripping water, listening to the long winds blow.

Cara had found her long-haired roan standing in the shelter of the dark pines, and she had slipped the hastily fashioned hackamore over its muzzle and swung onto its back, all without realizing what she was doing. It was automatic, as automatic as breathing in and breathing out, as the beating of her heart.

Her thoughts were centered on Ousa, only on Ousa. Fear was a constricting iron band around her head, the clawlike clutching at her heart by prickly little hands. Her chest was tight, her throat narrow. It was difficult to swallow, difficult to breathe, difficult to see. The storm froze wild tears against her cheeks, stinging her foolish eyes.

He was safe. Of course he was! Ousa was no fool. They would never capture him, strike down that tall black-eyed man. How could they?

She guided the roan toward the icy river, sensing the reluctance in the animal. Why would they kill Ousa? After all, he was not even war chief. He was only a single man. That would accomplish nothing. William was mistaken. She urged the roan on, kicking it savagely with her heels until it waded the river, belly-deep in the chilling gray water.

It was not far. Five miles, perhaps, to the Wolf Meadow, where Ousa had agreed to meet the general. Why, she would probably meet him returning from the rendezvous, and she would tell him why she had come. He would throw back his head and laugh, swing her from the horse's back in the grip of one muscular arm, and then he would kiss her, his mouth familiar, warm against hers. . . . She quickened her pace, kneeing the suffering roan, urging it forward, lifting it into a canter too swift for the weather conditions. The snow fell heavily. Dry, cold, all-obscuring. There was nothing but the snow, nothing but the cold, which crept into Cara's body and made her bones brittle with its icy touch. Her ears and nose felt lifeless, stiff; and if they were touched, she was sure they would snap away like icicles.

Wolf Meadow. She turned the roan northward, guiding it with the slight pressure of her legs. She became uncertain and halted the horse. Cara realized suddenly that she was not lost; the uncertainty had another origin. It was fear, stark and cold—colder than the most violent blizzard, colder than the breath of the stars on a clear winter night.

She was sitting, simply sitting, the snow falling around her, not so hard as it had been, but gently, soothingly. It was a cold, nearly welcome mantle which draped itself across the earth and cut off perception, denied the senses, dulled thought and painful anticipation.

"You are a coward," Cara said, sitting erect suddenly. "If Ousa could see you now . . . You are a coward, Cara!"

She turned the horse in the right direction, weaving her way through the snowy trees down the trail she knew so well, toward the valley which opened suddenly, a yawning gap in the deep virgin forest.

She wound her way down the hillside covered with snow-camouflaged brush, dead vines, and deadfalls. She could not see through the constant screen of snow, and she found that she was grateful for that. Recognizing this, she became angry with herself.

Silly woman. He is too clever, too strong, too knowing. Why would he trust Compton! A warrior all his years, a noble man. He would not be trapped. Look ahead. You will see him there, smiling, eyes bright, lips parted, ready to laugh. The man who has come forward to save his people; the man who has come from out of his safe refuge to negotiate freedom; the man who would risk himself for his people, who, through honor, would do what must be done so that the tribe—the source of life, of well-being, the breast of the Indian—might survive, as it must . . . as it must if man, the Kata Shawnee, the red man, is to survive; The man who has come to stand before their guns, their bayonets, and proudly say: I am he whom you seek. I am Ousa, the sachem, the war leader of the proud Kata.

They cannot kill such a man, for if such can be killed, then the world belongs to the savages, to the animals, to the guns, to the gods of chaos, to them who have no honor.

She was from her horse and running before the confused animal had stopped its rearing, its panicked sidestepping, tossing its head to fling the bitter, evil scent from its nostrils.

Cara crept through the storm, the snow to her hips. The wind was an intimidating weight against her shoulders and back, pawing at her face.

She knew. She did not want to know, but she did. He was there, and she found him. Black hair frosted with snow. Arms rigid, contorted. Deep purple ice across his chest. Lip curled back to reveal white teeth, the tip of a pink tongue. And eyes staring up into the whey of the storm, those black, black eyes, open to the whiteness of the day.

"Ousa!"

She got to her knees and went next to him. Her hand touched his, and she rubbed the hand, wanting to give it her warmth, wanting to see him stir, to laugh, to ask: "How long have I been asleep?"

He did not move. She heard the horse nicker, far away. Saw the snow tumbling down. "Ousa!"

You cannot die, it makes no sense if there is sense in the universe, if there is mercy in Manitou. For you, strong and laughing, honorable, loving, to die . . . it is sacrilege beyond sacrilege. While others like Compton live and congratulate themselves with doses of brandy, with tales told around a roaring fire, while their brains hummed, their blood flowed, their loins pulsed, their wretched ambitions grew and flowered . . . you lie dead in the snow.

It is not real, cannot be. Unless all of this is a vast, incomprehensible joke, unless the Great Manitou is a cruel hoaxer. And so he is not dead. It only seems that way—his arms crooked unnaturally, his chest motionless, with no strong beating of a great heart, with no rising and falling of the lungs within, and no warmth in those eyes— those black, black, haunting, loving eyes. The snow against his eyes no longer melted. Cara's head slumped forward, heavy, leaden. Her hands still held his cold, cold hand.

She lay against his chest. It was not fair. Her tears were hot, his flesh cold. They had not had enough time! There had been only turmoil, only contention. It had not been enough.

The snow fell, and she trembled.

The night came and the world was dark. You could survive it—the world could end and you might not die. There she lay, still breathing, some malignant spirit forcing her blood to flow on, to feed her body, which must already be dead, since, long cold hours ago, her soul had died.

It was snowing, but the weather was very hot. Probing, fiery fingers drifted down. Cara threw back her head and inhaled deeply, feeling the sting against her face. She had been cold for a long while, and now she felt none of it—heat, cold, fear, hate. She was emotionless, determined, a life occupying a body which had once been that of Cara, daughter of Crenna, the Oneida woman, wife of Ousa.

She stepped from her horse, leaving it, head hanging, before the lodge. Inside the shelter sat Dava and the children, appearing resigned, and William, who seemed battered, lifeless. Cara said nothing about it; there was nothing to say.

"I must speak to the Ghost Society. Will you remain, William? There may be trouble."

"Trouble." He repeated it without inflection; without, it seemed, understanding. He smiled briefly, a smile like that of a beast who did not understand the emotion behind the act. "Do what must be done."

Within the hour they were there: River Bird, Owl Eyes, Tak, and a dozen others, grim, uneasy, shifting their gaze from Cara to her pale brother, who sat, head hanging, eyes down-turned.

"We must fight. We must continue Ousa's battle. There is no peace to be had in this valley, in this life. There is only war, only death." Cara studied them, man by man. "I know why my husband chose you; I know why you stood by him. We understand one another. We will not give away an inch of our land. We will not bow to the French, nor to the English. We are Kata Shawnee, we are the people of Manitou. It must be an honorable life or we must suffer an honorable death. Choose now. There is no second opportunity."

River Bird was the first to agree. Since being told of Ousa's death, he had carried himself stiffly, the muscles of his shoulders bunched, his head erect, his eyes glowering. Cara did not know what his thoughts were, but she knew that his soul was vengeful. "It must be your way, Cara. I travel with you."

Owl Eyes demanded, "Who is this white man? Why is he here?"

"He is my brother, Owl Eyes. He was . . . a friend of Ousa's. He is here; that is all."

William now looked up and spoke. "Cara, this fighting leads nowhere. You can still travel to your winter camp. If you remain, many more will die."

"Yes. We will die until there are no more of us to die. It is this way, William. We may remain and fight and die with honor. We may run and live and die in disgrace, homeless and without honor. My husband dies an honorable man. I can do no less."

"You are sure?" he asked.

"It is right."

"Then I will fight with you, if you will have me," he said quietly..

"You!" Cara cocked her head to one side, not quite believing what she had heard. "Why, William?"

"I could say it was for honor, I could say it was because I have no place else to go, but I do not know. Not with certainty. Perhaps it is because there are only the two of us left. Neither white nor truly red, we stood no chance in this valley, in this world. . . . I do not know. I wish to kill no one, but I will. I do not wish to die, yet I know I shall. I wish to live with my son and watch him grow, but I cannot. Do not ask me why, Cara—I have no answer. I shall fight, that is all. Perhaps, like Ousa, it is because that is the only way I know. Perhaps, like Ousa, I know that if I put down my weapons, they will kill me."

Cara walked to her brother and knelt beside him. Taking his head in her hands, she kissed his forehead, a rare and touching gesture. Finally, smiling briefly, she rose.

"What about Shelokta?" River Bird asked.

"What do you mean?"

"He is leaving, taking his people—all of them, women, children, warriors."

"Going where?"

"I do not know."

"The French," Owl Eyes put in. "I have heard it said that he is going to fight at their side. They have cannon and many soldiers now. Shelokta seeks their strength. A coyote who wishes to run with the wolves."

"Let him go." Cara thought it was for the best. If he stayed, she was afraid of what she might do. He should have been killed long ago, simply murdered, but Ousa had been too noble to do that. Cara was not so sure of her own noble spirit. Since she had made her decision, she found that her heart was steely, her will implacable. She was not uncertain about this, although a moment's reflection should have made her so. She knew, with stark clarity, that they must fight. They would win or they would lose, but they must fight now. There could be no peace, there could be no retreat.

She ordered the village burned. There was no safety here—Compton knew its location. She turned to look at her people by the flickering firelight. There were pitifully few of them. The Ghost Society and a few others who had decided at the last moment not to travel with Shelokta. The men looked gaunt and severe, the women and children weary; no one seemed to fully comprehend what was happening.

What had happened was that their world had been taken away. Quickly, finally. The rug had been pulled from beneath them, and the reality they had avoided for so long had come up to slap them in the face. The British wanted their blood; the war was for survival. For their very existence.

"And so, they have accepted you at last." The voice was familiar, dry and throaty. Cara turned to find the shaman beside her.

"Do you travel with us, Sa-Miwok?"

"No, there is no point in that. I have a terrible gnawing spirit in my belly, Cara."

"You are ill?" she asked with concern. Why hadn't she known it before? He had always been small, frail-appearing. His head sat upon a thin, tortoise neck. His hands, seeming overlarge, trembled. But he had always laughed, always seemed to draw great strength from somewhere beyond this realm.

"Think nothing of that." He waved a hand. "I only regret that I am losing my student." He chuckled with deep amusement.

"I was not a good student. My mind was always with the world of people, not with that of the spirit."

"Yes. But you *were* a good student." Sa-Miwok watched the flames spread out against the snow, watched a lodge cave in in obeisance to the fire spirit's savage will. "You were a comfort to an old man, a bright flower. You would have been shaman if that was what you most prized. But you loved a man too much to put the world aside."

"And you knew all of that before you took me in." Cara smiled and touched the old shaman's shoulder. Firelight glossed his face and carved shadowy hollows in his cheeks. "You knew that I was not devoted enough."

"Perhaps. But I knew you needed to be accepted. Who else was there to help? You were so young, so beautiful, Cara. My withered heart came to life again when I saw you at my door. So . . ."—he shrugged—"I was selfish; I took you in to be near me, to let my eyes enjoy you."

"Now . . . now you will not go with me?"

"No. It is late. The dark sun ascends. The old shaman must prepare. It is time to make ready for midnight. Don't look unhappy, Cara! It is the way. We are not immortal. I join the many hundreds. I shall speak with my old friends, laugh with old Turtle Back and those I have missed. Time will cease to pass and we shall walk a long valley in sunshine. This I know."

"Then I won't see you again?"

"One day." He smiled and nodded. "One day you shall see a soaring hawk and it will fix eyes upon you, circling and crying out with joy, and it will be old Sa-Miwok watching over his student."

"Cara!" The runner burst into the clearing, his arm point-

ing in back of him even as he ran. "Redcoats! Across the river and advancing. They have cannon."

"In this weather!" William said in amazement. He stood staring that way even as Cara gave her orders.

"South a mile, River Bird, then back across the river. We shall leave our young in the pipestone quarry and return, circling behind them."

River Bird nodded and was gone, hurrying the Kata who were packing their belongings on the long-haired horses, sitting in small groups, or simply standing, standing and staring at the woman who would lead them.

"Now!" Cara told Dava, who stood, Cara's children bunched in her arms. "Leave now. I will carry Kokii."

"No!" The boy, his hair swirling about his face, his eyes coal black, hard, said firmly. "I shall walk. I am nearly a man."

Cara rubbed his head. "Nearly a man and already as brave as one." Kokii turned, walking taller now, glowing beneath his mother's praise. Cara watched him, smiling until he was nearly into the trees, and then she turned away, fighting back the tears. William was watching her.

"Well!" she demanded angrily. But his answer was soft.

"What do you want me to do?"

"Six men. A rear guard. Keep Compton a few hours behind us so that the snow will cover our tracks. When you come to the river ford, do not use it. Lead him to the west and away from the quarry."

William nodded, and without hesitation he turned to the assembled Ghost warriors. In his halting, somewhat flat Shawnee he asked for and got six volunteers, one of them Tak, who seemed smaller, thinner these days, whose smile was only a shadow of other days.

Cara waited, watching as the rear guard, under William, slipped silently through the forest toward the advancing British column; then she turned, and hurrying the laggards, made for the river ford herself, the massive River Bird at her shoulder.

The storm broke later in the afternoon, and Cara glanced over her shoulder at the blue sky, which showed brilliantly between stacked columns of white clouds.

"Now, when we need the snow, the spirits do not even give us that," River Bird said glumly. "It seems they too are against us."

"Then we must fight without them," Cara said, and River Bird glanced at the woman with new appreciation. Where had this strength come from, this competence? Her war plans were clever, clear-sighted, her determination evident. It was as if Ousa, dying, had given to his wife all of his strength, his cunning.

Cara spun around suddenly, as did River Bird. The Kata party was halfway across the river, which, swollen, swift, had made the ford treacherous. It was Owl Eyes, running heedlessly toward them, slowing only as the icy water became knee-deep.

He shouted, "They are on that side, Cara! They have split their force."

Cara spun back toward the eastern bank, seeing nothing yet but the haggard faces of those who had already crossed and who now stood cold and exhausted on the shaded bank.

"Back the other way!" Cara waved an arm. "Come back!"

She then turned and waded through the water, meeting Owl Eyes halfway. "You are certain?"

"Yes. Your brother saw them. He climbed a tall tree and saw the force split. Cara . . ." Owl Eyes hesitated. "Can your white brother be trusted?"

"Yes." There was no doubt, no hesitation.

"Then it is so. Compton has abandoned the cannon. He was going to shell the camp again, but knows it is empty. He has sent one party to the western bank while he marches south. The man," Owl Eyes said grudgingly, "is no fool."

"He knows about the quarry," Cara said with sudden certainty. "Somehow he knows."

The quarry, where the soft stone for their pipes was obtained, had long been a safe redoubt for the Kata. No enemy had discovered its location in a hundred years. There were high-rising bluffs of soft red stone where for centuries the Kata Shawnee had mined pipestone, stone used for the sacred calumets. Because of this mining, there were now caves in the bluffs, and tunnels which led to the peak. It had been used before as a hiding place, as a secure last outpost. Compton apparently knew of its existence, unless his actions had been purely instinctive, which Cara did not believe.

"How could he know?"

"Have you spoken to your brother?"

"Briefly."

"Not enough," Owl Eyes said. "Compton captured Wishosk,

Tamava, Komo, and . . ." He added with some hesitation, "Kalthipsa."

"Oh, no!" Not another brother dead. "Did he . . .?"

"Yes. But slowly. They were tortured, William says. They would have told anything at all. I believe Compton knows about the quarry."

"All right." Cara took a slow, deep breath. She looked back toward the river, where the last few stragglers were wading shoreward. She had counted on using the quarry to hide the children, the old, the infirm. Now that was eliminated as a possibility. "South, River Bird!" She waved an arm. "Keep them moving southward."

They heard distant shots, and Cara knew that William, after sending Owl Eyes as a runner, had begun a rearguard action. He would snipe at them, change position, run, and try to lead them off.

Nothing could be done about Compton's main force on the eastern bank. They would have to depend on Compton's army not knowing the ford, and upon the speed with which the Shawnee, born in the wilderness, could move through the rough country to the south and west.

"We could go to our cousins the Kaskinampo," River Bird said as they jogged southward, fighting through the brush, hurrying all before them.

"I have considered that." Cara had considered it strongly. A powerful Shawnee tribe, they had thus far avoided war with the British, refused to side with the French. Would they have them? Led by a half-white woman, bringing ragged hungry people to be fed from the Kaskinampo larder?

"Where else?" River Bird asked almost anxiously, although the giant warrior's face was as expressionless as ever.

"All right," she agreed finally. The skies were clouding over once more, and she looked worriedly toward them. If the snow would cover their tracks, it would also drive the game to cover, make travel difficult, bring cold to sap their energy. "Do you know their camp?"

River Bird nodded. He had been there many times. His family was closely related to the Kaskinampo Shawnee. Cara let them take the lead, and they traveled westward, ever westward, the clouds shadowing them. In the hour before nightfall, the snow began again, shuttering the skies, shading the world to a twilight gloom, the wind moaning and rumbling through the oak and pine forest.

At the hour of dusk, when a strange deep purple light colored the falling snow, William and his men caught up with the main party of Kata.

Panting, he reported to Cara. "We lost two warriors. Had a hell of a time finding your track. You should have sent someone back. Where are we going?"

"To the Kaskinampo Shawnee," Cara replied without slowing her pace. "Cousins to the Kata."

"How many Shawnee clans are there?" William asked.

"Many, many, William. The Shawnee are related to the Creek and the Cherokee. They are cousins to the Miami, the Fox, and the Chickasaw. There are Shawnee in the far south, along the Savannah River, taking their name from that river."

"So many . . ." William was thoughtful. "If only they would join together! There are many more Indians than whites in this land, many more Shawnee than British"

"There are too many chiefs, William, too many shamans, too many sachems with their own personal grudges and ambitions. It cannot be done."

"If it cannot," William said flatly, "there will one day be no Shawnee, no Indians at all in this broad land."

The snow fell throughout the night, drifting down through the trees, adding mass to the old snow, seeping into the clothing, freezing the will of the Kata. They rose with the gray, dim dawn and trudged on, fighting their way through the snow, which was thick, drifting even in the deepest forest.

"At least," Owl Eyes said, "Compton will not be following us through this!"

William said nothing; he let River Bird, who had been scouting with him, explain: "They are back there, my friend. We saw their red coats. They come. The winter will not turn them back."

But winter was carving at the determination of the Kata. The food was low. There were three cases of frostbite. Twice that day the snow became so heavy that no progress was possible—but the British would be coming still, traveling across the snow which the Kata had flattened and packed in their passing.

They plodded on after a terrible, swirling night, when the wind stretched tauntingly out of the darkness and tormented them with its icy talons. They sat huddled together, the

children crying, the old stolid and grim, their faces lined with the strain of discomfort.

"There it is!" It was Owl Eyes who called out. He was standing on a hillrise, rags wrapped around his hands and across his face. He was frosted with snow, as they all were, although the storm had lightened somewhat.

Cara struggled to where he stood. Following his line of sight with her own eyes, she saw the lodges clumped together near the small river.

"Are we there?" Stone Wolf asked. The old man looked terrible. His thin gossamer hair floated around his sharp mahogany face like a swirling mist. His eyes were clouded.

"Yes, Uncle," Cara said, placing a hand on his shoulder, "we are there."

Cara tried to make out the details of the camp, but could not through the screen of snow. She turned back toward the main party in time to see Tak emerge from the woods and lumber toward them, his mouth open as he tried to suck in great lungfuls of air.

"Tak!"

"We are bringing danger to the Kaskinampo," he gasped.

"Still back there?" Cara lifted her eyes to the deep, shrouded forest. It was incredible.

"Still coming. They have a good tracker, Delaware I think. Compton drives his men. Many have fallen."

"I'll slow them down," William volunteered.

Cara looked at her brother and nodded. "Be careful."

He grinned, tossed his musket to Tak, and took off at a loping run, clutching his bow. Cara turned back to the others. "Let us go down. We will tell the Kaskinampo what we have done. Perhaps they will not let us stay, but they may care for the ill."

"They will at least have food," River Bird said.

With that thought warming them, they started up the long, snow-deep slope, carving deep tracks against it. Compton would not need his Delaware guide to follow this trail.

They came onto the timbered western slope and dropped down into the valley, Cara leading the way. The village of the Kaskinampo was still only vague dark forms dimly seen through the slanting snow.

They were almost in it before Cara recognized what was wrong.

"Empty," River Bird said with disgust.

That was what had been wrong. There was no smoke; even had they not been able to see smoke, they should have smelled it. Cara stood stiffly in the center of the empty camp, looking dismally about. River Bird slumped into a crouch. Tak muttered something filthy.

"All gone!" The voice came from a nearby lodge, and as they looked that way, the woman walked toward them, arms outstretched. Her hair was a mad, matted tangle, her body shrunken and weightless. "They've all gone to the winter camp."

There was something wrong with the way the woman walked—slow plodding steps, arms outstretched—and it took a minute before Cara realized the hag was blind. Empty eyes looked straight ahead, lifeless and lusterless, as she shuffled to where Cara stood.

"No!" Cara breathed, for only then did she recognize the woman. It was Tadona. Battered, enfeebled, filthy, and blind. *Tadona*.

"Who is that? Who said that!" Tadona demanded. She was nearly in front of them now, and with one more awkward step her fingertips touched River Bird, and she halted. "Who spoke?"

"Tadona. It is I, Cara," she replied, trying to keep the pity out of her voice, but she knew she hadn't done so effectively.

"Cara!" Tadona made a sound which might have been the beginning of a laugh, might have been a stifled sob, but it broke off abruptly. "Who else is here? Why are you here?"

"The Ghost Society is here. We left the camp."

"Ah," she said, as if she had known all along. Her fingers worked up River Bird's arm. "I know you! There's only one so big. River Bird."

"Yes," the warrior said dully.

"Why are you here, Tadona? What happened. Where is Shelokta?"

"Shelokta!" She shrieked the name. "He did this. He did this!"

"But why?"

"Because I was angry with him," Tadona said, her voice becoming oddly childlike. "And I told the British where his new camp was." She started cackling, doubling up with laughter. River Bird looked at Cara and shook his head. "And so he put my eyes out and left me."

"But his camp?"

"All dead. He has twelve men, no more. The French were going to stand with him, but their government has decreed otherwise. The French have withdrawn to the Mississippi. The British have won!"

"And so you went to the winning side?" Cara asked with disgust.

"There was a man. A nice Englishman. He gave me things," she said, reverting to her childish tone. Cara turned away from the simpering.

"We are leaving now, Tadona," Cara said, still facing away from this wretched woman. She could not even feel sorry for her. "You may come with us."

"Why would I?" Tadona said with a flash of her old temper. "Stagger along through the snow, someone leading me, feeding me! I'll stay here. I have enough food for myself. In the spring the Kaskinampo will return. They will give me work to do and feed me. That is enough." She said no more. She turned and shuffled off toward the lodge, her arms outstretched. Cara could not bear to watch her go.

"Where now?" River Bird asked sharply enough to bring her out of her reverie.

"Southward, River Bird. Southward still."

"Some of them cannot go much farther," the big Shawnee said, looking back at the dismal line of ragged Indians.

"We will go until we can go no farther. Perhaps William can buy us some time, but we cannot count on that. We shall run, River Bird, and when we can run no farther, then we shall fight."

He was a ghost in the whirlwind of the snowstorm, flitting unseen behind the fine mesh of falling snow, listening to the eerie creak and moan of the wind in the pines, alert for the sounds which did not belong in the wilderness, alert to the first flash of scarlet.

His lungs were fiery, his legs leaden; the snow was heavy; to run far or fast in it was debilitating, but William Van der Veghe had to do just that. Run as quickly as ever in his life, attack swiftly, and move. He had to slow the British down, impossible as that seemed just now, or watch the Shawnee be run to the ground, watch the Kata Shawnee nation perish before the British guns.

Scarlet.

He hurled himself to the earth and notched an arrow. He saw nothing for a long minute, and so, taking a chance, he shifted his position, darting for the shelter of a huge old twin pine. There he paused, panting, squinting into the weather. Nothing.

Had imagination been playing tricks on him?

He saw it again. A flash of red and then a wave of scarlet, a tide flowing in, surging through the forest, flooding the land, staining it red.

William looked to the head of the column, searching for his man, for Compton. There he was—sitting a white horse, bundled in a fur jacket and hat. William drew his bow, sighting between the two trees. He found his hand was shaking, and he took a slow breath. His teeth chattered with the cold, and he silently cursed himself. The arrow flew.

Damn it all! Compton had turned in the saddle just at that moment to speak to the officer beside him, and William's arrow, grazing Compton's chest, embedded itself in the heart of the second man.

Compton roared, waving a hand as his men scattered, and William, leg-weary, dashed deeper into the woods. He leaped a frozen creek, scrambled up the far side, and heard the synchronous roar of a musket volley. Something red hot, agonizing, bit into the calf of his leg, and William pitched forward onto his face.

Careless. I'm getting damned careless. He saw now that there had been a flanking guard, and he had run right in front of their guns. Struggling up the slope, he made the shelter of the deep woods again, the following shots sending musket balls into the pines, tearing off bits of bark and low-hanging boughs.

Circling, William found temporary sanctuary in a pile of boulders. There he slit open his pants leg. Peeling back the cloth with shaking fingers, he examined the wound. It was ugly, but not serious, although blood trickled against the snow, staining it maroon.

He cut away his shirttails and bandaged the calf tightly. Then, knowing that he could not afford to remain in one spot for long, he continued his circling maneuver over rough ground until he was actually behind the long column.

He could see the last men, the stragglers, and he slipped

into the concealing forest to wait. Notching his arrow, he waited, throwing his head back to take in deep lungfuls of air. From somewhere ahead and to the north of him he could hear confused orders being shouted.

William waited until the last man was even with him, and then he sighted, somewhat reluctantly—this was only a common soldier trying to do a job. The arrow flew true, and William saw him clutch at his chest as if he had been stung by a bee. The arrow was broken off by the frantic waving of the soldier's arm, and then, curling up, knees to his chin in agony, the soldier lay against the earth.

"They're back here too! In the rear, sir!" someone shouted, and there was a rush toward the trees on the far side of the trail. William let another arrow fly; he could not tell if it hit anyone.

Now the British would assume there were Shawnee on all sides, and with any luck they would form up while Compton's slow mind decided what to do.

Grinning, William ran through the forest, his leg stiff and fiery. He was into the creek bed again, fighting his way through a tangle of dry blackberry vines and gray, weather-stunted willow. Emerging, he looked eastward, toward the column, and decided he had done enough.

Now to circle toward the Kata . . . The musket rang out, so near that William felt the heat of the muzzle flash. He felt his feet go out from under him, and he was cartwheeling down the slope. He was down in the snow, down and trying to rise. He could see the redcoats rushing toward him.

Careless. He reached for the pistol he kept in his belt and found he had lost it. He sat up, feeling as if he had been kicked in the chest by a mule. He could feel the blood seeping down his stomach, and he did not look, knew he did not want to look at this wound.

He sat there in the snow, the wind drifting his yellow hair across his face. He had himself braced with his hands, his teeth clenched, waiting for the first wave of pain, which would follow the shock. When it came, it was incredible. His chest was on fire. It felt as if someone had hold of a lung and was trying to tear it out. He suddenly strangled, and when he coughed, the pinkish blood frothed up.

They were around him now, and looking up, he saw Richard Dawes, his face engraved with grief. William nodded, coughed again, and clutched at his chest.

"Richard . . . I was . . ."

He said nothing else. He toppled to the side, his face against the snow, his blue eyes open to the day, and Richard Dawes could do nothing but turn and order his men back to the column.

13

The wind had ceased. There was a gradual clearing as the clouds drifted away to work their dark magic elsewhere. Cara looked down the slope toward the river valley below, watching them advance. Weren't they men, didn't they tire and halt, exhausted, to fall against the earth and replenish themselves?

Her head turned back toward the shelter of the cave. The old looked older, the ill more ill, the young very young and frightened.

River Bird had come up beside her to stand and watch. "We can go no farther," she told the warrior. "Here we will stand. The aged, the children, the ill, will have a chance to slip away if we can hold Compton long enough."

River Bird made no reply. He himself appeared tireless, as did the slender young woman beside him, who stood, blanket around her shoulders, sharp eyes peering upriver.

"Your brother did not slow them much," River Bird said finally.

"No." He was dead; Cara knew that as she knew many things. William, the warrior without a side, had been killed. Perhaps he had wished it without even knowing it. She thought of Louise and of James, with the bright, eager eyes.

Her thoughts turned to her own children. She walked back into the cave to find Dava. The Creek woman looked up wearily. Shanna was asleep on her lap. Lychma, blue eyes curious and alert, met the quiet gaze of her mother. Kokii, arms folded, warrior fashion, stared at her with small grim mouth compressed, with black, black eyes glittering too brightly. His childhood had vanished, his father had been snatched away from him; his nation was gone, his people wanderers on the earth. She walked to him and hugged him, and he did not protest it.

"Dava. You must go."

Dava looked up, her broad face uncomprehending. "Go where, Cara?"

"South. Along the high trail and through the canyon. I am sending all of the women, all of the young, the ill."

"Cara—"

Cara shushed her and crouched beside the Creek woman. "Take them with you. Take my children. Take them to your home in the south, Creek woman. They will have no life here."

"Cara, you must come!"

Lychma was wide-eyed now, frightened. Her tiny hands wrung themselves. Kokii stood by, being brave. Tears glossed his dark eyes. Shanna slept, her eyelids fluttering, her body moving in tiny unconscious jerks as she dreamed of running, playing, swimming the sunlit river.

"I must remain." Cara stood and walked away. She wanted to go back, to hug them, to gather them in her arms, to devour them with kisses, to stroke their sleek black hair, but she did not. It would only alarm them, would only alert them to the possibility that they would not see their mother again.

"I have told Stone Wolf," River Bird advised her. "He will be in charge of the party."

Cara nodded. She stared out at the white land. She felt a hand on her shoulder, and turned to find a grinning Tak. "It is time to set up our defense, Cara."

"Yes," she said after a moment's hesitation, a moment when many thoughts flitted through her mind, mingled, became tangled and confused. Rivers in the sun, long grass swaying in the wind, a dark and stormy night lying in a small bed, bundled to the nose in furs, her mother softly humming, the scent of her father's pipe, yawning, stretching small arms, falling off into a cottony world to dream of the man who would come on his spotted pony and take her away to his home; strong bronzed arms, healthy laugh, and bright smile, closeness in the night, his flesh merging with hers as the stars drifted past, the pain and exultance of childbirth, a dream, a completion, a beginning and an end. Black, black eyes.

Tak was still standing beside her. River Bird, his eyes questioning, was a little distance off. Owl Eyes squatted against the cold granite of the cave mouth.

"River Bird, you must design the defense," she said finally. "Perhaps men on either side of the canyon?"

"Yes, Cara."

"We may send out a party to flank them." Looking upward, she said, "If there is a place where the snow can be broken free, it might block their approach."

"Yes, Cara. I will look."

"Beyond that, the battle is yours, River Bird, and yours, Tak." Her own battle was done. Lost. Or perhaps not. She turned and watched the long ragged line of survivors work their way through the snow toward the pass beyond, the path which led to the south and to safety.

Shanna, with sleep still in her eyes, turned back, looking frantically for her mother, and Cara had to turn aside. Lychma, her blue eyes reflecting incomprehension, had been in Dava's arms. Kokii trudged forward up the winding trail, his head bowed, his heart filled with who knew what childish apprehensions, fears. Perhaps he would become a bitter man; but Cara knew this: he would be a warrior. A warrior with black eyes, with a catlike grace, a too-handsome face which would overwhelm the maidens, with strength and sinew in his arms, with the courage of another great warrior in his blood.

They would survive, and so the battle was a victory of sorts. They would survive, and so her life was a triumph; she had become, had done, had lived. What was there to regret? Lying in his loving arms, growing strong, becoming *Shawnee*, giving life?

It was growing dark now, dusk settling slowly across the earth, purpling the snow, staining the skies with deep, murky color. Her warriors had begun to slip down the slope to take up positions against the invader, the conqueror. With the dawn they would come; with the dawn. She stood and watched the night settle, watched the star-dusted sky go black. She stood, already knowing, as she had always known. She stood and awaited the dawn.

ABOUT THE AUTHOR

PAUL JOSEPH LEDERER was educated at San Diego State University. He now lives in Southern California with his wife, Sandra and their four children.

His interests include silent films, American folk music and Eastern philosophy.

Mr. Lederer is the publisher and entire staff of his own Cormorant Press, which releases literary efforts outside the mainstream "when funds are available."